Anna, Like Thunder

Anna,
Like Thunder

A Novel

P E G G Y   H E R R I N G

BRINDLE
& GLASS

Brindle & Glass
An imprint of TouchWood Editions
touchwoodeditions.com

Edited by Claire Mulligan
Cover design by Tree Abraham
Interior design by Colin Parks

LIBRARY AND ARCHIVES CANADA CATALOGUING IN PUBLICATION

Herring, Peggy, 1961-, author
Anna, like thunder : a novel / Peggy Herring.

Issued in print and electronic formats.
ISBN 978-1-927366-74-5 (softcover).

I. Title.

PS8615.E7685A83 2018   C813'.6   C2017-906536-X   C2017-906537-8

We acknowledge the financial support of the Government of Canada
through the Canada Book Fund and the Canada Council for the
Arts, and of the Province of British Columbia through the British
Columbia Arts Council and the Book Publishing Tax Credit.

The interior pages of this book have been printed on 100% post-consumer
recycled paper, processed chlorine free, and printed with vegetable-based inks.

PRINTED IN CANADA AT FRIESENS

22 21 20 19 18   1 2 3 4 5

For my mother, Irene, and my grandparents,
Anatolii and Marusya, with gratitude
for the stories that got me started

When I told her that her spouse would free the captives only on condition of an exchange for herself, Mrs. Bulygin gave us an answer that struck us like a clap of thunder, an answer we could not believe for several minutes, taking it all for a dream. In horror, distress, and anger, we heard her say firmly that she was satisfied with her condition, did not want to join us, and that she advised us to surrender ourselves to this people.

—TIMOFEI TARAKANOV[1]

You will hear thunder and remember me, and think: she wanted storms.

—ANNA AKHMATOVA[2]

CONTENTS

PREFACE

In November 1808, the Russian ship *St. Nikolai* ran aground off the west coast of the Olympic Peninsula near present-day La Push, Washington. According to records, the twenty-two Russians aboard came to shore and were enslaved and traded among coastal First Nations until the survivors were rescued a year and a half later. One of the Russians was eighteen-year-old Anna Petrovna Bulygina, the wife of the navigator.

There are two written records of this incident. One comes from Russian fur trader Timofei Osipovich Tarakanov, who was the supercargo aboard the ship. After rescue, he related the story of his experiences to Navy Captain V.M. Golovnin, who wrote it down and published it in Russia in 1874. The second is a Quileute oral tradition that was told by elder Ben Hobucket to federal Indian service official Albert Reagan around 1909 and published in 1934. In 1985, the two accounts were published together as *The Wreck of the Sv. Nikolai*, edited and with an introduction by the late historian Kenneth N. Owens. Despite their origins, there is a remarkable level of concurrence between the two versions.

Anna is a minor character in both accounts, though she plays a pivotal role. During an attempted rescue, she refused help and instead encouraged her rescuers to surrender. This set off a series of events that today illuminate an important period of history on the coast of the Olympic Peninsula.

This novel explores Anna's decision in the weeks before the event and the months that followed. This fictionalized version of what happened and why diverges at times from the written record, as she witnesses events from a vantage point not considered in historical documents. I've tried to remain faithful to the history as I understand it; nonetheless, this remains a work of fiction.

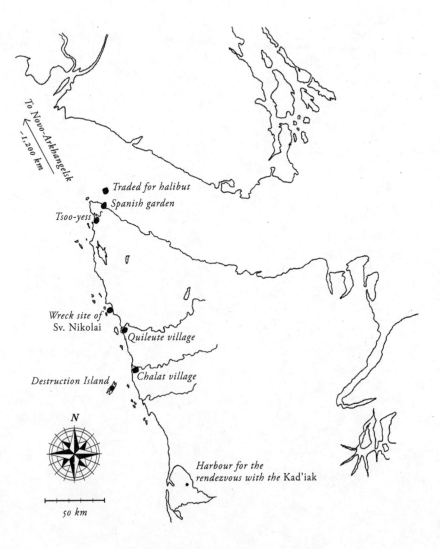

To Novo-Arkhangelsk
~1,200 km

Traded for halibut
Spanish garden
Tsoo-yess

Wreck site of
Sv. Nikolai
Quileute village

Chalat village

Destruction Island

N

Harbour for the
rendezvous with the Kad'iak

50 km

PRESENT-DAY OLYMPIC PENINSULA, WASHINGTON

AUTUMN 1808

CHAPTER ONE

I can scarcely see my beloved Polaris. The wispy clouds are like the sheerest muslin, and they stretch over the whole of the night sky obscuring the stars. But I keep my telescope pointed at her. If I wait, she may emerge: the brilliant beacon around which the heavens revolve. Navigators call her the North Star or the Ship Star. True amateurs like my father would call her Alpha Ursae Minoris: "alpha" because she is the brightest, and "ursae minoris" because she finds her home in the Little Bear constellation.

She will always be beloved, of course, for her role in guiding explorers and traders for centuries over land and sea. But I adore her for what most don't know. That she is not one star. Not two. She is three stars. Perhaps more. If not for the renowned astronomers Monsieur William Herschel and Mademoiselle Caroline, his accomplished sister, no one would know that. I aspire to make such discoveries of my own one day.

The brig groans and tilts as she climbs a wave. I wrench the brass telescope from my eye and fumble with my free hand. The bulwark is almost out of reach, but—here, I have it. I clutch the telescope to my chest. The ship tilts in the opposite direction as she slides down the wave and lands with a thud. I stagger. The frigid seawater splashes my face, and I shiver. With my shawl, I wipe the drops from my telescope, hoping no water has seeped through the seams and damaged it. As for my shawl, it's warm but not my best—grey wool with a peacock-blue fringe that's almost too pretty for it. If the salt stains it, I hardly care, and besides, nobody will be able to tell.

"Anya!"

My husband strides across the deck. Like the rest of the crew, he is sure on his feet, experienced after so many years working the ships for the Russian-American Company. Roiling seas are no trouble for him, but I'm still learning to live with their caprice.

"What are you doing out here? Come to bed." Nikolai Isaakovich slips his arm around my waist, and, because it's dark and the two men on watch can't see us, I release the bulwark and lean back. He's warm, and his body shelters me from the wind. His beard scratches my cheek.

"I just wanted one more look," I say.

He knows about my star log, and that it's modelled on the published tables my father pores over day and night. In Petersburg I helped my father with his log. Now I have my own, and it will be the first catalogue of the stars ever made along the vast coast that connects Novo-Arkhangelsk to the Spanish colonies in California.

Much to my dismay, there have been many cloudy nights, and the stars have often hidden themselves. There have been many cloudy days, too. Days when the grey sea and the grey sky merge, and the brig crawls along like a cart with a damaged wheel. I've not been able to log the stars as much as I'd hoped. So when tonight's sky looked promising, I tied my cap tight and pinned my shawl high on my neck to keep the cold out so I could extend my time on deck.

My husband releases me, and I latch onto the bulwark again. "Khariton Sobachnikov!" he calls.

"Yes, Commander?" comes the reply from the wheel. He's the tallest of the promyshlenniki—the sailors, fur traders, and hunters who work for the Russian-American Company—and, because of his height, our main rigger. There's not a mast or a spar he can't climb, not a bit of rigging he can't reach, even when the brig is tilted well over the waves.

He's also painfully shy. He can barely bring himself to address me, but when forced to, his face turns a livid red as soon as he opens his mouth. I believe it's because of his manner that he prefers the watch at night, when the rest of us are asleep and he doesn't have to speak with anybody. I leave him to his work when I'm out on deck, just as he leaves me to mine.

"Everything good?"

"Yes, Commander. The wind's coming up. But it's favouring us tonight."

"And our apprentice? Are you awake?"

"Yes, Commander. I'm over here," calls Filip Kotelnikov from the bow. Heavy, with a body as round as a kettle and limbs like sticks, he's sharp and ambitious enough that he's the only one besides Sobachnikov who'll volunteer for the night watch. Still, he's impatient and it irritates my husband, so I doubt his actions will lead where he hopes.

"That's what I like to hear. Remain alert. Both of you."

They give assent, and then Nikolai Isaakovich drops his voice. "As for you, my darling, it's time to come inside."

"In a moment," I say, raising the telescope again.

"In a moment. In a moment," he says and sighs, but there's humour in his voice. "You think we're sailing for your amusement? That the chief manager doesn't have more important work for us?"

The colony's chief manager, Alexander Andreyevich Baranov, has given my husband a special commission. Nikolai Isaakovich has been put in command of a crew of twenty and tasked with sailing south to further refine our empire's knowledge. He's to explore and chart the coast, and to look for a secure harbour where settlement might be established to facilitate the company's trade for sea otter pelts. He's to fill the hold with furs along the way. The *Sviatoi Nikolai*, this brig, is under his sole command for a few weeks of the expedition, after which we'll meet another Russian ship, the *Kad'iak*, at a predetermined location, to continue the mission together, as though we're not merely two ships but a great imperial fleet.

My husband has hung a wooden plaque carved with the Imperial Decree in our quarters. I see it every morning as soon as I wake up, and by now I've memorized it. It instructs us "to use and profit by everything which has been or shall be discovered in these localities, on the surface and in the bosom of the earth without any competition by others." It's well known in Petersburg that Tsar Alexander is obsessed with Russian America and that, if it weren't for Napoleon's aggressions in Europe, he'd sail the coast himself.

The cloud cover thickens, obscuring my Polaris. She tries valiantly to twinkle through the grey, but it's no use. I'll have to wait yet another night. I take her cue and follow my husband to our quarters.

The wind and sea are muffled down here, yet the thud of the waves that strike the hull and the answering grind of the timbers are still disquieting. The ship's dog, Zhuchka, whines and cowers on a mat next to the bed. She's on board to work—she's our sentinel when we go ashore, alerting us to danger, assisting the promyshlenniki in the hunt for game. But even when the seas are only a little rough, she's a coward, and she's become the source of much mockery among the crew if she happens to be on deck at such times.

"Don't worry, Zhuchka—it's just a little wind." I sit on the bed and pull her head onto my lap. She buries her nose into the damp folds of my shawl. Her russet-coloured tail, tipped in white like a paintbrush, thumps the floor. It has the most endearing curl, like the hair at the nape of a baby's neck.

"Would you leave that dog alone? You treat it like it's your child," my husband says.

"Are you becoming jealous?" I say lightly and kiss the dog's forehead with a big smack.

"Stop!" my husband cries. He leaps across the room and pries the dog from my embrace, pushing her out the door and slamming it behind her. The walls shake. He throws himself on the bed beside me and makes a big show of wiping my lips clean with his fingers. "Watch who you're giving your kisses to," he murmurs, and then he presses his lips to mine.

I pout and push against his chest. "I'm eighteen years old and can choose whoever I want to kiss." I lie back to get away.

But that's just part of our game. Nikolai Isaakovich flings himself down beside me and kisses me again. He slides his lips to my throat. I arch my neck to accept him.

He strokes my hair, my cheek. His slips one hand underneath my shawl and onto my bosom. He whispers, "Annichka." With his other hand, he clutches my wrist and pulls my hand to his chest.

For a short time and a long time, we continue, my arm around his back, his leg bent around mine, my mouth open to his shoulder, his mouth closed on my fingers. Something bony presses against my thigh. For an instant, I think it's my telescope. But no. I set that on the table. I suppress a smile.

He opens his trousers and pulls up my skirt.

He pushes himself inside me. His eyes close, and his face transforms. He thrusts and pants.

When I pull his hips to mine and thrust back, I feel his touch deep inside. It's a place I can't name. I think it's near where dreams take shape. It's a place created by romantic thoughts, and nurtured into bloom by the glances and brief meeting of fingers I've seen my parents exchange, seen men and women in Petersburg share while dancing.

Finally, sounds form deep inside him, as though some great beast is coming to life. He grunts and grunts and calls out: to me, to God, and to his mother. Then, he collapses atop me, sweaty and gasping, a lock of his hair between my lips.

After he rolls off, and his liquids dribble out, I can think of nothing except facing the old Aleut, Maria, in the morning. Thankfully, our quarters are far from the smelly forecastle where the promyshlenniki hang their hammocks. But we share a thin wall with Maria. She prepares the meals and washes clothing for me and Nikolai Isaakovich, and, since it would be impossible to house her with the men, she occupies a berth next to our cabin. The light from her lamp shines some evenings through the knots and cracks in the planks that separate us. If one were disrespectfully inclined, one could peer through these holes into the next room. I confess that I know how easy this coarse act would be because I did it. Maria wasn't there at the time. I could see clearly her bunk, a padlocked trunk, and a length of rope that ran from one corner of the room to another, though nothing was hanging from it.

Does Maria have such ill manners? It's possible, but it makes no difference, for what she can't see, she most certainly can hear. She could keep her own log book to mark the exact dimension and frequency of our passion, though why she'd care, I don't know.

When I wake in the morning, it's to near silence. I'm alone. The wind has died. In our dim quarters, I mull that over—how we say *the wind has died* as though it's a living creature. If it were a living creature, what would it look like? What would it say?

The peasants believe in such things. The spirits dwell every-where in their world and guide them through their lives. The domovoi lurks beneath the kitchen hearth. The leshii, disguised as a mushroom, tickles careless woodsmen to death in the forest. The long-haired rusalki lure young men to their watery graves in murky ponds. And the vodyanoy, who lives deep in the whirl-pools of the sea, kicks up storms and sinks little boats and big ships alike.

"The Enlightenment hasn't reached them yet," my father says. "The Tsar is right when he says as long as they can't understand science, they'll continue to lead deprived lives." Sometimes when he blusters against superstition, my mother leaves the room.

"What did I say wrong?" my father calls.

It's easy for him. He has his tables and logs. Three telescopes set up in a turret. He's invited to address the Imperial Academy of Sciences several times a year. When he was a boy, he went to the home of the celebrated astronomer Monsieur Mikhail Lomonosov just after his great discovery of the gases that swirl around Venus. "Everything in the world is rational, Anya," he tells me. "And if you think it's not rational, it only means you haven't thought hard and long enough about it yet."

I'm enlightened, too. I know that science governs the earth, the planets, the stars—everything. But does he never wonder? Has nothing ever happened to shake his faith in science? How is he so certain that everything can be measured and logged? I wish I were as steadfast, but it's too late. The doubts seeded themselves long ago, and after that, nothing he said or did could have stopped them from taking root and showing themselves at the least opportune moments.

I push myself out of bed and shudder when my feet touch the cold planks. I reach for my shoes.

As I emerge on deck, Zhuchka charges over. I stroke her head and look around. Just as I might have predicted from below, the sky is grey and seamless. The sea is smooth and glassy, though not at rest. A gentle swell rocks the brig. The sails sag, and the crew is idle.

I rub the soft place on Zhuchka's forehead, and when she seems satisfied, she runs back to where the American, John Williams, and the straggly-haired Kozma Ovchinnikov are teasing her with a dried fish head. They toss it to one another, letting her come close enough to smell it, but not to sink her teeth into it.

The American is pale and has carrot-coloured hair and freckles such as I've never seen before. He is the only man beside the Aleuts with no beard and his cheeks are so smooth, I don't think he could even grow one. His Russian is good, but his accent is flat, and he drawls out every word.

Ovchinnikov is a brooding beast of a man. His hair hangs to his shoulders and, unlike John Williams, almost his entire face is hidden behind a beard, which he keeps long and untrimmed. Only his small, dark eyes are exposed and it's unnerving the way he watches everyone and everything, keeping most of his thoughts to himself. I think he's best avoided; though he seems no different from the other promyshlenniki, there's something rough in his manner, and I think he could be a cruel man if provoked.

He's latched himself onto our prikashchik—the supercargo who oversees the company goods we trade and purchase—who seems pleased to order him around night and day.

Ovchinnikov throws the fish head underhand so it sails high up toward the top of the mast and then plummets down to the waiting hands of the American.

Zhuchka barks and leaps. She has much hope. Her white-tipped tail steadily wags, and her claws clatter as she runs and lunges at John Williams. She's drawing her own maps on the deck, lines stretching from man to man.

Encouraging her torment is Timofei Osipovich Tarakanov, the prikashchik who controls the dark Ovchinnikov. Timofei Osipovich is the most experienced man on the crew. He seems to know everything and doesn't hesitate to tell us that he does. His coat, trousers, and boots are all so new I wonder if he's helping himself to the cargo he's in charge of. And it's not just Ovchinnikov he's put under his spell. The Aleuts also attend to him and perform his bidding. I think my husband should pay more heed to these allegiances, but he's already told me he has it under control.

Timofei Osipovich cackles as Ovchinnikov pretends to throw the fish head overboard. He taunts, "Go swim for your supper, little Tsarina!" Zhuchka charges after the fish head. At the last moment, she catches sight of it still in Ovchinnikov's hand and reins herself in. They all laugh as she skids and hits the bulwark.

"Good morning, Madame Bulygina! Did you sleep well?" Timofei Osipovich says, leaving the dog alone.

When I know she's all right, I force my attention away from poor Zhuchka. "I did, thank you." Timofei Osipovich is jovial—as he always is before he makes an inappropriate comment or a joke at my expense. "And you?" I'm annoyed about the part he's played teasing poor Zhuchka, and don't care how he slept, but I can't bring myself to behave rudely.

"I slept delightfully," he says. "Thank you for asking. From the moment my head touched the pillow, I was asleep. I didn't lie awake for one single minute. I didn't toss and turn. I didn't groan and moan." He looks down and clears his throat. Then he narrows his eyes and looks directly at me with a wicked smile dancing at the corner of his lips.

My face floods with colour. He can't possibly have heard. Could he? Did everyone? Did Maria say something? She wouldn't have.

"And you? Did you sleep as restfully as I did?" he asks.

Before I can respond, a gull breaks through the grey with a screech, dips to the brig, and seizes the fish head in mid-air. John Williams screams. "Stop!" he cries, then explodes with laughter. Zhuchka barks and jumps, her body twisting in the air. Even brooding Ovchinnikov laughs, a deep, rolling rumble that transforms into a coughing fit as though he's not used to laughing and it's strained his system. He bends, his hands on his stomach. He can barely breathe.

The gull disappears with its prize.

"I guess your game is over," I say to Timofei Osipovich, and, though I would like a cup of tea, I go back to our quarters.

I sit at my husband's desk. It's an indulgence—an ornate secretaire from our house in Novo-Arkhangelsk, a thing far too fine for our plain cabin. He had its elegant feet screwed into the floor before our departure. Atop the desk are a few charts. The paper is as thick as serge. Smooth stones hold them down at the corners. His neat writing is on them everywhere—columns of numbers, symbols that I don't understand, and scattered place names—there's Novo-Arkhangelsk. Nootka.

I open his sharkskin case of tools. They're packed in precisely, a little slot for each. I slide them from the case, one by one. There are two wooden rulers, worn at the corners. A protractor, compass, and dividers, all made of brass. I know their names because my father told me. Russian girls are not normally taught such things, but my father saw no harm in it. He always spoke to me as if I were capable of a level of understanding no less than an adult's.

My husband is highly educated and accomplished. In Novo-Arkhangelsk, he's considered wealthy and cultured. He's already caught the eye of the chief manager, and he's known even to the Tsar. He works so fastidiously every day, studying the sky and the water. He calculates our movement with the navigation instruments he keeps near the wheel—his compass and quadrant, the log board and the knotted rope, and the leadline. Nikolai Isaakovich deduces and then tells everyone on board what must be done to keep us afloat and heading in the right direction. With extraordinary certainty, he records everything in his log book and on these charts. He is thoroughly enlightened.

I open the dividers and place one pointed end on Novo-Arkhangelsk. We departed from there September 29th, a clear day with a favourable breeze. I open the arms wider and extend them, placing the other sharp end somewhere on the coast of California. Our destination. What lies between is a faint, wandering line. The coast. Our path. But that's not what it's like. This coast is thick and certain. Like the barren north of Russia, it continues, unrelenting. Unlike Russia, it's fecund, rich with visceral odour and bands of dark blue water, pale sand, the black forest with its jagged top and, blanketing it all, the pervasive grey sky. The dark bands are broken up by the headlands of ocean-worn grey rock that sometimes take on rusty highlights on the rare occasions when the sun shines on them. The trees that rise beyond stone-strewn beaches loom unimaginably dense and dark, impossibly vertical.

Our watery path is dotted with stacks and stumps of rock, towering islands, some so small even Zhuchka couldn't stand on them, others big enough for a house. Nikolai Isaakovich has told me they pose grave danger for our brig. Beneath the surface of the sea, at the base of these stacks and stumps, there are many more rocks, jagged, barnacle-encrusted, and just waiting for a vessel to venture too close. He keeps the ship well back when they come into sight, though he allows us close enough so that he can measure the location and height of each one and mark them on his charts. As dusk gathers, he always moves the ship far out to sea, to a place many versts from shore, to where the coast is invisible, so there's no danger of running aground in the night.

I fold the dividers up. I want my cup of tea and a bowl of kasha. My husband always keeps a tidy desk, and so before I leave our quarters, I slide each tool back into its appointed slot and shut the case.

When I reach the deck, Main Rigger Sobachnikov nearly knocks me down.

"Madame Bulygina! Forgive me," he cries. He flings out his long arms and raises his hands in horror, his face redder than ever. "How careless of me. I never should have . . ." Before he finishes, he whirls away and dashes to the bow. Ovchinnikov and the Aleuts are reefing in the sails, their ostensible master, Timofei Osipovich, barking orders at them. Ovchinnikov's straggly hair covers his eyes and I don't know how he can see a thing. My husband is behind the wheel, his telescope to his eye, looking out to sea.

Through the grey, a shoreline reveals itself, a faint line demarcating the water's edge. Between it and us, there's a cluster of canoes. The row of heads and torsos jutting out from the vessels look like teeth on a comb. They're paddling toward us.

When he sees me, Timofei Osipovich turns away from his band of followers. "Opportunity has arrived, and so we open the gates," he says, with a grin.

With furtive glances to sea, the crew on deck prepares for our encounter. Zhuchka whines and paces, sensing apprehension. The canoes grow in breadth and length as they draw closer. They resemble the koliuzhi boats I've seen so often coming ashore at

Novo-Arkhangelsk, some of them immense, yet sleek as knives. These ones have long, curved bows and blunt sterns. They're mostly black but have been painted near the bow with symbols that look like faces, and some have gunwales inlaid with white stones that look like pearls.

When they reach us, the koliuzhi people call out. Their language bears no resemblance to Russian. It's crammed with popping consonants, with long, drawn-out vowels, and with thick rumbles that erupt from the back of the throat. It sounds unlike any speech I've ever heard before.

Surprisingly, Timofei Osipovich responds in their language. He says, "Wacush! Wacush!"

The canoes cluster around our brig and clatter against one another, forming a shape like a crystal pendant on a chandelier. The bow of each boat has a funny little carving on it that looks like a dog's head. In some canoes, the notch between the dog's ears supports several long wooden shafts, but I can't tell what they are. Most of the canoes hold only three or four men; a couple contain as many as ten. I count thirty-two men before I give up; the canoes are moving about too much to allow an accurate count. There are no women.

After a brief conversation, Timofei Osipovich says, "Shall we let them board?" He surveys the crew's faces and stops on my husband's.

"I don't know," Nikolai Isaakovich says. "They're armed."

Indeed, many are holding spears, while others have nocked arrows. Some have what looks like a cow's horn hanging from straps around their necks or over their shoulders. On closer observation, I see that these objects are blunt and carved with swirling lines. Are they weapons? Or just adornments?

"Their intention is clear," says the apprentice Kotelnikov, who's so impatient he's already concluded what's going on.

"Yes. They're here for trade," Timofei Osipovich says.

"Then why this arsenal?"

"You'd expect them to appear unarmed?" Timofei Osipovich says derisively, but he restrains himself as though the koliuzhi are carriage horses in danger of being spooked. "They don't know your intent any more than you know theirs."

"If they want to trade, they should put down their weapons."

"You put down yours first."

"Stop arguing," Nikolai Isaakovich tells them. "Timofei Osipovich Tarakanov, I will have a word with you." The two withdraw behind the wheel while the canoes stir and rattle against one another. Gulls screech overhead, a lone black crow darting among them. The Americans, it's said, are the only ones who let the koliuzhi board to conduct trade. The British think this rash and a temptation to fate. The Russians have no protocol, and so, in the end, my husband must choose how our trade will be conducted.

Eventually, my husband steps back and Timofei Osipovich calls to the koliuzhi again. "Wacush," he shouts. A brief conversation follows, and then two men in the canoes nearest the brig rise and work their way along the length of their vessels toward us. Then I can no longer see them. They're climbing the boarding ladder.

When they emerge, throwing their legs over the bulwark, I get a better look at them. They carry no weapons; I must assume Timofei Osipovich has insisted upon this. The first man is thin and limber with ropey muscles in his arms that swell against his smooth skin. He's around the same age as my husband, I think. His hair is knotted atop his head. Like the koliuzhi men in Novo-Arkhangelsk, he wears a cedar-bark breechclout and nothing more to protect him from the cold.

The second man is similarly dressed. His hair hangs loose and is much shorter. He has a slash across his chest, healed, but it's recent. He looks around and squints, and I wonder if he can see very well. He stops before an iron shackle, part of the rigging, and fondles it, running his fingers around its curve. I notice he's missing a finger.

Both men have painted themselves red and black. Most remarkable are their eyebrows—black half-moons that give them a look of astonishment. In all, unlike us, they've taken great care in their dress. I wonder if we've not understood one another's purpose here today.

Zhuchka is beside me. I hold her jaws so she cannot bark. She twists against me and whines, but I hold fast. "Calm yourself," I whisper.

Our crew has firearms aimed at the canoes and at the two koliuzhi on deck. The koliuzhi in the canoes point their spears and arrows at us. They hold their bows horizontally, in a fashion I find peculiar, and I wonder why they do so. With all the raised firearms, arrows, and spears, both sides resemble a hairbrush.

Our visiting koliuzhi stand so close to each other that their shoulders press together. Ovchinnikov stares through his straggly hair and drills his eyes into them. A heavy silence settles on deck.

The man with the scarred chest and missing finger watches me. How does he view me? Does he think me pallid and carelessly dressed? The clothing I wear is practical for a sea voyage but plain, a bit shabby, and badly in need of pressing. Thanks to the humid air, my dark hair is unruly—strands have escaped from beneath my cap—and my shawl hangs open, the pin carelessly left behind in our quarters, as though I don't value my modesty. The only ornament I wear is the silver cross my mother gave me years ago. Vines and leaves are carved into the three cross bars and a tiny tourmaline adorns a flower at its heart. The stone is pink in some lights but otherwise black. Zhuchka squirms, and I clamp down on her even harder.

Timofei Osipovich breaks the silence. The man's attention shifts. Zhuchka goes limp, accepting her confinement.

Timofei Osipovich's sentences are short, and he delivers them slowly. There's a long pause, and then the man who's been staring at me replies. After he finishes, Timofei Osipovich leaves a similar gap before speaking again. Each time he speaks, he repeats that same word, "wacush," and though I still don't know what it means, the koliuzhi respond favourably.

"Ryba, ryba!" somebody suddenly calls from the little boats. They know Russian? Two men in the longest boat lift a halibut about half my size. Maria cries, "My God!" and blesses herself. The men hold the huge fish aloft and wait.

We want that fish. We all want it. I imagine the meal Maria will make, the scent of it cooking in the galley, the steam that will rise from her iron pot as supper reaches perfection, the succulent morsels of the flesh in a salty broth tipped from spoon to mouth. Fresh food has been far from a daily affair on this voyage. My stomach, missing its morning tea and kasha, loudly confesses my hunger.

The negotiation begins. Timofei Osipovich says something, then sends his loyal Ovchinnikov to the hold below deck. Ovchinnikov returns with several strings of deep-blue korolki wrapped around his shoulders, and a string of glass pearls cupped in one hand. I've long admired these beautiful beads, though my tastes aren't as fine as the ladies in Petersburg who would've rejected them, not because they're unattractive, but because they're not the sapphires, rubies, and emeralds that make other women envious.

Finally, a deal is reached. Timofei Osipovich nods. Our impatient apprentice Kotelnikov shifts his weight and lets his musket sag a little. Zhuchka's tail wags tentatively.

The beads, pearls, and fish are passed over the gunwales at the same time. The Aleuts accept the fish with a grunt—it must be even heavier than I thought. Maria leads them away, her head held high as though she herself finalized the negotiation.

I expect the two koliuzhi to leave, but Timofei Osipovich is not finished with them yet. "Quartlack, quartlack," he cries, his hands open. The koliuzhi are impassive.

Sobachnikov blurts out, "They've got one, down there," and points to the canoes. Heads turn in unison. Sobachnikov's face floods, and he seems startled by his outburst. Timofei Osipovich gives him a withering look. He never has patience for Sobachnikov, and he's annoyed with the interference. Besides, he probably saw the beautiful sea otter cape long before Sobachnikov did.

A thick, fur cape rests on a man seated in the middle of the largest canoe. It's nearly black, much darker than my hair; as the man wearing it shifts slightly, he exposes its silver highlights. Everyone believes sea otter is the finest fur in the world. Back in Novo-Arkhangelsk, my husband showed me how its two distinct layers of hair render it thicker than what's found on any other animal. We call it "soft gold" in Russia, for the Chinese desire this fur over any other, and, fortunately for our empire, they're willing to pay ridiculous sums for it. I think the Chinese must be uninformed. Our Russian sable is far more beautiful and soft.

It occurs to me that what's happening—what has been happening ever since the canoes appeared—is about the black cape in the canoe. The halibut and the korolki have been a prelude to more important matters. We're here for sea otter furs.

"Makuk," says Timofei Osipovich, his eyes narrowing. "Makuk." He waits, then says again that word, "Wacush."

Timofei Osipovich sends Ovchinnikov back to the hold. Ovchinnikov takes a long time. The koliuzhi with the fur cape makes no effort to remove it. Throughout, the weapons on both sides remain aloft and no one speaks. Though the fish and korolki were successfully traded, any trust between us is only a half-cooked blin: batter poured onto the griddle and turned before it was set.

Ovchinnikov returns finally with our part of the trade: more korolki, more glass pearls, a fold of nankeen cotton, dark blue as the sea this day, and an iron bar, which must be poor quality or it wouldn't be offered so easily. I know this; surely the koliuzhi do, too. However, I still think it a favourable deal, better than what was offered for the halibut. But the koliuzhi remain unconvinced.

Then the koliuzhi man with the scar on his chest cries, "ʔupakuut! ʔupakuut!"[1]

Timofei Osipovich frowns deeply, and it's easy to predict what he'll look like as an aged man of forty years. In an instant, the frown transforms into a smile and a sharp laugh.

"They want your coat," he says to Nikolai Isaakovich.

"My coat? Whatever for?" He looks down at his chest.

"It's not the coat exactly. They want the cloth."

"Well, I need it. They can't have it," my husband says, somewhat petulantly. It's his black-green greatcoat, and it's been chilly enough throughout the voyage that he wears it every day. It nearly reaches his ankles and is adorned on the front and the shoulders with brass buttons stamped with the imperial eagle. With a tall collar and flaring cuffs that more or less reach his elbows, it's made of coarse broadcloth. "Tell them there's nothing wrong with the nankeen cotton, and that it's the best they'll ever see in exchange for that ratty, old pelt."

Calling the fur cape ratty is untrue and rude. What is Nikolai Isaakovich thinking? Does he want the fur or not?

Timofei Osipovich tells them something. When he finishes, there's much discussion in the canoes. Timofei Osipovich leans over the bulwark next to Ovchinnikov and they observe very closely. They remain so focused that they don't see when the koliuzhi men on deck make a move. They're halfway over the gunwales before either notices.

---

1   Coat! Coat!

Timofei Osipovich is startled. He cries out, "Quartlack! Quartlack! Makuk!" No one from the canoes replies. "Makuk!" he shouts again, shaking his fist toward the disappearing flotilla. "Makuk klush!"

As they paddle away, I release Zhuchka. Timofei Osipovich regains his composure. He says to Nikolai Isaakovich, "Well, the scythe has hit a stone. But they'll be back tomorrow. I will get you that pelt, and many more."

"They have more?"

Zhuchka puts her front paws on the bulwark. She barks and wags her tail at the disappearing koliuzhi.

"Of course they do. This is all a part of the trade. You wait until you see what they bring tomorrow. Your eyes will bleed."

Maria does justice to the halibut. In the galley, she saws through the fat flesh and tosses chunks into a pot of water. I stand away, for I don't want my apron to be stained. Blood and slime and shiny intestines and organs drip from the cutting surface. She ignores them, though Zhuchka does not. She devours whatever bits land within reach.

Maria chops each slice of carrot in half, frugal as she is. The fresh vegetables we carry—grown over the summer and sold by the bishop's own gardener in Novo-Arkhangelsk—won't last much longer. It's a testament to Maria's thriftiness and good planning that we have any left at all.

The smell of cooking fish wafts throughout the brig all afternoon. It's a relief when the meal's ready. Because there's so much fish, everyone's bowl brims with fat chunks of flesh.

Once the initial exclamations of delight are made, praise for Maria's skill expressed, and thanks to God offered, there's silence around the table, except for the sounds of eating and an occasional grunt of satisfaction. The men slurp the meal off their big, thick spoons. The bones are large and easy to find, and they extract them from their mouths impatiently while lifting another spoon of the oily broth to their lips.

Even I gobble the ukha as though I'm back home and my own mother has made it.

The sky clears in the evening. Content after the big meal, I wrap my warmest shawl around me, tie the ends loosely—I can't find my pin—and take my telescope on deck. It's breezy, and the air is so cool my face tingles. I look up. A few wisps of cloud remain. It's far from perfect, but as my father often says, the best astronomers always find a way to work with the seasons. I raise my telescope.

Polaris is faint. The tail of Ursa Minor is all that's visible of that constellation. Pisces, however, is clear. The two fish remind me of my supper. I follow the cord between them until I find Alpha Piscium, the star that holds them together.

"Anya?" my husband calls from across the deck.

"I'm here."

He approaches, and I lower my telescope. "Aren't you cold?" He folds his arms across his chest, burying his hands in those enormous cuffs, then grimaces and shivers. "Come inside."

I nod and snake my arm through his until we're latched together. "In a few moments." We huddle side by side and look to sea. Darkness surrounds us. The stars and moon and their insubstantial reflection that flickers on the edges of the waves provide the only point of reference. Without them, our direction would be unknowable.

It's easy to imagine how somebody would believe the vody-anoy, the old spirit man of the sea, lurks out there. Swimming just below the surface, hungering for human life, aggravated by the neglect of sailors who fail to make the proper offerings. One swish of his scaly tale would sink a ship. So the stories go.

"They'll be back," says my husband suddenly. "Tomorrow."

"Chief Manager Baranov will be pleased," I say, but only after a slight pause, because I thought he was talking about the vodyanoy, or perhaps the stars.

"Timofei Osipovich says they'll bring all the sea otter skins we want."

I squeeze his arm. "I hope he's right."

Nikolai Isaakovich pulls away. "Why would you say that?" he says sharply.

In the dark, it's hard to see what's in his face. "I meant nothing," I say cautiously. "Only that I await their return, with the pelts."

He relaxes, and, after a bit, he kisses me on the temple. "Come now, Anya. Let's go. That's enough for today."

There's no sign of life from the coast when we awaken. The morning stretches to noon, and still the koliuzhi do not reappear. Midday, we eat, and the leftover ukha warms my toes. Nikolai Isaakovich refuses his serving and remains on deck. He paces and watches the coast. He peers through his telescope, slowly scanning the shore. Zhuchka watches him, her eyes mournful, her ears flattened as though she already knows that he'll see nothing of what he seeks.

CHAPTER TWO

There are times at sea when everything seems favourable—the wind does not slow the ship, the current is advantageous, the sky is clear, and, if you're very fortunate, the sun warms the vessel and buoys everyone's spirits. Six weeks into our journey the brig enters a period of such favourable conditions. After having endured weeks of mostly grey sky, frequent rain, and capricious winds that either blew too strongly or diminished and left the brig becalmed, this ease is welcome.

The crew members work together like they're in a dance, each man knowing the next step and undertaking it with pleasure. The ropes groan, the rigging rattles, and the sails billow like they aspire to be clouds. The promyshlenniki's movements are graceful and generous as they manipulate canvas and cordage to move us closer to our destination.

"Destruction Island," says Timofei Osipovich, indicating a distant pan of land late one afternoon. "That's the English name."

"Why? What does that mean?" I say.

"Destruction?" He shakes his head. "It means ruin. Everything that touches that place is ruined. No good has ever come from it. No good ever will."

Rocky cliffs rim the island. The sea foams like a frothy dessert next to its westernmost edge. It appears harmless, even beautiful from this distance. As we pass to its south, we come closer and are afforded a fresh view. Like a hat, it sits atop the waves. Two long tongues of land bend away from its coast and thrust out into the sea. Behind it, in the distance, the shore looks mostly sandy and flat, except for a few stacks and the distant mouth of a river dotted with sea birds.

"Did they wreck their ships here?" I peer, wondering if I might spot the remains of a broken mast or hull, evidence of the calamities after which the island has been named.

Timofei Osipovich laughs. "It's not for wrecked ships."

"Then what?"

"You think—the vodyanoy?" he taunts. He curls his fingers into claws and bares his teeth. He lurches at me with a growl, then laughs when I recoil. "Don't worry, Madame Bulygina, I'm teasing." Then nonchalantly he adds, "It's only because of the koliuzhi."

The old Aleut Yakov is nearby, cap tilted away from his face, mop in hand, a bucket of seawater at his feet. He's grey-haired and grizzled, missing many of his teeth, easily the oldest man on the crew. According to my husband, he's been working for the Russian-American Company since he was six years old, so his Russian is quite good, though accented.

"It's better we don't speak of such things here at this time of day," he says, slapping his mop to the deck, and turning his back.

I stare hard at the island. Are there people out there watching us? People whose intentions are less than noble? What did they do to the English? I'm not pious—I place all my faith in rational thought and the scientific method—but I can't help but brush my fingers along the silver cross on my necklace, just in case.

My mother fastened the silver cross around my neck long ago. I was only eight years old. I had a raging fever and a hoarse cough, and she sat up with me for several nights. Her hand was cool and weightless as a feather against my forehead, against my cheek. Then a rash spread over my body, rolling hills of red blossoms that reached the ends of my limbs. It itched so badly I wanted to tear off my skin.

"It's measles," my father said. "Every child gets it. You must let it be." He cut my fingernails so short I couldn't scratch myself.

Within a day, I could no longer see.

The doctor insisted my father was right: it was measles, and the loss of vision, while troubling, would likely be temporary. He'd seen it before. He prescribed bitter medicine. He ordered the curtains drawn and the lamps extinguished; no light was to enter my room as it could render me permanently blind.

I was alone with my mother when the visions started. I bolted upright in bed, and I screamed.

"What is it?" my mother cried.

There were serpents twining around branches, fiery-eyed bears with unsheathed claws, a mushroom that transformed into a wolf that stalked me. These were from the stories all parents told their children to teach them caution. There was also a kitten that I cuddled in my coat only to have it die and transform into a skeleton. A hunter who lured me into the forest and tried to leave me with an old woman who wanted to chop off my fingers. These were strange beings from the even more disturbing stories my mother and her friends shared. The creatures had come alive at last, and I could neither close nor open my eyes against any of them, for they existed inside me.

"If you hadn't filled her mind with all that superstitious non-sense, she'd be fine," my father said. "It's just a fever."

He called the doctor back. My medicines were changed. He prescribed tonics that smelled so vile I gagged before taking even a mouthful. I couldn't sleep at all; the visions came whether my eyes were open or closed. My skin was on fire. Days ran into one another, with no change.

My father called the doctor for the third time. He brought a reeking bucket whose contents smelled of rotting fish. He told my mother to apply it to my rash twice a day and leave it for a half hour. Once the proscribed time had passed, she could remove the poultice and plunge me into an ice-cold bath.

My father had the servants carry the bathtub up the staircase and roll it into my bedchamber. They brought bucket after bucket of cold water until it was filled. I heard splash after splash, the servants' voices subdued.

When it was all ready, my mother said to my father, "I'll take care of it now." Her cool hand rested firmly on my forehead.

I detected my father's uncertainty. He wouldn't have completely trusted my mother to comply with the doctor's orders, and yet, his presence in the room while I bathed would have been unthinkable.

"Are you sure you heard the doctor correctly?" my father said.

"I did." She rose from my side and I heard her footsteps moving toward the door.

"You can't lift her into the bath tub. She'll be too heavy for you."

"I can do it." The latch clicked as my mother closed the door softly behind him.

No poultice of rotting fish was applied to the rash. I was never plunged into the bathtub. Instead, in the darkened room, my mother whispered to me of a silver cross on a chain. Her lips moved against my ear. She described its arms, the vines and leaves that adorned it, the jewelled flower at its heart. "Now," she said, "I will tell you what I'm doing with it. Listen."

She told me that she was dipping the cross in a bowl of water. I heard the splash, heard it knock against the sides of the bowl, heard the drip as she withdrew it. Then she told me she was lighting the wicks of three candles. I smelled the flare of the tallow. She prayed over the candles. "Coffin and grave, thrice I cleanse you," she said. Next, she told me she was holding the candles over the water one at a time and letting the wax drip into it. Then, I felt the rim of the bowl on my lips.

I sipped the water.

Afterward, she fastened the chain around my neck. The chain was too long for a child and it hung so low no one would ever know I was wearing it. Perhaps that was her intention.

I felt her kneel at my bedside and lean over the mattress. She began to pray.

She prayed for hours, her voice a low rumble of praise, pleas, and promises. When she finally stopped, she said, "Never speak of this night to your father." She kissed my forehead.

According to my mother, I fell asleep immediately and slept for the entire night. When I woke, my fever was gone, my eyesight had been restored, and I was very hungry. My parents embraced me and for many months afterward, indulged me with whatever I asked for.

As I grew older, and as my father continued teaching me the lessons of the Enlightenment, I dismissed the miraculous cure. It was coincidence. The illness had run its course, and the medicines had worked. While I didn't share my mother's view of the world, I knew that arguing would be disrespectful and, moreover, senseless. She'd never allowed enlightened thought to restrain her understanding. I allowed her to believe she'd cured me.

But no amount of rational thought was able to completely chase away the visions. They'd been so vivid and noisy that day, as though they were alive, and I wasn't certain they weren't still alive and wouldn't one day return. My father would have said they were caused by the fever or maybe the medicine, fuelled by a child's imagination. If we had ever spoken about them, I would have agreed. But just as my mother had warned me, I did not mention anything else about that night to my father.

The sun begins its descent into the sea, and the air has already cooled. My husband shouts orders from the foredeck. Men scramble with the rigging. The horizon swivels until we're sailing into the setting sun. Is Nikolai Isaakovich deliberately avoiding Destruction Island?

We sail into the dying light, and when the shore is a distant memory, we come to a halt. The wind that has favoured us for so many days has diminished but not died completely. We go to bed in this welcome quiet and wake to an ominous silence. The air is still, heavy as a decision waiting to be made. We're becalmed. The brig drifts. My husband and the others seem preoccupied, but there's nothing to be done except to wait for the wind to reappear. It's irrational to think it won't.

We pass a dull, windless day, rocked by the sea swell. Zhuchka is restless and petulant, and it comforts neither her nor me when I rub her ears. I polish my telescope and review my star log. I even while away some time embroidering the dinner napkins I brought. The linen was an unexpected gift from the chief manager. He must have paid dearly for it because it was fine and clear, and not the coarse linen that the promyshlenniki sometimes use to make their trousers and shirts. I'm embroidering an elaborate pattern in red and black, with a Б in the centre of one edge on each napkin. After I miss two stitches and must tear apart several rows, I throw my work back into its basket in a fury and sit and wish for the night to arrive. The movement of the stars will be a more gratifying diversion.

Much later, I bundle up under my shawl and take my telescope out on deck. But it's pointless. The sky is completely overcast. There's not a hint of wind. The sea is still dead calm and looks to remain that way all night. We pass a second windless night, and the next day, too, until late in that afternoon, Destruction Island comes into sight once more. The swell pushes us to the north of it, and we drift closer and closer to shore. The sails sag uselessly. We need wind. A storm. I chastise myself after this thought arises. We don't want a storm, do we?

As we helplessly float toward shore, Nikolai Isaakovich calls everyone on deck.

"We should drop anchor right now," blurts the apprentice Kotelnikov, impetuous as always. My husband's face barely moves, but I know what he's thinking.

"Don't be irrational. It's still too deep," drawls the American.

"Well, what about the skiff? Can't we use the skiff?" Kotelnikov counters, with an urgency that veers toward panic. "The Aleuts could tow us out to sea. What are we waiting for?"

"Ah, but to what end? There's no wind. How can we row all night?" says Yakov.

"Perhaps we could raise the sails and try?" Sobachnikov squeaks. He takes a tentative step toward the main mast and reaches toward the ratline. "There's a trace of offshore breeze." Timofei Osipovich frowns and the others either don't hear the main rigger or choose to ignore him. His shoulders droop, his face colours, and he steps away from the mast as if he'd never made the suggestion.

"If we can't get away from shore, we'll be pushed onto the rocks in the morning," says John Williams.

"If it takes that long!" says Kotelnikov. "We'll run aground before midnight."

Timofei Osipovich remains uncharacteristically quiet.

Finally, Nikolai Isaakovich waves his hand to terminate the

discussion. "Here are my orders: we'll steer through these rocks and reefs as best we can. The sea will determine our speed. As soon as we're able, we'll drop anchor, and we must do so before we lose what daylight is left. Then, we'll wait for the wind to pick up and, if we're blessed, it won't blow a gale. I should be able to steer back out through the same course to the open sea, and we'll resume our voyage."

"But the rocks," says Kotelnikov.

"If we can pass them once, it will be a miracle," says the American. "We'll have to pass them twice in order to get out."

An uneasy silence unfolds. No man knows where to look.

"As we all know, he who sits between two chairs may easily fall down," declares Timofei Osipovich finally. "Unfortunately, that's where we find ourselves. It's time to choose a chair. Our navigator is right." There's a stirring among the men, and I can't easily tell which side they're on. Then I see the tension dissolve from my husband's face, and I realize he's convinced them. We're going to steer through the rocks and anchor as soon as we can.

The crew whirls around like a waterspout, attending to this and that, and eventually they position themselves around the bulwark on the foredeck. There are no instruments, tools, or devices to help us now. We must depend only on what can be seen with the naked eye, a difficult enough task made worse by the dying light. There are twenty-one sets of eyes strung along the bow of the boat, for even Maria and I have joined the men.

"When you see a shoal or a reef, or a large rock beneath the surf, you must call out right away," Timofei Osipovich instructs us. "Don't wait. The survival of the brig may depend on you."

Nikolai Isaakovich embraces the wheel and holds it tight to his chest. He pushes himself onto his toes and uses the wheel to hold himself up. The men begin to call.

"Reef!" barks Ovchinnikov, peering through his hair.

"Rock!" cries the apprentice. "Be careful!"

We call out to my husband, our voices floating up one by one from all sides of the ship. "There's one here on my side!" exclaims Yakov. "Watch out!"

The water's surface ripples and glistens, making it difficult to see below the surface. When I do get a glimpse of the depths, I see shadow, and once, fish that scatter and vanish as quickly as they appeared.

My eyes strain against the moving water. I'm not sure I know what to look for. I don't want to call out in error, but I also fear my hesitation will cause the ship to run aground.

And then suddenly an object comes into focus. It happens just like it does when I'm trying to find a certain star with my telescope. That sudden clarity. I point. "A rock! Kolya! There's a rock!"

In response, Nikolai Isaakovich turns the wheel and steers away, along a passage so narrow even our tiny skiff couldn't navigate through it.

Kotelnikov points, his sizeable trunk pressed into the bulwark. "Look out! Look out! Are you looking out?"

Sobachnikov cries, "A sandbar!"

We're pushed even closer to shore.

I listen for the sound of a scrape. I listen for the splintering of wood. But neither come. The brig remains afloat.

"Drop anchor," my husband orders. The men release an anchor hooked to the aft of the brig. It splashes and the sea gulps it down. I hold my breath—we all do—but the anchor doesn't catch. The water is still too deep. The brig continues to drift toward shore, waiting for that anchor to reach bottom or hook onto something.

As the hazards slide into view the crew calls out: "Rock!" "Sandbar!" "Reef!"

Nikolai Isaakovich turns the wheel to port and to starboard as he's directed. The guidance comes fast, and he must concentrate.

Then, he orders again, "Drop anchor!" The second anchor goes over. It's slightly smaller than the first but fitted with the same pointed flukes, so perhaps it will work. We wait to feel the brig slow and stop, but no. We still drift.

"Again!" my husband orders. "Drop anchor!" This time surely we'll be successful.

But the brig lurches toward shore on the surf. "It's not working! Navigator!" cries the apprentice.

My husband orders for the last time, "And again!" That's our fourth anchor. There are none left.

Then—merciful God—the brig stops.

A cheer erupts. The crew members embrace, slap shoulders and backs. I catch the eye of Nikolai Isaakovich. He smiles weakly from behind the wheel. Zhuchka runs back and forth, nudging us with her nose as she passes. She yaps and though I know she can't possibly understand the peril we've evaded, to whatever extent is possible, I believe she feels our joy.

I turn my attention back to the water. Where are we? We're ringed by rock stumps. Not far from the bow of the vessel lies a patch of pale sea, visible even in the dim light. It's a broad shoal on which we would have run aground had we not halted when we did. Beyond this patch of sea lies a narrow, sandy beach that stretches away from us until it reaches the mouth of a river—the river we saw as we drifted in, the river that seemed to be pulling us ashore.

Tomorrow, the wind will return, and we'll reverse our feat. Nikolai Isaakovich will navigate back out through the rocks, and we'll safely return to our mission.

But the crew members haven't budged from their places ringing the brig's bow. They're quiet and watchful.

"Look," cries the apprentice Kotelnikov. He points.

The sea heaves. The swell is even stronger this close to shore. It lifts our brig, then releases it. Lifts and releases. Over and over again, and with each rise and fall, the brig strains against the creaking anchor cables that hold us steady. But one anchor cable rubs against a rock as the brig falls with the sea.

Timofei Osipovich and his faithful Ovchinnikov rush to the bulwark. Timofei Osipovich shoves the apprentice aside as Ovchinnikov brushes his hair from his eyes like he can't believe what he's seeing.

"Pull," cries Timofei Osipovich, and he and Ovchinnikov reach over and wrap their hands around the cable. I lean out over the bulwark so I can see what they're doing. Their fingers tighten around the cable. They twist and pull, trying to shift it away from the rock. They're fighting not only the cable. The brig and the sea pull against them, too.

"We need help," Timofei Osipovich shouts. Yakov and the Aleuts squeeze in beside them, but there's only so much room. One of the Aleuts climbs over the bulwark and hangs upside down, while Ovchinnikov holds him by the waist of his trousers. The Aleut stretches toward the cable. Perhaps from that precarious position he can add force to the others' efforts.

But whatever they do, it's to no avail. We helplessly watch strand after strand of the anchor cable wear through, each one shredding then snapping until only one fibre remains. When it goes, the broken cable flops into the ocean like a snake and the brig pivots. The ship comes to rest, held in place by the remaining cables.

Our new position is no better. The second cable ends up similarly compromised. The American, John Williams, climbs over the bulwark and gingerly steps onto the cable. He holds the railing, and the weight of his body is supported by the cable. He springs on it, gets it bouncing up and down.

"Be careful," says Yakov.

"Get back on board," orders Timofei Osipovich. "You're making it worse." He reaches for the cable. His hands are bleeding. The Aleuts are at his side once again.

This cable doesn't last as long as the first, and it soon breaks, leaving us with only two anchors.

Night has fallen. Nikolai Isaakovich calls for the lanterns. Sobachnikov takes the first one and leans out as far as he can—farther than anybody else can reach since he's so tall—and dangles it from a crooked finger, casting light and shadows in the area around the third cable. Eventually, under the weight of the lantern, his extended arm begins to shake, until he has no choice but to retract it. The men take turns and struggle, fighting against what I now believe will be our fate.

When it's completely dark and Orion is directly overhead, visible without the telescope, I find the three stars of his belt. As if to mock us, strong and solid, it fixes him and his sword to the firmament forever. We don't need forever—we just need the cables to hold until the wind comes up.

Then the third cable snaps.

As dawn approaches, Orion slips down toward the sea. He'll disappear soon, as every astronomer knows. But on this occasion, his looming departure feels prophetic.

Then—wait! "Commander!" shouts the American. He's not the only one who's noticed. A nearly indiscernible breeze has come up from the southwest. Nikolai Isaakovich jerks to attention. He scans the sails, looking for response, but they only droop. Still, each little gust tickles my cheek, and each time, it feels slightly stronger than the last. Silently I urge: blow, wind! If not now, then when?

We finally lose the last anchor. Whatever noise the severed cable makes when it gives way is consumed by the sound of the surf; I feel the loss immediately as the brig pivots like a dancer unleashed from the grip of her partner.

This breeze is the only thing that can save us now, this inconsequential and capricious breeze blowing from the southwest— that and the skill of my husband. Nikolai Isaakovich orders the sagging sails hoisted. Again, he leans into the wheel and spins it all the way to one side. Stout Kotelnikov thrusts a flickering lantern as far out over the bow as he can stretch, but his reach is inadequate. As the sky brightens in the east behind the black trees, the light his lantern casts is faint, too diffuse.

"Can't you hold it farther out?" says Yakov. "The navigator can't see."

He presses himself tighter against the bulwark until his round body bulges against the wood. Eventually, his lantern lines up with those of Yakov and the American, and I can't help but feel glad to see Orion's belt mirrored here on the brig. Maybe we're going to make it.

The sails flutter in the light wind. There's a hopeful rattle from the rigging.

"This passage is so narrow," declares Timofei Osipovich, "no navigator but ours would dare to attempt to find a path through it in the light of day, let alone now."

For once, there is nothing in his words for me to disagree with.

We pass rock and shoal and rock and reef again. With each wave that breaks, I'm buoyed. I wait for the thud, the splinter, the crunch—but they don't come. We're moving into water that's increasingly deeper. My husband sends the apprentice for the leadline. "I want to know how deep it is before we extinguish the lanterns," he says. He's beaming—he knows we're safe.

Behind the wheel, he stands tall and navigates through what may be the trickiest passage of his career, the most awkward, with the greatest stakes. Dear Nikolai Isaakovich, you're proving your worth to the company. How I wish Chief Manager Baranov were here to witness your astonishing skill! I squeeze Zhuchka until she coughs and squirms.

But then, the sea and the wind are nothing if not unpredictable. I'm a fool to forget this.

With a groan and a crack, the foreyard breaks.

Twenty-two sets of eyes roll up, drawn to the noise. A length of the yardarm falls and swings, attached only by shards of wood. The once-billowing foresail collapses and flutters uselessly.

Sobachnikov, the main rigger, dashes to the base of the mast and, like a spider, begins to pull himself up.

"Stop! Wait!" cries Timofei Osipovich. "There's nothing you can do now. We have no spare."

The brig was to have dropped anchor several days ago so the crew could go ashore to replenish our supplies. The barrels of fresh water needed topping up. The promyshlenniki were to take Zhuchka hunting for ducks or, if they were lucky, a deer. Nikolai Isaakovich also wanted them to cut a few timbers that could be used to repair or replace the masts and yards if they should break. The weather prevented us from getting close to shore that day. The next day, there was no acceptable place to anchor. I don't remember what happened the third day. The water barrels were low, but the situation wasn't desperate. Then the brig was becalmed.

"But—" cries John Williams. "You can't tack against this without the foresail!"

"Our fate is sealed," Timofei Osipovich declares. For once, there's no mockery in his tone.

The crew tries valiantly. They manipulate the sails as best they can under the direction of my husband, with Timofei Osipovich offering assurances and advice. Even I, knowing nothing of sailing, can see the futility. Without the foresail, we can only head in one direction. For a long time and a short time, the surf pushes us toward the shore.

Mid-morning, a swell lifts the brig—the most powerful swell to hit us all morning. We rise, rise, rise—and pause. The brig teeters. My husband freezes, his hands clutched to the wheel. Old Yakov removes his cap and blesses himself. Then, with a *whoosh*, the water recedes. We fall gently. The hull grinds into the sand. The brig stops. We meet our fate.

It's not noisy. It's not dramatic. It is merely the end of our voyage.

Zhuchka gives a joyful yap, happy perhaps that we're finally not moving.

But her joy is short-lived. The surf, finished its inhalation, now exhales. The waves strike us broadside. The brig tilts. Seawater sprays the deck. I flinch when it hits me. Then the water rushes out and the brig levels. A moment later, the waves crash against us again. Our vessel groans. How I wish the force were strong enough to dislodge us from this sandy perch and carry us back out to sea. But we have no such luck.

Then the ship is struck by two terrible waves in succession. There's no lull, no time to catch my breath. The brig tilts to shore at such a precarious angle that I'm certain we'll capsize. I press my body against the foremast and hold with all my strength. The ship tilts to the other side when the water recedes. Poor Yakov slips on the wet deck and falls. His cap goes flying. His body slides until it hits the bulwark. Sobachnikov rushes over, helps him up and hands him his cap.

Nikolai Isaakovich should give orders, but latched to the wheel he's like a sleepwalker—his eyes open and staring but vacant.

"Navigator!" Timofei Osipovich cries.

His one word forces Nikolai Isaakovich from his stupor. He surveys the questioning faces on deck and shakes his head like he's coming out of his dream. His confusion slips away, replaced with an authority he must have learned in the naval academy.

He calls on the ship's carpenter, Ivan Kurmachev. "Is there water in the hold?" Kurmachev scurries below deck as fast as he can, given his age. His footsteps bang down the ladder.

Then he addresses Timofei Osipovich. "Where in the name of heaven are we?"

"We're north of Destruction Island," he replies.

"I know that," my husband says, exasperated. "Does this place have a name?"

Timofei Osipovich shakes his head slowly. "It might. You could check your charts."

Just then, Kurmachev comes clattering up the ladder. "Commander! She's filling!" he shouts hoarsely and pants.

"How much time do we have?"

"Not long."

"Then we have no choice. We must abandon ship," my husband says. He leans in and renews his grip on the wheel, contrary to what he's just said. The members of the crew are equally insensible. They continue to cling to the bulwark, the masts, or whatever holds them steady. The waves continue to wash in and out.

"Abandon ship!" he insists. Again, no one moves.

Timofei Osipovich intercedes. "First, the arms and the ammunition," he orders. "Keep the powder dry."

"We can't take the skiff out in this surf," says the apprentice Kotelnikov.

Timofei Osipovich gives him a withering look before he issues orders. "Kozma Ovchinnikov, John Williams—and Yakov—and the rest of the Aleuts—you'll carry as much as you can manage." He tells them to jump overboard, run to shore and drop their loads, and, as soon as possible, return to the ship where the remaining crew members will have their next load ready.

"Now, on my mark," Timofei Osipovich advises. Another fierce wave breaks against the brig, and she tilts alarmingly toward shore. When the waves reach their furthest point up the sand, they turn around and start back toward us. The instant the ship starts to swing back, Timofei Osipovich shouts, "Now!"

The crew jumps, arms loaded and held well above their heads. Zhuchka can't help it. She flings herself into the sea right behind them.

Dog and men, they surge toward the shore as if pursued by the devil. My arms remain wrapped around the foremast.

Nikolai Isaakovich orders the men to remove the sails. "These will be our tents," he says. They climb and begin to unfasten the shackles and draw rope through the blocks.

Some of the crew return. They take the next load, more arms and ammunition and, I'm relieved to see, a barrel of buckwheat.

In this way, lifting, leaping, landing, and running in waves timed against the surf, they ferry the necessities onto shore. Timofei Osipovich even gets them to salvage a cannon. They roll it off the deck. It splashes into the shallow water, lands on its barrel, and is impaled in the sand. Much time and great strength are required to dislodge it and get it to shore, but the men manage.

I remain latched to the foremast. The more I look at it, the more the distance between the brig and the shore expands. I can't swim well, and, as irrational as it seems, I can't leave without my telescope and star log. I must go get them. But then what? I don't think I can just jump into the sea. I must save myself, it's the sensible course of action, but when I look at all I need to do to reach land, I'm immobilized. I dig my nails into the mast.

"Anya," shouts Nikolai Isaakovich. "What are you doing? Go to shore."

"Now?"

"Yes now! Hurry up."

"But I want my telescope!"

"For God's sake, Anya. Go to shore."

"No. I want my telescope."

Flustered, he pounds the air with his fist. "This is not the time!"

"I'm going to get my telescope." I let go of the mast; the brig shifts violently to one side. I stumble and grab the mast again.

"I'll bring it to you. When I come to shore. I promise. Now go, Anya. Before it's too late."

"And the log! Don't forget my star log."

"Oh, Anya," he groans. I wish I didn't sound so petulant, but these things are important.

I stagger to the bulwark and throw one leg over. I hold tight to the railing. It steadies me. I wait, as I've seen Timofei Osipovich do, for the surf to break. It crashes against the side of the vessel, releasing an arc of spray that pricks my back. The brig tilts and the timbers moan.

I must wait.

Wait.

The sea makes a terrible sound as it retreats, like a million grains of wheat pouring through the fingers of the mighty hand of God.

Now.

I jump.

My feet meet unyielding sand. The water's done nothing to cushion my fall. Rather, the sea catches at my skirt and tries to pull me out. The sand washes out from beneath my feet. The ground collapses. I dig in my toes. It's no use. I'm being pulled out to sea.

It's cold. Colder than the Neva during a Petersburg spring.

"Run, Madame Bulygina, run!" somebody screams from the brig. I try to see who, but when I turn, the next wave is upon me. It's a grey wall charging like an angered bull.

I run.

I never could have imagined this. The cold water will break my bones. I'll go under and drown. My corpse will float all the way back to Russia. The shore is shifting, and it's so rimmed with froth, I can't tell how much farther I need to go. My shoes are packed with sand and filled with water. One shoe starts to slip off.

I can't go on without my shoes. I must not lose this shoe. I reach down. If I can just tug it back over my heel—

The surf knocks me over.

I tumble. Cold envelops me. The sea pulls me up, pushes me down. I've nothing to latch onto now. My body is jumbled like coins at the bottom of a pocket. I can't tell where the sky is. I'm overcome with the irrational fear that something down here is trying to get me. Somebody's screaming. There's a rough tug on my arm. And then another on my other side. I'm up. I cough and spit out water. It burns inside my nose. I can't see for the hair in my eyes, but I know two people are dragging me to shore.

Over the roar of the sea, I hear shouting, but there's water in my ears and everything's muffled. It's as though the person addressing me is in another room, a distant place.

Finally, I'm lugged completely onto shore. Water streams all down my body and pools on the ground at my feet, at my shoes. Both shoes. My ears clear.

My old grey shawl is gone, thanks to my lost pin, presumably still somewhere in our quarters, gone to be with the sea and sky, as though all grey things have an irresistible affinity for one another. I touch my head. My cap has floated away, too, and now I'm bareheaded like a little girl.

Zhuchka leaps around me, barking.

"Madame Bulygina, you almost killed yourself!" Maria scolds.

"Go dry yourself by the fire," Timofei Osipovich says. "Help her," he orders Maria. He turns and strides into the sea, strong legs plunging through the surf and propelling him back toward the brig.

"Did your mother teach you nothing?" Maria chastises. She takes my arm and leads me to where the promyshlenniki have built a fire in a ring of smooth stones. A plume of smoke rises into the sky and bends toward the forest until I can no longer see it. I lower myself onto a piece of silvery wood and wait for warmth to enter my body. I can't wait for night to fall. Perhaps I'll be able to bear the inconceivable misfortune that has befallen us if my beloved Polaris is there watching over us tonight.

CHAPTER THREE

———————

The fire crackles like a hot frying pan, and my clothes steam as they begin to dry. I adjust the folds of fabric, spreading out the layers around my legs. I extend my arms and turn them like I'm roasting them. The crew has erected two tents with, under the circumstances, a strangely respectable distance between them. I just can't fathom that I'll be sleeping in one of them tonight.

Zhuchka doesn't care about drying off. Unlike us, she's spirited and good-natured. She noses about the beach, compelled to examine every rock, every shell, every log. She chases the birds bold enough to land. They easily fly out of her reach and return once she's not looking. Despite our circumstances, it's impossible to begrudge her this joy. Every once in a while, she raises her muzzle and chews, having found some morsel.

It must be well past the time for our midday meal. I glance at Maria; she's staring into the fire with a muted expression. I feel reluctant to mention hunger—it seems trivial in the face of our present adversity. I try to concentrate on the warmth from the fire and the comfort it brings.

My perch on this log faces the sea. It's a convenient place from which to watch the crew finish unloading the boat. They haul barrels and sacks of ammunition, tools, and food through the foaming surf. They fight against the forceful sea, which pushes and pulls them in opposing directions. They make trip after trip after trip, labouring as they drag everything across the stones and through the sand, and then place it beneath the large tent to ensure it stays dry.

Mercifully, there's no rain falling now, and it doesn't feel as if it's imminent. Light clouds blanket the sky far above us. The smoke from our fire merges with it and disappears. I hope we have a dry night.

My husband stands thigh-deep in the ocean, just beyond where the surf breaks, near to where a bobbing flock of black seabirds warily keeps an eye on our activity. He shouts commands to the Aleuts who are still on deck. One of them is high up the mainmast and continuing to dismantle the sails from the rigging. I'm not sure why; perhaps Nikolai Isaakovich intends to erect more tents.

Has he retrieved my telescope and star log and sent to shore yet? I hope he hasn't forgotten. Otherwise, somebody will have to make a separate trip to fetch them.

Most of the rest of the crew is here beside the fire. The apprentice Kotelnikov sits and stands and sits again, lacking the patience to find a comfortable enough seat on the logs and rocks. Carpenter Kurmachev earlier opened his flask, but when he found it empty, he began whittling a piece of wood. He dejectedly flicks the shavings into the fire. Timofei Osipovich opens his palms to the flames. The bleeding has stopped, but his hands are raw and bruised.

He's ordered his steadfast Ovchinnikov and the American to stand sentry. They're a short distance away, facing the forest, their firearms loaded and resting over their shoulders. It's the koliuzhi they await, but there's no sign anybody's nearby. We haven't seen or heard anything other than what you'd expect from such a vast and desolate wilderness.

We've run aground in a place that's empty and beautiful. The edge of the beach closest to the surf is covered with smooth stones. Bundles of tangled kelp mark the tideline and brilliant white seashells glow even though it's overcast. Above the stones, there's powdery, pale sand. A few silvery logs, tossed up on shore and dug into the sand, set up a barricade along this upper edge. Beyond this, beach grass nods in the gentle breeze, and beyond that, dense black forest beckons and threatens at the same time. Birds drift overhead and keen and call out to one another. Their cries echo eerily off the trees and rocks, rising above the incessant sound of the sea.

Ovchinnikov stops. He slips his musket off his shoulder and aims it at the forest, spreads his legs wide. Timofei Osipovich sits up and takes his hands away from the fire. The bushes at the edge of the forest begin to quiver. Then, from the darkness, six people emerge.

Zhuchka, nosing around a bundle of kelp, looks up. Her hackles rise. She barks, and then charges toward the people—all men—who don't even glance her way.

"Steady," Timofei Osipovich warns in a low voice. No one at the fire moves or makes a sound. Zhuchka, on the other hand, leaps in circles around the newcomers. They pay her about as much heed as if she were a swirling mote of dust.

As the koliuzhi draw closer to the fire, everyone rises, even Maria and me. Two of the six strangers advance, one a tall, moustached man carrying a spear, the other a slightly smaller version of him who is hardly an adult. This boy has a blunt object hanging from a sinew around his neck, identical to the horn-shaped objects carried by the koliuzhi who gave us the halibut. I'm no closer to knowing its function. This one is so ornately carved I wonder now if these objects are ceremonial, like the sceptre carried by the constellation Cepheus, the king who keeps one foot planted on my beloved Polaris as he spins around her.

Their heads are covered with wide-brimmed hats woven with a material very much like bast. Our peasants, however, fabricate nothing like these hats, which have angular designs woven right into them. More remarkable than the bast hats, however, are the men's faces and shoulders, which are painted red and black and sprinkled with fluffy white feathers. I've never seen anything like it. Their appearance is strange and beautiful, striking and intimidating.

"Liʔatsḵatsdoʔóli,"[2] says the moustached man.

Timofei Osipovich replies—thank goodness he knows this strange language.

The koliuzhi brightens, and says, "Kʷokʷósas hokʷachiyólit táʔad."[3]

Timofei Osipovich gives a short nod and waits.

Nikolai Isaakovich watches us. Timofei Osipovich waves to say the situation is under control. My husband takes two steps toward the beach, then stops, hesitates, and eventually turns back to his tasks on the brig.

The moustached man and Timofei Osipovich continue their conversation. Timofei Osipovich's face is a stone; I can tell nothing from his expression. Does he really understand what the man is saying? Is he pleased? As for the moustached man, sensation and thought flit across his features. I think he's surprised to find us here, but why wouldn't he be? I can't yet tell if we're welcome—or if we're under threat.

"Ḵʷópatlich asítsḵal taɫáḵal o x̣áx̣i?"[4] he asks.

Timofei Osipovich smiles and bows his head before replying briefly. Then he slips into Russian and says, "Madame Bulygina, Maria—come with me. The rest of you, stay here and remain

---

2   Greetings, strange ones.

3   Your floating village is stranded.

4   Do you wish to ask to stay? If so, I will advise the elders to decide whether they will allow it.

alert." We follow him into the smaller tent. The two koliuzhi in the hats join us.

It's colder in the tent without the fire. However, I wouldn't leave even if Timofei Osipovich ordered it. The moustached man wears a sea otter cape dark as a moonless night at sea. When he shifts, the fur's silver highlights gleam even though only a sliver of light enters the tent. Plump tails of fur dangle from the hem. The boy, on the other hand, is dressed simply in a plain breechclout and a cedar bark vest that hangs to his hips. Beneath it, his chest is bare. He stares at Maria and me, his eyes bulging. His gaze latches onto my silver cross. There is no more space than the span of an open hand between us.

The conversation continues. Timofei Osipovich doesn't say much, but he listens while his eyes flit around the tent, jumping from the older man, then to me, then to the young man, then Maria, then the sand, and once again the koliuzhi, then the ceiling of the tent.

The older man leans in, one hand open, moving up and down in the same rhythm as his speech. He seems earnest and concerned. About what? Is it us? Is it something happening at his home? Where is his home? There's not a house in sight, not a sound, not even a trail of smoke leading into the sky that I can see. If he doesn't live here, how did he get here?

Timofei Osipovich is impassive. Why isn't he responding? Is it possible he doesn't understand everything the man is saying?

The moustached man is mid-sentence when Ovchinnikov thrusts his head through the opening of our tent. His face blocks our narrow view of the sea, his hair obscures his eyes.

"The koliuzhi are in the other tent," he says quietly.

Timofei Osipovich's eyes widen. He frowns and presses his lips together. He glances at the moustached man who's stopped talking and is watching with an intensity like smouldering coals.

"What are they doing?" asks Timofei Osipovich.

"They're looking at our things. They keep touching them and picking them up. I don't trust them. They're going to steal something."

"Watch them. I'll talk to this one."

Timofei Osipovich addresses the moustached man. He speaks calmly, and smiles frequently. When the man finally replies, I think I've been wrong. Timofei Osipovich must know how to speak their language.

In their faces, in the tone of the conversation, I feel something come to rest like when a bead of water rolls across the deck and arrives at the bulwark. Timofei Osipovich turns to Maria and me.

"Everything is fine. He'll talk to the others," he says. "He's the toyon."

"What's that?" I ask.

"You don't know toyon? It's—a kind of emperor. Their version of it anyway." Timofei Osipovich pauses. "There's usually more than one. It depends on where you are. This one's friendly."

Whatever disaster has befallen us, it seems it's not about to get worse. I look at our toyon who is serene and maybe even, dare I hope, a little sympathetic to our circumstance. I don't know what's happening in the other tent, but I suddenly have confidence in this toyon to make everything right.

Timofei Osipovich exhales decidedly and announces, "I'm going away with him."

Maria stiffens.

"Where?" I demand.

"His house. It's not far."

"You can't leave us here."

He smirks. "Then come with me."

Maria and I exchange looks.

"Madame Bulygina, you'll be fine. Ovchinnikov will be in charge here until I return. If the apprentice tries to convince you to do other than what Ovchinnikov tells you, ignore him."

"What if they turn on you?"

Timofei Osipovich raises his eyebrows and smirks again.

"Nikolai Isaakovich would never allow you," I continue. But my logic is flawed. These matters are secondary. What's most concerning is that he's the only man here who can communicate with the koliuzhi. He mustn't leave.

"In fact, Madame Bulygina, your husband would insist upon it, if he knew. But, as you are aware, he's occupied. Would you like to ask his permission on my behalf?" I lean sideways until I can see my husband through the opening in the tent. He's still thigh deep in the sea. His attention is on the crew members who are lowering the empty skiff into the ocean. It swings helplessly from its cables, banging against the side of the brig. Between Nikolai Isaakovich and the shore, the surf roars. Between the froth and me are stones and sand. Timofei Osipovich will be gone by the time I get to the edge of the beach. And I'll never be able to shout loudly enough to be heard above the sea.

"He's a friendly man," says Timofei Osipovich, rising. The older man and the boy both rise with him. "He wants to help us. I'll come back in a little while. I'll settle the rest down before we leave."

"Timofei Osipovich!" Ovchinnikov calls.

Timofei Osipovich pokes his head out of the tent. "Stand fast, men," he says quietly.

"What's happening out there?" I cry.

I can't see, but it's certain something's going on. The koliuzhi outside the tent have raised their voices.

"Do the best you can. Try somehow to get them out of the camp without fighting." Timofei Osipovich and the koliuzhi sit down again and begin to talk once more. Timofei Osipovich has a lot to say now. The toyon squints and listens thoughtfully.

In the middle of their discussion, a rock flies across the tent opening. Another follows, coming from the opposite direction.

"They're throwing stones!" I cry. I don't know who's responsible. I can't see.

Timofei Osipovich leans toward the opening in the tent and shouts. "Control yourselves! Don't retaliate!" He assumes it's the koliuzhi throwing the rocks.

Then, a gun fires. The birds shriek.

Timofei Osipovich rushes from the tent. He catches his foot on one of the cords. "Damn," he cries, extracting his foot. The tent shivers violently. It might collapse. The fabric springs back and forth. But the tent stays up.

The toyon leaps over my folded legs. I lean back, believing he'll fall on me. The boy follows seconds later. They leave behind a cloud of spinning white feathers as they fly out of the tent.

There's another gun shot.

I duck and cover my head with my hands. Maria shrieks, throws herself down, and curls up on the sand. Outside, there's shouting. Thuds. Grunts. Screams. I snake to the narrow opening and when I muster enough courage, I raise my head.

Timofei Osipovich staggers backward, then twists toward our tent. The shaft of a spear vibrates in his chest. He's been struck.

Hardy prikashchik—he grabs the shaft and with a grunt, he pulls out the spear. With his free hand, he raises his pistol and turns to the big tent where all our supplies lie. A man with a mouth contorted in rage has a spear in one hand and a rock in the other. He throws the rock at Timofei Osipovich. It strikes him in the head. The blow spins him around so he's again facing the tent. A stream of blood trickles down his forehead and into his eyes.

The toyon's empty-handed. What happened to his spear? He streaks around, runs from man to man, shouts and tears at their arms, urging them to leave.

The apprentice Kotelnikov strikes him across the back with his musket. Something cracks. The toyon screams.

Where's my husband? I can't see him. I need to find him, but I can't leave the tent. I can barely breathe.

Timofei Osipovich trips and falls across a huge log. He doesn't move. He lies there like some hideous mat on a tiny table.

The man who threw the rock at him is on the ground. I can't tell if he's alive or not.

Zhuchka barks wildly. I can't see her.

I must find Nikolai Isaakovich. I rise to my knees. As soon as I do, another gun fires. And another, and another, and another. I throw myself away from the opening and down onto the sand beside Maria. I press my body against hers. I hug my knees to my chest. I hear a wail. It's me and it's not me.

Outside, there's the sound of running feet. They pound the sand and shake the earth. I feel it rumble up into my body. It's moving away from the tent, in the direction of the forest. Finally, it ceases.

Quiet descends like a bank of fog and smothers everything.

I wait. And wait.

I hear a groan. Somebody sobs. Is it one of us? Is it the koliuzhi?

I look at Maria, but her face is turned away, and she's still as an old rock.

I leave her side and tentatively approach the tent's opening. Slowly I push my head through the narrow vee.

It's over. The battle is over. The only people outside are us.

I immediately find Nikolai Isaakovich. He's face down on the sand. There's a spear in his back.

I run from the tent and fall to my knees before him. Zhuchka butts up against my side and whines. I shove her away.

Dear God. My husband is dead. I'm a widow, and I'm not even twenty years old.

I look up, weeping, and there's Timofei Osipovich, bloodied but alive, standing over us. "Don't worry. He's fine. Aren't you?"

"Get that thing out of me, would you?" my husband mutters.

Timofei Osipovich grasps the shaft and pulls. My husband groans. The spear easily slides from near his shoulder blade. There's a wide rent in his greatcoat, but it seems the thick wool prevented the spear from penetrating too deeply.

"Kolya?" I cry. "Are you all right?"

He rolls over. Blood coats half his face.

"Oh. Oh." The sight of so much blood tangles my tongue for a moment. Finally, I find my words. "My darling, what happened to you?"

"It's nothing. Don't worry." With difficulty, he pushes himself up to a sitting position.

"I thought you were dead." I clasp his arms, but he grimaces, and I let go. "Oh, Kolya." I blot at the blood with my apron, with the hem of my dress. It instantly blooms across the absorbent fabric, painting big red petals. "Does it hurt?"

The American, John Williams, holds his head and groans. There's blood oozing down his ear. Yakov limps toward us. "Commander?" he says. "Are you badly injured?"

Kotelnikov has blood drying beneath his nose. He swipes his pudgy hand across it and cries, "They're filth! Scum!"

Maria crawls out of the tent. She looks around the beach in disbelief. It's strewn with the spoils of our battle: spears and rocks, cloaks of cedar, and the woven hats. Many of the crew have been injured.

"What happened out here?" cries Timofei Osipovich. He looks at the men one by one. "Can't I leave you alone for a minute?"

We're bloodied and beaten, but not seriously. None of us is dead. However, the koliuzhi haven't been so lucky. Two koliuzhi bodies lie on the beach.

"They carried away another one of theirs when they ran," says Yakov. "He couldn't walk."

One of the dead men is the one who threw the rock at Timofei Osipovich—somebody, perhaps even Timofei Osipovich himself, shot him. The other body belongs to the boy with the blunt, horn-shaped object who accompanied the toyon into our tent and stared at my silver cross. The blunt object is still attached to its cord, still wrapped around his neck.

I've seen dead bodies before, at wakes and funerals. As an enlightened young woman, I never allowed them to disturb me. I know the body is a shell. It holds life—and then it doesn't—and when the life is gone, that's it. There is no eternal life. That's the nature of mortality. It's the biological ebb and flow of a person's life.

But I've never seen a body like this boy's. Fluffy white feathers still cling to his face. His eyes are open and vacant and there's a piece of down caught in his eyelashes. His hat is gone. His hands lie limp, open and empty at his sides, the fingers slightly curled. With all the life gone from him, he's diminished. He looks like a little boy.

However, it's the red-rimmed cavity in his chest, the size of a dinner plate, bigger than his head, all out of proportion to his tiny body that I can't comprehend. I see it one minute. The next I don't, and I wonder why he doesn't roll over, as my husband just did, sit up, and say, "It's nothing," rise to his feet and head home. How despairing his mother and father will be when he doesn't come back this afternoon.

Zhuchka thrusts her nose into the hole in the boy's chest.

"Get away!" I scream and she cowers, paws over her bloody nose.

How did this happen? What transformed the goodwill I saw in the tent into this?

The crew begins to stir. There are wounds to clean. Bloodied sleeves to rinse in the sea. And the spoils of the battle, which we will collect and add to our belongings in the big tent.

In the meantime, the watch cannot rest. Firearms are reloaded. Sentries are posted. Night will arrive shortly, and when it does, for once, I will turn my gaze away from the heavens. Today my world has shattered, and its remnants have been strewn along a cold beach in a strange land. The order and beauty of the constellations offer no comfort; instead, they only mock.

CHAPTER FOUR

———————————

Late in the morning, Nikolai Isaakovich gathers everyone outside the big tent. The men have scabs on their foreheads and chins, soot on their hands and faces, and torn clothing. Did anybody sleep last night? I didn't, even though I was exhausted from the wreck and the battle. Nikolai Isaakovich told me to rest, to get some sleep, in preparation for the trials ahead. He was right, of course, but who could sleep? The roar of the sea was so close, I imagined every wave crawling into the tent and soaking us. Other noises, creaks and scratches, were muffled and unidentifiable. Each one made me believe the koliuzhi were just on the other side of the canvas and about to attack. Far worse than these, what made sleep impossible, was the image of the maimed body of the koliuzhi boy on the beach. He wouldn't leave me, no matter how tightly I closed my eyes. That soft skin ripped open, the shredded flesh, bloody as minced meat, and those eyes, glazed and empty. He's still with me this morning. I think he'll never leave me. I don't know when I'll ever sleep again. *Ever. Never. Forever.* But I mustn't allow myself to think such despairing thoughts.

Shortly after we'd woken, my husband organized a small group to take stock of our surroundings. Their goal was to find a protected place where we could establish ourselves until our rescue. Would it take a week before somebody came looking for us? A month? When would the captain of the *Kad'iak* realize we weren't going to make the rendezvous? Even if someone came next week, could we manage until they arrived? The beach had grown narrower overnight as the tide came in, and though we remained dry, it was a very calm night. Debris showed that at its highest, the tide wouldn't leave enough space on the beach for the tents. We'd have to find a drier area up or down the coast, or we'd have to take shelter among the trees.

"Keep your muskets ready," my husband advised as he divided the men into groups.

He sent old Yakov and the carpenter Kurmachev up the beach, in the direction we'd come from. I don't know what he was thinking sending two old men together. If either one ran into trouble, neither would be of much help.

The apprentice Kotelnikov and Main Rigger Sobachnikov were directed down to the river. "You two be especially careful," the prikashchik warned them. "We can't see what's upriver from here." Sobachnikov paled.

Timofei Osipovich was sent into the forest with his loyal Ovchinnikov and the Aleuts.

"What about me?" cried the American.

"You watch the camp," said my husband. "Your hair and skin—dear God, you're a walking target."

The men dispersed. Timofei Osipovich and the Aleuts fanned out and were swallowed by the hungry forest. Zhuchka hardly knew which group to follow, but in the end, she chose the forest. They returned first, each man emerging from the woods with the same grim expression on his face. Ovchinnikov brought back a handful of shrivelled purplish-black berries, which he said the Aleuts found soon after entering the forest. I'd never seen these berries before, not in Russia, not in Novo-Arkhangelsk.

He offered them to me. I put one in my mouth. It was starchy and bitter. Others spat out the skins and seeds because, as hungry as the men were, the berries were unpalatable. Zhuchka jammed her nose into the ground and licked up the remains, and rolled her tongue, trying to get rid of the sand that inevitably stuck there.

The crew members who'd been sent to scout along the beach returned much later. I watched them through the mist, dragging their feet in the sand, and long before they reached us, I knew they'd been unsuccessful.

Now, outside the big tent as we wait for my husband to speak, a cold mist rolls in from the sea. It mutes the cries of the birds. Timofei Osipovich gave me one of the woven cedar capes left from the battle. It smells of smoke and fish. It's a bit coarse, but softer than I expect and pliant enough to wrap around my shoulders and keep the mist at bay. It disturbs me to think of whose shoulders it covered before mine. But I must not let that stop me from wearing it—my survival may depend on it. I only wish I knew how to fasten it closed. There are no long ends to knot as there are with a shawl; there is no pin.

Mercifully, my shoes dried before the fire last night. They're practical shoes—mostly flat, with only a small heel that clicked on the deck and announced my arrival wherever I went. The only ornamentation is on the vamps, which are embossed with a circular pattern of curling vines and feathery leaves. While we were aboard the brig, Maria cleaned them and kept the mould at bay. She sometimes polished them with grease to keep them soft. Though fine for life on a ship, they're inadequate for this wilderness. They slip on and off my foot too easily, as the teal Morocco leather they're made with has stretched over the weeks. They fill with sand wherever I go. It compacts between my toes until I have no choice but to empty them. The sand pours from them in a stream, like it does in the sandglass the crew uses to measure the watch. At least I still have shoes.

Out at sea, our brig rocks gently, rhythmically, keeping time with a small flock of seabirds that floats nearby. The ship's broken foreyard still dangles from the mast and sways and creaks with the motion. High tide has come and gone, and the ship remains grounded. Many more things need to be brought ashore. My telescope and star log are among those that were left behind yesterday. Nikolai Issakovich thought they'd be safer there, away from the salt and sand. He's promised me he'll fetch them as soon as our camp is better appointed, and I have a place away from the elements to keep my things.

My husband has attempted to clean himself up. He's brushed his greatcoat. He's run his fingers through his hair and beard. He perches atop one of the driftwood logs, facing us and the forest. Behind him, the waves break and fingers of froth creep up the beach, but he pays them no heed. My husband leans just slightly. I can tell he favours the side of his body where he was struck by the spear. Still, he looks the picture of authority; he bears it well, as he should. All twenty-two of us have survived and, despite the unfortunate skirmish with the koliuzhi, that's an auspicious beginning.

"According to the instructions given me by the chief manager of the colonies," he cries, "the company ship *Kad'iak* is coming to the shores of New Albion. Its destination is a harbour lying not more than sixty-five nautical miles from where we now stand."

Sixty-five nautical miles. No one breathes. Everyone knows how far sixty-five nautical miles is.

"Between these two points," my husband continues, "the map shows no bay, no cove, nor even a single river."

Every head turns left then, to the river Kotelnikov and Sobachnikov surveyed only a short while ago. Even from this distance, a churning tongue can be seen flowing from its mouth. Where that wild water meets the surf, a turbid tangle of whitecaps, whirlpools, and currents that reverse one another forms. Between here and there, brown birds with pointy beaks scuttle along the sand.

The maps on my husband's secretaire are incomplete. That's why the company had him sighting, measuring, and marking more precisely this coast's features. What lies to the south is largely uncharted. We can't depend on what the maps say. So why does my husband insist on it? Every man can see that what he says is false.

Nikolai Isaakovich ignores the skepticism that shows itself on each face and carries on. "If we stay here, we expose ourselves to the threat of almost certain death. We'll have to fight day and night to stay alive. They'll besiege us. We'll have to battle until we have no ammunition left. And then, these dikari will exterminate us without a second thought."

I think about being in the tent with the two koliuzhi, about sitting so close to them, no weapons, no voices raised, nothing but a conversation between us. The battle has changed everything, even the way we speak. Now, they're no longer just koliuzhi. They're dikari. Savages.

"And so, we must leave. We should be able to reach that harbour quite easily."

"They'll follow us," cries John Williams, his face even redder, enflamed with his outrage. "They'll try to kill us."

"They may . . . or they may remain here to plunder the ship and divide the spoils," says Timofei Osipovich quietly, picking at the scab on his forehead. "Who can tell?"

My husband looks at him gratefully. "Yes. Timofei Osipovich is right. Most likely they won't pursue us, for we'll carry nothing they want, and so they'll have no need come after us," my husband adds. His eyes shift to the forest. "Most likely."

There's silence, except for the persistent, rhythmic murmur of the sea. Every man is imagining the walk we're about to set out on, through a land we don't know, during the onset of winter. Every man is imagining the alternative. Waiting. For what? If there's no ship, will there be a grand carriage pulled by six horses on its way back to Novo-Arkhangelsk? A peasant with his donkey cart who'll make room for us beside his sacks of grain? Will the vodyanoy intervene and instead of drowning us, take us home? Every man is imagining our demise. How we'll fall—from illness, battle, hunger, cold. We'll fall, one by one by one, until none is left standing. No one in the world will ever discover what's become of us.

"Then, we place ourselves in your hands," pronounces Timofei Osipovich. He flicks away the scab he picked.

The doubt instantly washes away. Brooding Ovchinnikov cracks a smile now that his ostensible master has given his approval. Old Yakov nods and readjusts his cap. Nikolai Isaakovich folds his arms across his chest and looks pleased with himself. Sobachnikov shyly meets my eye, and I smile to let him know everything will be fine.

Will everything be fine? I think it would be wiser to stay with the brig. Everything we own is onboard the *Sviatoi Nikolai*—and we may need it all if our rescue takes a long time. Despite the koliuzhi, I'd place greater faith in staying, building a shelter suitable for the winter, and hunting and fishing for our sustenance. Maybe we can make peace with the koliuzhi. Perhaps they'll leave us alone. I think waiting is a wiser choice than hiking sixty-five miles in near winter, over terrain we know nothing about. But no one asks me. So, I must follow. I'll go where Nikolai Isaakovich leads.

We begin preparations for our long march. First, the rest of the supplies we'll need are retrieved from the brig. More ammunition, more food, some knives, bowls, cups, and cooking pots—two wide vessels and a kettle.

The carpenter Kurmachev carries a small keg of rum to shore, thrashing through the waves with the weight on his shoulders. In Novo-Arkhanglesk, every man is allotted four to five cups a month because the company believes spirits, when taken moderately, offset the hazards of living in a wet and unhealthy climate. They also keep away the scurvy. Kurmachev takes this advice to heart and his breath often reeks of drink.

Fortunately, the sea is less turbulent than it was yesterday, and the tide is out. The trips back and forth are less arduous.

Maria and I watch these labours mostly from the side of the morning's fire, which we stir and feed to keep alive. Timofei Osipovich has ordered his favoured Ovchinnikov and the apprentice to stay onshore and guard us. They stand poised not far from the tents, eyes trained on the forest and the ends of the strand. Occasionally, Ovchinnikov patrols far up the beach, skimming the forest's fringe, watching for movement behind the trees. The forest is as quiet and brooding as he is. I worry that the koliuzhi are waiting in the shadows and his presence, so near the woods, will precipitate another confrontation.

Later, when the fire's dying down, I walk up the beach toward the river with a mind to collect a few pieces of driftwood. "Madame Bulygina," calls Ovchinnikov, "don't go any farther." When I turn back to our camp, I notice Sobachnikov near the big tent, fussing with a barrel instead of heading out to the brig again.

I return as instructed and throw the wood I've collected onto the fire, watching Sobachnikov the while. I wonder if we could burn the wood from the barrel he's opening. I'm about to call out to ask when he looks up and beams at me. In one hand, he holds my telescope. In the other, my star log.

"The commander asked me to give these to you," he says when I approach. He's flushed, and his hands, as he extends my things toward me, tremble. I receive them. The star log is dry. The telescope doesn't have a drop of water on it.

"How did you manage to keep them dry?" I exclaim.

He blushes. "I thought to wrap them in an old coat, and then I put them in a barrel of gunpowder where I knew they'd be safe."

He must have opened the barrel, then resealed it, before carrying it to shore. Once here, he pried it open once more. "I've inconvenienced you. I'm sorry. Thank you for undertaking such an effort for me," I say.

"Madame Bulygina, I . . ." he fumbles. I wait, though it pains me to see him in such agony. "I see you every night on deck. I know you value it."

"Yes. My father gave me this telescope," I say.

My telescope was built in Germany; it's of the same design as Mademoiselle Caroline Herschel's first telescope—the one she used to discover many galaxies and comets, when she was not much older than I am now. It's a solid instrument, reliable, and though I'm not superstitious, I imagine it will bring me the same luck. I would never dream of leaving it behind.

Sobachnikov fidgets and opens his mouth as if to say something. Instead his face flares as he thinks better of it, and he turns abruptly and heads back to the brig for his next load. I watch him until he enters the surf again, and then I return to the fire.

When the crew finishes bringing in all the provisions we'll need, my husband orders the rest destroyed.

"We won't make it easy for those dikari," he says. "They must not profit from our misfortune."

The men wade back out to the brig. They drive iron spikes through the barrels of the cannon—each strike rings out as though delivered by a blacksmith, and I warily watch the forest wondering if the koliuzhi will be drawn out by the noise. They next heave the cannon, one by one, overboard. Each one falls with a tremendous splash and then disappears beneath the waves. Then the crew moves onto smaller objects: iron tools deemed too heavy and of too little use for our trek. Pikes and axes, inferior firearms—they break the locks on all the guns and pistols first—even the remainder of Maria's cooking pots and utensils. All the knives and forks and spoons. The rest of the rum. My half-embroidered napkins and my sewing kit. They toss everything into the sea as if making offerings to the vodyanoy. In the hold are a stack of Russian possession plaques—iron plates engraved with the Holy Cross and the bold words "Country in Possession of Russia." We were to bury them along the coast when we went ashore for provisions. We haven't had the chance to leave a single one behind. One by one, the crew flings them all into the surf. The powder—what we can't carry—is tossed overboard too.

It troubles me greatly to see our things thrown so carelessly into the sea. Is there no way to bring them? Granted, we can't carry such weight for sixty-five nautical miles. But couldn't we improvise a kind of cart or sled using our skiff and tow or drag our things along? What about hiding them? The forest is vast and empty and surely there are many hiding spots. If bad luck befalls us and we're forced to return to this beach, we'd have these things to help us. Unfortunately, there's no time to plan. Destruction seems to be the only choice.

The final act involves the single cannon that took so much effort to roll up onto the sandy shore. The Aleuts roll it back out to sea. They struggle for some time to push it through the surf into deeper waters until it's completely submerged.

My husband, with the assistance of Timofei Osipovich, divides up the load. Each man is given two guns and a pistol. The boxes of cartridges are evenly distributed. The least injured men will also carry the three kegs of powder. The rum is decanted into each man's flask until the cask is dry—the wood flares in the fire. Everything else is wrapped in torn sailcloth bundles that are tied closed, to be slung over our shoulders.

The bundles of food are very small. We've eaten a lot in the hours since the brig ran aground—big bowls of kasha and cups of sugared tea. Sobachnikov and the apprentice Kotelnikov made an extra trip out to the brig at Maria's request to look for more food. They returned with stale bread, a withered onion, and a tub of pickles. They also found strips of the leftover halibut that Maria salted and was starting to dry. Within a few minutes, all of it was eaten.

Now, all that remains is some bruised potato, turnip, and a few carrots, a paltry quantity of buckwheat, flour, sugar, yeast, salt, and tea. How this will feed twenty-two of us, I can't imagine.

"We still need more," Maria says, overseeing the packing of the food. "Somebody has to go back to the brig again. I know we have more."

"There's nothing left," says Kotelnikov.

"Old woman, stop worrying! We'll hunt and fish," Timofei Osipovich cries. "There'll be plenty—berries, mushrooms . . ."

"It's almost winter, you fool. There are no berries and mushrooms. And if you're such a good hunter, why didn't you get us some venison last night?"

"You want venison? Why didn't you say so?"

"What am I supposed to make with this? For twenty-two people? We need to go back and get more."

"There are limits to what can be carried."

"And yet you make allowance for—trinkets?" Maria gestures dismissively at the pile of korolki, handkerchiefs, and folds of fabric waiting to be tied into a bundle. The edge of a blue nankeen cotton robe pokes out from the heap.

"These *trinkets* will buy you a fish or a haunch of good venison," Timofei Osipovich says. "You'll thank me later, old woman."

The bundles and barrels are loaded into the skiff, and, in fours, we ferry ourselves across the mouth of the river. Zhuchka wades in. When it becomes too deep to walk, she paddles, but not for long. Once we've all crossed, Timofei Osipovich and the Aleuts push the empty skiff into the middle of the river. It twists one way, then the other, then makes a pretty circle before choosing a direction and heading out to sea. Does any man wish to be on it? It's conceivable, though he'd have to believe that the fate that awaits him alone at sea would be preferable to the fate that awaits him on shore.

We don't wait to see our little boat disappear.

Timofei Osipovich pushes aside a few branches and finds an opening into the forest. He ducks in and disappears, Zhuchka on his heels. Half a minute later, they return, Zhuchka panting.

"I found a trail," he says. "It's quite muddy, but not terrible. It will be easy enough to see anyway." Zhuchka trots back to the bank of the river and laps at the water.

"Maybe we should follow the beach instead," my husband says.

"We'll be safer surrounded by trees and brush," counters Timofei Osipovich. "On the beach, we'll be too exposed. We need sentries, in front and bringing up the rear."

I look up. Low grey clouds promise rain before long. Perhaps the forest offers shelter from that as well.

As I shoulder my bundle—mostly food, but my telescope and star log are cushioned in the centre of the load—I notice my husband watching. I stop and smile, and I wonder what he's thinking. He looks wild and hopeful and handsome. His cheeks are ruddy, chafed by the wind and salt air. I feel a longing for him deep in my heart—to be close to him, to hear his voice in my ear, to feel his beard brush against my cheek. How reassuring his arm, tight around my waist, would be before we enter this sombre forest and begin an unimaginable voyage.

He smiles briefly, then turns his attention to his bundle. Despite his injury, he has a load as big and heavy as anybody else's. As he pulls it up on his right shoulder, he winces. I stifle a cry. He'd want no man to notice.

As commander, he's the first to push aside the branches and enter the forest. Timofei Osipovich, his loyal Ovchinnikov, and the American follow immediately, while the rest of us trail behind.

I follow Sobachnikov. He pushes aside a springy branch of a low shrub with his hips. I'm so much shorter than him, I must duck underneath it. I lift it and step into the gloom, letting the branch fall behind me.

And I stop. A reverential hush has fallen over our group as if we've just entered a beautiful old cathedral in Petersburg.

Green surrounds us, a soft and luscious green as I've never seen before, not even in the finest tapestries. Leaves hang heavy with moisture, and everything else seems covered in moss and lichen.

Every tree is oversized. The tree trunks tower distantly to the sky. At the base, they are gnarled and peeling, with roots that push up through the earth, as though there's no room left for them down there. These trunks are so broad that not even four of us hand in hand could circle them. Even the fungus that clings to the trees is unnaturally large, crusty, and coloured like pretty beze cookies.

The air is fragrant and silky. Though I know it irrational, I feel I could touch it. Hold it in my hand. After so many weeks on the brig, where sea breezes could not dissipate all the foul odours of a vessel at sea, this air makes me think about the courageous and worthy things that people fight for and are capable of but somehow rarely get and even more rarely do.

Tears well up in my eyes, surely from my exhaustion, but also because I've never known anything as beautiful as this exists, and I realize how poor my life has been without this knowledge.

Timofei Osipovich's trail winds through this splendour, then peters out into nothing after only a few minutes. We spread out looking for it again. I walk around a grove of ferns with brilliant green leaves on arched spines that spill over like streams of water in a fountain. Behind the ferns lie spindly branches covered in thorns. I edge around them to avoid being scratched. The ground is spongy. Cold water seeps into my shoes.

Nearby, tall Sobachnikov pushes aside another branch, and this time, when it springs back, it knocks old Yakov's cap off his head. A small flock of birds as tiny as buttons flit overhead as though launched from slingshots.

Just ahead, Maria skirts along an old fallen log covered in moss. The log is wide like the trees that surround us. She's dwarfed as she walks its length. Smaller trees and plants grow on top of the log as if it's a garden. Maria has to walk some distance before she finds a place to cross over it.

"Over here!" John Williams cries. "The trail's over here." I head toward his voice.

Big beards of moss so long they could be braided garland the trees. Is it alive? How does it sustain itself without killing the tree? Fixed to the branches as it is, it makes the trees look like a congress of fat, bearded priests, gathered to discuss profound questions of faith and sin.

I follow the others. I walk as well as I can with one hand clutched to the neck of my bundle, and the other trying to hold closed my cedar bark cape. Most of the time, I can't see Nikolai Isaakovich. But I yearn to be with him. I want to see his face to know if this forest surprises and moves him, too.

As I predicted on the banks of the river, it begins to rain. It's soft, misty rain that makes me believe we're walking through a cloud. It continues, soaking my hair and my skirt. I clutch more tightly the opening of my bark cloak. My bundle feels heavier. I wonder if the food I carry is being spoiled in the rain. But it will be even worse if my telescope and star log are becoming wet.

I enter a thicker part of the forest, and the trail grows vague again. I hear the others just ahead; I must be moving in the right direction. After a few minutes, I come upon the crew waiting in a grove. "It's too dark to go on," my husband says. "We'll stop here."

"How far do you think we've come?" I ask.

"We've made good progress," he replies and turns to Timofei Osipovich. "What do you think?"

"I would think perhaps a good three nautical miles."

No one smiles. Three. Leaving sixty-two more to go.

We drop our bundles and the Aleuts start to put up our tents, tying cords to the trees and branches that surround us. I walk the perimeter of our camp area. My feet sink into the mossy ground, but perhaps this is as good a place as any we might find in this drenched forest.

Timofei Osipovich sidles over and points. "Look, Madame Bulygina, here's my supper." Mushrooms have pushed up around a rotting log. They're orange, with upturned caps in the shape of a jaunty hat I'd once yearned for in Petersburg. "Cook them for me, will you?" And when I frown, he adds, "You do know how to cook, don't you?"

"Cook them yourself," I mutter.

"They're poisonous," says Maria. "Don't touch them."

Our fire is very small—just big enough for Maria to prepare another meagre meal of kasha and tepid tea. Though we haven't seen the koliuzhi all day, such a tiny fire won't draw any attention should they happen to pass nearby. Still, my husband doubles the size of our watch. Four men guard us at once, four more taking their place after a few hours.

Nikolai Isaakovich sits beside me, tired and sagging toward his injury. I'm tired as well. My feet are achy and blistered. My loose, wet shoes have rubbed the skin off my heels and toes, and they bleed in several places. However, I'm so exhausted, I'm sure I'll forget as soon as I lie down. Tonight, I'm destined to sleep the deep and bottomless slumber of little children.

Zhuchka is on my other side, pressed into my leg. Her steady breathing offers as much comfort as the heat she generates.

The night looms over us the way the mountains hang over

Novo-Arkhangelsk. There are no stars to be seen overhead. It's too overcast, and even if it wasn't, the canopy would block any view. It will be many hours before the sun rises again. The men slouch and sigh, and if it weren't for their full flasks—thanks to the carpenter—I'm sure they'd have given up and retired for the night.

The fire sighs and pops.

"Long ago," Timofei Osipovich says, breaking our silence, "not near, not far, not high, not low, the Tsar sent me to sea, alone." The American peers at him. With one hand, the carpenter stirs the fire with a stick, while he takes a swig from his flask with the other. The other men shift. "I was on a secret mission. Don't ask for details—I'd be put before a firing squad if I were to reveal its true nature." The men sit up.

"The winds howled, as they do, and the seas were higher than these trees, as they sometimes are, and I was forced ashore to an island so small and rarely visited that it fails to appear on any navigator's map." My husband stiffens and looks as though he's being accused of incompetence, but no one's paying any attention to him. Everyone is mesmerized by Timofei Osipovich.

"It was a merciless piece of land forsaken by God. A barren rock in the middle of nowhere. Even the birds stayed away. There was hardly anywhere to land my little baidarka. I fought the waves until I came to a stony beach, scarcely wider than this." He holds up his hands to show us. "I didn't think my boat would fit through the opening, but I forced it. I had no choice.

"Then, I made a horrible discovery. I'd been wrong. The island was not abandoned. A hundred men jumped out from behind a rock. They waved their swords and spears and screeched like the devil's army as they came for me."

Every man leans in. In the fire, a burning log collapses with a soft thud. The fire crackles and a few sparks rise and then extinguish themselves.

"I'd walked right through the gates of Hell. I couldn't fight those savages on my own. I'd drown if I tried to go back out into the sea. I thought for certain that day I would die.

"And so, having no other choice, I raised my empty arms high above my head." He throws his arms aloft, slapping the jaw of his loyal Ovchinnikov who doesn't so much as wince. "I faced the charging savages. And I hoped that one of them would understand that I was surrendering, and placing my fate in their hands.

"Much to my astonishment, my assailants immediately stopped. They were no farther away from me than Ivan Kurmachev is right now."

Every head turns to see where the carpenter is, to gauge the distance and estimate how long it would take if one had to withdraw to save his life. Kurmachev takes a nervous swig from his flask, and when he lowers it, he reveals eyes as round as full moons. Timofei Osipovich continues.

"I didn't budge. Neither did they for a long, long time. It seemed a lifetime or two. Finally, slowly, one man at a time, they lowered their weapons. And then two of them approached. They inspected my boat. They began to take everything out, running their filthy fingers over each item, discussing the ones that interested them. You know the koliuzhi way—you've seen it yourselves. All the while, I did and said nothing, for fear of driving them, once again, into a savage rage.

"When they got to the end of my belongings, and seemed not to know what to do next, I realized immediately that I had to do something to distract them. Otherwise, they might think that the next best thing to do would be to kill me."

"What did you do?" Sobachnikov says, in awe.

"What could I do?" Timofei Osipovich laughs. "I made a kite."

The men around the fire shift, but no one laughs with him. No one wants to miss his next words.

"I found two sticks about this long." He shows us with his hands. "I lashed them together with a piece of kelp that was there on the beach beside my baidarka. I attached a piece of paper to it. And when I was finished, I held it up to show them.

"No one spoke. I tied some thin rope to it, and threw it into the air."

He makes a motion like he's throwing something into the wind. Old Yakov flinches.

"At that moment, I realized I might have misjudged and placed myself in even greater peril. The koliuzhi leapt back in fear. The wind caught the kite. They raised their swords and spears. Some pointed them at me and others at the kite. I thought I was about to breathe my last.

"But then—as I released more of the rope—they lowered their weapons. They began to smile. One laughed. Then others joined in. As they watched the kite climb, they rejoiced. And by the time it reached its full height," he pauses long and hard and swivels his head around the fireside, meeting the eye of each and every person here, "we were best friends. All of us.

"'You Russians are clever people,' they said over and over again. 'Surely you can reach the sun.' 'Oh no,' I said to them, 'no one can do that.' 'But you are so intelligent. Is Russia full of geniuses like you?' 'You flatter me much, and I thank you for such consideration, but no. I assure you I am a very ordinary man.'

"So remember: if you find yourself in terrible trouble with the koliuzhi, with nowhere to turn, find a distraction. They're such little children at heart, all of them, and very easily amused. In this part of the world, that may be the only thing that will save you from the hungry jaws of death." He slaps his knee. "There's a tale for you and crock of butter for me."

They laugh. And laugh, and laugh—that familiar line from the old tales, how often I'd heard my own mother append it to her stories. The men closest to him smack him on the back and nudge him with their shoulders. Even Nikolai Isaakovich laughs.

But why? His story is not rational. Right from the beginning—why would the Tsar trust a serf with a secret mission? And why would he be out on the stormy sea by himself? He's tough as an old piece of dried meat; still, he wouldn't be so foolish as to venture out into the open ocean by himself.

Does an island such as he describes exist? Does anybody live there? From where would he get paper? How could he speak so fluently the language of a people he's never seen before—and who, it must be presumed, if they're that forsaken, couldn't have learned Russian? When you think about it, his story is like a quilt coming apart at the seams because the seamstress hadn't thought beyond the basting.

Yet the others are charmed. Tomorrow, they'll heed and follow him. They'll think fashioning a kite is going to save their lives. Kotelnikov is sharp; so is the American. Can't they see through his embellishments? Doesn't anybody understand that he's treating us like we're children? He has such high regard for himself, and so little regard for us and the truth.

When the men have finally tucked away their flasks, we settle in for the night. I wait, cold and achy, for sleep to overtake me. But then somebody calls out in his sleep, and I'm wide awake again. Eventually, I feel myself drifting off. I'm once more ready to fall deep into slumber. But somebody rolls over and bumps the tent and the walls shiver. I awaken again. How I wish I were a little girl, my mother with me, holding my hand until my restlessness leaves me. This goes on all night, so that when I wake in the morning for good, I don't feel restored.

We're a ragged troupe carrying our bundles and our hopeless spirits. I don't know which is heavier. Early this morning, as we packed up, everything damp from the mist, my husband announced we'd head back to the seashore and walk along the beach for the day. So, as we set off, we turn toward the coast and after only a half hour or so, we break through the forest's edge and see the water.

The ocean is calmer today than it was yesterday. It's dark grey and, even though it's placid, the water still rushes up along the beach and floods back out again. The sky remains overcast, though the clouds are high and light, and so there's no rain. My husband orders a brief rest. Timofei Osipovich and his devoted Ovchinnikov clean their muskets. Maria and Yakov enter into a brief discussion that ends with them redistributing the contents of their bundles.

I look for a place where I can wash my hands and face. I locate a small pool on a rocky outcropping at the edge of the beach. A purple sea star droops its arms over a rock in one corner, and I take it as a sign of welcome.

When I put my hand into the water, the pool comes alive. Small fish dart away. Tiny snail shells quiver and then totter off as though they have legs. Things I thought were rocks or seaweed begin to wave their arms and curl into tight little balls. I pull my hand out and wait. The creatures grow still. Then, I dip only my fingertips in. I rub them around my eyes, across my cheeks, and over my lips. When I wash off the layer of mud and dirt, I feel a little less tired.

I loosen my hair and let it fall. I try to run my fingers through it, but it's choked with knots and tangled with leaves and twigs. When our ordeal is over, I may have to cut it. If the sacrifice of my hair would end our suffering today, I'd gladly make it.

"Madame Bulygina—we're leaving! Hurry!" Maria calls. The men have risen and shouldered their burdens. My husband has already turned and set out along the sand. I finish tying up my hair again. I'm the last to join the procession. There's a gap between me and the last man. After a moment, Timofei Osipovich steps aside. He waits and, after I pass, he rejoins the line, walking right behind me. His musket rests on one shoulder.

"That's a big load you carry, Madame Bulygina." Mine is less than half the size of his. He must be mocking.

"I can manage," I say. "Like everyone else."

"You could manage better if you fastened your cloak properly."

"I prefer to do it my way." My words sound childish, and I redden.

He laughs and says nothing more.

Out at sea, a bed of kelp rises and falls with the waves. Gulls float nearby, unperturbed by our presence.

Once more, my shoes fill with sand. It becomes harder and harder to walk. My one hand holds my bundle, the other holds my cape closed. I wonder about my shawl pin. Whatever happened to it? How I long to have it right now.

We follow the shore until we reach a rocky headland. On the side closest to the forest, it's navigable. I scramble over the rocks, following the others, Timofei Osipovich just behind me. "There's a passage to your right," he advises. "See where it flattens? You can put your foot just there."

It annoys me that he's right. I'm eighteen and capable of finding my own way across the rocks. I don't need anybody's help, especially not his.

On the other side of the headland, the sand on the beach is replaced by loose pebbles, even more difficult to walk on. Each step forward requires two steps of effort. I fall farther behind. I wish I could run like Zhuchka who appears and disappears at will, moving easily over the little stones. How much time would she need to spend here before she became as wild as the wolves? Not long I suspect.

Judging by the crunch of gravel on my heels, Timofei Osipovich is right behind me. Each step he takes matches mine and it irritates me. I stop, and the cedar cape slides off one shoulder. When I try to pull it back into place, my bundle falls to the stones.

"Show me," I grumble.

Timofei Osipovich looks around and picks up a twig. I allow him to adjust the cloak around my shoulders and pin it in place with the twig. The twig slides easily between the bark fibres. I redden—so simple and I didn't think of it myself. He tugs the hem to make sure it's secure.

"Let's go," is all he says.

The crew is now far ahead, beneath a rocky headland at the other end of this pebbly beach. They've lined up and it looks like they'll wade into the sea to pass around it. The tide is coming in. They'll have to go quickly if they're to get to the other side before the opportunity is lost.

The tide is also narrowing the strand on which Timofei Osipovich and I walk. The straight path between us and the crew is being bent into an arc that lengthens as the water advances. My shoulders burn but I hurry. Each minute I'm delayed, my path grows longer. I, too, must pass the headland before the water gets too deep.

Then I slip, turn my ankle, and stumble. I throw my arms out and catch myself just before I fall.

"Steady, Madame Bulygina," says Timofei Osipovich. "Don't injure yourself now."

I cautiously flex my ankle. "I'm fine," I say. "It's not like I've been speared and struck with rocks."

He laughs. "Thank heaven for that. If you had, no doubt your husband would have ordered us to carry you. Perhaps it would have been your good fortune if he had selected me for the task."

I bristle. "Even if I was injured, I'd do the same as any man here, the same as you. I would not add to anybody's burden."

I turn back to our path. The others are very far ahead now.

"What are you doing?" I cry. "Put me down!"

Timofei Osipovich has picked me up and slung me over his shoulder like I'm one of the sailcloth bundles. He laughs, and I feel it ripple through my body. His feet dig into the small stones, and we set off toward the others.

"We're falling behind, Madame Bulygina, and we need to catch up."

"Put me down!" I repeat and push against him. How does he manage to carry me, my bundle, and his own load all at the same time? Is this his injured side? He gives no sign that he's in pain.

I wish Nikolai Isaakovich were here. I wish Zhuchka would come back and bite his legs. But everyone is so far ahead, no one sees us, and with the sound of the surf masking everything, no one can hear me call for help.

"I'll put you down once we catch up with the others." He's fast. He trots. I bump along, my body pressed into his bony shoulder. My silver cross bounces into my mouth, and I spit it out.

"If you don't put me down now, you'll have to deal with my husband!"

"I have to deal with him anyway. He's in charge. Or hadn't you noticed?"

Then I see them. Three koliuzhi. Emerging from the forest.

"Timofei Osipovich! They're back!"

"Who?"

"The koliuzhi!"

He stops, slides me down his shoulder and turns to look. He takes his gun in hand but doesn't raise it. I wish he would. Our entire crew has disappeared around the rocky headland. I don't know how Timofei Osipovich alone will be able to defend us against three koliuzhi.

The koliuzhi call out, "Likáḵɬi."[5]

They carry bows and arrows. They wear vests and breech-clouts, but no paint, and no feathers this time. They have no shoes. How do they manage on these rocks without shoes?

I recognize one—it's the man who was in the tent on the beach with me. The moustached toyon. He looks different without the paint and feathers, without his sea otter cape. He doesn't limp as he approaches. It wasn't him they carried off the beach. I think about the dead boy, again and dread creeps down my limbs.

The toyon says, "Hílich hawayishka okiɬ ḵiʔ ixʷatiliʔlo t́siḵáti."[6] Timofei Osipovich frowns and squints.

"What did he say?"

He shrugs. "I think it's about hunting."

"I thought you understood their language."

"Some of it. Sometimes they understand me better than I understand them." He smiles at me. "Don't worry. Your Timofei Osipovich also knows a thing or two about hunting."

He asks them a question. The toyon responds. As he's speaking, Timofei Osipovich shifts his musket and the toyon stops. We all grow still.

In a low voice, Timofei Osipovich says, "The scoundrels have been stalking us all day. I knew it."

He asks another question and after the toyon responds, our prikashchik turns to me. "He wants to know where we're going. I wouldn't tell him. He also says there's a better trail in the forest. He wants us to follow them so they can show us."

"We can't do that," I cry, colour burning my cheeks. "Do they think we're stupid?"

"Madame Bulygina, compose yourself. They can't understand

---

5 Stranger!

6 You are acting like a deer in the hunters' grounds.

what you're saying, but if you look and sound angry and frightened, they're not going to respond favourably."

He's right. Our strength right now is our language. We can say anything we want. They won't understand. This may help us escape, or at least hold off an attack until my husband realizes we're missing and sends somebody back.

Timofei Osipovich turns again to the koliuzhi. I can tell the toyon is adamant about us following.

"I think this toyon needs a hunting lesson," says Timofei Osipovich coolly. "Watch me—but stay calm, please, Madame Bulygina."

He says something that seems to please the toyon, and they stop talking. Timofei Osipovich steps away from us and picks up a piece of driftwood. He sets it atop a larger log stretched on its side, just a short distance away. He jiggles the driftwood until it's balanced on the big log.

"Be still, Madame Bulygina, no matter what. I'm going to step away now, but don't worry. I'll kill them all if anybody touches you."

He takes a few steps away. He turns to see where he is. Then he walks farther. The stones clatter under his feet. When he's a distance away, he turns, loads his gun, aims, and pulls the trigger.

The shot echoes through the forest. My ears ring. I understand now. He's giving a demonstration—a demonstration to instill fear and respect—and at the same time, to signal to our group that we're in trouble. It won't be long before the others return.

The koliuzhi look sideways at one another but say nothing. Once Timofei Osipovich lowers his gun, they go to the driftwood. One of the men—not the moustached toyon—picks it up. There's a hole punched through the wood. Splinters jut out at all angles like lightning. He gives it to the toyon.

Then they walk toward Timofei Osipovich who hasn't moved. They walk with purpose—I think they're counting their steps. They want to know how far Timofei Ospiovich's musket can shoot. It takes more than a minute before they reach the prikashchik.

I don't know what they say. They don't even wave before they disappear into the forest. They take the shattered piece of driftwood with them.

At that moment, our group appears down the beach. They're running as fast as they are able to on loose rock, while dear Zhuchka bounds along at their side. Timofei Osipovich hollers and waves his gun in the air.

"They're late for the party," he says, grinning. "In such a hurry, they miss all the entertainment." He looks to the grey sky, which is still light. "Come on. Maybe we can manage another mile or two before night."

CHAPTER FIVE

This cave is wet and smells like mushrooms and fermented cabbage, but we're better off in here than out in the snow. The firewood is damp, and though we wave our caps and cloaks to direct the smoke outside, the cave has other ideas. My eyes water and old Yakov has a coughing fit—still, no one leaves the fire's side for long. No one wants to know the exact depths of this cave and risk meeting the creatures that sprout and grow in perpetual darkness.

The mouth of the cave frames the falling snow. The flakes are as big as feathers but judging by the way they fall, they're heavy. Snow ought to be a delight, but this fills me instead with dread. Much more of this lies ahead. It is only November, and it will only become colder.

I already miss being dry and warm under the covers of a bed where I can sleep properly. My house in Novo-Arkhangelsk is full of holes, and it leaks as bad as a barn. It's an ugly grey block of a house, perpetually dark inside, one of many arranged so randomly they appear to have been inadvertently dropped into that outpost. The houses are clustered atop a hill dwarfed by mountains whose peaks are always concealed in cloud. The furnishings are austere and uncomfortable. But I'd rush up the rough path to its front door right now if I could, unlatch it, and enter, throw myself onto the first piece of serviceable furniture I could find and never complain again.

The men are also tired, cold, and hungry. The food we salvaged from the ship is indeed not enough. Maria's already reduced our portions in order to stretch out what's left. She's asked the brooding Ovchinnikov to go hunting or fishing so she can make something instead of plain kasha and tea; he looked to Timofei Osipovich who shook his head, no. Even our prikashchik is too dejected.

The old carpenter Kurmachev emptied his flask and asked the others to share. Only Sobachnikov agreed. He poured some of his rum into the carpenter's flask, and Kurmachev nodded his thanks before fixing himself a place away from the smoke, and quaffing a mouthful or two. Or more.

Not an hour ago, Zhuchka began to act strangely. She hovered at the opening of the cave and whined. Finally, just when John Williams offered to go see what was bothering her, something crashed outside. I looked up. A boulder landed at the mouth of the cave. It was followed by a second boulder and a third. They were falling from above the cave entrance. At first, I didn't understand what was causing this landslide. Then my husband said, "It's the koliuzhi again."

"What are they doing?" grumbled the apprentice Kotelnikov.

"They're throwing rocks."

"Rocks again? Are they trying to kill us?" said Kotelnikov.

"No. They want to scare us," said Timofei Osipovich. "If they wanted to hurt us, believe me, they would have done it by now. They know we're cornered in this loathsome prison." He picked up a loose rock and sent it flying out into the daylight. "I thought I made it perfectly clear to them . . ."

"It seems all you did was challenge them to a contest," I said. "Perhaps they're not as scared of your little gun as you think."

He glowered but then laughed. "Clever girl."

The falling rocks stopped. We waited. Then a rustling began outside. Zhuchka raised her hackles and growled. A koliuzhi ran by. He moved so fast, it was impossible to say anything about him—how big he was, whether he was armed, what he was wearing, whether he was somebody we'd already met. Then another man dashed by in the opposite direction. There was a third. Timofei Osipovich and Ovchinnikov raised their guns in preparation for the fourth, or even an invasion. It seemed Timofei Osipovich's mistaken assessment of their intentions had brought into being what we most dreaded. But there wasn't another sound, and no other koliuzhi disturbs us all night.

When we rise the next morning, it's to discover that the snowstorm is over. The light that streams in the mouth of the cave is intense. Blinded by the brightness, I cautiously follow the others outside. No rain. Vibrant-blue sky peeps through the forest canopy. The air is as crisp as a freshly starched cuff. Patches of snow are scattered here and there. It seems most of it has already melted. I scoop up a small handful and put it in my mouth. It's as cold as the light is bright. I scoop again and wash my face with it. It stings, but I'm revived. If this weather holds, perhaps the stars will be visible tonight.

While we're outside exploring our surroundings and clearing our lungs of last night's foul cave air, John Williams locates a trail. My husband announces that we'll follow it for as long as we can, for as long as it heads in the right direction. He doesn't mention what happened on the beach yesterday. I know he's worried. He wants us to stay together; he also wants us to maintain a brisk pace, which is nearly impossible when crossing sand and gravel beaches. The farther south we can get, the warmer the weather will be, and hospitable weather means a better chance of survival.

Near mid-morning, our trail ends at a narrow, but deep, stream. Zhuchka is already halfway in, up to her belly, lapping up water, and snapping at debris carried from upstream. The water turns her fur nearly black, except for the white tip of her paintbrush tail, which retains its brilliance and its curl even when wet.

"Look—the track turns this way," says John Williams. The path he indicates follows the riverbank upstream, into deeper bush.

"If there's a path, we should take it," says Nikolai Isaakovich.

"With caution," Timofei Osipovich concurs. "Remain alert, men."

We follow the path. Sunlight reaches us in fingers through the trees. Maria finds some edible mushrooms. Though slimy and well past their prime, she boils them when we stop for a meal, with some purplish berries like the ones I tasted our first day on shore. The broth is dismal, but I'm so hungry and the broth is so warm that I gulp my entire portion except for a few pinches of mushroom that I offer to Zhuchka. She gobbles them.

"I don't know about this trail," my husband says as we shoulder our bundles for the next stretch.

"It's going in the right direction," says John Williams.

"The koliuzhi trails are all like this," says Timofei Osipovich.

We march on through the afternoon. I hobble a bit. The blisters on my heels sting, but I try to forget about them. Eventually callouses will form if I give them time. Maria walks with me. Ovchinnikov, whom Timofei Osipovich charged with guarding our backs, is the last man in our queue. Zhuchka returns periodically to insert her wet nose into my hand before plunging back into the undergrowth.

We leave the little stream. Its burbling disappears, and the trail starts to climb. Maria and I slow to a crawl. The path is muddy and uneven; gnarled roots protrude from the soil. It grows more and more slippery as it weaves up the hill in short segments that snake back and forth on one another. Maria and I stop often to catch our breaths. Ovchinnikov has no choice except to slow to match our pace. The way he watches us when we stop makes me shorten our breaks.

My bundle pulls against my shoulder, and though I shift it often, it makes no difference. The sailcloth digs painfully into my shoulder. In the mire, I see evidence in the footprints of how others before us have slipped.

My mother once told me that on the day God and the devil made the world, they had to decide whether to make it flat or mountainous. The devil chose flat, but God chose the mountains. "Why?" asked the devil. "Why would you choose mountains and hills? What good are they?" And God said, "They're for the people—so they'll remember us. When people want to descend from the hills, they'll think, dear God, help me get down. And when they want to climb, they'll think, what a devil of a hill. So you see—mountains ensure they'll never forget either one of us."

"You're treating her like a child," my father had said that day. "Don't fill her head with nonsense."

"She is a child and that's not nonsense. If you're so smart, tell me—where do hills come from?"

"I don't know," my father cried, exasperated. "But I know there's a rational explanation. It has nothing to do with God and the devil."

A certain smile stretched across my mother's face; she looked away and said nothing more.

My mother has her own way of making sense of the world. She knows all the old stories, and when she starts telling me one, it's my father's turn to leave the room. I don't really believe her stories but her faith in them is unshakeable, even in the face of the Enlightenment. On this long climb, I miss her so much it aches. What is she doing right now? Does she know where I am? When the news of the lost brig reaches her, she will most likely think me dead. I think of her praying over my bed for so many

hours when I had the measles. I can't bear to imagine the grief
I'll cause her this time.

When Maria, Ovchinnikov, and I reach the top of the hill,
Nikolai Isaakovich is waiting.

"Is everything all right?" he asks.

"Yes." I smile. "Just—that was a devil of a hill."

He smiles back, and falls into line behind me. We follow flat
terrain for some distance, then we descend. Toward nightfall, as
we squeeze out the final minutes before it becomes too dark to
continue, Timofei Osipovich shouts from far ahead, "Navigator
Bulygin! Hurry!"

"Coming!" he cries and leaps over the roots and mud, leaving
us alone again.

Long before we reach them, I hear their voices—loud and
laughing, bubbling over with a joy I don't expect. I can't distinguish the words, but I know they're happy. When we arrive, I
see a tiny fire in a clearing. It throws light on a hut that sits on a
riverbank. The crew is inside the hut.

The grounds are deserted, but the people who belong here
can't have gone very far. In the river, a net stretches from bank to
bank. It shivers in the water current.

This place makes me think of the Baba Yaga. She would keep
a dwelling like this—a wooden hut in the middle of a clearing
with a small fire to lure unexpected visitors inside. My mother
told me all the Baba stories, too. I don't believe in the old hag or
her power. Still, something about this place, a kind of eeriness,
makes me wonder if perhaps I'm foolish to ignore our lore.

The apprentice Kotelnikov comes out of the hut, laughing,
and waving an object dull and flat.

"Kizhuch!" cries Ovchinnikov. His beard opens up to reveal a
broad smile and a rarely shown row of uneven teeth.

Maria grins, and her eyes become slits in her wrinkled skin.
"Ryba," she says. It's fish.

Hanging from the rafters of the little hut are many more fish. They're dry, dusty orange, and they've been split. I touch one—it's hard and unappetizing, but still my mouth waters. It smells like warm honey in the hut. There are fish heads, too, grotesquely pierced on stakes, as though confirming the Baba's presence. The crew pull the salmon from the rafters, stack them up, and cradle them against their chests. Some are taking two, even three entire fish.

I leave the hut empty-handed.

Outside, Maria says, "Aren't you hungry?" Her arms are wrapped around two salmon. Nikolai Isaakovich has one flattened salmon.

"Whose fish are these?" I ask.

"Whose? No one's. There's no one here," my husband says.

But before we leave, he instructs Kotelnikov to leave behind a small heap of korolki and the blue nankeen robe we brought from the brig. He sets them alongside the wall near the entrance, so that whoever comes back won't fail to find them right away. In return, we've taken twenty-seven pieces of fish.

"As the old saying goes—God is on high and the Tsar is far away," Timofei Osipovich says to me and smirks. My hunger is stronger than my need to respond.

We must leave before anybody returns. So, with our stolen fish, we head back into the forest, following no trail. We ascend, then find a hollow surrounded by thick brush. Here we set up for what's going to be another cold, damp night. I wish we were back in the cave, but at least we have food. What Maria does to the kizhuch smells miraculous, and despite the weight of my moral unease, I accept the portion offered. I drink the broth, and eat the fish, sharing little bits with Zhuchka. Not once does anybody complain about the little bones.

"Commander! The koliuzhi are back!" cries Kotelnikov.

In the middle of the forest, we're surrounded. They stand silently as though they're shadows attached to the trees. They're armed with spears, bows, and arrows. I stop and wait. How did they manage to get so close? John Williams's hair is a beacon in this dim forest. We must have been too distracted—tearing down last night's camp, packing our bundles, getting ready for another day of marching through the wild. Why didn't Zhuchka bark? Is it possible that she didn't notice them?

The koliuzhi watch us watching them. There's an old man with a harpoon on his shoulder who looks like he's a peasant with a long-handled hoe. His harpoon has slender prongs better suited to fishing than battle. Another man carries a tiny bow in one hand and an arrow in the other, but neither is raised. The man closest to Kotelnikov, the one who must have startled him, has a dagger with a long, carved shaft. The sheath droops from a cord around his waist. He holds his dagger at his hip.

"Hold your fire," says Nikolai Isaakovich.

But Timofei Osipovich raises his gun and fires a shot into the air.

It thunders, the sound coming from everywhere at once. The koliuzhi scatter into the forest.

"Why did you do that?" my husband says. "I told you not to shoot."

"I didn't shoot. I was just scaring them away. It worked, didn't it?" To me, he says softly, "Distraction. It works every time. I told you, didn't I?"

Zhuchka comes running from deep in the bush.

"What kind of people are these?" drawls the American. "You said they'd be looting the ship and would leave us alone."

"Ah, the ship's probably gone by now," says Timofei Osipovich. "You can bet once they finished plundering it, they burned it to ashes."

I picture the brig, its graceful hull, its towering masts, the line of the bowsprit pointing us forward. The beautiful wheel carved from mahogany. The deck the promyshlenniki mopped every day. The place beside the skiff where I often stood when I watched the stars because it was sheltered from the wind. Gone to ashes. It seems impossible.

"As for you—you could try covering your head. Where's your cap?"

John Williams reddens and touches his head, as though he'd just noticed the absence of his hat.

"Hurry up and finish your packing. We need to get as far away from here as possible," Nikolai Isaakovich instructs. I turn back to my bundle. I rewrap and reposition my telescope and the star log, whose pages are becoming wavy in the damp. It's going to be difficult to keep them safe and dry until we reach the *Kad'iak*.

We leave the grove where we spent the night and trudge back down to the river, then head upstream, plodding along through the mire until we find a shallow place to cross. The stones in the river's bed are smooth and round, so I take care. My husband waits on the other side and offers me his hand. I take it, and he pulls me up onto the bank.

The trail disappears again, and though we search, no one, not even John Williams, can find it. So we head into the forest once more. Without a trail, our progress is slow. Every once in a while, the brush rustles, and a shadow flits by and vanishes. I'm sure we're being followed, though no one says a word about it.

What do they want? Why are they following us? I knew nothing good would come from looting their fish. Perhaps we should offer them what remains of our beads and cloth. Would they leave us alone if we did?

When we finally stop for the night, my husband increases the number of sentries. Seven men guard us, forming a tight ring not far from the fire. A mist settles over the camp, making it impossible to see much beyond the trees that circle us. I look up, searching for the last of the day's light, but the trunks just fade into the grey. It's impossible to see the canopy. It will be another night without the stars, without my beloved Polaris, another night for my telescope to stay wrapped safely in my sailcloth bundle.

Maria cooks another proper and satisfying meal with the fish. The flavour infuses the broth, and there's the thinnest shimmer of oil on top. It surprises me to see it; the fish was so dry when we took it from the rafters.

For a long time after the meal, the promyshlenniki sit around the fire without saying much. There are no stories tonight, no jokes. They drink desultorily from their flasks. Considering how easily we were surprised this morning, everyone is nervous about going to sleep, even with all the guards. Timofei Osipovich half-heartedly stirs the coals every once in a while and a few sparks rise. Finally, it can be delayed no longer. It's time to sleep.

For the first night since the brig ran aground, Nikolai Isaakovich had the Aleuts set up a tiny tent at the edge of our circle, slightly apart from the others. "We'll sleep here tonight," he murmured to me. I was undecided about this closeness. While it would bring me comfort to lie next to my husband, I felt concerned about what the others would think.

We lie on my cedar cape, though there's barely enough room for one. We face each another. He opens his greatcoat and pulls me into his chest. I feel uneasy, but his body radiates warmth. Light from the fire ripples over his face.

"Kolya!" I whisper, startled by his expression. "What's wrong?"

He whispers back, "Anya—we're in trouble."

"Hush." I press my finger to his lips. "Go to sleep."

When I remove my finger, he says, "I don't know what to do. We're lost." He cups my silver cross and slowly runs his thumb across each of the bars. His hand trembles. "It's hopeless."

Our situation is terrible. It's worse than any of us ever could have imagined. If it's not the koliuzhi who kill us, it'll be the cold or a wild animal or we'll starve to death. No one dares to speak it, but it's the truth. I'd hoped my husband believed in his plan and in the wisdom of the instructions he's been bravely issuing to the crew. They depend on his confidence, and so do I, and without it, I don't know what could happen.

"Everything will be fine," I whisper. "It's hard. But we'll get to the *Kad'iak*."

He drops the silver cross and cradles my cheek. I smile. "Now go to sleep. You'll feel better in the morning."

His hand slides from my cheek to my shoulder. "Annichka," he murmurs. The firelight flickers in his eyes. His fingers glide down my arm to my waist. He tugs at the ribbon on my skirt and leans in to kiss me.

"Kolya," I say quietly. I pull back. I shove his hand away from my waist.

"Come on." He slides his hand around mine, and pulls it to his groin.

"No!" I push hard against his chest. But not before I've felt his stiffness.

He's lost his mind. No. Not here, not now. I sit up and roll out of the tent.

"Where are you going?" he demands.

"I have—ladies' business." I scurry away, heading for the forest. Ovchinnikov, on sentry duty again, grows alert as I pass beyond the ring of guards. When I stop and reach for my skirt, he knows to discreetly turn away. Zhuchka's awoken and followed me into the darkness.

I squat in the bushes. I can't see far through the mist, but I know Zhuchka will let me know if there's any threat. Like all animals, she's acutely aware of everything surrounding us. I finish relieving myself. But I remain squatting, curled into myself, because I don't want to go back in the tent with Nikolai Isaakovich.

"Anya?" he finally calls.

"I'll be right there," I reply. But I wait.

"Anya? Where are you?" he calls again after a few minutes.

"Coming." But I still wait. Zhuchka whines and tilts her head at me. Funny girl. What does she want?

Finally, I rise. I go slowly back toward the fire. How am I to avoid this mortification? When I reach the little tent, much to my surprise, Nikolai Isaakovich is asleep. He lies on his back, in the centre of my cedar cape. His limbs are flung wide. He snores softly.

I don't dare to wake him. I lie down as close as I can. At least part of my body is off the damp ground. Zhuchka curls on my other side. I can count on her and her fur to keep me warm.

CHAPTER SIX

On the trail, far ahead, leaves shiver and there's the quiet crack of a branch. Ovchinnikov and the apprentice Kotelnikov, who are protecting us from the front, raise their weapons.

"Wait," says Timofei Osipovich. "Don't shoot."

A woman and three men emerge through the trees and quietly approach us. The men are armed with spears, but they remain lowered. The woman is young—younger than me. She wears a cedar-bark skirt and over her head and shoulders, a bark cape that, unlike mine, has no front opening. She has boots made of brown animal hide. A soft-sided basket curls into the curve of her back. It's strapped to her forehead. From the tightness in her neck, I presume the basket is not empty. She smiles.

The instant she does, I'm reminded of a girl from Petersburg named Klara. Klara was never without a dance partner. She knew all the steps before anybody else—the ecossaise and the anglaise and even the mazurka when most people had only just heard of it—and she never once looked my way. I tried several times to earn her kind regard by smiling at her. There were always rumours of her engagement—to a handsome prince, to a wealthy count, to whichever man was deemed the most eligible that week—but

I left the city before anything was announced.

The men scan our group, looking, I think, for our toyon. Nikolai Isaakovich notices this too, and steps forward, but it's Timofei Osipovich who greets them in that language he knows. "Wacush."

They look surprised, but they answer in a cordial way, then pause. Timofei Osipovich replies and asks a question.

Only six days ago, the koliuzhi on the beach had been friendly when we first met them, but that changed so quickly. These koliuzhi also appear to be well intentioned, but how can we really tell? If Kotelnikov becomes impatient again or one of the Aleuts becomes too nervous and raises his weapon, the koliuzhi are so close that any one of us could be killed.

Then, with a swing of her hip and a dip of her shoulder, the woman rolls her basket around to her side. She withdraws several pieces of dried fish and offers them to Timofei Osipovich. He accepts them, says something—presumably he thanks her—and he hands the fish to Maria.

After more discussion, Timofei Osipovich turns to us. "Well," he begins, "they're different. Another clan altogether. And it seems they're at war with the koliuzhi who've been tormenting us."

"A different clan? They look exactly the same," says Kotelnikov.

"What about the woman?" says the American. "There was no woman before."

"Do you believe them?" Isaakovich asks Osipovich.

He shrugs. "Who knows? It wouldn't be the first time some impostor has tried to fool Timofei Osipovich Tarakanov, would it? But they say terrible things about the other koliuzhi—how they raid their villages, capture their people, and then force them to work. They told me those koliuzhi steal their food and tools. They also claim that they're more peaceful."

"Are they at war with the other koliuzhi?"

"Who knows? They could be."

My husband ponders this news before finally he shrugs, too. "I guess we should believe them," he says. "After all, if they were treacherous, they probably would have attacked us by now."

"And they wouldn't have offered us food," says Sobachnikov awkwardly. Timofei Osipovich gives him another withering look and the main rigger looks away. I pity him. No matter what he says and does, Timofei Osipovich finds fault with it.

"I don't know," says the apprentice Kotelnikov. "I don't trust them."

"Well, I don't know either," my husband says briskly. "But there are only four of them, and this woman is as scrawny as a plucked grouse. What do they want?"

After further conversation with Timofei Osipovich, it seems what the koliuzhi want is to help. They'll walk with us, protect us, and guide us through the forest. Would they take us all the way to the *Kadi'ak*? A wave of fresh hope washes over me. Perhaps the worst of our ordeal is over.

"I think we should go," says Timofei Osipovich. "If they try anything funny, we'll kill them." Ovchinnikov barks a cruel laugh.

I flush. I'm still not used to the fact they can't understand us.

We don't stop until midday when everyone's hungry. We've made good progress through the forest partly because the koliuzhi know where they're going but also because their pace is faster than what we're used to. Koliuzhi Klara—in my mind, that's how I'm thinking of her—sits at the fire near Maria and me. She watches us openly, in a way that's nearly impolite, but she can mean nothing by it. I can't imagine what she thinks of us—how filthy we are, our clothes muddy, our hair unkempt. Does she think this is normal for us? I hope not.

She seems especially curious about John Williams. He's the only one in our group with such pale skin, freckles, and a thatch of red hair. She stares as though she's never seen red hair before.

John Williams frowns and looks away. He keeps checking to see if she's still staring and mostly she is.

She also watches Maria as she cooks. Her eyes widen when Maria sets the pots of water on the hot coals. When Koliuzhi Klara detects the scent of the cooking fish, her eyes dart away from John Williams and back to the pots.

When the ukha is ready, Maria ladles it into our bowls. "Give her some," she tells me, and nods toward Koliuzhi Klara. I cradle the bowl in both hands and lower it to the woman. She takes it, looks at it, then looks at me. Doesn't she understand?

"Wacush," I say, attempting the word Timofei Osipovich always uses with the koliuzhi, always with positive results.

Koliuzhi Klara jerks back. A few drops of ukha spill. Her eyes grow wide, then crinkle at the corners. A laugh bursts out of her. She says something to the koliuzhi men and they look amused. I blush and turn away. I have no idea why what I said is so funny.

She tries the ukha and grimaces. She says something to the men again and they laugh; they all eat it anyway. Timofei Osipovich converses with the koliuzhi men, and translates their conversation for my husband. They've had a mild winter so far. They caught a lot of fish in the summer. European ships have visited before, but they don't come very often. Though the discussion is slow, with the translation flowing in two directions, the men appear to enjoy one another's company, and I become convinced that we're right to trust them.

❧

When we've finished, we begin to walk again. Koliuzhi Klara leaves Maria and me and joins her own people in our long line. From behind, I can watch her without appearing rude. With the basket strapped to her head, her shoulders and arms are free.

She swings them as she walks and uses them, when needed, to push branches from her path. She's light on her feet and fast, almost like she's skipping down the trail. She doesn't stumble over exposed tree roots or rocks.

Very late in the afternoon, a clearing emerges in the distance. When we arrive, I see it's not really a clearing. It's the wide mouth of a river. The water ripples and gurgles over a stony riverbed, and, to the right, only a short way from where we stand, it empties into the sea. I didn't know we were so close to the ocean. On the other side of the river sit five broad wooden buildings. They appear to be empty.

"Where is everyone?" Nikolai Isaakovich says.

"I'll ask," replies Timofei Osipovich. He speaks with the koliuzhi and then translates. "They say everyone's gone to another village, but I don't understand why. What they say—it doesn't make sense."

"Well, can we get across?" my husband asks.

I wonder if we can sleep in one of the empty houses. If no one's here, then they couldn't possibly mind.

"They say it's too deep, and the current is too strong."

"Is there a boat? Ask them if they have a boat."

Timofei Osipovich turns his head slightly. The koliuzhi can't see his expression of skepticism. "Apparently, it's not deep enough for a boat right now. This is low tide."

"Too deep, not deep enough—what is it then?" my husband demands. Then he sighs and says, "Will they bring a boat at high tide?"

"They say yes, they'll bring one for the next high tide," Timofei Osipovich says, with a pointed gaze to the heavens, one corner of his mouth turned down.

Every man here can count. Every man here knows—as do I—that the next high tide will fall in the blackest part of the night. The one after that won't come until midday tomorrow.

My husband taps his lips as he considers this news. "We'll set up camp, but not here," he says finally. "Tomorrow, we cross this river, in daylight, high tide, low tide, no matter. Tomorrow, we'll be on our way first thing in the morning, with or without their help."

Timofei Osipovich says something and then we turn back toward the forest, leaving our guides on the riverbank. My Koliuzhi Klara doesn't watch us leave; her face is turned to the grey sea, to the sky woven into it, and to the soft yellow ball of the dimming sun as it sets.

Just as he did so often on the ship, Sobachnikov takes the shift no one else wants and guards our camp until the early morning hours. Then he wakes us. The air is damp, as usual, but there's no rain. The birds chatter and flit overhead. We each eat a small, grimy helping of kasha that tastes of fish—the pots haven't been cleaned since yesterday morning—and a mouthful of dried kizhuch. Then we return to the riverbank.

A much different scene faces us this morning. Our guides are gone, and the deserted settlement is now dotted with men. There are at least twenty, but not more than thirty. Each is armed—I see spears, daggers, and bows and arrows—but their weapons remain lowered.

"What's going on?" says my husband. "I thought they were going to help us cross the river."

"That's what they said," says Timofei Osipovich and shrugs.

The crew spreads out along our grassy side of the river, a narrow band of water that separates stage from audience as if in a grand theatre. But who's performing here? Who's paid for the show? If only somebody on either side would move, I might be able to tell.

Where are the people who helped us yesterday? There are no women on their side. Koliuzhi Klara is gone. I can't tell if any of the three men from yesterday are among those on the riverbank this morning. We're too far away.

On their side, on the stone-strewn shore, two canoes rest, their bows pointing toward us, as though the boats are about to be launched.

Timofei Osipovich calls out, "Wacush!" His voice thunders and echoes off the trees. He must raise it if he's to be heard. A moment later, his greeting is returned, and he responds with a long speech. The river performs a soft score that plays beneath his words. He finishes with a question, and waits. The koliuzhi don't answer. He asks again. Once more, he waits, but it's clear they're not going to answer.

"Why don't they say something?" my husband asks. "Don't they understand you?"

"I don't know," says Timofei Osipovich. "They understood me yesterday."

"I don't think these are the same people," says Sobachnikov, then flushes.

"What would you know?" Timofei Osipovich snaps, impatient as he always is with the main rigger. He kicks at the moss and an egg-shaped chunk rolls into the water. It bobs away with the current, spinning around the rocks.

We stand and wait for a long time and a short time. Zhuchka, who's back in the river again, chews at something. She dips her nose in the water whenever something interesting catches her eye. She heads upriver, her tail a rudder floating on the surface behind her.

Finally, my husband stirs. "Let's go then. No point wasting any more time. I said we'd cross today and cross we will." He shifts the bundle on his back, turns, and sets out following the riverbank away from the ocean.

Somebody from across the river shouts. Another man calls out. Three or four koliuzhi advance to the river's edge and wave to get his attention.

"Commander," says Timofei Osipovich. "Wait."

The larger of the canoes is launched with only two men onboard. It's sleek and plain, and takes only a minute to cross to our shore. It scrapes against the bottom as it comes near our grassy bank, but they don't land it. Instead, they manoeuvre it into a spot where the current is not so strong, and paddle so that it flutters in the channel and moves neither up nor downstream. The paddlers' faces are turned up to the crew as they wait for us to do or say something.

"That boat is too small," my husband says. "We can't all fit."

"Then we'll split up," Timofei Osipovich says. "Cross in two trips."

"That's reckless!" cries the apprentice Kotelnikov. "They're trying to trick us!" He puffs up his big chest in outrage like a cockrel on the wrong side of the fence.

My husband throws down his hands in a fury. "Tell them to bring us another boat," he sputters, raising his voice. "I demand another boat."

Timofei Osipovich lowers his voice to a purr. "I will *ask*, Commander, but if you let your frustration show, we'll have far more than a river crossing to deal with."

My husband grumbles but defers.

Timofei Osipovich speaks with the men in the canoe. That's followed by shouting between the canoe and the people on the opposite shore. Eventually, the other canoe is launched, but it's smaller than the first and most certainly won't solve our problem.

The little canoe is proficiently paddled by one person and has a passenger. As it draws close, I'm startled. The passenger is Koliuzhi Klara. She sits quietly. Nothing on her face acknowledges that she's seen us before. It's peculiar. Still, I'm happy to see her. Even if we must be divided for the crossing, now I'm sure nothing untoward will happen.

Nikolai Isaakovich, however, isn't happy. "What is this mischief?"

"You can see for yourself," Timofei Osipovich says dryly. "If it doesn't please you, we can try to find another way across." He gestures upstream. "All rivers, no matter how long, have a source—somewhere."

"No. We've wasted enough time." He looks at the crew, one by one. "Remain vigilant! Do you hear me? These are my orders!" Sobachnikov colours, and shifts nervously. John Williams looks away, his pale eyes hooded. The apprentice Kotelnikov exhales loudly and frowns at my husband.

The nose of the little canoe is pulled up to shore.

"How many people can fit?" my husband asks.

"Only three," says Timofei Osipovich. "I assume the woman is staying."

"Filip Kotelnikov—you go," my husband says. "And control your temper." Kotelnikov looks startled. "Old Yakov. You, too. Make sure he causes no trouble." Yakov nods, but we all know that no one can stop Kotelnikov. "And Maria, leave your things. We'll take all the provisions in the larger canoe."

Yakov slides down the muddy bank and into the boat in one motion. He's directed toward the stern, to a seat in front of the paddler. Maria follows. She climbs into the small canoe like she's done this many times before, and she seats herself in front of Yakov. Kotelnikov is next. He submerges a foot but otherwise steps neatly into the canoe. It rocks with his weight. He sits beside Maria.

There remains one more seat between them and Koliuzhi Klara, who occupies the bow.

"Madame Bulygina should go with this group," says Timofei Osipovich.

I jolt, then turn red. Is he serious? The little canoe is already heavily loaded, and looks so unsteady. I want to cross with Nikolai Isaakovich.

My husband looks from him to me and back to him, and says, "Why?"

"It's safer," he replies. "There's only one man and he has the paddle. What could possibly happen?"

My husband deliberates, and makes his decision quickly. "Anya. You go."

"Are you sure? Maybe somebody else . . ."

"No. He's right. It's safer. You'll be fine."

I turn to the riverbank. The others' feet have left long, thin marks in the mud. It's slippery. I take a careful step.

"No, Anya," my husband says. "Leave your things."

I stop and look over my shoulder at him. "But my telescope— and the star log." I wrap a protective arm around my bundle. "I can manage."

"We'll take them in the big canoe."

"I think it would be better if I took them."

"Anya," he cries, exasperated. "There's not enough room. Can't you see?"

"I'll bring it to you, Madame Bulygina," says Sobachnikov. "I promise." He blushes.

My husband looks at him quickly, then back to me, and says, "Are you satisfied now?"

I carefully set down my heavy bundle, and, because it also seems awkward, I remove my cedar cape. With only one step, I slide right down the riverbank and into the water with a splash. Now my skirt is wet. I stand in the river, clinging to the gunwales, feeling my feet sink in the soft muck. I'm not sure how to get into the canoe now, but I'm glad I left my bundle, which could have landed in the water with me.

I hear a quiet laugh. "Be careful, Madame Bulygina," says

Timofei Osipovich, "unless you've decided it's an appropriate time for your bath."

"You're a pest," my husband says to him. "Be quiet." I give Nikolai Isaakovich a thankful look.

"Come," says Kotelnikov. I use his pudgy hand to steady me while I climb back onto the riverbank. It's easy with his support to step over the gunwales. When I put my foot down, the canoe rocks violently as it did when Kotelnikov boarded. Koliuzhi Klara grabs the gunwales. The koliuzhi man in the canoe leans to one side and dips his paddle into the river. "Sit down, Madame Bulygina," cries Kotelnikov. When I do, the canoe rocks, then settles. I'm backwards, facing Maria and Kotelnikov. "Just stay where you are," Kotelnikov says. "Don't move."

"Anya? I'll see you on the other side," Nikolai Isaakovich says.

"Don't forget my things."

"Don't worry."

Our canoe is pushed into the river. The instant we're afloat, I feel how unstable the little boat really is. I cling to the gunwales. The balance is so delicate that every ripple of water, no matter how small, unsteadies us. If we capsize, who will save me?

I hear a scrape and glance over my shoulder to see what it is. Koliuzhi Klara has taken a paddle from the hull—I didn't realize she had one. She dips it into the water and pulls.

Zhuchka swims beside us, her head a wedge that cuts through the flow. She's so close I can hear the heaviness of her breath. Her eyes roll as they watch me. I smile to reassure her, but I don't dare call out in case she gets it in her mind to climb into the canoe.

Facing backward, I see everything happening on our shore. They're boarding the large canoe. They're loading some of the bundles, passing them from man to man along a chain that runs down the riverbank and into the vessel. There'll only be enough space for half the remaining crew. The others—and the bundles left behind—will have to wait for the second trip.

My bundle lies where I dropped it, right beside a tuft of reeds. They won't dare forget it. I'll go back myself if they do.

My husband is the last to board. As commander, he should be among the first to be greeted by the koliuzhi who wait on the other side. Timofei Osipovich, on the other hand, remains on shore though my husband probably could use his skills to translate once he debarks. They push their canoe out. It's loaded so heavily it barely rides above the water.

The water divides and flows around our little canoe. The koliuzhi man labours with the paddling. Thanks to the extra weight, even with two people paddling, the way forward isn't easy. His arms strain, the muscles bulge, and his neck is tight and sinewy. His breath comes in quick puffs. He bends and pulls, bends and pulls. The large canoe begins its journey back to the koliuzhi side. Despite also having only two men to paddle, and being so heavily laden, it advances more quickly than ours.

We enter choppier waters. Froth curls on the water's surface like a confection. Trees line both sides of the river, drawing to a deep, shadowy vee upstream. I turn away and look back downstream to see how the larger canoe is progressing.

From the sea, a grey wall of water advances. It rises steadily, alarmingly, heading for the river. What is it? It narrows, the riverbanks funnelling it into a bulging mass of water. I want to scream but I'm mute. I raise my hand and point.

Maria, Kotelnikov, and Yakov look. In the big canoe, John Williams leaps up and also points.

"No!" I finally cry.

The wall of water curls over like a serpent then falls in a huge sweep that swallows the big canoe. The boat disappears. An instant later, our little boat is lifted like a feather. We're turned around.

What's happening to the ocean?

In a rush, the water recedes. Our canoe stays afloat. But the big canoe is half submerged, and it tilts as though the hull has been breached. Not many men are still aboard. Those that are have no paddles, no way to stop their vessel from drifting toward the sea. Where's Nikolai Isaakovich? A few heads bob in the water, fighting the current that pulls them downstream. Two people stand waist deep near the bank as the water swirls around them. They're Russians. They hold their guns above their heads. Is one my husband? Three other men swim toward the koliuzhi's shore, where everyone has lined up along the riverbank. I can't tell anybody apart.

Zhuchka swims frantic circles around the bobbing heads.

"Kolya!" I shriek. I don't know where he is.

It's impossible to know who throws the first spear or shoots the first gun.

Maria slides down in the canoe, cowering in the hull. Yakov clutches the gunwales.

"Go back! Take us back!" Kotelnikov shouts.

Our paddlers ignore him and head away from the gunfire and the soaring arrows. They continue toward the koliuzhi shore. "Turn around!"

Kotelnikov lunges for the paddler behind him. He's pushed away. Our little canoe rocks threateningly. Kotelnikov lunges again and this time, the koliuzhi man knocks him down with the paddle.

One end of the big canoe sinks and the other swings around toward our shore. The remaining men jump out and make for land. John Williams is the first to climb out of the water—he's the easiest to see with his red hair. He aims his musket; nothing happens. He shakes it. In a fit, he throws it on the riverbank. The musket must be wet, useless. He picks up a stone and throws it. But the river swallows the rock before it reaches the midway point. It's too far. Still, he takes another and tries. He re-enters the river to get closer, and when knee-deep, he stops and positions himself. The riverbed has hundreds of rocks. He bends to get one, throws it, then reaches for another. Arrows plunge into the water all around him.

Zhuchka climbs out of the river. She runs up and down the bank on our side, barking. She jumps back in, chasing a flying rock.

Our little canoe crunches against the koliuzhi shore. Our paddler tries to steady the boat. Kotelnikov turns on him again. This time, three koliuzhi men emerge from the trees and rush over to help. Kotelnikov grabs the paddler's neck, but the men easily pull him off.

They drag Kotelnikov and Yakov from the boat. While they're distracted, I wonder if Maria and I should push the canoe back out. But there's no sense to that. We'd drift right into the crossfire. We meekly climb onto shore.

Koliuzhi Klara is gone. I didn't see her disappear. I'm certain she didn't go overboard but in all the confusion, I didn't notice her leaving the canoe.

We're now a safe distance from the thundering battle. The fighting has shifted into the forest on the opposite side of the river. Where's Nikolai Isaakovich? I glimpse men darting between trees, but none is my husband. Timofei Osipovich still has his musket. So does his dependable Ovchinnikov. They shelter behind the trees while they load their weapons, then lean out to shoot. John Williams has climbed a tree. He hides his red head in the foliage and shoots down on the koliuzhi. Somebody must have given him a dry gun. The carpenter Kurmachev and one of the Aleuts burst from the forest. They drag Sobachnikov between them. He's limp as a wilted violet, and his long arms and legs flop uncontrollably. He's unconscious, and there's blood on his jacket. The trio line up like the three stars in Orion's belt and disappear into the trees.

But where's Kolya?

The battle moves deeper into the forest, away from us, until we can no longer see anybody. Where's Zhuchka? Has she been hit? Is she dead? I hear a bark and a yelp. Poor girl. She must dodge fire from both sides of the battle.

The sound of gunfire echoes off the trees and riverbanks, as do the cries of men shouting to one another, and the men who've been struck. I cover my ears. I can't stand to hear another sound—every scream sounds like it's Nikolai Isaakovich. But we're not allowed to leave. Instead, we're made to sit together, back to back, these koliuzhi pressed up against us with their spears and arrows and daggers. Helpless to do anything to prevent it, we four are forced to listen to the long, low howl that marks the end of our world.

WINTER 1808–1809

CHAPTER SEVEN

Poets describe vividly the sensation of the falling heart, but I've never experienced it. I know it's irrational—as if a heart could plummet from heaven, spinning end over end, toward the hard earth and an inevitable, tragic destiny. Only children and the superstitious would believe such fancy. But when the koliuzhi focus their attention on us on the riverbank, I wonder if the poets might be right.

One of the men speaks to us, hard consonants thrown in our faces. Without Timofei Osipovich, we don't know what he wants. The man's voice becomes louder, and his lips twist and contort around his words. Does he think we can't hear? Doesn't he know that we don't understand?

Finally, the man growls. He nudges stout Kotelnikov with his knee, then again, and when the apprentice glares at him, the man pulls him roughly to his feet. Kotelnikov cries out, writhes, and tries to get away, but the man won't let go. "Ḵʷópatichásalas siwáchal, ichaḵłí axʷółkadídot́sa!"[7] he screams.

Guessing, we rise and stumble into a line behind Kotelnikov—Yakov, Maria, then me. We are led down a rugged path that skirts the river. The paddler from the canoe taps his paddle on the backs of my legs, herding me like I'm a goat.

---

7   If you wish to live, you better act like you're a puppy!

From the battlefield, there's neither movement nor sound. Where is everyone? I haven't seen my husband since the wall of water struck his canoe in the river. Did he drown? Has he been shot and killed? I strain to hear the smallest sound, to see the slightest movement, but it's as still as a painting across the river Nothing, not even a bird, dares to disturb the calm.

As we advance along the riverbank, we're also drawing near the sea. I begin to hear its murmur. Its voice grows louder and more insistent the closer we get. Then, beneath it, there's something else. A faint sound rises, then disappears. Then it's back. It goes away again. The wind plays games with it, with us, until at last the rhythmic sound swells so that nothing can blow it away. We round a bend in the river and the sound erupts like exploding cannon. What beats like a hundred drums? Roars like a thousand thunder claps? The noise rises through the soles of my feet. It fills my head until I can think of nothing else, then my heart until I believe it'll burst.

We reach the clearing with the five houses, the one we gazed upon from the opposite shore only a short while ago.

Koliuzhi, perhaps a hundred or more, ring the houses. Everyone strikes the walls with staves, pounding as if intent on demolishing their own homes. Even atop the houses, people lash out with batons violently enough to break the very roofs they stand on. The houses quiver, as if constructed of nothing more than a scrap of cloth or hide stretched over a wooden frame.

Is this their victory celebration?

Across the river, we'd been safe together such a short time ago. Now, in the tall trees and shadows that stretch as far as I can see, there's no sign of anybody. There's nothing I wouldn't expect to see in this overgrown forest—except for some of the sailcloth bundles, white as shells, scattered across the earth, many torn open—is one mine?—and a grey-brown mound collapsed at the foot of a tall tree. I can't take my eyes away from it. I look for movement, any movement at all. But it's lifeless.

"That's not him," Maria says, leaning near my ear to be heard.

"How do you know?"

"He led the men away. I saw him."

"Quiet," Kotelnikov snaps. "You'll provoke the koliuzhi."

The drumming stops suddenly, and everyone rushes to the doorway of one of the five houses. They squeeze through the yawning opening, men, women, children, even babies in arms.

We ought to escape. Run. But to where? All directions are the same when you're doomed.

Finally, Kotelnikov's captor pulls him toward the same door. The koliuzhi man strains against the apprentice's weight, but he's muscular. With a look at the man who herded me up the path, I say, "Come," to Maria and Yakov.

Like the little house we stole the salmon from, this one is made from wide, wooden planks that run the entire length of the building. Unlike that little house, this one is enormous, as big as a Petersburg mansion, perhaps bigger. There are no windows. The broad door lets two or three people enter at once.

Inside, darkness blinds me. All I see is the harsh glow of a fire, which verifies its presence with smoke scented like a Christmas feast. I sense movement all around. When my vision begins to adjust, I start to notice faces emerging from the gloom. They're lit partly by the fire and partly by the outdoor light creeping in through the door, chinks in the walls, and a hole in the roof, the purpose of which must be to release smoke.

Novo-Arkhangelsk and the hills that surround it were filled with koliuzhi. They lived there. They worked, traded, fished, and who knows what else? Others knew, no doubt, but not me. I didn't speak with them. I didn't enter their homes. I didn't ask after their mothers and fathers, their brothers and sisters, their children. I didn't seek their advice, nor did I offer my opinions. It's not that I didn't wonder about them. But I was uncertain how such overtures could have been made. I lived in a cloud of not knowing.

What is to be made of our situation? Will I die today? Will we all? None of us moves. We stand for what seems like an eternity with no one speaking. I strain to read the faces of the koliuzhi. I expect anger, but they keep their distance and watch. I remember those two koliuzhi men surrounded by our crew on the brig on the day we traded for the halibut. How long we forced them to stand before us in silence! Now, the table has turned.

"Híli Chabachíƚa, ƚib ťisíkʷƚ ókiƚ Chalaťilo ťsiķáti,"[8] says a man from deep in the shadows of the house. It's difficult at first to locate who's speaking. When I do, I see a man opposite us, dressed in a cape unlike any I've seen on this voyage. This cape catches the firelight and glows soft gold. It's not fur. It's made of bark, just like mine was, though the gold is natural, not paint. Glossy black fur trims its edges. The cape is tied at his waist with a wide belt into which is tucked a dagger. He stands in a manner that reminds me of the towering trees firmly planted in the spongy soil of this forest.

He thrusts out a strange cylinder, then shakes it. It rattles like a cart running over a rutted road. What is it? It's shorter than a telescope, and I think it's made of wood. Huge eyes, ringed in red, and the pointed beak of a bird have been carved into it.

"Hakótƚalaxʷ sisáʔwa boyókʷa hótskʷať,"[9] he continues. His voice rumbles and reverberates off the plank walls. I try to understand, to identify any familiar word, but there's none. He continues to speak, directing his words at everyone in the house, not at us alone.

Before long, a woman steps forward. I think she's about to speak, too, but instead she kneels and tends the fire. My eyes shift from her to the speaker and back again. It's hard to know where to look. A second woman bends near the fire and lifts the lid

---

8   I am Chabachita, a name that has passed down through five generations.

9   Some drifting village people have come to our land before.

of a wooden box, one of several scattered about like toy blocks, unnaturally large versions of the ones I played with so long ago when my father was teaching me about gravity and the physical properties of objects in relation to one another.

When the lid is lifted, this wooden box releases a plume of steam and the aroma of stewing fish. The woman dips a big spoon—it's a seashell lashed to a handle—into the box and stirs. She's cooking. In a box? A box can hold water? Steaming water? A third, then a fourth woman soon join them, and together they fuss with the fire and the contents of the boxes with sticks and spoons and stones. With long wooden tongs, they move stones from the fire into the boxes. The stones sizzle when they hit the water and more steam billows to the rafters and spreads among the grasses, stalks, coils of cord, baskets, and skewered objects hanging up there.

The speaker's voice drones in the background while the women cook. One woman rises slowly from her fireside tasks, wipes her hands on her skirt, and walks behind us. The hair on the back of my neck prickles, but she just slips out the door. Immediately, the children become restless. They fidget, whisper, and giggle, drawing my attention away from the women. A boy makes faces while two girls pretend not to notice him and smother their laughter with their hands. One of those girls cradles a sleeping baby in her lap and curls a tendril of the baby's hair around her finger.

After a long time and a short time, the speaker finally stops. I'd like to sit down. I catch Maria's eye—she must be tired, too. But she only shrugs, shifts, and looks away.

It's not over yet. Another man steps into the ring of firelight. He's as wrinkled as Yakov, with eyes that glitter like stars in the night sky. His voice sounds much younger; its pitch and rhythm rise and fall, much like the river outside clambering over the rocks.

"Wáʔalaxʷ chaʔáḵalosalas hiḵítxli xʷaʔ didíʔdal ƚatsáʔ," he says.

"Histilósalas ish híx̣at ishatash tiɬal. K̓ʷíxʷa álita. Xʷokʷódis."[10]

Yakov tilts his cap back and squints and frowns as he listens to the old man, but it's clear from his face that he understands nothing. Kotelnikov is alternately sullen and defiant as he huffs, shakes his head, and puffs out his burly chest. No one interrupts the old man who continues as though he's telling a long story. However, two or three men slide along the walls to the doorway and leave the house.

I try to concentrate but my feet ache and soon my attention also drifts.

There's a heavy pillar in the corner, not far behind the head of the man who's speaking. Just like the rattle, it's carved, but with designs and images that look as though they've been plucked from a madman's feverish dreams. They're creatures. That much I can tell. Eyes, yes, hands, yes, mouths upturned or deeply frowning—but horns and claws and pointed teeth and tongues, too—and too many of everything, not attached where they should be, all encased in ovals. What these creatures represent is impossible to say. I look around me. Every pillar in the house—there are eight altogether—is similarly carved, but all the designs differ. In the firelight, though I know they're only blocks of wood, I expect the eyes to shift, the lips to part, and the tongues to unfurl as they come to life.

Maria nudges me, and I shift my attention back to the man and try again to concentrate. After a long time and a short time, the old man's story or speech finishes. Surely, the talking is over.

But no. Here's another man coming forward. Younger than the first two, this man has enormous half-moon eyebrows. At first I think he's painted them on, but then I realize they're real. Tangled and dark, they hood his eyes and resemble the eyebrows of the

---

10   Those strangers didn't kill the Indians with their thunder sticks. They gave us gifts and bought fish or animal fur.

carved figures on the posts. The rest of his body—his face, arms, and legs—are smooth. His legs are muscular, thick like tree trunks.

As with the first speaker, he addresses us. He starts with Yakov, who nods at him but says nothing. Maria won't meet his eye, and so he turns to Kotelnikov, who scowls and opens his mouth as if to say something but thinks better of it. Kotelnikov's lost a brass button and his black-green jacket gapes open, his big belly straining against the fabric, the white of his linen shirt like a feather easing its way out of a pillow.

Then, the man with the eyebrows turns to me. He says, "Xʷaʔ wíɫpaƛot χiʔ čhíḵa, chiʔ titsíʔyaɫ, halakitkatasalaxʷ čhikástoli."[11] Then he waits.

I look away, but he continues to watch me. "Wacush," I finally say. It's Timofei Osipovich's word and I don't know exactly what it means—it didn't work when I gave the ukha to Koliuzhi Klara—but the koliuzhi seem to respond to it.

The man with the eyebrows startles. Smothered laughter ripples through the house. My hands tremble.

Kotelnikov turns on me. "Madame Bulygina! You will provoke him!"

This eyebrow man is most certainly not provoked. The corners of his mouth twitch. Is he, too, about to laugh?

"Yakov? Help me, Yakov," I say softly.

Yakov looks down and shakes his head.

The eyes of the eyebrow man flit like dragonflies from me to the others, and eventually come to rest on me. Then he begins to speak again. He's not angry—of this I'm certain—but equally he's not happy. He's telling me something. When he finally pauses again, I have no choice.

"Wacush. We can't understand you. Do you understand me? We come from Russia. We're stranded here. We didn't mean

---

11   The families of those you killed will probably ask me to kill you for revenge.

to . . ." I think of the battle. What word is right for what happened? ". . . *disturb* you. We have no way to get back home, except if we can get to another Russian ship—it's waiting about sixty miles away. If you'll just let us go, please, in the name of God, we'll go and leave you alone.

"We're very tired and hungry, and we left everything on the ship. Keep it all. We have no use for it now." They don't need to know we've jettisoned so much. "We carry only what we need for our journey—a few things to eat, our muskets—"

"Madame Bulygina! Stop!" Kotelnikov snaps.

"They don't know what she's saying," Yakov chides softly. And he's right—I can tell by their puzzled looks that while they may have understood "wacush," that's all.

The gathering then, inexplicably, breaks up. Where's everyone going? I can't understand anything. All the signposts I possess have been torn from the ground and thrown in a river; they float away beyond reach.

We don't move, we four, until finally two little boys take Yakov by the arms and pull him to the other side of the fire. Old Yakov looks down at them with surprise and bemusement, and does not struggle. The boys giggle and offer the big, toothy smiles of children whose milk teeth have fallen out, but whose faces have not grown big enough to accommodate their new adult teeth.

When they arrive at the side of the man with the golden cape and the rattle, who's seated, the boys gesture to Yakov to sit down. The man with the golden cape looks up at Yakov and gives a short nod. Yakov sits and removes his cap. The young boys then come back for the rest of us. We sit on a cedar mat. The earthen floor is dry and slightly warm from the fire.

Then, Koliuzhi Klara sets before us a long tray.

She pushes it forward until it presses against my knees. "Wacush," she says mischievously, looking pointedly at me. She smiles when I blush.

The tray contains a mound of unidentifiable pink-brown mush. Maria cries, "Kizhuch!" I take a closer look—she's right. It's salmon again. Chunks of fish swim in a shiny broth. Steam rises from the tray. Why are they feeding us? Is this a trick? I look to Kotelinikov, Yakov, and Maria; they've already plunged their fingers into the food. Kotelnikov is gobbling like a half-starved pig at a trough.

Is this entire tray meant for us? Or are we to help ourselves and then pass it to others? I'm starving, too, but I don't know what to do.

A woman sitting on the opposite side of the fire has noted my hesitation. She was cooking earlier; clamping tongs around the hot stones and sliding them into the boxes of water. Does she think I don't want her food? That I don't find it good enough? I hear my mother's voice chastising my manners—so I pinch a scrap of fish between my fingers.

Once the food touches my tongue, I can't stop. I cram handful after handful of fish into my mouth. The wiry bones slow me down a bit, but with my tongue, I push them from between my lips. Having nowhere to put them, I hold them in my other hand.

The hunger I've been staving off for so long raises its head to ask: where have you been, Anna Petrovna Bulygina? I feed it, feed myself, eat and eat until there's nothing left on our tray, every little drop of oil has been licked from my fingertips, and my hand is full of small bones.

That night, I lie on a coarse cedar mat on the smooth earthen floor. Broad wooden benches rim the walls, but they're occupied by others.

Cedar mats, propped upright, divide some of the sleeping areas and provide a little privacy. But I can still see into most of them.

People in these compartments sleep in clusters looking like bumps along a treacherous road. Men, women, and children are heaped alongside one another. Are they families? Are they random groupings?

I'm quite far from the fire and I'm cold. Maria shares the cedar mat and a soft cedar cover that's far too small for two people. I'm fatigued but too chilly to sleep. I listen to Maria's breathing. I can tell she's awake.

"Maria?"

"What is it?"

The dark and the cold and my exhaustion feed one another. Questions form, and the answers are shadows in my mind. I try to suppress them but they're hardy and insistent. Finally, I say, "What are they going to do to us?"

She doesn't respond for a long time. Then she says, "That is written with a pitchfork on flowing water."

"What's that supposed to mean?"

"It means I don't know. And neither do you. Now go to sleep."

"I can't."

"Your worrying won't change a thing."

"I can't help it."

"Well, I can. I'm tired. Good night."

Though it's not like me, I pray—something I haven't done before bed since I was a little girl—and ask God to grant us our prayers, if they are good, and bring us all back together again in Novo-Arkhangelsk. But it's futile, and I'm no closer to sleep.

Long after Maria has succumbed, I lie on my back, my eyes wide open, recreating the night sky on the ceiling. Polaris is overhead. Is my head pointing east? I think so. Cassiopeia would be over there near the post. Orion would be there, where the bundles of dried grass stir in the fire's rising heat. Pegasus would be over there, near the door, which has been covered with some sort of screen for the night. I worry about my telescope and star log—was my bundle saved? Are my things safe and dry?

It's not just my thoughts that keep me awake—the night noises also disturb me. I've never slept in a room with so many people. There's coughing and throat clearing. Some people snore. Some call out in their sleep. One child laughs, caught in a dream.

And then, after I've lain awake for a long time and a short time, a certain rustling begins. Right away, I know what it is, and I'm not surprised when, before much time passes, it progresses to shameless grunts and moans. I put my fists over my ears but it's fruitless—my imagination furnishes the imagery.

I don't know what to do with the fish bones from our supper. My fist closed, I squeeze them lightly in my palms, feel their bend. If there were a way to reassemble them, to put the flesh back on the fish, to turn the clock back, how far back could I go? Could I identify the one miscalculation that brought me to this place—and undo it?

※

The next morning, I wake with empty hands. The bones slipped away in the night and they're now woven into the cedar mat and half-buried in the thin layer of dust that coats the earthen floor. I very badly need to relieve myself. What is the koliuzhi way? Do they have some kind of gutter or a cesspit? If not, where should I go, or does it matter? I ask Maria what I should do, and she tells me to find a private place outdoors.

"Are you sure?"

The corners of her mouth turn down, and she studies me like I'm a child who ought to know better.

"Then come with me. Please."

She shrugs. "I may as well."

We slowly cross the floor toward the door, taking small,

tentative steps. Many people watch. Then a man around my age with hair longer than mine springs to his feet. He remains right behind us as we pass through the doorway, and stays only a step back as we begin a search for a secluded spot. He must know what we're doing; he makes no effort to prevent us from wandering away from the house. I look around the sodden forest. Drops of water as big as pearls slip one by one from the boughs overhead and plop as they hit the ground. The ground sucks at our feet. Humps of moss that look like velvet pincushions dot the forest floor.

"Should we stop here?" I say. The dripping water and the cool air aren't helping. I can't wait much longer.

Maria nods and says, "He thinks so." The young man looks uneasy. He glances from us, to the house we just left, barely visible through the tree trunks, then back at us.

Before I lose my courage, I step to the side of a small shrub, turn my back, and pull up my skirt.

The long-haired young man scurries away and waits from a distance. Everywhere it's the same: even the most courageous men are scared of ladies' business. Maria squats on the other side of the shrub.

I try to release my water quietly, but it resounds as it hits the earth. Steam rises through my legs. Relieving myself takes forever. And when I've no more water to release, I wipe my hands on the moss, and then on my apron because I don't know what else to do.

"Ready?" I ask Maria. She nods.

The long-haired young man follows in silence and leaves us only when we're back in our corner.

We don't have breakfast. Instead, we again assemble for speeches. Because I didn't sleep well, I struggle to pay attention. A meal is prepared while the talking progresses. We eat fish once again and when it's finished, there are more speeches.

The treatment we're receiving from the koliuzhi is most unexpected. It tempers my anxiety and leads me to what I believe is the only rational conclusion. If they've not harmed us, and continue to feed us, they must intend to release us. I just can't comprehend why they haven't done so yet.

The house is warmer on our second night. Tired from my poor sleep the previous night, I easily drift off. But I wake suddenly at a much later hour to the sound of rain pounding on the roof. The din inside is as loud as the house-drumming that we witnessed the day of our capture. At least I'm dry and warm. I wonder where the crew is and how they're managing. The tents would be useless in a deluge this heavy.

Oh, Kolya, what are you doing right now? Are you awake and wondering what's happened to me? You're not out in this storm looking for me, are you?

Dear Kolya. I'm all right. I'm safe.

Are you?

❧

That day and the next and the one after are no different from the two we survived. More talking, so much talking—and not just from the three men who spoke that first day. Others also present speeches and stories long and short that unravel in the house, spin themselves around the listeners, the fires, and the things hanging from the rafters—but can't find their way to me, Maria, Yakov, and Kotelnikov. Even after so many days, we understand so little of what is happening.

People come and go, bringing firewood, water, and food. In a corner, some women weave on queer little looms that sit on the floor. They aren't weaving with wool; but I can't tell what fibre they're using. They each have baskets at their feet. Every once in a while, a woman withdraws a stick or a tool with teeth that she uses on her work.

One woman is making a basket. Her hands ripple like flowing water as she weaves thin branches together. She has a cord attached to her ankle. It leads to the head of a cradle suspended from an overhanging bough. Two babies nestle inside like fledglings. When the basket weaver moves her leg, the cradle rocks. The babies sleep on.

Older children play and whisper during most of the speeches, and we eat twice a day—more fish, and then clams and mussels, and after that, a tangle of small starchy roots, and then a hard, dried cake of berries I don't recognize. The cakes are tough to chew, and drenched in that same fishy grease. During the long speeches that follow, I dislodge the gummy bits stuck to my teeth.

I miss Nikolai Isaakovich terribly. I miss the way he stands behind me on the deck of the brig and keeps me warm while I look through my telescope. I miss our long talks in the evening, poring over his charts, discussing the places we'd seen and the places that lay just ahead.

Why hasn't he come for me yet? There has to be a good reason. I won't accept that he might have been killed. I also won't accept that he's given up and headed south without us. What am I supposed to think? Everything I imagine is unbearable.

The days unfold in the same strange routine. Koliuzhi Klara gives Maria and I each a cedar cape. I thank her, knowing she won't understand. The cape will keep me warm, but it will also serve as a blanket at night. Never again will the cold keep me awake.

Maria and I continue to relieve ourselves together, always under the watchful eye of the same long-haired koliuzhi man. Our trips together to these private places remind me how mortifying it will be when my monthlies arrive. I plan to tear my apron into strips, but I can't begin to consider how and where I will wash and dry them.

Each time I go out, my eye is drawn to the grey-brown mound on the other side of the river. The crows are equally preoccupied with it. Black shadows, they flutter over it, pick at it, tear bits off it, and squabble and screech over the shreds. Before long, the scent of death hangs in the air. I can't understand why the koliuzhi seem not to notice.

One evening, just before the meal is ready, I say, "I wonder what's keeping them."

Yakov and Maria look sideways at one another. Kotelnikov, who's cleaning his nails with a twig, wipes it on his sleeve and says with confidence, "They're planning a surprise attack. They're going to settle the score with these koliuzhi and shoot them all."

"Shhh," says Maria and blesses herself.

"Why would you say such a cruel thing? They're feeding us and treating us kindly," says Yakov.

"But that won't go on forever, will it?" I ask. "It can't."

"Don't worry, it won't," says Kotelnikov. "The crew might come back anytime. Any minute now, they could charge through that door . . ."

"Be patient. There are many things we can't understand," says Yakov. "Everything will become clear soon."

"Maybe they're waiting for us," I say. "Maybe they want us to try to escape."

"Give it time, Madame Bulygina. Rest and eat well. Take these days to build up strength," Yakov says. "When they come, we'll have a difficult voyage ahead of us."

"No," says Kotelnikov. "She might be right. We should go."

"I don't think so," ventures Yakov.

"Well, I do," says Kotelnikov. "They can't stop us."

Yakov looks at him, his expression in shadows. "If you must, then go," he finally says. "I'm staying."

"You're too trusting, old man. They mean to kill you first."

"If you flee, you'll be killed first."

I decide that instant Yakov is right. At least we aren't hungry. Our lodgings aren't luxurious, but they're a great improvement over a tent. The blisters on my feet have begun to dry and harden. We need to remain patient and wait for answers.

As each day unfolds, I pay more attention to the koliuzhi. This place has been carved out of a Baba Yaga story, with its dense forest, the gloom, the impossible houses in the middle of nowhere, the burbling river, and always the way that fire draws us together in the dark.

Koliuzhi Klara appears and disappears throughout the day. Once I see her with a large, open-weave basket, but it's empty. Next, I see her with her arms full of small sticks. Then I see her with a basket that has the image of a bird woven into it and I wonder what might be inside. Koliuzhi Klara is thinner than many other women, and her hair is less well-kempt. Her clothing is adequate but plain. If we were in Petersburg, I would assume she comes from a family that, while not exactly poor, had fallen into difficult circumstances. In society, she wouldn't be highly regarded, though some would take pity upon her.

But they don't treat her like that here. She talks often with a woman with a round, stern face, who, I notice, is much better dressed than many of the other women. Most remarkably, her hair is pinned back with a comb of fine, filigreed silver. Where did she get it? Other women wear combs in their hair, but they're carved of wood or bone, maybe antler. No woman has anything so sophisticated. Is this woman Koliuzhi Klara's mother or aunt? I think not—their ages are too similar. However, they're most certainly not friends. They speak frequently and courteously, but without the warmth of close friends.

The man with the rattle and the golden cape is the toyon. He's often at the centre of a group of men who listen respectfully as he speaks. He's not the only man treated this way, but there's something that elevates him above them all. In my mind, I call him the Tsar.

The long-haired young man who follows me outside when I need to relieve myself is often away, and he returns after dark. I was wrong about his age. He's older than I first believed, closer perhaps to my husband's age. It's not just Maria and me that make him skittish and nervous. The slightest sounds, even the shadows on the wall distract him, as though he were a kitten. I call him the Murzik for he behaves like a kitten in many ways.

"What do you think that Murzik does all day?" I idly ask Maria one day. She laughs. She knows of whom I speak.

"He's playing with his mouse," Maria says and gestures crudely. I redden and ignore her.

I start thinking. What is he doing? Hunting? Could he be hunting the crew? We hear nothing, not a single gunshot, not a cry to indicate the crew is anywhere nearby. Yet I feel uneasy with the Murzik's frequent absence.

There is so much about the koliuzhi we don't understand. The way they live is beyond imagination. Some things I admire—like being able to cook in wooden boxes, the versatile bark mats that serve as skirts and tunics and capes and bedding and walls and tables and yet are quite soft and beautiful, the houses' rafters festooned with so much salmon it's easy to believe the structures are made of fish. They aren't—but they're no less miraculous, constructed with logs so thick three men hand-in-hand couldn't encircle them. How do they stand them in the ground? How do they fall them in the first place? I start to make a list and try to remember these novelties, so I can tell Nikolai Isaakovich and perhaps even my parents one day when we finally get back to Novo-Arkhangelsk and I can write them a letter.

But other things are less pleasing—how I feel damp even when I'm not outdoors, how the smoke backs up into the house when the rain is heavy and the clouds are low, the lack of privacy when I must relieve myself, the way fish is served at every meal, no matter what time of day or night. The indecent sounds at night—the children must hear them. What do they make of those sounds?

I wonder whether the koliuzhi would like to see how we live in Novo-Arkhangelsk, or even in Petersburg. I wonder what they'd make of private bedchambers. Steaming bathtubs. Feather beds. Silk. Butchers and bakeries. Letter writing. While we think these the pinnacle of civilization, I wonder whether the koliuzhi would find them novel at first sight, and then tiresome. Such things seem meaningless here. A man who does not eat bread has no need of a bakery. A cathedral is useless to a man who does not worship. And a man who does not read and write has no use for a letter, no matter how beautiful its penmanship.

What would they think of the hours I spend marking the position and measuring the brightness of the stars, writing it all down for others who will do exactly the same thing?

This reflection on our differences reminds me of our inability to communicate. It's language, yes, but the gap stretches beyond simple words. I'm beginning to believe certain elements of my world are so fundamentally different from theirs that I couldn't begin to describe our odd customs and ways even if anybody were to ask. As they go about their lives, they could never imagine ours. The converse is equally true. They have and do things for which we have no words. The pool into which we must plunge to understand one another is infinitely deep and, as irrational as it seems, perhaps for all of us, immersion would be impossible.

CHAPTER EIGHT

———————

Six days after the battle, we wake to heavy, steady rain. It traps us inside with fellow prisoners, darkness, and dreariness; time slows in this confined space. The children fare best with our imprisonment. They bound around as though catapulted from wall to wall, gamboling like they have learned their play from lambs. What fun Zhuchka would have with them, chasing them, yelping to get their attention, and then running from them while they chase her. I half expect a reprimand from the Tsar and the men deep in conference in the corner or from the women tending the fires and handling hot rocks as they prepare the food, but no one speaks a harsh word or lays a corrective hand on them.

In Russia, there's no such lenience. Though we love children, we believe they'll be spoiled if not taught to be good. My own parents always tried to be fair but firm because they knew proper discipline would determine my future, and, like all parents in Russia, they aspired to raise a responsible adult. I feel ambivalent about how the koliuzhi children are behaving. Part of me is enchanted by the purity of their joy and I feel nostalgic for the times in my childhood when I felt so free. Another part of me is more cautious and I wonder if this lack of discipline will harm them.

Though the children play, the rain is no excuse for idleness among the adults. Several women are once again crouched before their looms, weaving slowly and purposefully in this dull light. Talk and laughter wrap around them like a transparent shawl. The looms are decorated with stones or shells, maybe even teeth—I don't know which—that are set into the upright posts like jewels. Some women work on looms of three sticks lashed together at the top with their legs spread wide like the tripods my father uses in his turret observatory. After some study of their work, I realize the tubes they're weaving will be skirts.

Other women sew, their white needles small fish that dart up and down and flash when they catch the firelight. One of the women is plump-faced and thick around the waist. She's expecting a child. She pulls her needle aloft, then lowers it, draws a bead onto its point and once more lifts it. The bead slides down the thread. An instant later, she does it again. She barely looks because she's engrossed in the words of the woman with the silver comb in her hair. Her previously stern face has relaxed. She's making a basket as she speaks. Her hands are swift, and she, too, never looks at her work. Suddenly, all the women burst into shrieking laughter and the beading woman drops her needle in her lap.

I recall the day on the brig when we were becalmed for so long that I turned to my embroidery project with the napkins to pass the time. How easily I let my patience fade and allowed myself to give up. After six long days of waiting here with nothing to occupy my time, I would relinquish my supper to have that napkin and needle back in my hands today, and if it could be instead my telescope and star log, I might give up a week's worth of suppers.

The beading woman wipes tears from her eyes, finds her needle, and resumes her work. What's she making? It's too dark and I can't tell. I sit up on my knees and lean to the side.

"Korolki," I cry. "Maria—they have korolki!"

The blue Russian trading beads are piled on the mat where the women work. There are heaps and heaps—more than what we brought on the *Sviatoi Nikolai*. They have the ones as small as a baby's fingertip and the big tubular ones that are nearly black. Their facets glitter.

Maria opens her eyes and I point. "Look! Korolki!"

"Korolki," repeats the beading woman. She says something to the other women and they laugh. The woman with the silver comb in her hair turns and looks at me expectantly. Her fingers rhythmically work the basket fibres. As she watches me, a slight smile on her lips, she doesn't once look down at her work.

Again, I will disappoint them. I have nothing else to say. I'm as helpless and unable to express myself as an infant. I flush but contemplate this: though neither is destined to get us very far, there are now two words we share.

The rain persists through the night and into the next morning. Kotelnikov dozes off, snoring, and Yakov brushes his cap while he and Maria talk about an Aleut they haven't seen in a long time. Yakov thinks he's left the Russian-American Company and gone home, but Maria heard he died in Hawaii. Around midday, I can no longer bear the boredom. I take advantage of a lull in the storm and leave the house. Ostensibly, I'm going to relieve myself, but I plan to go far from the house, and return slowly, cutting downstream if the guard will allow me, and stopping to watch the river empty into the sea.

The trees are dripping. The leaves of the bushes are luxuriant with beads of moisture. The air is a misty veil and the earth is covered in puddles. I avoid the trail—it's all mud—and pick my way around mossy, decomposing logs and boggy hollows.

Despite the rain, the Murzik is out somewhere. I'm followed instead by a child. He's small, with wrists as thin and knobby as the legs of a bird. It looks like a wind could blow him away. How old is he? His face is as smooth as a baby's, and he behaves nervously—walking too closely behind me, lurching to my side with his arms raised when I jump over a puddle as if to prevent me from fleeing.

High in the trees where lacy crowns caress the clouds, a fragment of blue sky emerges. It's the colour of hope itself. I know my Polaris is up there, invisible in the sunlight, and that when night falls, she will again reveal herself. I wonder for an instant if I could escape. I'm alone with the boy. I'd only have to outrun him. If I couldn't? Then, I'd have to knock him unconscious with a stone. I look around—are there any stones nearby? Once he's knocked out, I'm sure I could go far before anybody notices.

I'd have to look for Nikolai Isaakovich and the others. How? Where could they be in this forest? Which stars would lead me to them? How long would it take me to find them—and what would happen to me, alone in this vast forest, while I was searching?

When have I ever knocked anybody unconscious with a stone?

My eyes fill. I'm trapped here until they come to rescue us. What's taking so long? Has Nikolai Isaakovich forgotten me? I need my husband. I need to see him, to be near him, to breathe in the scent of him in his damp greatcoat, his breath warm against my neck as he whispers, "Anya," because he needs me, too.

A boom resounds through the forest.

Gunfire.

My thoughts slip from my fingers like a crystal goblet that shatters when it strikes the floor.

Another shot. There's another. Then another.

They're coming from far upriver.

My husband is near. My heart floods with hope and dread.

The boy looks sideways upriver, staring hard, as though he could bend the course of the water and fell all the trees with his thoughts. He shouts at me. He hammers and twists his skinny fists in my direction. No words are needed. I know what he wants. Without relieving myself, I run back to the house.

At the doorway, I'm engulfed in chaos. People push in and out of the house, nearly knocking me down as I try to squeeze inside. The looms have all been tipped over. The contents of the baskets of tools are scattered among the spilled beads. A baby shrieks. Men carrying spears and bows and arrows push their way outside.

I can't see Maria. Then I spot her, huddled on one of the benches behind me. I go and crouch beside her.

"What happened?" she asks.

"I don't know," I say. "I didn't see anything."

Across the house, a man strikes Kotelnikov across his back. He howls. He and Yakov are pushed toward the bench on which Maria and I cower. Kotelnikov's pushed against me, and I feel the force of his weight as he half-lands on me. I can't breathe. I shove him away. Yakov's knees ram the bench and he cries out. He turns until he's squeezed between me and Maria. He bends, holds his knees, and rocks.

The gunfire continues. The women and children alongside us scream with each shot as though they've been hit. An old woman crushes a wrapped baby to her chest. The baby's hysterical shriek rises above the din and the old woman tightens her embrace. Koliuzhi Klara's back is pressed up against one of the carved posts. She's frozen, her gaze pinned to the doorway. A carved figure with an open mouth and sharp teeth looms over her head, whether to attack or protect her, who can say. The Tsar shakes his rattle and shouts, but his booming voice cannot pierce through the chaos.

The shots become less frequent. Then they stop altogether. Outside, there's not a sound. Inside, children sob. A few women try to comfort them, and the rest wait.

Is the crew getting closer? Are we finally going to be rescued? Yakov, Maria, Kotelnikov, and I watch the door.

Then I hear a voice outside. The footfall of a person running. The woman with the silver comb rushes to the door. She calls out. Somebody outside replies. Voices join in. The woman with the silver comb veers away from the entrance. A cluster of people bursts into the house. The light from outside is too bright and I can't distinguish their faces. Is that us? Is that Nikolai Isaakovich?

"Kolya!" I scream and wave. "Over here!"

The bodies swarm together like clouds in a storm. Everyone's talking, yelling, and some are shrieking. I climb up on the bench.

As they move away from the harsh daylight, I see it's not Nikolai Isaakovich. It's not even our crew. It's koliuzhi men. They're dragging a body.

The man, limp as a fallen petal, groans. His head hangs, and his arms drape over the shoulders of two men. There's blood, dark and glossy, on his leg. He's been shot in the thigh. His wound is the size of the small celestial sphere my father keeps on his desk. The blood drips all the way down his naked leg and onto his foot. It leaves a trail on the floor.

The koliuzhi hoist him onto the bench. He's flat on his back.

He's the eyebrow man, the one I said "wacush" to on our first day. His eyes are shut. His mouth gapes as he struggles to breathe. The koliuzhi close in around him. I can't see what they're doing. He bellows.

I collapse down on the bench. I can't bear to look. Yakov has put his hand over his mouth, and pulled his cap down. He, too, has turned away from the injured man.

The sound of a man singing rises through the tumult. He wails, long ays and ohs, and cries out. As his voice grows louder, the people quiet. Then somebody begins to beat a drum. The chaos around the injured eyebrow man transforms into order, governed by the beat of the drum. The house itself joins in, its planks and beams coaxed into vibration. I stand up and the rhythm rises through my feet until my heart is no longer only a part of my flesh, but a part of something large that demands compliance. Near the door, four men with sticks as long as their arms pound the wooden bench that, I realize, is hollow and empty as a drum.

Then a rattling begins, sounding similar to the Tsar's wooden cylinder carved with the bird's head, but harsher and more clattery, like the wheels of a coach. Wood is not making that sound. I can't see who or what is.

I look to Maria, then Kotelnikov, then Yakov. Where is Yakov? He's no longer beside us. Across the house, I spot his cap. Surrounded by koliuzhi men who grip his arms, he's beside the injured eyebrow man. The koliuzhi speak urgently.

Through the drumming and rattling and singing, Yakov cries loudly, "No!" Kotelnikov and Maria turn toward his voice. "I told you—I don't know what you want!" He's flustered and confused. The more he objects, the more they insist.

The singing, drumming, and rattling add to his confusion. He tries to twist away, but they push him back toward the injured man. What do they want? How is Yakov supposed to know?

"Take the musket ball out," Maria shouts.

Yakov squirms and recoils from the men who nudge him forward. He doesn't hear her. So she shouts more loudly, "The musket ball! Yakov! You have to take out the musket ball."

Yakov hears this time. His face crumples. "How? I can't. I don't know how."

"For Lord's sake, Yakov, just do it. It can't be hard."

"No!" he shouts. "I can't."

The singing soars, the beat of the drum grows more urgent. With a shake of her head, Maria pushes forward. She slips sideways between two koliuzhi. She nudges another with her shoulder. She steps around a woman older than she is. Eventually, the koliuzhi crowd divides and allows her to pass until she reaches Yakov and the injured man.

I strain to hear their conversation. It's almost impossible with the drumming and singing, but the words eventually rise above the clamour.

"Poor boy," Maria says. "He's not awake, is he?"

"He won't live," Yakov says. "How could he? The blood . . ."

"Shhh! Are you mad?"

"They can't understand me."

"Don't summon the devil."

"Not even the devil would dare to come here."

"Then go ahead. Call him. Perhaps you'll be next."

This silences Yakov. Under Maria's oversight, he bends and examines the wound. His head shakes.

"Oh, you old fool." Maria bends, and I lose sight of her.

"Maria!" Yakov gasps. "Maria, no!"

The eyebrow man bellows so loudly I expect the walls to fall. Others wail. A man near me shouts and tears at his hair.

Maria's turned to the crowd. Her arm is raised, her hand bloody to the wrist like a midwife's. Pinched between her fingers is the flattened musket ball.

"Maria!" Kotelnikov cries. For once, there's no sharpness and impatience in his face. He's shocked.

Silence falls throughout the house. The eyebrow man must have fainted from the pain and no one knows what to say about the sight of Maria with her raised, bloody hand, holding the musket ball as though it's a baby she has just delivered or perhaps an amulet she's conjured up like she's a sorceress.

"Bring some water," Maria says firmly. "Warm, if you can. We need to get cleaned up."

The mood changes from that moment, as though having stumbled upon a crossroads, we blindly chose a path and through a miracle it turned out to be the right one. The eyebrow man is alive, and if he survives the night, perhaps we will, too. If she's saved his life, perhaps Maria will also have to her credit saving ours.

When it's late, the fire is stoked and most of the koliuzhi drift to their sleeping places. Only a few remain at the side of the eyebrow man. One is the singer. Even after most people have retired for the night, he sings in bursts, and sometimes, he shakes a staff decorated with feathers and black bones or shells that dangle from cords and rattle together.

The door is heavily guarded, though I doubt the Russians will come back so soon after today's battle. The fierce rain that's started to pound the roof will also keep them away.

From my place on the mat beside Maria, my mind clambers over tonight's events and weighs the possible outcomes. I try to think rationally but it's hard to fight the terrible ideas as they occur to me, one after the other. I try to think instead about what I love. Nikolai Isaakovich. My mother and father. Zhuchka, dear little Zhuchka with her paintbrush tail and her simple joy. My telescope on a clear night, the searing feeling of the cold brass against my fingers. The comfort of a feather bed and a warm cover. A book. I miss reading a book. Dancing in a room so full of people the ceiling swirls and you think it will lift at any moment.

I'm not the only one who can't sleep. There's rustling everywhere. Whispering. Sighs. Babies' cries as they try to settle, parents' reassurances as they try to hush them. Any sleep tonight, if it comes, will be troubled.

I am half asleep when I feel our cedar blanket shift. I think it's just Maria turning in her sleep but when I look, I see a koliuzhi man. He's kneeling beside Maria and gently shaking her shoulder. She turns her head, looks, and freezes.

"Baliya," he whispers.

She doesn't move and neither do I. What does he want?

"Baliya," he whispers again, "Ƚ̓áxʷal akʷ."[12]

Baliya. That's how he pronounces Maria's name. There's silence and it's evident that most of the koliuzhi are asleep. No one's listening. Nobody is going to help us understand what he wants.

"Ƚ̓áxʷal akʷ! Chiʔalik̓ʷáyolilo lobáʔa,"[13] he says. Assured she's awake, he rises and waves his hand as though he wants her to also get up.

She and I sit up. On the other side of the fire, across the house, two women and several men who've gathered around the eyebrow man call out and gesture when they see us. "Baliya!" they cry.

They want Maria. The watchmen around the door shift nervously and glance back and forth between the eyebrow man and our corner.

"The koliuzhi want you," I say. "They're calling you over there."

The man standing beside our bed continues speaking with some urgency. The man with the staff of feather and bones, who's still posted next to the injured man, shakes his staff as if she might understand that instead of the spoken words.

Maria's eyes flit back and forth among the koliuzhi, but she remains next to me, her fingers curled around the edge of the blanket, refusing to let go.

"You better go find out what they want," I say, "before they get angry."

---

12   Wake up.

13   Wake up! We need help.

Stiffly, Maria rises to her feet and lumbers across the floor. When she reaches the bench, she bends. I can't see her anymore. The fire in the house is burning low and there's almost no light.

Finally, she comes back to our sleeping place.

I hold up her cedar bedclothes so she can slide in more easily. "What happened?"

"Nothing. I think they just wanted me to look at that man."

"Is he dead?"

She shakes her head. "He's asleep now. But his wound is terrible."

"Is he bleeding?"

"No. It's stopped—but it's black. They put medicine in it." She pauses. "And he needs a splint."

"Is he going to live?"

Silence answers. Lightly I touch my silver cross.

"They know your name."

Maria grunts.

"They called your name. Baliya, they said. Now they know your name."

"Go to sleep."

As soon as I awaken the next morning and sit up, the koliuzhi call out. "Baliya! Hák^wotłi ak^w!"[14] They want her back again.

She rolls over right away, and pushes herself up until she's sitting on the mat. She must have been awake. "You come with me this time," she says.

"They're asking for you."

"You have to come," she insists. "Come and see. You have to help me."

---

14 Come!

"There's nothing I can do." I'm afraid to see the terrible wound up close, but I feel sorry for Maria. The eyes of the watchmen at the door follow us across the floor.

Sweat is beaded on the eyebrow man's forehead and upper lip. His eyes are red and filmy, and they don't shift toward us. His eyebrows look lifeless. The wound is covered loosely with a small hide. A woman rolls it back. Maria is right. Something black has been crammed into it. The surrounding flesh is white and swollen, and water oozes from its lip. Maria places her hand on his forehead, drags it down to his cheek, and tenderly cups his face for a few moments. "He's feverish."

"You already took out the musket ball. Isn't he getting better?"

She shrugs. "He needs medicine."

I point to the black substance that fills the hole. "He has medicine. Their medicine. Isn't it working?"

"I don't know. I don't even know what medicine it is."

The peasants use rustic medicine. Onions. Old bread. Concoctions made of wild plants and roots they harvest from the meadow and the forest. Even magic spells and pagan chants. My father believed these were foolish—the ways of the superstitious—and he would always rather call the doctor, just as any adherent to the Enlightenment would. The doctor's ways and the elixirs and powders he compounded in his chambers seemed just as mysterious to me, but they were, of course, based on science.

"Can you do anything for him?"

"He needs a splint."

"Then give him one."

"After that—I don't know where to start."

"You have to save him," I insist. "You have to try. Or they might kill us. Give him some medicine. Some herbs or something. Some roots."

"Where am I supposed to get medicine?"

Her iron stubbornness is impenetrable. "Where you usually get it."

She waves a hand dismissively. "I don't know anything about what grows here. Or about their medicine."

"Lamestin," says the koliuzhi woman. "Baliya lamestin?"

I'm not really listening—I think it just more words that we can't understand. Then the face of an old tutor flits to mind—long, dreadful French lessons, conjugating verbs and struggling to wrap my tongue around a language that never fit.

"Maria," I say. "It's French. I think she's speaking French."

"How would she know French?"

I ignore her question. Instead, I turn to the old woman—she's silver-haired and wearing a belted cedar dress that covers her neck to ankle but leaves her arms free and bare. She has a ring in her nose and a long necklace of feathers, beads, and shells that rattles as she moves. I point to the black tar in the wound. "Le médicament?" I exaggerate my lips the way the tutor showed me.

"Lamestin," she says and smiles, showing gaps in her teeth. She lisps a bit because of the missing teeth, but I'm sure I heard correctly. It's not exactly French, but it's close.

What is this lamestin? Did they make it? Where did it come from?

"Maria, it is French. I think she's trying to say medicine."

"D'où est-ce que vous avez trouvé lamestin?" I ask the koliuzhi. *Where did you find this medicine?*

"Lamestin," she repeats. She has no idea what I've just said. If she knows French, it's maybe just this single word.

"If you could find the right herbs and roots, could you help her?" I ask Maria. She furrows her brow, presses her lips firmly together. "Would you at least try?"

"Don't get hopeful. This isn't my home and I don't know anything about this place or their ways."

꧁꧂

It takes gestures, pointing, and repeating this single word, but finally the old woman leads Maria and me into the forest. A koliuizhi man, armed with bow and arrow, accompanies us. He may be here to ensure we don't flee or harm the old woman, but it's more likely he's here to protect us all.

The lamestin woman has a knife with an iron blade tucked into her belt. She also has a small, soft-sided basket of tools made of stone or shell or bone—impossible to tell without examination. Our watchman has a breechclout of hide and a cedar mantle, but it's ragged and short and barely reaches his waist. I wonder that no one has given him a new one or even a simple shirt to keep him warm outdoors. The lamestin woman leads us along a path that skirts the river.

Maria and this old woman know what we're looking for. I don't. Plants, even the ones in our garden in Petersburg, are strangers to me. When I look at them, they blur into a swathe of green, and if they're flowering, blotches of red, purple, pink, yellow—whatever the colour of the blossoms. To me, plants are pretty, and sometimes sweetly scented, and that's all.

Across the river, the grey-brown mound still lies waiting for somebody other than the crows to pay it heed. Today, it gets its wish; a gull battles for its share. The reek of death has grown heavier. It's spreading to our side of the river. Again, I turn away.

The sky's heavy and promises rain before long. The lamestin woman stops before a cluster of tall plants with jagged leaves. "T'łópit,"[15] she says. Many of the stems are brown and bent and the remains of the huge flower heads are dried. Some still contain seeds.

"Putchki?" Maria says. "Is it?" She very gently fingers the

---

15   Cow parsnip or wild celery

leaves and kneels. She digs out earth from around the stem. The lamestin woman passes her a knife that's a shell with a sharpened edge and she cuts two stalks. The lamestin woman picks a broad leaf growing on a nearby plant and wraps it around the stalks before picking them up. Then she looks at me.

"Is that enough?" I ask Maria.

"No," she replies. "Let's keep going."

"Lamestin," I say to the old woman. "On y va?" *Let's go.*

She leads us until we come across a little creek emptying into the river. We follow the little creek until it vanishes into a bog. A black bird squawks and springs sideways from a tall reed as soon as we appear. The reed sways long after the bird is gone. The spongy bog is hungry and sucks at my shoes. The heels slip off with each step, slowing me.

"It's hamidux." From far ahead, Maria says the word as though she doesn't expect to find it here.

"Há?t̓aliċhiyił,"[16] says the old woman. She and Maria kneel next to one another. In a low voice, the old woman continues to speak to Maria.

By the time I approach, Maria's dug out a couple of plants, roots and all. The leaves are round with a jagged edge that's turned reddish-brown. Mud clings to the roots.

"I have enough," Maria says. "We can return if we need any more. Let's go back."

"Lamestin," I say to the old woman and I point to Maria's hands. "Baliya a fini lamestin. On y va." *Maria is finished with the medicine. Let's go.*

The old woman looks confused. She walks away, leading us around the marsh area. On the other side is a small grassy meadow. "Sisi?bátsɬwa,"[17] she says.

---

16   Avens

17   Yarrow

Maria kneels almost immediately before a plant with fringed leaves. "Look! Cingatudax. It looks different but—" She rubs the leaves between her fingers and smells them. "This might help close the wound." Then she snaps off all the leaves that show a hint of green. "That's enough. We should go back now."

"How fortunate you found everything you need," I say, and then I chide her. "And you said you didn't know anything about the koliuzhi plants and their ways."

Maria looks at me like I'm mad. "I didn't find anything. She led us here," she says. "She brought us right to the plants I need. Didn't you notice? She knows."

The lamestin woman smiles, showing the gaps in her teeth, then turns down the trail. I've lost my sense of direction so I'm not sure where she's going. After a few minutes, the trail mysteriously twists, and we approach the houses from the back, bypassing the grey-brown mound. Thankfully, I don't need to see it, though the stench reminds me it's gone nowhere.

Inside, the koliuzhi women bring utensils to Maria. There are knives like the one Maria used to cut the putchki—sharpened shells, and also rocks whose edges have been honed thin as the paper of my husband's charts. There are scoops and spoons and ladles with differing lengths of handle, some carved out of wood and bone, some made of large seashells. Koliuzhi Klara brings a mortar and pestle of heavy grey stone. She can hardly lift them. Maria tells me to grind up some of the leaves we collected. I press down and twist the pestle, bruising and shredding the leaves and stems until they turn into a mash. As I grind, Koliuzhi Klara fills the cooking box with water and puts hot rocks into it.

While the medicine cooks, Maria applies the splint. Somehow, she makes the koliuzhi understand what she needs, or perhaps, as it was with the plants, they already know what's needed. I can't see what she's doing but I hear the eyebrow man groan. I hear the rattle of the singing man's feathered wand and his voice rising in song.

When the medicine is ready, the koliuzhi sit the eyebrow man up and hold him while Maria brings a small ladle to his lip and makes him sip the broth she's made. After four sips, some of it running out of the corners of his mouth, he's laid back down. The lamestin woman watches that they're careful not to hurt him. Maria and the lamestin woman then wash the wound, removing the black medicine. I hold a small woven bowl into which they fling the ooze to be discarded. He groans when Maria must go deep into the wound. The splint holds his leg steady as they work. Finally, Maria replaces the black medicine with a warm green poultice. The lamestin woman holds the sides of the gash while Maria packs it in. They leave the wound uncovered.

When they've finished, the singing man with the staff begins again, this time accompanied by drums. During his song, the eyebrow man suddenly goes limp. At first, I think he's died; then I realize he's fallen asleep or perhaps simply passed out.

⁕

The eyebrow man is our Lazarus. He makes it through another night. Maria tells me his fever is no longer raging. She feeds him more broth. Again, I hold the little woven bowl—a basket, but the weave is so tight it doesn't leak—while she and the lamestin woman clean out the wound and press more warm poultice into the opening. The wound is less swollen and inflamed. The Tsar with the golden cape looks less worried. The singer waits until we're done before he rattles his staff and begins another song.

We're nine days into our trial and finally have found a way to start communicating. Yakov decides we should introduce ourselves. He lines us up before the Tsar and begins by pointing to Maria and saying just as they would, "Baliya. Baliya."

Several people notice and, curious, they approach. The Tsar says, "Baliya," and others echo him. "Baliya. Baliya." I'm certain Yakov's been understood.

Yakov then points at me. "This is our dear navigator's wife, Madame Anna Petrovna Bulygina." Silence. He tries again. "Madame Anna Petrovna Bulygina." This time, the Tsar frowns and others mutter, but no one tries my name. So Yakov makes another attempt. "Madame Bulygina," he says with exaggerated pronunciation. People smile, then look at one another, and a few of them laugh. Perhaps my name doesn't translate appropriately.

Yakov looks uncomfortable. He must address me in a much less formal way. In Russia, that's never done. That name is reserved for use by family and closest friends. But we're not in Russia, are we?

"Go ahead," I say. He says nervously, "Anna Petrovna."

There's still nothing more than a broken murmur. His only recourse is to cross a final social boundary and speak to me like a husband or parent. I nod my consent.

"Anna. Anna." Kotelnikov flinches when he hears Yakov. The name sounds unnatural and disrespectful coming from this Aleut.

"Ahda," says the Tsar. Then I hear others repeat it. "Ahda. Ahda." I feel my face redden. The woman with the silver comb in her hair smiles at me.

Yakov then lays his hand on his chest and says, "Yakov. Yakov."

"Hálas 'Ya ḱop?'"[18] says a woman. Muffled laughter spreads through the house. "Ishkida! Bayílo t̓ísikʷoł."[19]

The koliuzhi laugh loudly. Kotelnikov hesitates for a moment, then a smile spreads across his face and he joins in. He points at the old Aleut and says, "Yah-kop. Yah-kop. May I introduce

---

18   Did he say, "Feel the urge to fuck?"

19   Ha! Crazy name!

Monsieur Yah-kop?" He has no idea what he's saying; only that it amuses the koliuzhi and annoys Yakov.

Yakov doesn't wait for the laughter to die down completely. As soon as he can be heard, he points to chubby Kotelnikov's stomach and says, "Kotel."

The koliuzhi stop and look disbelieving. The Tsar is wide-eyed. Then the koliuzhi screech with laughter that's magnitudes greater than how they laughed at Yakov's name.

A laugh dies on Kotelnikov's lips and his face twists with anger. "No!" He straightens and thumps his sturdy chest. "Kotelnikov! Kotel-NIKOV! Don't forget the Nikov part."

It's too late. The koliuzhi repeat, "Kʷóxʷal. Kʷóxʷal."[20] And with each repetition, the laughter grows.

I have no great affinity for Kotelnikov, and I share my husband's belief that his impatience and ambition cloud his judgment. But I try not to laugh because he's so offended and no one will listen to him. The koliuzhi cannot possibly know they have called him a cooking pot, a name that cruelly draws attention to his stoutness, and yet they've made sense of his name, sense that they find amusing. Many koliuzhi wipe tears from their eyes, they laugh so hard.

It's impossible to resist. His overreaction is as funny as his new name. I give in and laugh, too.

"Listen! Kotelnikov! It's Kotel-NIKOV!" He stomps around, gestures wildly, and looks for anybody who'll listen.

He circles back and turns on Yakov. "Tell them! Tell them my proper name!"

"You tell them yourself," Yakov says dismissively and frowns. He turns away from the apprentice and smiles slyly. The laughter explodes anew.

Then Kotelnikov grabs Yakov's arm, and pulls so hard that Yakov, caught off guard, falls.

---

20 Scrawny. Scrawny.

He lands hard, cries out, and reaches for his knee. "What are you doing?" he shouts at Kotelnikov. "Stop it!"

Kotelnikov kicks Yakov's backside.

The laughter dissolves. The koliuzhi descend. Several men pull Kotelnikov away from Yakov. They lift Kotelnikov onto their shoulders. They struggle a bit with his girth. They carry him toward the door while the singer with the staff helps Yakov up.

"Where are they taking him?" I ask Maria.

"I don't know," says Maria. "Come on."

Kotelnikov jerks with all his strength, but outside there's more room, causing other men to join the effort. They hold him high as they head toward the river. They immobilize his kicking legs and swinging arms. "Put me down, you savages!" cries Kotelnikov.

When they get to the river's edge, they launch Kotelnikov like he's a sack being thrown from the deck of a ship.

His body lifts. His arms and legs thrash. Then he changes direction and plummets. The river cracks when he hits the surface and swallows him whole. Huge waves ripple out.

The river's not very deep, and he's up in a second. He stands. Water streams down his body.

"I'm going to kill you all!" Except for Maria and I, no one understands him, but translation isn't necessary. He spits out a string of curses, most of which I've never heard.

"That fucking goat will pay for this! He's going to regret what he did! You tell him," he cries when he notices Maria and me, "Filip Kotelnikov is going to get even."

Many of the koliuzhi walk away. Surprisingly, two men don't. They enter the river and wait at its edge. Perhaps they want to make sure he neither hurts anybody else nor escapes.

"Let's go see how Yakov is doing," Maria says, and we head back to the house, followed closely by the watchmen.

CHAPTER NINE

———————

In the misty afternoon, the Murzik follows me when I venture out to relieve myself. Before we reach a secluded spot, he shows me a startlingly white handkerchief.

"Where did you get that?" My voice squeaks, raspy as a rusty gate. I reach for it.

The Murzik grows uneasy and pulls the handkerchief closer. Its folds lie stark against his dark, worn hands. He starts to crumple it into his fingers.

"Let me see. Please." Before he can put it away completely, I snatch it.

He protests, but I turn my back on him and examine it against my apron front. This cheap Russian trading handkerchief, fresh and undamaged, is white as new snow against my filthy clothing. However the Murzik managed to get it, it hasn't been with him long.

He snatches it back.

"No," I cry. "Give it back. Just for a moment. I promise I'll return it. Please." I hold out my hands. "Wacush. Korolki. Lamestin. Please." He laughs. Then he dangles the handkerchief before me, flicking it beyond reach. After a minute he releases it and the tiny white scrap flutters back into my hands.

I pull it to my nose. It reeks of smoke and fish. "How did you get this?"

"Híli hílils kíwa kiyáʔli ti'l xʷaʔ hótskʷaƚ," he says. "Óχas xʷoʔó yix ƚichaʔakʷóɬwa."[21]

He points and gestures, but I understand nothing. Has he stolen it? Killed somebody and taken it? Has he been given it? His story is long, and he mimes many things—one moment, he's carrying something burdensome, the next, it's vanished, then he's embracing himself and rocking back and forth. Sometimes he laughs. Other times he frowns as if annoyed.

"Kiyáʔli xʷaʔ hótskʷaƚ 'χat hidáʔťot histáʔalach χiʔ ƚicháʔat,"[22] he says.

"Come," I say, and I turn back toward the house. He reaches for the handkerchief. "No," I say. "Come with me." I crumple the handkerchief in one hand and gesture with the other to urge him along.

The crows lift from the grey-brown mound on the opposite side of the river as we run past, cawing their annoyance at the disruption. When I enter the house, I find Maria and Yakov. There's no sign of Kotelnikov.

"Look!" I cry. "The Murzik has a handkerchief."

Yakov takes the crumpled handkerchief and inspects it.

"How did he get it?" asks Maria.

"I don't know," I say.

Yakov ponders. Of the many ways that this handkerchief might have come to the Murzik, some are frightening, while others bring hope.

"He's stolen it," says Maria, eyeing the Murzik suspiciously.

"Maybe," says Yakov. "Perhaps it was given to him."

"Why?" I ask. "Why would they give something to the Murzik? A few days ago, we were shooting at them."

---

21   I helped the white men. This is my own cloth.

22   I helped them, and my father said that I could have this for my own.

"Maybe it was given in trade." Yakov passes the handkerchief back to the Murzik.

This pristine handkerchief is a sign our crew is alive and not far away. If the handkerchief has been acquired in trade, then they'd have to be talking amicably to the koliuzhi. Are they talking about us? If they can trade a handkerchief, what else might they be able to do? Perhaps we won't have to wait much longer for our rescue.

The handkerchief tucked away, the Murzik extends his closed fist. Slowly he opens his fingers to reveal korolki of varying shapes and sizes. He cups them like seeds. The faceted surfaces catch the light as he rolls them around with his thumb. He also has some silver beads. He watches our faces.

Yakov frowns, puzzled. "It must have been a trade. I wonder what he gave in return."

"Are they coming for us?" I look to the door.

"More likely they needed something to eat."

Of course. Though I understand, I'm disappointed.

Very early the next morning, before we eat, we're brought before the Tsar. The Murzik is already here. The handkerchief, less pristine than it was yesterday, droops from the Tsar's hand

The Tsar questions the Murzik. The Murzik fidgets and replies in bursts, his eyes darting around the house, as though he might scoot away like a startled cat. There's no doubt—he's come into possession of this handkerchief through mischief, and now he'd do anything to be rid of it.

Then a woman with a baby on her hip shows a second handkerchief to the Tsar. He's surprised. He speaks sharply to the woman. She shifts the baby to her other hip and gives him the handkerchief. The Tsar clutches both handkerchiefs in his fists, shakes them toward the woman and raises his voice.

The baby cries. The Murzik hangs his head. The woman shouts back. When she does, the baby wails. The Tsar glowers and says nothing. From behind us, a man yells and the woman with the baby bellows back at him.

Suddenly, somebody pushes me down. I fall hard. My chin strikes the floor. I bite my lip and taste blood.

I try to get up, but I can't. My skirt is tangled in my legs. Everyone's shouting now. "Yakov?" I plead.

I come up on my hands and knees, and look up over my shoulder. Who is this furious man glaring down at me?

The Tsar cries, "Wa ťaʔakʷóla xʷóxʷa!"[23] He directs these angry words not at the man who pushed me, not at the woman who produced the handkerchief, not at the Murzik—but at me. He shouts at me a long time and a short time, and when he finishes, he gives back the handkerchiefs—one to the Murzik, and the other to the woman with the baby who's now screeching and bucking against her grip.

A hand closes around my arm and heaves me up like I'm weightless. I cry out and my sleeve tears. The furious man pulls me toward the door.

"Let go of her," cries Kotelnikov. He leaps over and reaches for my captor's hands. Another koliuzhi man pulls Kotelnikov away and pins his arms behind his back. "Get your shit-covered hands off me!" Kotelnikov twists.

"Be careful, Madame Bulygina! Don't fight! You won't win!" cries Yakov.

What he doesn't realize is that even if I wanted to fight, I couldn't. Every part of my body has turned to jelly.

---

23 This is not our way!

We paddle upriver in a small canoe. I sit on the frigid keel, my hands clutching the gunwales. The blood on my lip is drying, tightening the swollen skin. The man who pushed me down is in front of me, pulling hard against the current. As our vessel slices through it, water rises up and folds over in a voluptuous, glistening lip.

We're accompanied by two other canoes and six more koliuzhi. Why has the Tsar sent so many men? Where are we going, and why?

The river bends gently. The canoe tilts a little as they steer through the curve. Ahead, a fallen tree, half-submerged, pokes its many branches through the surface. Should I jump in? If I could reach the tree, maybe it would help me to pull myself to shore. Would they kill me first? Before I can decide, we pass the tree and it's too late.

The river has a stony bottom that reveals itself where there's no light reflecting off the water's surface. A feather twirls by. Rushes lining the riverbanks bend as though bowing their heads for a passing funeral procession. Beyond, the forest is black in all directions. If this is to be my end, let it be quick and free of pain. I close my eyes. The canoe lurches forward against the current.

Then I hear a crunch, followed by another. I open my eyes. The canoes have come to shore. Ours squeaks against the reeds as it, too, stops.

From the opposite bank, a man's voice says, "Over here!" I turn, and I can't believe what I see.

Nikolai Isaakovich. The American. Timofei Osipovich and his loyal Kozma Ovchinnikov. Everyone is here. Everyone. Timofei Osipovich pushes through the reeds and stands at the river's edge.

"Madame Bulygina, are you hurt?" he calls.

His voice is strong and, for once, addressing me he's serious. I look at my husband. He stands behind the reeds and stares. His face is rutted with pain. He looks shrunken and, with his untrimmed beard, almost beastly. Where is his overcoat? His eyes are too shiny—is he about to cry?

"Fine," I shout finally. "I'm fine. Kolya?" I begin to cry.

"Anya!" he shouts, his voice breaking. "Oh, Anya!" He stumbles to the edge of the riverbank and leans so far out I think for a moment he intends to jump in.

The entire crew looks filthy and exhausted. They all have sunken cheeks and black circles under their eyes. Their clothing is worn and ripped in new places. The Aleuts are barefoot.

I rise to my knees in the canoe and force myself to stop crying. "Nikolai Isaakovich, I'm fine. I'm perfectly fine."

"You're bleeding!"

I touch the newly formed crust. "It's nothing," I say.

"What have they done to you? Who did it? I'll kill him."

"It was an accident," I say. "It doesn't hurt." I fear for the outcome of this meeting if he doesn't calm himself. "Everything is fine." I manage a small smile.

"Are the others all right?" says Timofei Osipovich.

"They're fine. They're back at the house. We've been waiting."

Everything makes sense now. The koliuzhi are letting us go. I'm to go first, and though I don't know why, it doesn't matter. "Let's go. We still have time to get to the *Kad'iak*. Timofei Osipovich, please tell them to bring me to shore."

The crew begins to fidget. Something's amiss, something that's been set in motion by my words. And then I notice.

"Where's Khariton Sobachnikov? And where's Zhuchka? Zhuchka!" I call. She does not bound forward, but before I call her again, Timofei Osipovich shouts.

"Madame Bulygina, remain quiet now while we negotiate your release."

"What do you mean?"

"We have to negotiate your release. Be patient. They're asking a lot, but I might be able to talk them out of it."

"Kolya?" I try to control my tone. "What's he talking about?"

"Be quiet now, Anya."

At the edge of the riverbank, Timofei Osipovich says, "Makuk." I recognize this word—he used it when trading for the halibut. A man in one of the other canoes answers. Our prikashchik responds.

John Williams steps forward. His shock of red hair is plastered to his head and his cap most certainly is gone now. In his arms he cradles a fold of nankeen cotton. A string of beads is curled on top of it. He glances nervously at my husband.

Timofei Osipovich continues to speak, his hands moving to give emphasis to his words. The koliuzhi are silent. Finally, the man in the other canoe shouts something.

Timofei Osipovich shrugs and then nods to the carpenter Ivan Kurmachev. He steps up beside John Williams. Folded in his arms is a black-green greatcoat. It's Kolya's.

Timofei Osipovich addresses the koliuzhi again but whatever he says is useless. The koliuzhi remain unconvinced. Finally, the koliuzhi in the other canoe snaps at him. Timofei Osipovich sighs heavily and orders Ovchinnikov, "Get the broken one. They won't know any better."

Ovchinnikov fusses in his bundle and pulls out a musket. Nothing would indicate it's broken. He lays the musket in his extended arms and takes his place beside John Williams and Ivan Kurmachev.

The koliuzhi exchange glances, then lift their paddles. Our canoe pushes away from the bank and turns into the current.

"Stop," cries my husband.

"Stop!" I cry. "No!"

We stop. The canoes are pulled back to the riverbank. But we're a sazhen or two farther downstream on the opposite bank.

Don't they want what we have to offer? Why not? They can't possibly know the musket is broken, so it must be something else.

"Let me go!" I plead. I point back upstream to where my husband stands with the others. "Paddle! Come on, paddle." I mime for them, an invisible paddle in my hands. "Please!" But we remain where we are.

"Give them the muskets," my husband screams. "I command you. Now!"

"That would be foolish," says Timofei Osipovich.

"I want my wife released. Give them the four muskets," he insists.

"My dear navigator, as you well know, we have only one good musket for each man. We've not one single tool to repair them if anything should break. They're all we have to save us."

"We have plenty of guns," shouts my husband. "We don't need one for every single man."

"Maybe you're right," says Timofei Osipovich coolly. "But if we give them four guns, they'll use them against us. Maybe even tonight. Who would you like to see killed first by our own weapons? Him?" He points to the carpenter Kurmachev. "Or him?" He points to John Williams whose face turns even paler.

"Stop!" cries my husband. "You go too far."

"Forgive me. I will disobey your order."

My husband runs and plants himself before Kurmachev. "Give me your musket. Give it to me." Kurmachev squeezes his musket to his chest. His old face is knotted in despair.

"If any man follows our navigator's commands," says Timofei Osipovich, "I'll leave. I'll get in the canoe with Madame Bulygina and join the koliuzhi. You can fend for yourselves until you find the *Kad'iak*."

Kurmachev doesn't move.

Nikolai Isaakovich faces John Williams. "Give me your musket. I command you." His voice is hoarse with the threat of tears. But the American is defiant. He looks at Timofei Osipovich and waits.

"A person's life and liberty are the most precious things on earth," says Timofei Osipovich. "We have no wish to lose them. We have spoken."

Four muskets stand between me and freedom. Four. How many muskets did we senselessly destroy and toss into the ocean when we abandoned the brig—while we packed another fold of cotton and another string of beads? "Give them what they want! Please!" I shout.

"Be quiet, Madame Bulygina. Your words only make things worse," says Timofei Osipovich. My husband buries his face in his hands. My heart breaks, but his tears are worthless to me right now. Why doesn't he do something? Not a single word passes his lips. No reprimand for the crew who cling to their muskets, nor for the prikashchik whose insolence would earn him severe punishment from the chief manager if he knew. I'm not worth four muskets. My life and liberty are much less precious than any of theirs.

A crow calls out twice from downstream. Its squawking voice carries through the trees.

Timofei Osipovich speaks to the koliuzhi, but they don't let him finish. They twist their paddles and the canoes respond. The current pulls us downriver, back toward the houses and the ocean.

My voice is as loud as thunder as I wail into the trees. If I survive now, I'll never let them forget this betrayal. They'll never forget this day, how they chose their freedom over mine and how they abandoned me for the sake of four muskets.

I jump from the canoe when it touches shore. "Maria! Yakov!" I call as I run, my skirt tangled in my legs. "Yakov!"

They're standing when I burst through the doorway.

"What happened to you?" Maria cries.

"I thought we'd never see you again," says Kotelnikov.

"We're never getting out of here! Never!" I sob. "I hate them all!"

Yakov nudges Maria, and she puts her arm around me. She awkwardly pats my back, and then, with her fingers, pinches the edges of my torn sleeve together and holds it closed. I fold in to her, and put my arms around her shoulders. She's so tiny but I let her support me like a mother would support her daughter.

"What happened, Madame Bulygina?" Yakov says.

I tell them everything—from the canoes, to the arrival at the riverbank, to the nankeen cotton, Nikolai Isaakovich's greatcoat, and the four muskets. From Timofei Osipovich's defiance, to the crew's submission. From the koliuzhi's refusal to bend from their demands, to my husband's relinquishment of his command. When I finish, I press my face into the crook of Maria's arm. My shoulders shudder. I know I should show more courage, but I can't restrain my despair any longer.

We're offered food, but I can't eat. Maria tends to the eyebrow man, while I lie on the mat and cry until I fall asleep, exhausted. Late in the afternoon, Kotelnikov calls us over to a bench in the corner. The koliuzhi watchmen turn their heads from the doorway as we cross the house to him, but no one stops us.

"We need a plan," Kotelnikov starts.

"What for?" says Maria.

"We need a plan to get back with the others. Before they leave."

"They won't leave! They have to wait for us," Maria cries. "Don't say such foolish things!"

When they hear her raised voice, the koliuzhi watchmen peer at us.

"I think the negotiations are not finished yet," Yakov says. "The crew shouldn't move until they are—or until the worst of winter has passed. It would make no sense."

"But Yakov," I say, "it's no longer a matter of sense or no sense. Timofei Osipovich won't give them any muskets—and no one has the courage to confront him." It saddens me to think how quickly the others aligned themselves with Timofei Osipovich and against my husband, and how easily my husband then capitulated. "What kind of negotiation is that?"

"The kind that takes a long time," Yakov says.

"We're fools to think these negotiations will come to an agreeable conclusion, let alone any conclusion," says Kotelnikov. "The koliuzhi are playing games. If we were to give them four muskets, they'd turn around and demand four more. They're unreasonable."

"What's unreasonable is offering them less than what we were willing to give for a sea otter pelt—and expecting them to hand over the commander's wife," says Maria.

"No. Circumstances are different," counters Kotelnikov. "The rules have all changed. We must act while we're strong and the snow's not deep."

"You're wrong," says Yakov. "Now, more than ever, we need to be patient. Let the negotiation continue. I predict that in one or two days, we'll be released, and then we can be on our way—less perhaps a musket or two."

"If you want to take your chances, you go ahead. I'm leaving. At the first opportunity," says Kotelnikov. "And I'll take anybody who wants to come. Maria? Madame Bulygina?"

How can I? If I go with him, we may wander the forest for days before we find the crew—days during which we're pursued by the koliuzhi, days in which we'll need to fend for ourselves with no food, no shelter, and no firearms. It's the middle of winter. The cold alone could decide our fate.

Besides, I don't want to see our crew. I hate Timofei Osipovich. My husband is a coward. How can I forgive them so easily? I know these are the vengeful thoughts of a little girl who imagines she's been betrayed, and not an eighteen-year-old married woman, but I don't care. I don't.

"They don't want us," I say. "There's no point."

"That's not true," says Kotelnikov. "Be rational. We can't stay here. They're going to kill us eventually."

"They're not going to kill anybody," Yakov points out.

I agree with Yakov. The koliuzhi have shown no inclination toward murdering us. If Kotelnikov were to go and the rest of us were to stay, would that change? And if I decided to go with him, leaving Yakov and Maria behind, what would the koliuzhi do to them? I can't leave them to the mercy of the koliuzhi.

"I'm not going," I decide, "and I don't think you should either, Filip Kotelnikov. We should stay together."

"Then come with me. All of you. There's no other way."

"We wouldn't even get to the river," Yakov says.

"Please, Filip Kotelnikov," I beg. "Please don't go. At least wait a few days before deciding. Maybe Yakov is right."

"Two days then," he says. "I'll give you two days to make up your mind. Then I'm leaving, and you will too if you have any sense."

The dense forest repels the rain but traps us in its twilight. We left mid-morning and except for one break to eat, we haven't stopped. We've been walking for hours at a brisk pace, so I'm sure we're a long way from the Tsar's house. I haven't walked this distance since the days after we abandoned the brig, before we were captured. My feet have blistered in the same places. Though it's not raining, we're walking through mist. My clothes are soaked, and my hair is so wet and straggly I don't even bother to push it from my eyes.

I have no idea where we're being taken, or why, or what's happening with Maria and Kotelnikov, or where Nikolai Isaakovich and the rest of the crew are.

Except to urge us on, no one speaks to Yakov and me.

Kotelnikov's two-day deadline proved meaningless. Early this morning, before we were offered food, he was pulled to the door by three men.

"Let go," he cried. He tore one arm from their grip and struck one of the men. The man wrenched Kotelnikov's arm back and Kotelnikov screamed.

"Let go! I told you to let me go!"

I looked at Maria, then Yakov. The koliuzhi dragged Kotelnikov through the doorway. Perhaps they intended to try and negotiate his release with the crew. But I knew that made no sense. Eventually his shouting faded in the distance.

I waited for them to come for the rest of us. Instead, the morning routine resumed. Koliuzhi Klara offered us fish and grease that she scooped from a round, shallow dish shaped like a bear or wolf, its tail the handle. I could barely eat.

Once we finished, Yakov was pulled to his feet and nudged toward the door. When halfway there, a man pulled me up as well. "Ahda," he said, and I yielded. I didn't know what was happening, but it gave me shaky confidence that Yakov was to be part of whatever it was.

I turned when I reached the doorway. "Maria?"

She'd stood but the man who'd pushed me down held her forearm. The lamestin woman was beside them. "Baliya," she said, followed by an incomprehensible chain of words.

"She can't stay here by herself!" I cried. "Yakov! Do something!"

"The eye can see it, but the tooth cannot bite it," he said. "What can an old man do?"

Yakov and I were led to a small canoe on the riverbank and nudged into its bowl. I sat backward, facing the house. I looked for Maria, but the doorway was blocked with koliuzhi. I saw the woman with the silver comb. I saw Koliuzhi Klara and the Murzik. From the distance that stretched between us, I couldn't guess what any of them were thinking.

We landed on the north side of the river. I gagged. The reek of the grey-brown mound was stronger on this riverbank, and the squabbles of the crows much louder. But the decomposing corpse itself seemed to have disappeared. I didn't want to look but it puzzled me, and so, I did, and when I couldn't locate it, I concluded it was my perspective. I just couldn't see it from where I stood.

The koliuzhi led us into the gloomy forest.

"This is the wrong way," I said to Yakov. "Nikolai Isaakovich and the crew are upriver."

Yakov shook his head and said nothing.

The trees thin out a little and allow the silver light to reach us. The forest floor here is covered with crisp leaves, yellow, orange, and brown, which rustle as we walk through them. The trees are neither as tall nor as imposing as the conifers. A few have silvery bark that reminds me of the birch forests I'd visited often with my parents.

My father liked to wander in the forest. He'd see something— an unusual fork in a branch or an abandoned nest or freshly dug earth that suggested an animal might have had a den nearby— and he'd wander off the path. My mother preferred to stay on the trails and insisted always that I stay with her.

"I knew this girl," she began one day when my father had disappeared on one of his diversions. "She lived in a certain village—not far, not near, not high, not low. She was walking in a forest just like this when she came across a necklace lying on the path."

"Where did it come from?" I asked.

"I don't know," she said dismissively, and continued. "The necklace was extraordinarly beautiful. So beautiful that she forgot about the incantation."

"What incantation?"

"I will tell you. I will teach it to you. But you must promise me that you'll never forget it." She waited. "Well? Do you promise?"

Warily I said, "I promise." I hoped my father was too far away to hear.

"Good," my mother said. "Now repeat what I say:
Earth, earth, close the door.
One necklace, nothing more.
Earth, earth, I command,
One necklace, in my hand."

When I was able to recite the whole thing by myself—it was easy—she continued. "Without the incantation, she took the necklace. She put it in the box with her other jewellery. That night, when she was asleep, a voice woke her up. 'Give me back what is mine,' the voice said."

"Who was it?" I asked. "Voices have to come from somebody."

"Ah, you sound like your father. Listen. I will tell you," she said. "There was a man beside her bed. It was his voice. She was terrified, so she said yes, she would give it back. When she opened her box to get it, the necklace was gone."

"The man took it?"

"I don't know who took it."

"This is not a real story. It's not possible."

"It is a real story. It happened to my friend," she said. "Don't you want to know how it turned out?" I nodded.

"The man was very angry. He said, 'You've taken what belongs to me. Now I will take you.'" I was old enough to know what she meant, but I still didn't believe it. "He told her never to tell anybody or she would die.

"Every night, it was the same thing. I know it sounds crazy but—my friend said he would show up as a flying serpent. He'd transform into a man and then—take my friend as though she was his wife. Until finally one day, after a long time and a short time, she couldn't take it anymore and she told me."

"And? What happened?"

"Anya—she died the very next day."

My mother wrapped her arm around me and pulled me close. "That's what the leshii does if you're not careful when you go to the woods," she whispered.

I knew my mother's story was untrue. It was absurd. Even when I was young, I knew there were no flying serpents. I knew men didn't appear in women's bedchambers unless invited. I knew jewellery didn't disappear. There were no magic incantations. And there was no leshii. As we continued along the path, her arm tight around my shoulders, I heard sounds, and when something lying on the ground ahead of us glittered, I fought the compulsion to grasp my silver cross through the thin fabric of my dress and apron and cry out, "Earth, earth . . ." as she'd taught me. I refused to give in to my mother's irrational fear. The sparkle was probably just dew on the leaves where the sun struck. The sounds were probably just my father rustling around with the object that had caught his fancy that day.

Probably.

This part of the forest is just like that forest, and I feel the same sense of uncertainty as I did after my mother told her story. This time, I readily touch my silver cross, trying to bring her closer, trying to keep the leshii, in case there is one, away.

I trudge on, following Yakov, unable to elude my fears. They swarm around my head and refuse to abandon me. Much later, we emerge into a flat valley. We follow a smooth, wide trail that, if our crew had found it, might have cut our travel time by days. Mountains command the land as far as we can see; their tops disappear in the cloud.

It's very late in the day when we finally emerge at the edge of a river too wide and deep to cross. The sky is brighter toward the west, but it won't be long before it's too dark to see where we're going. The koliuzhi walk downstream toward the light until the shape of a few houses emerges.

"Where are we?" I ask.

Our koliuzhi draw close to the houses and call out, "Yiʔátsḵal chiʔ łiḵal xóxʷaʔ."[24] A person appears in a doorway, and then another, and another, until many people are watching us.

We are led toward the doorway of one of the houses. Just before we enter, I look straight up into the darkening sky. Through an opening in the trees, I see Polaris valiantly trying to shine; she'll be bright and sharp as crystal in a few more hours. I follow the others inside.

Yakov and I face a row of old men, a crowd of curious koliuzhi, and a routine whose rhythms we know well.

"Xʷasáka, hótskʷaɾ,"[25] says a man with a moustache and a sea otter cape that has a hem fringed with plump fur tails.

It's not the flickering light.

"Yakov," I say. "It's the toyon. The man who's speaking. We know him."

"Who is he?" he whispers.

"He's from the tent. When we were on the beach. Just after we ran aground. Remember? Timofei Osipovich took Maria and me into a tent to talk with him—and then there was that battle."

---

24   Hello, the house (lit.)

25   You've returned, drifting village people.

Yakov peers. "I don't remember him."

"That's because he was in the tent and you were outside. Timofei Osipovich and I saw him again, later, on the beach. None of you were there. That's him. I know it."

We've returned to where we abandoned the brig. It's only been a handful of days, but it feels like years since we were here. Was Timofei Osipovich right about it having been burnt to ash, or is there a chance it has survived? I'd like to go aboard. Would they let me? Could I sleep in my own bed? Change my clothes, comb my hair? Maybe I'd discover my missing shawl pin, fallen between the planks of the deck. What else might be left, what other precious objects escaped our frenzied destruction, and how could it be that I'd never understood how precious they were?

The toyon begins to speak. Undoubtedly, he knows who we are. How angry is he about the battle? I watch for signs.

Yakov and I are separated. We sleep at opposite ends of the moustached toyon's house.

After we eat the next morning, movement suggests this house is not our destination. We must have farther to walk.

"Where are they taking us now?" I ask Yakov.

He shakes his head. He's weary. Another day on the trail will not do such an old man any good.

One of the koliuzhi who travelled with us yesterday stands before me. "Ahda," he says, and gestures.

We follow a path down to the river. Its mouth seems narrower than it did when we ferried ourselves across with our bundles and released our skiff to the mercy of the sea. Two canoes beaded with moisture from last night's rain rest on the stony beach.

These canoes are much bigger than the other tiny canoes I've been in. I climb into one. It's the schooner of canoes. When I sit, unless I stretch I can't see over the gunwales, which are dotted with bits of luminous shell that have been polished and set into the wood. I don't know how it will float—the river is too shallow for its size.

The moustached toyon is already seated in front of me. His sea otter cape falls in folds before my face, the hair furrowing and bristling as he shifts. Our canoe is boarded until it fills. I'm the only woman.

The canoe enters the stream, followed by a second canoe. The paddlers flick their pointed paddles as if they're hens scratching the earth. The sea looks calm, though it still roars and crashes against the beach. The humped island plugs this river's mouth; the trees are a jagged-edged shadow atop it.

The bow of our canoe turns toward the island. I thought we were crossing the river. We reach the turbulent place where the river and sea meet. The waves and currents slam into one another; peaks of white water form, merge, and disappear. The paddlers fight against it. Their paddles plunge in unison and they efficiently move us beyond the tumult.

The canoe turns parallel to the shore and heads north. We're in deep water, and I feel nervous. A flock of birds rises from the ocean's surface. After only a few minutes, I'm positive this is the place we ran aground. I recognize the stumps and stacks. But where's the *Sviatoi Nikolai*? There's nothing here. Not a mast, a plank—nothing. Not even debris washed up on the beach. Did the tides push it against the rocks until it broke apart and then pull its remains out to sea? Perhaps Timofei Osipovich was right after all when he said the koliuzhi would have burned it to ashes.

"Yakov?" I turn my head, wondering what he thinks. But he isn't here.

I look to the other canoe. He's not there either. Is he still on the riverbank?

No. He's not there either. He's gone.

"Yakov!" I shout. But no one pays any heed to my cry. The paddlers maintain their rhythm.

The canoe's bow slices through a cresting wave. Seawater cold as a winter night sprays my cheek.

CHAPTER TEN

———

The sea lifts and tosses us, while the wind whistles and buffets our canoes. The paddlers struggle to find a rhythm. In each boat, the men slide long, smooth poles from the bow where they were held in place in a notch that looks like the pointed ears of a dog. They fix the poles in slots midship, and attach sails made of cedar bark—another use for the woven mats—and rigging made of bark rope. The sails swell in the gusts, just as though they were canvas, and send us careening over the choppy surface.

On one side, the ocean opens to infinity. On the other, vague features of the shore are shrouded in mist: the beaches, arced like half-open eyes, delimited by rocky headlands, and the velvet black forest outlining the land, dark as kohl on a dancer's eyelid. We're heading north.

We're going away from Yakov, Maria, and Kotelnikov. Away from Nikolai Isaakovich and the rest of the crew. Away from the *Kad'iak*. We've been divided as if we were a measure of wheat or a bushel of apples.

We're returning along a shore we passed so long ago when we were aboard the *Sviatoi Nikolai*. We sailed around this headland and past that white beach. We saw this tiny cluster of stacks topped with scraggy growth against which the sea now throws itself in a tantrum.

Ahead lies a foam-capped ocean. We'll drown if the canoe should capsize. We slide up a wave several times the height of the boat and slam down on the other side. Water splashes into the canoe. I have no cape—it was left behind. But there's no time to dwell on my wet clothes. Looming ahead is another monstrous wave.

We surge to its crest and plunge down the other side with a thud. Another fan of water sprays me. It's so cold, it bites.

Water begins to accumulate in the boat. Around my feet, rivulets stream back and forth along the length of the canoe as we climb and descend the mountainous waves. From behind, I hear the rhythmic scrape of somebody bailing.

Then a paddler starts to sing. "Wála hiiiiiii!"[26] he cries.

Without hesitation, others join in. "Wála hiiiiiiii! Tikʷotsláli."

Music slides into the bowl of our vessel, then curls up the other side, and is pushed overhead where it hangs for an instant before the wind takes it away. But the "wála hi" refills the boat again and again, and eventually it seems like the canoe itself is singing. The voices of the koliuzhi in the other canoe rise faintly above the sound of the storm as they, too, join in. The men match their paddling with the cadence of the music.

Abruptly, the canoes are steered out to sea. The bow of the canoe is pointed directly into the waves and it slices through them, opening a path for us. The men continue to sing and dig deep with their paddles, taking us farther and farther away from land. When we're directly across from a distant headland that resembles a fortress, the paddlers pull the nose of the canoe sharply toward shore. Within two strokes, everything

---

26   This lyric is from a "Song for delivering brides (or women) to Neah Bay." It is believed to have been found by Young Doctor, a noted Makah shaman and finder of songs. The words are thought by the Quileutes to be "song syllables" that don't mean anything—like the "scoobee doobee do" found in several American songs of the 1960s.

smoothens. The waves flatten. Instead of fighting us, the wind pushes us along. The singing ends as suddenly as it began. The paddlers drive us, like an arrow, toward the shelter of a long and shallow bay.

On shore, four totem poles overlook the cove. Like the ones outside Novo-Arkhangelsk, they're immense. The silhouette of one pole, with open wings near its top, resembles the Holy Cross. Dwarfed by the line of poles and nearly lost in the trees, a dozen low buildings squat. They're well above the sand, well away from the sea, merging with shadow.

As we draw closer, I see people gathered on the beach. Are they expecting us? The wind shifts and carries music out to us. The people on the beach are singing us onto their shore. Are they celebrating? The other canoe heads toward them, but we stay at sea beyond the line where the surf breaks, and bob in the water like a dry leaf.

A basket-laden man from the landed canoe follows a line of koliuzhi into one of the houses. The rest of the men from the canoe remain on the beach with two watchmen, one holding a bow and arrow, the other a spear. Despite their appearance, their weapons are at rest and they converse with their visitors. After a long time and a short time, a crowd emerges from the house and returns to shore. The basket-laden man is among them, but he's left behind whatever he was carrying. My canoe is beckoned to the beach.

"Wacush! Wacush!" I hear the koliuzhi shout as the canoe scrapes against the beach.

After I disembark, I follow everyone up the sand and over the rocks. We pass between two of the totem poles. They're each as high as six men, and, astonishingly, for I've never before seen any totem pole closely, each is made of a single piece of wood. Carved by whom? Erected how? The eyes, hands, and feet, the paws, claws, toothy mouths, and nubs of rounded ears or peaks of pointy ones, all flowing into one another, follow the grain of the wood. Why are they here, facing the sea? What do they represent? Everyone enters the shadowy doorway of a house, and I have no choice but to follow.

Upon entering, I'm again blinded by darkness. A fire burns in the centre of a sunken floor. When my eyes start to adjust and my surroundings emerge, I see how similar this house is to the Tsar's house: wooden plank walls that stretch between heavy, carved posts; the entire perimeter ringed with imposing benches; the rafters garlanded with fish, skeins of dried grass, ribbons of bark, coils of rope, and bulging baskets. The only difference is in scale. There are ten carved posts and the ceiling soars like in a great hall in a royal palace. This house is mammoth.

I hear giggles and whispers in the shadows. When my eyes have finished adjusting, I see the people. There might be two hundred of them.

The man who must be the toyon stands beside the fire. He has a rattle in his hand. But everything else about him is unlike any koliuzhi I've ever seen.

Shaven and short-haired, he's groomed like an Englishman. A fashionable beaver hat is perched atop his head, tipped back, exposing his young face. His shoulders are covered by a sea otter cape that reaches to his knees. Through its opening, the rest of his clothing is visible: a red broadcloth jacket, double-breasted, with long tails. And trousers. He wears trousers.

"Good day," he says, in English.

I don't know English, but I recognize these words. In the mansions of Petersburg, I've heard them often enough, mostly in the funny anecdotes meant to contrast the fine breeding of the French with the coarse manners of the English. "Good day," I reply awkwardly.

I look down. His boots are made of soft hide, just like the Tsar's, and seem out of place with the rest of his clothing.

He speaks to me in English, the way the English do, barely opening their mouths and slurring together all their words, softening the consonants until they all sound the same, so unlike my language. He arrives at a question, asks it, and waits for my response.

"I'm sorry," I say. "I don't understand." Is there any point? "Russian," I say, though I know it useless. Our conversation is finished. "I speak Russian."

"You speak Russian?" he says in Russian. "Fine," he continues. "My Russian is tolerable. However, you must pardon me when I make an error."

He speaks with an accent just like Yakov's, but he appears more like an English nobleman than a worker for the Russian-American Company. I shouldn't be so surprised. The koliuzhi who gave us the halibut knew the Russian word for fish. And what about the lamestin woman speaking French? Still, I never would have imagined hearing my language spoken here. "How could you know Russian?"

He laughs. "I like different languages," he says. "They interest me. But your people—I think you do not. Long ago, I decided it would be best if I learned some words."

Some words? He makes mistakes but he's conversant.

"Who taught you?"

"Do you know of the *Peacock*? There were some good-humoured men on board. Right after that, it was the *O'Cain*. I cannot imagine why your Tsar thought it wise to get mixed up with the Americans, but who am I to say so? Your men were good enough teachers of your language."

"I've never heard of those ships. I come from the *Sviatoi Nikolai*."

"Yes, Captain Slobodchikov said there would be more ships—Russian ships—but we haven't seen any yet. Mostly it's the English and the Americans."

"Our brig passed this coast about two weeks ago."

He smiles. "We have much to discuss. Welcome to Tsoo-yess."

⚜

He has a complicated name crowded with hard consonants and long vowels. I attempt it, but he laughs and tells me to call him Makee. Now I want to laugh—poppy seed!—but it would be unkind and rude to laugh at his name. He mangles Anna Petrovna Bulygina—such a simple name!—and we end with agreement that he'll just call me Anna, like the others. He pronounces it "Anna," in the Russian way.

He invites me to sit beside him on a bench and lays his rattle between us. His is carved in the shape of a fish and there's a person clutched in its jaws. Four men, including the moustached toyon who came here with me, sit alongside us. Others—including women and children—either sit or stand in a semicircle before us. A baby nearby fusses until its mother pulls it to her breast. I can hear the sucking, gulping, and a happy chirping sound coming from the baby.

"I wish I could offer you tea," Makee says. "Your people are quite obsessed with it, aren't you? But this will have to do." A woman with her hair tightly tied back offers me a small wooden bowl of warm liquid that smells like tree needles. There's a white, crescent-shaped scar on the back of her right hand. I sip the drink—it's hot and bitter—and cradle the bowl to my chest. After the journey, the drink and the hospitality are comforting.

"Thank you," I say to Makee. "That's very kind. Now—if you would allow me to speak bluntly for a moment—where am I?"

He smiles sympathetically. "You're in Tsoo-yess."

"And why am I here?"

"The Chalats have brought you." He points with his chin toward the men who were in my canoe.

"But why? The others—the people I'm with—they'll be wondering where I am."

Makee smiles again. "The people you're with, so I am told, are quite hopelessly lost in the forest."

"We're not lost. We're trying to get down the coast to meet a ship that's expecting us. But . . . we've run into some . . . unfortunate difficulties."

Makee peers at me, his brow furrowed. "If you will now allow *me* to speak bluntly—what are you doing in our territory? What do you want?"

"We're on a mission—with the Russian-American Company. We're here to trade with you; we're also looking for an empty place where we might be able to build a settlement."

"I see." Makee's smile disappears.

"We're here in the name of the Tsar."

Makee turns to the four men sitting around him and speaks to them in his language. They look at me, then him, then back at me again.

When he finishes, Makee turns to me once more and says, "Did your Tsar tell you to take all their salmon?"

It takes me a moment to figure out what he means. He means the dried slabs of fish we took from the little abandoned hut we discovered that day on the riverbank. "We didn't." It wasn't *all* the salmon. "We were hungry. We didn't know it belonged to anybody."

"They were going to eat that fish this winter. Do you understand what will happen to them now?"

"I'm sorry. We didn't know," I stammer. "We left them some beads. And a robe. Didn't they tell you about the beads?" I remember the inadequate piles we left behind. How I said nothing.

"Did your Tsar also tell you to shoot at them with your muskets? And before that, what you did to the Quileutes on the beach?" He doesn't allow me to respond. He speaks again to the four men and while he does, everyone listens.

I think again about the dead boy with the ragged hole that opened his chest. Sand lay on his cheek and in his hair like dust. We left him there so the koliuzhi could come back for him.

Makee finally turns back to me. "There have been so many problems since your ship arrived."

I open my hands and plead to Makee. "Then let us go. If you let me go, I'll tell the others what you said, and we'll leave. We won't cause you any more difficulties if you'll just take me back to the others."

"But Anna—I can't."

"Why not?"

"The Chalats need food for the winter. To replace what you took."

"We have no food!" I cry. "We have nothing to eat ourselves!"

"They know that. They've come to us for food."

"Then why can't you tell them to take me back?"

"You've misunderstood."

"Then what's the problem?"

"You're staying here now. This is a trade. You're what they've brought in exchange for this food."

Makee explains the terms of the trade. The Chalat Tsar has two problems: he needs food for his people, and he wants to stop the stealing and the attacks. He thought the easiest way would be to trade us back to our own people, and to encourage us to leave. So, starting with me, the Tsar tried to exchange us for muskets and powder. According to Makee, the muskets would solve both the Tsar's problems. They'd make it easier to hunt through the winter—and help the Chalats to protect themselves from any further attacks we might launch.

When the crew refused to trade, Makee says, the Tsar had no choice.

"The lady doctor is staying with the Chalats. One man has gone to the Cathlamets and the other will stay with the Quileutes. And you're here."

By dividing us up, Makee says, the Tsar ensures no village is the sole subject of endless attacks. And no single village will have to trade away much of its winter supplies to make up for what we stole.

"You can't do this!" I say. "It's wrong."

Makee turns to the four men and speaks. An old man whose sunken, bony chest is visible from beneath his cedar vest says something and pauses. Makee replies at length.

When he finishes, he says, "Anna, it's better you stay here. Besides—I'll get you home. Maybe even Russia, if that's what you want."

"How?"

"The next time we see a ship," he says, "we'll go out to meet it. If they're willing, I'll trade you and they'll take you to your home."

Home. Maybe even Russia. There might be a way out of here that doesn't depend on the *Kad'iak*. I'd never dreamed such a thing could be possible. But at what cost? Trading in human life is wrong. People are born free and equal. Our Tsar has embraced this and many other principles of enlightened thought. Slavery was abolished before my parents were born. And though the condition of serfs has improved with reforms for the state's peasants and the free agriculturalists, I've heard my father's friends arguing long and hard over how much further the Tsar must go.

Even Timofei Osipovich knows about egalitarianism, though he'd use a simpler word for it. He said on the riverbank that a person's freedom is the most precious thing on earth.

Still, regardless of the lofty principles debated around my parents' dinner table, Makee offers what may be the only realistic way out of this horrible predicament. My father would see the practicality of the arguments right away. I think I know what he would say.

"I want to go home," I say, "but . . ."

Makee bristles. "You have no choice. Anyway, you wouldn't be the first stranger whose passage home I arranged. Too-te-yoo-hannis Yoo-ett—you must have heard about him."

I can hardly understand. "Who?"

"Too-te-yoo-hannis Yoo-ett. He was with the Mowachahts for many years. Mokwinna wouldn't allow him to leave. But I helped him."

Makee speaks to one of the four men and the man disappears. When he returns a moment later, he hands something to Makee. Makee holds it out to me.

It's one of the blunt, horn-shaped tools that I've seen hanging from the neck and shoulders of koliuzhi men. The dead boy on the beach had one attached to a sinew. But this one is different. It's made of burnished metal, engraved with the same eyes, mouths, and hands that are found on the totem poles, house posts, and wooden boxes.

I take it from Makee. It's heavy, but its weight is balanced along its length. It curves with exquisite gracefulness. Other than the silver hair ornament worn by that woman in the Tsar's village, I've never seen anything like it here. Only the finest metalsmiths in Petersburg, the ones who make the samovars and tea trays for princes and princesses, could have crafted it.

"What is this?"

"It's a čiṫuˑɫ. It's a war club."

"Cheetoolth? Did you make it?"

"No, not me. Too-te-yoo-hannis Yoo-ett made it for me. He was going to make me a harpoon too, but Mokwinna wouldn't let him."

"Who was this man—this Too-te-yoo—" I hesitate.

"Too-te-yoo-hannis. He's American. He was captured by Mokwinna long ago. He spent several years with the Mowachahts. Mokwinna wouldn't let him go because he made so many nice metal things. Mokwinna became quite rich trading them.

"But the American wasn't happy. He wanted to go home. And when I was visiting Yuquot, he secretly asked me to help him escape. He wrote a letter and begged me to give it to any sea captain I met. Mokwinna would have been furious if he'd known. I gave it to the captain of the *Lydia*. I heard later that he convinced Mokwinna to release Too-te-yoo-hannis Yoo-ett."

I turn the object over. I believe Makee's story.

"When could we expect the next ship?"

"It's hard to say. There aren't any ships in winter. The sea is too stormy; later, in the spring, they'll be back."

"And what about the others? My husband—and the rest of the crew."

"Your husband is with you?"

"Of course. Could you arrange his rescue as well? Could you arrange for us all to be released?"

"I can try. If I'm not successful, perhaps you'll be able to arrange it yourself once you're free."

He speaks to the four men, and then the people who've been watching and listening. When he finishes, they all get up—Makee included—and leave me on the bench with my now-cold bowl of tea and a feeling that everything might work out after all.

When it's time to eat that evening, I'm ushered to Makee's side. The moustached toyon sits on his other side. A woman with two plaits as thick as the rope on the brig sets a tray of food before me.

Makee says, "This is my wife." She's older than me but not as old as my mother. She has a broad and certain face, lips that turn up at the corners even when she's not smiling, and she wears a cedar dress that covers her to her ankles. There are round shells in her earlobes and bracelets on both her wrists.

"Wacush," I say, and she looks to Makee. He says something briefly to her, and she smiles before she returns to the cooking boxes.

The tray contains fish and grease. There's also something brown that looks like a crooked finger. I find another, and another, barely concealed by the grease. They appear to be roots. I cautiously squeeze one. The skin opens and something dry, flaky, and white appears through the crack.

Potato. It's roasted potato.

When I look up, Makee's smiling.

"You may also have onion and cabbage—but you'll have to cook it yourself. We don't like them, and no one knows what to do with them."

"Where do you get these vegetables?"

"We take them from the Spanish garden. They left our coast many years ago, but their garden still grows. I'll take you there soon."

The idea of a garden of vegetables seems as strange and wonderful as boarding a ship bound for Russia. "Thank you."

Makee's wife returns, then sits beside me. We start to eat, sharing the food in the tray. I watch her from the corner of my eye, aware that she's also watching me.

Later, the young woman with the crescent-shaped scar on her hand gives me a woven mat and a soft animal skin. It's thin and frayed at the edges. The bristly brown hair has worn off in patches and it's too small to cover me and my legs. She indicates where I'm to make my bed. When I go outside to relieve myself, no one follows, but it's so dark, and the sea, so much closer here, roars. I take care of my business, then locate my Polaris. She's extra bright tonight, as if all the stars she's made of have aligned. I bid her a good night before I run back inside.

When I wake in the morning, I notice that the moustached toyon is nowhere to be seen, and when I go outside to relieve myself, I see the canoes that brought me here have gone. They'll carry back my news to share with the others. I only regret that they have no way to tell Maria what good fortune I've stumbled upon. I wish there was some way to tell Nikolai Isaakovich, too. Perhaps he'd be more resolute if he knew there was hope.

"Anna?" Makee calls me to the bench later in the morning. He flicks back his coattails before he sits and tips his hat back so his eyes are no longer hidden in the brim's shadow. "Did you sleep comfortably?"

I nod, thinking about how Maria and I had shared bedclothes when I was with the Chalats, and how even though my covering here is so thin and small, the space I had last night was unexpectedly large.

"Good. As I said yesterday, it could be some time before a ship appears, and I can't predict whether the captain will be willing to trade. So your rescue could take longer than any of us expect."

"I understand the situation," I murmur. "I'm content to wait until the circumstances are right."

Makee smiles. "You will be treated well here and though it may not meet the expectations of a Russian noblewoman, perhaps you will be comfortable enough. You may find our ways odd. Nonetheless, you will feel better if you do as we do."

Not far from the bench where we sit, the woman with the crescent-shaped scar on her hand watches us. She's dressed differently than she was yesterday. Her cedar bark cape is wrapped tightly around her neck, and a cord holds it around her waist. Her skirt reaches her ankles. Her feet are bare. Her hands are folded around some coils of cords.

"Go," Makee says, indicating the woman. "Go with—" And he says a name that sounds like Inessa.

"Go where?" I ask.

He says something to the woman and she replies briefly.

"She'll show you where we collect wood for the fire. And after you come back, you'll go out with her for water."

"I don't understand."

"Anna, you have work to do. Today, you will gather firewood and bring water with—." And he says the name again, but I can't quite catch it. It still sounds like Inessa.

"But—I can't do that. I don't know how."

His face looks like my father's when he's disappointed in me. "Even a child could do such simple tasks," he admonishes. "But she will show you, if necessary." He frowns when he sees my expression. "You did not expect to be idle here, did you?"

"No," I say, aware that I sound peevish but unable to stop myself. "Isn't there other work I could do?"

"Like what?" He waits, but I've seen enough of the koliuzhi way to know that my accomplishments have little meaning here. Nobody is clamouring to keep a log of the stars. Nobody is embroidering dinner napkins. Nobody is conjugating French verbs or learning the steps to the mazurka.

"If you are going to stay with us, you will have to work with us." He rises. "Everyone here has responsibilities. You will need to do your share. Now, go with her. Go, and do whatever she does." He heads for the door and his form disappears into the daylight.

I follow the woman I now think of as Inessa. She doesn't even look to see if I'm behind. Her hair is freshly combed, and again, very tightly tied back. Her single plait bounces against her cape. The cords swing from her left hand as she walks down a trail that leads into the forest. Just like Koliuzhi Klara, her movement through the trees is easy, even with bare feet.

There's wood all around us, but for reasons I don't comprehend, she walks right by it.

As we go deeper into the forest, the ground becomes spongier, and the light dims. We tread past lofty trees and drooping moss. The sound of the sea disappears, replaced by the sighs of the wind in the canopy far overhead.

Inessa leaves the trail. I follow, climbing over rotting logs and roots that buckle up out of the soil. Ahead, she stops and drops the cords. She leans over a fallen tree. With one foot planted squarely on the trunk, she twists a thin branch until it snaps. She throws it down, then wrenches off another, and throws it onto the pile of wood she's started.

There are so many sticks everywhere. They're probably wet, but they'll dry soon enough. This should be easy. I choose one—it's not heavy—and I add it to Inessa's pile. The next one is slightly thicker and dappled with curls of pale lichen. I untangle it from the thatch and place it on our pile.

Inessa looks at the thick branch, then me, and laughs. She kicks the branch.

"What are you doing?" I cry.

My branch shatters, flaky as pastry. It's rotten. It could never burn.

I wander away looking for better wood. I try to find a tree like the one Inessa is working on. As I search, I hear snap after snap of breaking branches as she builds her pile. The snaps grow distant, but I still can't find a fallen tree that's not completely rotten. I pick up a small stick that looks good. Then Inessa calls.

"šuʔuk!"[27]

I have only one stick, but I start to head toward the sound of her voice.

She calls out again. "hitakʷałšiƛeˑʔisid! waˑsaqiˑk?"[28]

When I get back, she's standing beside two huge bundles of sticks that have been wrapped in the cords she brought. She looks at my single stick in disbelief, grabs it from my hand, then throws it into the bushes. She swings one bundle of wood onto her back and slips a band that I hadn't noticed around her head. The band's attached to the bundle of wood.

She leaves the other bundle for me.

Before she gets too far away, I lift my bundle and try to roll it onto my back just as she did. But when I finally do, I can't reach the headband. How did she do it? I can't remember which step comes first, which hand goes where, and I also can't take the time to figure it out or I'll lose her.

I lift the bundle of sticks into my arms and crush it against my chest. I can hardly see over it. But if I lose sight of Inessa's back, I will have much greater trouble.

Inessa and I make several visits to the same grove in the forest. Each time, she collects and carries back most of the wood; each time, I also manage a little better. I'm very slow compared to her, but she doesn't stomp on, or throw away, any more of the sticks

---

27 Come here!

28 We're leaving! Where are you?

I gather either. I watch her and figure out the series of moves it takes to successfully get the sticks onto my back.

When we're done, Inessa gives me a basket as big as a coal scuttle, takes one for herself, and leads me along a path in a different direction.

We stop beside a small pond. A flock of ducks takes flight as soon as it sees us, calling *krya-krya* as the ducks disappear over the trees. Inessa walks into the water, bends, dips her basket in, and as she pulls it up, in a fluid motion, she rolls it along her shoulder and onto her back while slipping the band over her head.

"You can't put water in a basket," I say. I laugh in disbelief. "What are you doing?"

It's the basket, not Inessa, that responds. Water runs down its sides and stops. From the way she walks, I can see the weight of her load. When she passes me, standing by the side of the pond, I look inside her basket. It's full.

I brush my fingertips over the surface of my tightly woven basket. It seems illogical, but then I think of the woven bowls we used in the Tsar's village. They were watertight. I just didn't think you could make such a large basket that wouldn't leak. I wade into the cold water, just as she did, soaking my skirt to the knees. I fill it, heave it onto my back, and slip the band around my head, all the while trying to imitate Inessa's movements.

The full basket pulls at my neck muscles and seems to grow heavier as we get closer to the house. My wet skirt tangles in my legs, forcing me to take tiny steps that slow me down. Back at the house, we pour the water into square wooden buckets, the same size and shape as the cooking boxes. It seems all fresh water is stored in these containers. Then we go back to the pond, once, twice, and after that, I lose count.

CHAPTER ELEVEN

————————————

My days fill with wood and water, water and wood. Whether it pours, or tendrils of mist wrap themselves around the trees, or the sky clears and sunlight mottles the moss cushions scattered on the forest floor, Inessa takes me out, and we return, as reliably as the tide, with water and wood, wood and water.

We need firewood all the time. The fires here don't rage as they do in the stone hearths of Petersburg, but still it takes much wood to maintain the intense flames that produce enough heat to warm the stones to cook, as well as to make a modest difference to the temperature inside. The need for water is similar. The women use basket after basket of water to wash for and feed these many people. A near-empty storage box is a disheartening sign that Inessa and I need to make another trip to the pond.

I've never worked so hard, so physically, in all my life. I'm weary at the end of every day, fatigued in a way that's completely unfamiliar. Responsibilities I understand. I have duties to my husband, as he does to me, to the crew, to the company. Even when I was a girl in Petersburg, my parents would never have allowed me to be idle while they were themselves busy. But I lack the natural inclination needed for this kind of heavy labour. My mind has always been stronger than my body. Perhaps Makee could give me more suitable duties. "Like what?" he'd asked. I still can't imagine what.

I'm a prisoner—and I have been since the day of the battle on the river with the Chalat Tsar's people. I cannot go where I please. I've been traded in exchange for food. And now I'm compelled to work. Hard labour.

This is slavery, or, at best, some koliuzhi version of serfdom.

But then, like my father's friends in debate, I argue with myself. I'm a prisoner—but I'm not locked up in a cell. I cannot go where I please—but where would I go? I only want to go home and Makee said he'll arrange it. No one torments me, mistreats me, or withholds food. The work is hard—but who around here is not working hard? I see no idle man or woman, not even an idle child.

I think that whatever I am here—slave, serf, or a working guest, like a girl hired to be an old woman's companion—there is no word in Russian to describe it.

⁂

I spend my days with Inessa and yet know so little about her—not even her real name. In the evenings, after our work is done, she eats her meal in a corner with other young women and children. They talk and laugh—who are her friends? What amuses them? Is she married? I think not, but surely she favours somebody. I watch to see if there's a young man she gazes at, or who gazes at her with that kind of longing.

Where is Nikolai Isaakovich? Did he get his coat back? Is he missing me, looking for me? I pass the hours walking to and from the forest thinking about the last time I saw him, his beastly beard, without his coat, his thin shirt no shield from the cold, and the way he hung his head, impotent before the men who, only a few weeks before, had obeyed his every command. I am so disappointed for him, and, frankly, disappointed *in* him. But I know he's not a coward—not really. Something's happened with the crew to influence him, but no matter how hard I try, I can't imagine what it might have been.

I picture his face when we meet again. How surprised he'll be if the next time he sees me I'm hailing him from the ship that's come to rescue all of us. How tightly we'll embrace one another and how sweet his kisses will be when we're finally alone again.

One grey morning, before Inessa and I head into the forest again, Makee calls me.

"I will show you the garden today," he says. "Come."

We head out along a path that leads away from the sea. Two men, one carrying bow and arrows, the other a spear, accompany us. The path is narrow and muddy, so we walk single file. After a long time and a short time, the sound of the surf vanishes beneath the twittering of birds and the soft breath of the wind in the trees.

It's a relief to be in the forest with a purpose other than searching for firewood. I can nearly imagine my parents here, my father off wandering in the underbrush, my mother beginning one of her cautionary tales about the leshii. This forest is so different from the one in the hills that surround Petersburg. I wonder if she'd sense the leshii's presence here, too.

At a bend in the path, two tiny birds flutter away when they see us. Startled, the man with the spear lifts his weapon, then lowers it when he sees there's no danger. Around the corner, right beside the trail, grows a strange tree with a short trunk that splits into many branches that all grow straight into the sky. Together, the branches form a bowl; the tree resembles a chalice.

"How long did the Spanish live here?" I ask.

Makee shrugs. "Not long—in the end. But they intended to stay much longer than they did. They constructed houses, sheds for their cattle, and even a building where they made metal things—a whole village. After it was built, they surrounded it with cannon. I was a young boy then, but I remember there were six. All facing outward and pointed at us."

"Why? Were you at war?"

"We should have been. They built it all on top of our houses."

"On top? How?"

"They came when the people were away. It was summer and naturally everyone was in the forest and up in the hills. When the people came back, their village was occupied. The Spanish men didn't care, and they even insisted the people stop trading with everyone else. But the Spanish had almost nothing anybody wanted. No one wished to restrict trading like that."

"So what did the people do?"

"There was no choice. They had to find somewhere else to live. Some of them came to Tsoo-yess—the rest to other villages. That winter, the Spanish suffered a lot and eventually they went back to their country. And when they did, they left everything. So, the people came back to their community. They tore down the Spanish houses. They burnt what they didn't want, or threw it in the river. The garden is all that's left."

We walk until, in the distance, the horizon brightens, and the sound of the sea returns. Gradually, through the trees, the ocean emerges once again. The men with us hold their weapons more casually, and the hard readiness of their arms melts away.

"This is it," Makee says, and we stop before a tangle of vines and overgrown plants that bolted long ago. It's hardly a garden. It lies just outside the edge of the forest, a short distance from the sea, at one end of a huge bay that's empty except for a floating flock of black birds. A lone gull glides overhead.

I kneel and pull aside a desiccated mesh of stalks and vines. Beneath them, life is taking its course: many small plants huddle together. Their stunted leaves are dark but green, so I know they're alive. Makee squats beside me and pulls the debris even farther back. There, nestled in pale, oversized leaves, is a tiny emerald jewel.

"Cabbage?"

"You take it. Nobody wants it—only the insects."

The outer leaves have been nibbled at the edges. I fold them back, exposing the core, which the beetles and caterpillars haven't yet found. I pull it out of the earth, root and all. It smells sweet, like most cabbages when just picked, but a bit sharp, too, like it's been left in the ground too long.

Makee shows me where the onions grow. Using a pointed stick, I gouge the earth in a circle around a bulb hoping to make it easier to pull up. Makee and the two men watch.

When I rise, I fold over my apron and sling into it one cabbage and three onions with their spiky tops bent over. My cheeks feel warm from the wind and the exertion.

Makee looks overhead to the darkening sky. "Come. The clouds are aching. We should go back."

We pass the tree that looks like a chalice, and head along the trail that crosses the forest. The wind picks up and, indeed, each minute, the sky grows darker. The air is heavy with the promise of rain. I pull my vegetable-laden apron a little closer and try to keep up with Makee.

"I'll be giving a big feast soon," Makee says, over his shoulder. "I'm inviting people from the nearby villages but also some people who live much farther away on the coast."

"Will there be many guests?"

"There always are. We're known to be generous with food, and some even call us by that name: 'Makah,' is how they say it. But that word comes from another language, not ours."

"So what do you call yourselves?"

"Qʷidičča?aˑtx̌."

"Kwee-dashch-awt?" I say, trying my best to make the sounds.

"Kwih-dihch-chuh-aht," he says, emphasizing the syllables, and gives a short nod.

"Does it have a meaning?"

"It means that we are the People of the Cape. That we live among the gulls on this rocky land that extends into the ocean." He stretches out an arm to take it all in. Many more words are needed to say it in Russian than in Makee's language.

"Will I be at the feast?"

"I insist upon it! My guests will want to see you," Makee says. "Some have seen a babałid before, but almost no one's ever seen a babałid woman."

"What's a babathid?"

"It means you—your people. The Russians and the Spanish and the Americans and all the rest of you. Who only have houses on the water and who float to different places with no particular origin or destination." Once again, it takes many words to express in Russian. Even still, the idea is mistaken.

"I have a home," I say. "In Russia. And another one in Novo-Arkhangelsk. And I *am* going back."

"Of course you are," Makee says.

The rain starts to fall while we're still in the forest. My hair quickly becomes wet but my shoulders, under the cedar cape they gave me, stay dry.

When we get back to the house, I'm offered a place near the fire to prepare my vegetables. The heat helps dry my hair and the damp hem of my skirt. The women give me a sharp shell knife just like the one Maria used preparing the medicine. I use it awkwardly to cut the cabbage and onion into smaller pieces to hasten the cooking. Then, the women give me a cooking box containing water. They move rocks in and out of it until the water's steaming. It takes many rotations until the vegetables are soft. I ladle everything into a small tray on top of a chunk of dried white fish and I shake my head, no, when they offer me the usual dollop of grease.

I eat slowly, alone, thinking of the Spanish and their six cannons, and the taste of my mother's shchi cabbage soup.

I'm unprepared for a feast, especially one where people will want to see me. My clothes are dirty and torn; my shoes are disintegrating. My hair needs grooming. Makee tells me his wife will assist. So, when she comes for me one morning, I'm equally relieved to get a reprieve from collecting wood and water, and curious about how she'll help me prepare for the feast.

Makee's wife and three other women take me to a sediment-filled pond. At its soggy edge, they demonstrate that I will have to, for the first time since the ship ran aground, wash my clothes. The youngest woman gives me a short cedar robe to wear while I'm laundering my skirt and blouse. I keep my chemise on. The robes gape and I feel ashamed that these women might be able to see me unclothed. The women stifle smiles when they see my strange costume, my stained and wrinkled chemise drooping from below the hem of the robe, but Makee's wife shushes them.

The oldest woman, who has thin greying hair that falls to her shoulders, shows me some coarse reeds I should use to scrub my clothes. I rub so vigorously, I chafe my fingers, and I worry that my skirt and blouse will come apart. Despite my efforts, some stains won't wash out.

After my clothes are as clean as I can get them and have been draped over bushes to dry, I discover that I ought not to have fretted about my modesty. My body is next. The old woman tugs at my cedar robe and then at my chemise.

"wi·k̓ qʷa· wi·widačik! hała·da·x̌—hała·disubʔic!"[29] she says loudly.

---

29   Don't be cowardly! You bathe now—you need to bathe!

Reluctantly, I turn away and slowly drag each one over my head.

I've never been outdoors and completely unclothed. I fold my arms but there's no way to hide, no way to stay warm. I enter the pond. My feet sink into the mucky bottom and tiny bubbles creep up my legs. Cold rises over my womanly parts, and then my bosom, until only my shoulders and head remain dry.

The old peasants fear the rusalki who live in ponds in Russia just like this one, waiting for young men to approach. The rusalki know who's weak and easily lured by a pretty face, and those young men are never seen again. What if I see a lock of hair, a billowing sleeve, a fingertip through the murk? I'm not a young man but would they want me anyway, want me to become one of them? I know it's foolish but the muddy water I've stirred up makes my imaginings more real.

I splash a bit of water on my face, and wonder how, with so much sediment, I'll achieve what they wish. I'll come out dirtier than I already am. After a long time and a short time of watching my half-hearted effort, the old woman cries out and throws off her robe. She scoops up the coarse reeds I'd been using to scrub my clothes and enters the water. Her breasts are two empty sacks hanging to her waist. I've never seen the bare breasts of an old woman before.

"da·ʔukʷa·čixsubaqa·k?"[30] she asks as she draws close. Her tone is coaxing. "šuʔuk, ti·ƛti·yayikdi·cux̌."[31] She takes me by the arm and scrubs my skin with the reeds. Then she turns me and scrubs my other arm. The reeds bite. I feel like a bride being washed for her wedding.

She splashes water on my back and then I begin to clean other parts of my own body. Finally, she tugs my head back and

---

30 Do you need help?

31 Come here, we'll scrub you.

washes my hair. Her fingers are fierce, and she kneads my scalp like it's bread. When that's finished, she leads me by the hand out of the pond.

We stand dripping before the other women, and she still doesn't release my hand. With the sweat and dirt washed away at last, my skin tingles. The youngest woman wraps me in the cedar dress again and I begin to warm up.

Back at the house, I'm given a bone needle threaded with a coarse fibre. I'll be able to mend the sleeve that was torn so many weeks ago. Being along a seam, the repair is easy. I also sew the hem where it's coming loose. The faint rusty bloom of a stain remains, my husband's blood from the day of our battle on the beach.

Finally, on a clear afternoon when the clouds and mist have vanished, and the blue stretches lazily from one end of the sky to the other, I go to the beach with a bowl of fresh water. There's one more step to take to prepare for the feast. I must do something about my tarnished silver cross.

I unclasp the long chain. I hold the cross out and let it twirl in the breeze and sparkle in the sun. Even though it's badly in need of a polish, it still glitters like a star. I consider that other cross in the sky, Cygnus the Swan, and how she spans the expanse of the Milky Way, and how Mademoiselle Caroline Herschel and her brother counted the stars there, drew the first diagram of our galaxy, and marked our tiny sun's place among the others. Unlike the pink tourmaline on my cross, we're not in the centre. My father always reminded me of this and of the ancient men who argued that we were until, one by one, science proved them wrong. "Only a fool knows everything," he said.

I rinse my silver cross in the bowl of water, then rub it in the fine, warm sand. I rinse it once more, then hold it out before me again, letting it dry. Without the tarnish, it's even more brilliant, as shiny as the day my mother gave it to me, and fit for a feast.

I fasten it around my neck once again.

A dancing man who wears a mask bounds out from behind a wooden screen that's as big as the front of a mansion and carved and painted with koliuzhi figures. The creature in the centre has eyes on its face but also eyes on its hands and knees and feet. On either side of the figure there are more eyes, and also ears and mouths and snubbed noses, all encased in ovals, all floating away from one another as if they were bubbles. The pointy shape that looks like a wave or maybe even the fin that rides on the back of a fish repeats itself inside and around the creatures. Each half of the screen is a mirror image of the other. Firelight casts rippling shadows that make the figures come alive.

The dancing man dips close to me and freezes. His head swivels and the carved and painted eyes of his mask bore into me. He dances away, turns his head, and again, the mask's eyes turn to me. Then with a leap he spins around and though I expect to be released from his gaze, I'm not. There are eyes on the back of his mask, too.

Makee has a tall chair like a throne with a carved back and arms. It's so tall, he needs to climb up to sit down. But right now, he's standing and blowing into a funny little pipe that plays a single squeaky note, keeping time for the dancer.

When I think I won't be able to bear the dancer's gaze any longer, he moves to the other side of the house. Like the first snow, down that's scattered on the floor floats and settles behind him, marking a white path across the house.

Makee's skin sparkles. His face, arms, and legs are painted and powdered with something reflective. His lower arms are ringed with bracelets that dance and rattle as he moves. The bracelets are made of leather and a shiny orange metal that appears to be copper. Could it be? Where would Makee get it from?

All the men have painted their bodies, some in red and black squares that bring to mind the harlequins and jesters who sometimes entertained us in Petersburg. Some have adorned their faces with oversized black eyebrows in the shape of half-moons or triangles, just like the injured eyebrow man. Their hair, greased and piled atop their heads, is decorated with cedar boughs and sprinkled with white down. The best sea otter capes, black as coal, are draped over the shoulders of the most regal-looking men.

The women's bodies and their clothing are also covered with adornments, every one of which eclipses my silver cross with its single jewel. Korolki are stitched onto the fronts and hems of their skirts, often strung next to long, white beads that look like skinny bird's bones. These white bones dangle in rows and rattle as the women move. Though most women are wearing dresses of cedar bark, there are many with clothing made of fringed animal hide with fur trim. Their skirts are white and painted with designs of fish and animals and red and black patterns that run along the hems and look like my cross-stitch.

Even Inessa wears a hide skirt; hers is painted with a repeating pattern of birds with outstretched wings that seem to fly along the hem. She also wears a beaded necklace and many bracelets. Her hair, for once, is not tightly tied back, but spills over her shoulders like a glossy waterfall.

I've never seen such robes, furs, and jewellery. I don't even know where they came from—I never knew the Kwih-dihch-chuh-ahts had such things in the house. The sight of them is no less majestic then anything that would be seen in the grandest ballrooms of Petersburg. I would never have imagined there could be such lavish clothing in a place so remote.

When the circling man finishes his dance, some little children take his place. They are five or six years old and so their older sisters or maybe their mothers lead them in a circle while they sing, their voices nearly lost in the big, noisy house. One of the little girls wears a headdress made of the same skinny white beads that look like bird bones. The children are just like pretty, garlanded girls dancing a khorovod in the spring. My mother would get tears in her eyes watching them, and she'd always applaud wildly when they finished, sweaty and panting, for the dizzying dance is much harder than it looks.

Conversation dies down as the children attract more attention. The people watching call out, and the children pick up their pace. Just when I think they must be dizzy and about to fall, they stop. They remain in a circle, facing one another. The older women start a song, and the children join in, moving their hands up and down, their mouths Os of surprise, their eyes wide and serious. I think they might be telling a story.

As Makee had promised, some of the guests came to look at me. There was no formal ceremony. Most just passed in front of me, their eyes lowered, their glances furtive. I smiled, wanting them to meet my eye. After all, I'd prepared for this. A few stopped and stared in disbelief before saying something to one another and moving on. One woman laughed; a baby, thrust up before my face, cried.

Two men paused before me. Their faces were painted red and black and their hair, tied atop their heads, was garlanded with cedar boughs. I smiled and lowered my eyes. But not before I saw something that drew my gaze right back to them. Recognition. They had seen me before.

They spoke in low voices to one another. I studied them. They weren't from Makee's village. Had I seen them before? Where? Were they from the Tsar's house?

One of the men shifted and the cedar vest he wore opened a little. His chest was slashed with a long, white scar. He adjusted his vest and when he did, I saw a missing finger and I remembered.

I remembered how, many weeks ago, he'd fondled a shackle onboard the brig. I remembered how the man beside him had hooked a long leg over the bulwark before descending to the waiting canoes. And I remembered how surprised Timofei Osipovich had been with their sudden departure and his failure to get the sea otter cape that my husband had said was ratty.

We stood for some moments staring at one another. Were they surprised to see me here? Or had they expected it? When they heard about the babathid woman, did they think it might be me? How much had changed, and yet the very unconnected threads of our lives had once again wound around each other.

"Wacush," I said, and smiled tentatively.

The scarred man furrowed his brow and after a short pause said, "ʔeˑʔeˑ, kʷisasiɫakɫʔitʔuc! babaqiyuk̓uˑk?"[32] I nodded but had no idea what he was saying. "ʔuˑšuˑbisdakpiˑdic,"[33] he continued, with a look of concern.

Finally, the tall, muscular man nudged him, and he stopped.

"I'm sorry," I said and flushed.

They walked away, their necks bent together in conversation, the cedar boughs in their hair interlacing.

Later, I saw the scarred man speaking to Inessa, whose eyes were averted, whose brow was deeply furrowed. But it didn't stop him from leaning in and continuing to speak to her.

For two days, the singing and dancing continued with only a brief pause at night when most people slept. There were playful dances that delighted the audience as much as the dancers themselves. There were men in masks who whirled in dark dances in which they pretended to kidnap and kill others. The Kwih-dihch-chuh-ahts cried out. The stories—I concluded that's what they were—unfolded as in an opera, and just like in an opera, I could hardly understand the narrative.

For two days, we ate all we could: trays of sour caviar, dried salmon, roasted roots, steamed leaves and stems, some bitter,

---

32 My, you have changed a lot. What happened?

33 You must be having troubles.

some sharp like onion, and cakes of sweet, dried berries. Everything was, as usual, served with grease ladled from ornate wooden serving dishes. They were shaped like fish and four-legged animals just like the everyday serving dishes I'd been seeing in Makee's house, but these were far larger and more decorative. Empty trays were refilled immediately, refusal being, as it is in Russia, out of the question.

Late in the afternoon of the second day, everything stops. Makee installs me beside him and a heap of objects. Attendants hover, waiting for instructions. Makee begins. He speaks and when he stops, the attendants move. One man extracts a basket from the heap. Another man takes it and lifts it above his head. He parades in a small circle, turning slowly to give everyone a look at the basket.

It's a medium-sized basket with four red canoes woven into it as though they're chasing one another in a circle. Around the base, a pattern that might represent waves has also been woven in. There's a tight-fitting lid with a knobby handle. The attendant locates an older man whose sea otter robe skims the ground and hands the basket to him.

Makee speaks again. This time, the attendant pulls out a bladder filled with grease. The same man who held up the basket raises the bladder, his arms straining under the weight. Once again, a recipient is located—this time, it's an old man with a cedar robe who accepts the gift.

Makee gives away more baskets, more bladders. Cedar mats, capes, and dresses. Beads and necklaces. Elaborately woven hats. Sea otter pelts and other animal furs and hides. Mirrors, which I'm startled to see. Several caskets of gunpowder, which I'm even more shocked to see. He gives away slabs of dried fish and roe wrapped in cedar boughs and ferns. Each item is lifted high for everyone to behold before being given to a guest.

When the pile has all but disappeared—there's only a box, a basket, and a thick coil of rope remaining—dancers take to the floor once more. A drummer and singers join them. The attention of Makee's attendants is drawn to the music.

Makee watches for a minute and then, without taking his eyes from the dancers, he says, "I have something for you, too."

From a wooden box at his feet, he draws a pair of floppy boots.

They're made of brown hide, stitched together with sinew. They haven't been dyed and decorated, they have no heels or silver buckles, but to me they're the most beautiful pair of shoes in the world.

"Thank you. I didn't think anybody noticed."

"We say: ʔušu·yakšʔalic."

"Oo-shoo-yaw—" I stop, shake my head. "I can't."

"Yuksh-uhlits. Go ahead."

"Yuksh-uhlits." I smile apologetically.

"I hope you'll be more comfortable outdoors."

They slide on. My feet feel warmer and drier than any time since we abandoned the brig.

There's a hush over the house that night. I go to bed believing I'll sleep deeply. Instead my slumber is broken, coloured by outrageous dreams of a ball in Petersburg that transforms into a shipwreck and then into the crazy, whirling dance of a disembodied mask that sees and speaks.

It snows two days later, huge feathery clumps that thrill the children and melt as soon as they hit the ground. It falls furiously for a few minutes, then is followed by an abrupt downpour of cold rain. Christmas is coming—soon. But when? I lost track of time long ago. I have missed my own name day and Nikolai Isaakovich's too. Unless I make a plan to mark Christmas Day, I'll miss it as well. So, I randomly choose a day to have my own Christmas feast.

That day, I harvest one potato and pick the last cabbage. It's smaller than my fist. I prepare them as always, struggling with the curve of the shell knife, uncertain still of where it's supposed to fit in my hand, nervous about cutting myself. When the food is ready, I bless myself and remember the clatter of forks and knives, the clinking of glasses, and the irresistible aromas that would signal that start of the Christmas feast in my parents' home.

I bow my head. It feels wrong to eat alone and I want to share my food with Makee and his family, with Inessa, but I have so little, I'm ashamed. It's nothing compared to their feasts. I tell myself they wouldn't like my food anyway, but that argument is a thin veil and I'm pretending when I say I can't see past it.

I miss my husband. I miss everyone.

Salmon spill from a barrel-sized open-weave basket onto the ground and slither over one another, forming an ever-expanding heap. The women cry out in dismay and call the children to help keep the fish in a more orderly pile.

This week, I'm with the women, deep in the forest on the bank of a stream. It ripples over rocks and gurgles, then turns a corner not far from where we're working. There's a hut where we're hanging salmon to smoke, and there's a small house where we sleep. Wooden vats as big and round as cabinets squat in a row at the edge of the clearing. A scaffold of thick, straight branches lashed together looms over the vats. This is our camp.

On the first day, Inessa and I naturally fetched many bundles of wood. Late in the morning, when we'd apparently brought back enough, I was given a new job.

Inessa started by indicating that I must choose a fish from the heap. She showed me how to scrub it with ferns, until the coarse leaves removed the slime and scales.

She then gave me a shell knife. It was much larger than any I'd used so far. My whole hand could not cover it. The cutting edge was shiny and freshly sharpened. I wondered if a knife like this had given Inessa the scar on her hand.

Inessa cut into the fish just behind its gills, slicing off its head. Next, she slit open the belly, crooked her finger deep into the cavity, and pulled out shiny entrails.

She then filleted the fish. I could hardly see around her elbows and hunched back. In an instant, she unfolded two boneless halves that remained attached at the tail. She picked it up to show me. Her fish resembled a drooping reticule.

She trimmed the fins and fatty pieces, and then tossed all the scraps into one of the large vats. She called one of the children. He took the fillet from her, scrambled up the drying rack, and threw it over the highest crossbar.

At the end of the process, Inessa said, "ɬaẋa·ʔal, wa·ɬsu·qƛa·k čabuɬ qʷisi·ẋu·?"[34]

My first fish ended up ragged. The edges were rough, the tail that was supposed to hold the halves together had almost been severed, and there were strings of skin and flesh hanging loose. My second was better, and my third fish contained skeins of glossy roe. Inessa showed me how to pull them out without breaking them. She tossed them into a different vat.

Over the days, the fish on the rack accumulate, and they begin to dry. When the women decide they're dry enough, the fish are slung over the rafters in the small hut. Fires inside the hut are fed green branches that Inessa and I gathered especially for this purpose. The branches create acrid, slow-rising smoke. We attend to the hanging fish, turning it, moving it farther away or closer to the smoke to ensure everything will be ready at the same time.

---

34 So, do you think you can do that?

Whenever it's my turn to work in the smokehouse, the harsh air irritates my eyes. But the sweet scent of the salmon is comforting, like an old memory.

The women and I work hard, but we are rewarded—some fresh salmon is set aside for our meals. These fish are cut differently, opened like butterfly wings and skewered flat with cedar splints, then propped before a very hot fire until they bake. The taste of the cedar enters right into the flesh.

There was a ceremony for our first meal of baked fish. When it was ready, it was laid on fresh cedar boughs on a mat and sprinkled with down. The women sang a song. After we finished eating, the bones and all the small scraps were gathered, paraded down to the river, and thrown in the water, just like the offerings fishermen make to the vodyanoy.

I try to remember how many days have passed since we came to the smokehouse and how many days since I arrived in Makee's village and how many days since the brig ran aground. I can't. I think it's nearly two months since the wreck, but the passage of time feels fluid here, as fluid as the flow of the little stream we're working alongside. Two months reminds me that it's been a long time since my monthlies. I haven't had one since I was onboard the brig. I pray they won't return until we're rescued.

Every day I see Makee. He's busy speaking with the other men, or joking around with the children. Sometimes I see him outside, down on the beach by the canoes, and other times, he comes out of the forest carrying a bow and arrow. He's busy but he often speaks with me, asking after my health or telling me about fish they've caught or a herd of seals nearby or any other piece of news from the house that he thinks I should know about.

But then a day passes, and I don't see him. I wonder if he's gone away—no one seems disturbed. Then, there's a second day when I don't see him, and a third, fourth, and fifth. He must have gone to another village up the coast, though I have no one to ask. His wife has stayed in bed since he's disappeared. She barely moves under her cedar blanket, and no one disturbs her. What if Makee's dead? No one would be able to tell me. But I refuse to believe it. Wherever he's gone, he's coming back.

CHAPTER TWELVE

"Anna!" Inessa shouts from far ahead. "Anna!"

I drop the firewood I'm carrying. It clatters to the earth. I hurry down the path that leads back to the houses as fast as I can, heading for her voice.

As I draw near the village, I see people streaming through the doors, going in and out, some stopping to embrace one another. Where's Inessa? Young men on the rooftops lean over and pull their friends up beside them. Once up, they pound the roofs with staves, and with so many young men on the rooftops, it's not long before the rumble of their enormous drums thunders through the whole bay.

A crowd has gathered on the beach; Inessa must be there. They're gazing toward the rocky headland. Out on the headland, a smaller group waits, their faces turned to the sea. When they begin to cheer and cry out, the crowd on the beach joins in. I head down to where celebrations unfold.

A canoe glides into sight. Everyone on board sings. The paddlers take two strokes then strike the gunwales. Two strokes again, then thud. When their paddles are lifted, I see how they're as narrow as sticks, and how they end in a long point. They're not like other paddles I've seen.

Another two canoes appear. A cheer swells up while the pounding on the houses grows even more frenzied. Laughing children chase one another along the beach nearly knocking me over. Gulls spiral overhead and shriek.

"Anna!" I turn. Inessa beams. "čiłapuwiq! ʔuda·kšiʎʔu čiłapuwiq!"[35] She laughs and hugs me, then pushes me away and runs off.

At the front of the fourth canoe, Makee sits. Instead of his beaver hat, he's wearing the kind of woven hat he gave away at the feast. It has a wide brim and a jaunty knob on top that makes it look like the lid of a basket. A rope stretches behind his canoe. Whatever they're towing is surrounded by pale floats that bob in the water and keep the towed object just below the surface. It traces a broad wake in the grey sea.

Slowly the canoes near the shore, and men on the beach hurl themselves into the ocean. Some reach for Makee and his canoe, while others pull the tow rope and, as soon as they can, push the towed object toward land. The surf crashes around them, and the water rushes back out, each time revealing a little more of the towed object until finally it's so close that when a wave recedes, I see.

A whale.

They've captured a whale.

The way the men work with the force of the sea makes me think of the day the brig ran aground and Timofei Osipovich guided us to do the same as we shuttled our belongings to shore. With each wave, they advance the animal in tiny increments, straining to prevent it from sliding back with the retreating water. Finally, a powerful wave coupled with a forceful push brings the whale up onto the beach. When the sea subsides this time, rattling the stones on its way out, the whale's grey body is exposed.

Like a rock, the whale is speckled with barnacles. In colour and texture, it blends into the gravel beach. It's dotted with

---

35   A whale! He got a whale!

wounds—it's been stabbed many times. Its eye is open and glazed. Its long beak of a mouth has been sutured shut with thick cord that's been looped around the tow rope. An incision circles the whale's tail. There remains not a twitch of muscle. This animal has been dead a long time.

White down is scattered from baskets over the whale's back. An older but agile man from Makee's house hoists himself upon the carcass. With both hands, he raises a spear above his head and plunges it into the animal. The blade sinks in while blood and clear liquid dribble out. He saws through the flesh making a rectangle across the back and down the sides of the body toward the sand. Once he completes three sides of the rectangle, he abandons the spear for a much smaller knife with a wide blade, which he inserts into one of the slits. He cuts beneath, pulling away and rolling a slab of cream-coloured flesh down the animal's side. The warm scent of fresh slaughter rises.

At the whale's side, a man opens his hands and reaches for the roll of flesh. He guides it down, and when it's reached the beach, he cuts the slab free and it sags to the ground in folds.

Several men heave the chunk onto a pole that rests on the shoulders of four men. The pole bows as it receives the weight. They carry the pole up to the house, navigating slowly along the path. The agile man with the spear follows them. Makee watches and I know he's satisfied, even a little proud.

Now that he's close, I see the pattern woven into Makee's hat. There's a whale, and when he twists his neck, I see the men chasing it, their canoe floating atop waves that encircle the brim. Makee calls out and another man climbs onto the whale's back. That man also cuts off a slab of flesh, and then follows the procession as it's carried to the houses. There's a third man, and a fourth, and so on. Each slab disappears into a different house. When eventually the skeleton is visible and then the organs spill, the stench is powerful. It draws flocks of crows and gulls, even white-headed eagles. Overwhelmed, I leave the beach.

Outside Makee's house, four fires blaze. Each is filled with the smooth stones used for cooking. Rosy-cheeked women laugh and joke with one another as they tend the fire and, with their tongs, move the stones around in the flames and hot coals.

Other women are helping one another carry dripping containers of water that they lift and pour into four huge vats that stand like stout men on guard. A woman with a knife calls out to Inessa, who says to me, "šuʔuk. ʔusubʔi ƛaʔu· ʔatkse·ʔi· ƛaʔu."[36]

She grabs my hand and pulls me toward the forest.

We set out along the path heading for the place where I dropped the firewood. The trail is a bit drier—it hasn't rained since the day before yesterday. Everything is cast in a green hue as light reflects off the soft moss that coats the trees and nests in the forest floor. Just ahead, something rustles in the bushes. A russet-coloured squirrel whose fur looks like Zhuchka's scampers across the path ahead. It leaps onto a tree trunk and scrambles up, chattering and scolding us.

When we reach the dropped wood, Inessa and I work together to divide it into two piles. As we distribute the sticks, I ask, "What does whale meat taste like?" I know she won't understand. Even if she could, is there a comparison that would make sense?

Her eyes slide over and she waits.

"Is it good?" I point back to the beach. I pull my fingers to my lips and pretend to chew. "Does it taste nice?"

Her eyes flicker with recognition. Has she understood?

"čabasaps. čabułeyiks haʔuk ti·kaʔa· du·bačeyał ʔiš wi·y pu-sakšiƛ haʔuk ti·kaʔa,"[37] she says, her eyes enormous, one hand near her mouth, the other on her stomach. She smiles. Then she takes the larger of the piles of wood and we head back to the house.

---

36 Come on. She wants more wood again.

37 I love it. I could eat this every day and never grow tired of eating it.

By the time we return, steam is rising from the vats. After we drop our wood, I peek into a tub: the surface glistens. I look into the next one. It's also shiny. I check the third. It's no different. A woman with a shallow basket skims the surface of one vat and pours it into a different vat. I think I understand: all that grease we eat, the bladders and boxes and dishes full every single meal—how else could they get so much? It's from the whales. We're going to render every drop from the carcass and store it away for the months ahead. I had no notion of it, but I've probably been eating whale every day ever since I was captured on the river so long ago.

In the evening, the Kwih-dihch-chuh-ahts celebrate, and we feast. There are strips and chunks of whale meat, roasted and boiled, in soup, wrapped in leaves, covered in grease, all laid out on the best wooden dishes. There's one dish with carved handles that resemble wings, its rim inlaid with a row of pearly teeth that twinkle when they catch the firelight. There's a big bowl in the shape of a man lying on his back, a braid of hair dangling from the crown of his head.

The slab of whale flesh that had been draped over the pole and carried to Makee's house is on display inside near the fire. The pole is suspended between two notched timbers, and the meat is decorated with feathers, cedar boughs, and the whale's eyeballs, still attached by the sinew that held them together. A shallow wooden tray collects drippings.

Though I've eaten plenty of whale grease, I've not tried the flesh. I take a small bite. It's both strange and familiar. It resembles venison but smells and tastes like brined herring, and I take a second, larger bite. As I'm chewing and trying to decide whether I like it, I notice Inessa watching me. When I catch her eye, she smiles and, just as she did on the trail, she lays her hand on her stomach.

A man beside her nudges her, and she looks away and raises her smiling face to him. He takes something out of the tray and puts it in front of her. It's the man with the scar on his chest— who came aboard the brig, who came to the last feast. She rises and walks slowly toward the cooking boxes. Her hips sway. The man's eyes follow her.

There's no koliuzhi celebration without singing and dancing, and this one is no exception. Makee, in his whale hat, and his wife, in a resplendent cape with two whales painted on the back, dance. To the slow beat of a drum, the two turn toward one another and circle, taking big steps. As the beat of the drum picks up, their circles grow smaller and they move closer together. When they reach the centre, they whirl around one another like they're dancing the Polish mazurka that everyone was learning when I left Petersburg. Makee and his wife send white down spinning in all directions. When they finish, they each drink deeply from a water box that's been decorated with feathers.

A number of women gather in the centre of the floor. Many of the cooks are among them, their faces still flushed from their labour, wisps of their hair flying loose. When the drumming starts, they circle, shuffling their feet, their hands open before them, palms up, their arms pumping in time to the beat of the drum. It seems as though they're lifting the sky.

Next, four men carry a thick, heavy plank into the centre of the floor. The people must move to let them pass and many cry out gleefully when they notice the arrival of the plank. Drumming begins, the beat urgent and aligned with the drumming of the benches.

The four men raise the plank. Then, they let one end plummet. They tilt it, twist it, and then raise it again in big slow circles like they're drawing figure eights in the smoky air. They move slowly, trying not to strike any of the people at the front who are watching.

Sweat glitters on the foreheads of the four men. When the plank is held at a certain angle, I notice a flash of colour. There's a small red dot painted on it, no bigger than the size of a berry.

Makee steps into the circle. He carries a stiff white feather. People cry out.

He stops, raises the feather, and examines it. He strokes it, pressing flat its vanes. Then he begins to dance alongside the plank.

He follows it. When it rises, so does his arm. When it turns, he follows. When it falls, nearly to the floor, he drops and creeps along behind it.

The plank, I understand, is the whale. The feather is his harpoon.

With no warning, Makee aims, snaps his fingers, and throws. His aim is true. The feather hits the red dot on his first try, and bounces off the plank, fluttering to the floor. Cheers rumble off the walls like thunder.

When I go outside later to relieve myself, the sky is clear. Though I wish I had my telescope, the constellations are brilliant enough tonight. It seems proper that I look for Cetus the Whale. Her big belly is turned, as always, to Orion the Hunter. I think Makee would be pleased to know that tonight the entire sky is a mirror for his successful hunt. I say good night to my beloved Polaris before I head back along the path to the house.

This period of gruelling work and fervent celebrations lasts four days. On the morning of that last day, when there's nothing left on the beach but the skeleton, it, too, is dismantled. Men saw apart the huge bones. The largest are laid in shallow trenches that surround the houses. Makee tells me they direct the flow of heavy rain away, while keeping leaves and needles from clogging the gutters. The big scapula that look like wings are set aside, and Makee says he'll use them next time there's a crack in one of the walls of his house.

"All the outside bones of the skeleton are solid, but the inside ones are quite porous. We need them, too. We can make combs and ornaments from them. And they're good for certain tools. Spindle whorls need to be light and strong. We also use them to make a tool we need to turn the cedar bark into threads."

"Aren't they too fragile for tools?"

"Not really. The pores are what makes them so sturdy. They're harder to carve than wood, and so, usually the carver decides what to make only after he sees the bone he's working with."

When the four days are over, everyone is full. I can hardly imagine being hungry ever again. We've produced many bladders plump with whale oil that are stored away in the house. At night, the foot of each building is lit up by moonlight reflected off gleaming new bones. But it's not just tangible gifts the whale's left behind. There's also a mood of contentment that continues for many days.

"Anna, drop your wood," Makee orders. His face is pale, his voice strained. He's wearing his red jacket, his trousers, and his beaver hat. He's come into the forest, partway along the path, to meet me. "We have to leave." I release the bundle of wood from my arms. "Hurry."

He strides ahead, and I scramble to follow. "What's wrong? Where are we going?" Either he doesn't hear or he's ignoring me.

After a short time and a long time, we arrive at the beach where men are boarding two canoes. "Makee—excuse me—is there a ship?" Hope swells in my heart, and a powerful longing for my husband pushes every thought from my head. If there's a ship, I'll see him very soon.

Makee looks at me distractedly. "No. Get in. Please."

I climb into the canoe he indicates, but he gets into the other one. There are many other men coming with us. They steer the canoes out to sea and turn south.

The ocean offers little resistance; we're aided by a current that hurries us along. I'm less nervous than I was on my last canoe voyage. The men sing as they dig into the water, paddles plunging deeply to the song's rhythm. We pass the same jagged-edged coastline, the same kelp-strewn beaches, the same defining headlands, the same wide-open sea that bleeds into the sky. The light on the horizon is almost gone when the canoes steer for shore. We'll have to weave through rocky stacks lined up like chimneys along our path. There's a flat-topped island, and behind it, the yawning mouth of a river.

I've returned to where the *Sviatoi Nikolai* ran aground—to where the moustached toyon lives. I'm like Zhuchka chasing her tail around and around.

We land just beyond the river's mouth. These koliuzhi—I remember Makee told me they're the Quileutes—welcome us and lead us by foot up the river to the place just inside the edge of the forest where their settlement lies.

This is where I left Yakov. He should still be here.

Makee joins the moustached toyon on the bench. I can barely see them through the crowd that mills about and presses forward. No one's smiling or laughing. We're not here for a celebration. I scour the heads, looking for Yakov's cap.

Then I see Maria.

No one pays attention as I approach her. She starts when she sees me. "What are you doing here?" she whispers. She pulls me close and holds me for a long time. I kiss her cheeks.

"I came with him," I whisper back, indicating Makee with my chin. "What are *you* doing here?"

"Those people we were with—that wounded boy and the old woman who makes the medicine and the others—they brought me here."

"Where's Yakov?"

She shrugs. "They took him away when they left. I think he went back with them."

"Do you know what's happening?"

Again, she shrugs. "Everyone's been upset for days but I don't know why. Where have you been?"

Softly I tell her how I live now. How hard I work with Inessa. The things I've had to learn to do. "I'm nearly a slave now," I say and give a short, wry laugh. A quick glance at Maria makes me realize I've said something wrong. She looks at me sharply. I redden.

I change the subject. "I have other news. Their toyon speaks Russian."

"What?" Maria cries. A woman peers at us. "How?" she says more softly.

"He learned it a long time ago from some Russian sailors."

Maria frowns at Makee. She's assessing his jacket, trousers, beaver hat—and his boots. "He looks very strange," she finally says, "as if he's walked out of a house from far away."

"He's very kind, in spite of how odd he appears."

Makee speaks and he's even more distressed than he was before we left Tsoo-yess. He's angry, too. The moustached toyon responds with irritation. Is he unhappy with Makee? I can't be certain. I turn back to Maria.

"What about you? Do they treat you kindly?"

Maria nods. "I also work every day—just as you do. Sometimes I help the woman who does the medicine here. But it's fine—maybe even a little better. There's much less work than on the ship, and what they ask me to do—it's not as wearying."

Nikolai Isaakovich told me that the Russian-American Company was very generous with Aleuts like Maria. It offered them a way out of their remote villages where eking out a living was almost impossible. It gave them food, clothing, medicine, and good jobs. Once they paid back their debts to the company, many went on to live very comfortable lives. I didn't argue, but I knew from the discussion among my father's friends that it wasn't quite like that.

Until now, I never thought Maria aware of these abstract debates. I thought her willing to perform her duties until she earned her freedom, and maybe even a little grateful for the opportunity. My work with Inessa has changed the way I see the things my father's friends debated night after night. I peer at Maria.

"Where are the others? Have you heard news?" she asks.

I shake my head. "I haven't seen anybody. You're the first."

In the morning, Makee seeks me out. He looks like he didn't sleep all night. "Anna, I need your help," he says. "Something terrible has happened."

"What is it?"

"It's my sister. She's been taken by your people."

"I beg your pardon?"

"Your people have captured my sister. Her husband is frantic."

So—this is the source of Makee's distress, of the moustached toyon's irritation, of the upset that Maria said had plagued the

Quileutes for days. But is it possible? It makes no sense. "Are you certain?"

"She was seized a few days ago. Everyone's tried to negotiate her release, but your people won't let her go."

What's come over the crew? Why are they still battling the koliuzhi? I'd have thought they'd be trying to get to the *Kad'iak*, or at least settling in for the winter until fairer weather made the voyage south possible.

"What can I do?"

"They wish to exchange her freedom for yours. Yours—and all the Russians'. Once you're released, they'll free my sister and the other prisoners."

"Others? How many are there?"

"Three. My sister, a young woman, and the man guarding them. Anna—the life of my sister is more valuable to me than anything I own. Please help me."

My rescue is within reach. Before the end of the day, I could be back with Nikolai Isaakovich, with my beloved Zhuchka. I could hold my telescope up to my eye once again, turn the pages of my star log, and go over the sightings I made from the brig's deck. No more long days spent scouring the forest for firewood. No more struggling under the weight of basket after basket of fresh water.

Could we make it to our destination? We're as far away from the *Kad'iak* as we were on the day the brig ran aground. Conditions have become worse. It's colder, rainier, we have nothing to eat, and, most importantly, we do not know where we're going. I'm almost certain we're neither strong nor well-equipped enough to make it. Or, even if we were to make it, would the *Kad'iak* still be waiting for us? So much time has passed.

"I have other news—I've been told there are two European ships sailing the coast right now," Makee says.

"Isn't it too early?"

"It's earlier than ever before but it's possible."

Ships! Two! And from Europe!

"I've asked the Chalats to give you some food and show you the trail. Everyone's been informed—if they see those two ships, they will tell them where to find you. If you see the ships first, then you can arrange your own passage. No one will disturb you for the rest of your journey. Anna—please."

I nod my head slowly, considering my release and how, at last, it's so close to being within my grasp. "Then take me to my husband."

Maria and I and about twenty koliuzhi—Kwih-dihch-chuh-ahts and Quileutes—follow a trail that winds through the forest. We meet countless streams; some we follow for a time, while others we cross by balancing along narrow, fallen trees that span the water's width or by leaping to the opposite bank. Maria is slow and falls behind. I stay with her. I offer her my hand when there is no choice other than to jump. She's as light as a child and shockingly easy to pull across.

Eventually, we ascend along a steep, slippery path that leads partway up a slope. It levels out and we follow it as it skirts a mountainside. The trail here is dry and clear of foliage. An expansive valley widens below us, with a river snaking through it.

This is the route I took in the opposite direction with Yakov when I was sent to Tsoo-yess.

We descend into the valley and start to walk its length.

Just ahead on the trail, I see that the others, including Makee, have stopped. Maria and I catch up. What's drawn their attention is a ring of charred wood and several planks leaning against a clump of scrubby trees.

The foliage in this grove has been flattened as though the planks had lain on top of it. The broken stalks of dried grass are folded over in layers that lie atop one another. All the small sticks are gone, too, probably for the fire. The men are disturbed by what they've found, and I feel it, too. There's something haunted about this place, and if my mother were here, she'd say the leshii was nearby.

I try to catch Makee's eye but he's deep in conversation with one of the other men. So I look to Maria but she's staring wide-eyed at the edge of the charred ring.

There's a vivid white bone pressed into the earth. Against the black cinders, it glows. Farther away, scattered at the men's feet, there are tufts of russet-coloured fur. Something struggled and died here. I look down at my own feet. There's a big clump of that same russet fur attached to skin that's attached to a curl of white fur.

Zhuchka?

I fall to my knees. I touch it. It's her tail. It's cold and damp. The edge of the skin is straight and clean. It's been cut with a knife.

Somebody used a knife.

"Makee," I cry. I point to the remains of my beloved Zhuchka. "This was my dog."

Makee looks at me with pity in his eyes and the instant he opens his mouth to reply, before he even speaks the words, I understand what happened. "Your people must have been very hungry," he says softly and lowers his eyes.

I cover my face and bend until I'm folded over my knees and just a small ball, another layer atop the trampled grass. I wish the earth would swallow me. I want everyone to go away and leave me alone. I want this nightmare to be over.

I know none of them cared for her. None of them even looked at her other than as an tool that helped them do their work, or as something to torment when they were bored. Couldn't they see that it was not like that for me? When I held her head in my hands, when her eyes met mine and her tail thumped on the deck, I knew she was much more than that.

What is the sense of being released? We're never going to make it out of here on our own.

I won't trade my new life in Tsoo-yess with the certainty of rescue for some meaningless freedom that ensures nothing except that I'll be lost in the wilderness with those brutes until we all die.

Across the river, Timofei Osipovich shouts, "Madame Bulygina!"

Like shadows, the men emerge from the trees. Brooding Kozma Ovchinnikov is hunched over, his hair stragglier than ever. Everything about him that once scared me has diminished, and he seems pathetic now. The carpenter Kurmachev is barefoot, his cheeks so sunken he looks like an old man with no teeth. Has he still got his flask? I doubt it. He must be faring poorly without his rum. The American John Williams has stringy hair that now reaches his shoulders and a pale beard that's growing in patches. His greatcoat is missing all its buttons. Everyone is shockingly filthy and spiritless, and for a moment, I pity them so much I almost forgive them for eating Zhuchka.

Then I catch my breath. "Where's Kolya?" I cry.

"He's upriver—at our camp. Not more than a versta from here," replies Timofei Osipovich. "He's fine."

"Why isn't he here?"

"He's coming. Don't worry." But the men shift uneasily, and I begin to sense something is wrong. Others are missing, too. Where's the main rigger, Khariton Sobachnikov? He's so tall, I should be able to spot him among the men, if he's here.

"Where is my sister?" Makee says. He's right beside me on the riverbank. Two canoes rest on our shore, waiting for the exchange to take place. "Ask them where my sister is."

I turn back to Timofei Osipovich. "I've been informed that you've captured three koliuzhi. Where are they?"

The prikashchik nods at his loyal Ovchinnikov. He slips behind some bushes and when he comes out, he's pulling a cord attached to the wrists of Koliuzhi Klara, the woman who wore the silver comb in her hair, and the Murzik.

Koliuzhi Klara has a black eye.

I cry out and cover my mouth. I look to Makee. "That's her," he says. "She's alive."

I know instantly who he means. Her silver comb. His metal cheetoolth. Of course, that's his sister.

"Anna—tell them," Makee urges.

The captives stare dully across the river. Ovchinnikov jerks the end of the rope and they stumble together.

"Anna!" Makee cries out.

"Timofei Osipovich," I shout. "One of those women is the sister of this toyon." I gesture toward Makee. "His name is Makee, and he's a fine man, a gentleman as you can see." I point to his groomed hair, his red jacket, his trousers. "I'm living with his family, and he's been taking good care of me. He's a virtuous man known everywhere for his generosity and kindness and I have no doubt his sister possesses the same qualities. You must release her—and the others as well."

"Let's shoot them," says Ovchinnikov. "All of them."

Makee yelps. All the koliuzhi rush to the edge of the river and nock their arrows.

"Kozma Ovchinnikov! This toyon speaks Russian! He understands everything you say," I cry.

"Shut up, you nattering magpie!" Timofei Osipovich slaps Ovchinnikov, who cries out, as shocked as the rest of us to see his master turn against him. He claps the hand with which he's holding the cord over his ear. Koliuzhi Klara's wrists are jerked up to her chin.

Timofei Osipovich slides into the language I don't understand, his eyes fastened on Makee. Makee listens, then says something to the koliuzhi, and they lower their bows.

Timofei Osipovich reverts to Russian. "We'll free the prisoners once the koliuzhi release you. Your husband insists that you be released first."

"Tell him we accept," Makee says in a low voice.

"In the name of the Emperor, I vow to finish our mission," cries Timofei Osipovich, "and it will not be over until we get you, Madame Bulygina, home. Come now—rejoin our expedition."

"No," I cry. "I will not." Ovchinnikov's mouth gapes, opening up his bushy beard. He looks like I just kicked his shins. "I'm satisfied living with these koliuzhi," I continue. "They've given me a warm place to sleep and plenty to eat. This toyon is arranging my rescue."

I know with certainty the *Kad'iak* is gone. Even if it were still there waiting, there's no chance the crew will ever reach it. A sixty-five-mile walk down this coast is not a summer stroll down Nevsky Prospekt. They'll never survive the rest of the winter.

Tsoo-yess is not Petersburg, and I'm not a free woman while I'm there, but I'll be comfortable enough until I can go home. If anybody can guarantee that I'll get home, it will be Makee, and not these fools. They're lost in many ways, some of which they can't even fathom.

"There are two European ships travelling on this coast right now. As soon as we see them, this toyon will release me into their care, and I'll make my way back home. So I won't join you—and if you have sense, instead you'll join me and these koliuzhi.

"Surrender. And release your prisoners. It's for the best."

The river gurgles in the silence that follows. No one dares move.

"Anna, what are you doing?" Makee says.

"Madame Bulygina, you don't know what you're doing!" shouts Timofei Osipovich.

"I've made up my mind," I call back across the river.

"But your husband—he's a madman ranting day and night about you. You wouldn't speak so callously if you could see him—is this not the truth?" The others nod and grunt in agreement. "You must come. You have no choice."

"I've made my choice. Now you release the prisoners."

"Come to your senses!"

"You come to yours. Release the prisoners. And give up the delusion that you're going to survive without the koliuzhi."

"This—negotiation—is—not—finished," Timofei Osipovich declares. He stomps into the forest. The others follow, pulling the prisoners behind.

"Anna, what have you done?" Makee cries.

"I'm sorry. I'm not going with them. They're fools."

"But you said you would. Now they won't release my sister."

"Don't be so certain. They'll release her. I know they will."

Makee speaks to the koliuzhi men. Four of them launch the canoes and cross the river. They follow Timofei Osipovich and the others into the forest.

Makee and I stand in uncomfortable silence. The shadows are lengthening, and the birds have started their evening song. He turns on me. "Why didn't you go? You said you would."

"I said I'm sorry. They'll release her. Don't worry." I cast aside doubt. I'm an eighteen-year-old woman and I know them all. I know exactly how they'll respond.

Just then we hear voices from the opposite side of the river. Timofei Osipovich bursts onto the river bank, followed by the crew and the koliuzhi. Nikolai Isaakovich is still not with them. Neither are the prisoners.

"Anna Petrovna Bulygina," Timofei Osipovich begins, "I beg you to take pity upon your husband! He was so distraught, he wept! He wept so severely, he decided—God help him—to take your life. I had to stop him. I pried his musket from his grasp. I held him down until the others came to my aid. We tied him up so he wouldn't come here and murder you."

"Your threats are hollow! Nikolai Isaakovich has no intention of murdering me."

"Your husband has lost everything. And when a man loses everything, he can no longer be held responsible for his actions."

"I scorn all threats."

"Anna—please—" Makee says hoarsely. "Please go."

"By orders of this toyon, release your prisoners now!" I add.

"You will force his hand Madame Bulygina if I convey your words," calls Timofei Osipovich.

"And you will force this toyon's if you don't release the prisoners now!"

"As you wish then," Timofei Osipovich says coldly, and heads back into the forest with the rest of the crew. Makee's men follow him and I wonder if they'll return with the prisoners in tow. I think they will.

Evening is upon us and I'm chilled through when the koliuzhi return—alone. Timofei Osipovich isn't with them, nor is Nikolai Isaakovich and his musket. Nor are the prisoners. Makee asks them several questions. Then they board the canoes and return to our shore.

As we begin the long trek back to the village where we spent last night, Makee again turns on me, his voice raised. "I trusted you, Anna. You said you would go. They'll never release my sister now."

"Maybe they'll release her tomorrow," I say timidly. I'm cowed by the anger I've never seen in him before, and confused by the crew's failure to release their prisoners.

"I don't believe that."

The damp night air settles on us. The sky is black, and the few stars strewn overhead that we glimpse through the trees twinkle distantly. I don't have the heart to look for my Polaris. The moon was full only a few days ago, so there remains enough light that we can follow the trail easily enough.

When we reach the village, Maria and I are directed to separate houses. I'll go to bed alone, but will I sleep at all? I've let Makee and his sister down. The Murzik and Koliuzhi Klara, too. The image of her black eye is burned into my heart.

They'll release everyone tomorrow. They must. And if they're smart, they'll join Makee at the same time.

The next morning, Makee and the koliuzhi men from yesterday disappear down the trail. I'm not asked to accompany them. No one tells me what they intend to do once they see the crew.

I'm confined to the house all day. I don't see Maria. With nothing to do, I scrape dried mud from my boots and my dress and watch the familiar routines of this house. A woman leaves with a basket—she's going to collect kindling. Another pours water into the cooking boxes—she's preparing a meal. There's a baby strapped into a cradle suspended in a quiet corner of the house. Some women in a circle play a game with curved dice that look like they're made of teeth. Children play their own game with paddles and a twig with feathers they knock back and forth until the twig lands in a cooking box and they're sent outdoors.

Nothing breaks the day's dullness except the thoughts that hound me.

Late in the afternoon, there's a disturbance outside. A cluster of people bursts through the door. It's Makee and his men. People rise to their feet. Some rush to the door, calling out. Makee beams. I don't see his sister, Koliuzhi Klara, or the Murzik. Makee pushes through the crowd and inserts himself before the moustached toyon. They embrace. The crowd and the news flow around the house and one by one, I see faces light up with joy.

Then, entering the house: Timofei Osipovich. Grinning.

Brooding Ovchinnikov and two Aleuts.

And, right behind them, there's Nikolai Isaakovich. Glowering.

As they approach, my feelings fall like Tarot cards one on top of the other, each fortune cancelling out the one beneath it. When Kolya draws near, despite all that's passed these last few weeks, there's an involuntary tug at my heart.

"Good evening, Madame Bulygina," blusters Timofei Osipovich. "How soon we get the pleasure of your company once again." His hands open in a gesture of welcome incongruous with his mocking tone.

"I'm not going with you," I say. "I told you yesterday."

Timofei Osipovich laughs. "Yes, you made that perfectly clear. But don't worry. You're not going anywhere. No one is."

Nikolai Isaakovich cuts him off. "Anna Petrovna, you've made a mess of everything. Do you know what you've done?"

"Nikolai Isaakovich, I don't understand. Why are you here?"

"Madame Bulygina, we've taken your advice," says Timofei Osipovich. "We've released our prisoners. They're back where they belong. As for us—we've come to join your toyon."

"You have?"

"You said we should. We decided to listen to you. Why are you so surprised?"

"Where is the rest of the crew?"

"They've decided not to join us. They want to try to get to the *Kad'iak*. Their fate will be wrought by their own hands."

Nikolai Isaakovich looks as though he really would murder me now. But whatever misgivings he may have, their change of heart is for the best. Eventually my husband will understand. We're on the right path now. In the end, we'll all get back home.

SPRING AND SUMMER 1809

———————

CHAPTER THIRTEEN

Tonight, we're split up. Nikolai Isaakovich and the crew remain in this toyon's house while Maria and I are sent to a different house to sleep. We're like spinster sisters once again sharing a mat and some bedclothes. When I lie down, thoughts whirl around my head like untethered shadows. The decision I made on the riverbank seemed so clear, but in the dark, where not even the stars can reach, it's transformed into a restless spirit that won't let me alone.

When Maria settles herself, her silence is too much.

"Joining Makee is our only choice," I say. "You see that, don't you?"

She doesn't budge, and I think she's already asleep. But then she mutters, "I see everything—and nothing."

"That's impossible. You can't."

"No? Well, I'm too old to do otherwise."

"Well, I believe Makee," I insist.

"I hope you're right."

"I am. He's going to get us home." My decision is sound and well-considered. The prisoners were released—Makee's sister is free—and we're going home as soon as a ship arrives. Eventually Nikolai Isaakovich will agree. "I just don't know how to make my husband understand. He's so stubborn."

She's quiet for so long I wonder if she's fallen asleep. Then she murmurs, "You seem so certain. Perhaps he doesn't share that. Perhaps he thinks you're not seeing the whole picture."

"What picture? Without Makee, our situation is hopeless."

If only she would offer some reassurance, perhaps I could rest. I lie still, waiting for a sign. But all I detect from her side of the mat is her breath, so slow and measured. Finally, she speaks. "You say joining that toyon is the only choice. And you might be right. But why are you surprised your husband doesn't see it that way? Surely he's ashamed that his own wife forced him to give up command. And perhaps he's worried about the ones who didn't surrender. Is your decision going to help them?"

"You don't know my husband," I cry. "You don't know anything about what he thinks and how he feels."

"Then what about that toyon? He doesn't seem very happy with you either."

After she's spoken, I feel even more confused. Try as I might, sleep evades me all night.

I'm awake in the morning before everyone else, and when I go out to relieve myself, no one follows. After I finish, instead of going back inside, I walk along the river's edge toward the sea. The sky is clear, and the western horizon indigo blue. As the sun rises, my shadow is thrown out before me, tall and rippling over uneven ground as I walk. It's like I'm breaking apart.

At the river's mouth, the sea glitters where the early morning sun reaches it. The waves rise and tumble over themselves, drawing white, lacy lines along the water's surface. The sea is calm today but, even so, it never rests.

I stop beside several pools of water that have collected at the base of a rock carved smooth by the waves. In one pool, purple and pink sea stars are wedged together, their arms clinging to one another and the rock. Waves wash over them, bathing them in salt water. I climb the rock. An eagle flies into view, swoops over the sea, wings yawning. With a flap and a pivot, it lifts itself and sails over my head, drawing a wide arc that leads it back over the forest and out of view.

I imagine it's going home.

After Maria and I eat, we're called to the water's edge where the canoes sit. My husband huddles with the rest of the Russians. They're like moths gathered around a lamp. My husband raises his eyes as I approach, and glowers.

Makee speaks quietly with our hosts and does not look at me.

Then, the moustached toyon declares, "Liʔátsḳal axʷół xabáʔ. Watalik ti asʔostoʔó,"[38] and Makee's people move toward the canoes.

No journey ever begins, and no visit ever ends without singing. An older man on the beach delivers a line, everyone responds, and then he sings another. Back and forth, they're like priest and congregation during Mass. We stand at the edge of the water, where land, river, and sea all meet, but I imagine I smell incense and feel the chill of old stone just as I would if I were in Vladimirskiy Cathedral on a winter day.

Maria lightly touches my shoulder. "You're going now," she says.

"Back to Tsoo-yess," I say. "Aren't you coming?"

"No. I'll stay here. I won't see you until next time."

I turn my back to the people boarding the canoes. I close myself from the music and the sea and face only Maria. Trying to understand what she means by "next time" is like trying

---

38 Thank you and farewell. You did everything appropriately.

to imagine a Sunday afternoon at home with my parents in Petersburg.

"No. We're not leaving you here," I say.

She embraces me. "You'll need the forbearance of the old trees," she murmurs and then releases me with a decisive push. When she does, I realize she really is staying.

"We'll be back," I promise. "We'll be back for you."

"The koliuzhi are waiting."

I climb into the canoe to which they direct me. It's not Makee's. His is already well into the channel, and paddlers are pulling against the surf and inching the vessel to sea. My husband, Timofei Osipovich, and the rest of the surrendered crew are in that canoe, too.

Into the mouth of the river the singing follows us, strong as the sea and the wind, as if it, too, will help carry us home. I wave for as long as I can see Maria on the shore. She does not wave back, but she remains until we pass beyond the headland and I can no longer see her.

As we disembark at Tsoo-yess, we're received into song. Women, children, and men have gathered on the beach to welcome us home. Others are drumming on the rooftops, the thunderous sound shaking the ground beneath our feet. White down that, from a distance, looked like snow has been strewn plentifully for our arrival.

"Wacush! Wacush!" the Kwih-dihch-chuh-ahts cry.

The festivities that mark our return spin around us like a whirlwind crossing a field of dry grass. The gulls shriek, disrupted by our arrival. In the chaos, my husband is nudged over until he's at my side. "How was your journey?" I ask. He looks me up and down before allowing himself to be swept back up into the throng.

Makee's family has prepared a feast—fresh halibut and clams and roasted potatoes. Everyone's wearing their finest clothing and jewellery. Makee's wife wears a white dress with a beaded bodice—korolki in the pattern of a star. Inessa has a woven band of bark around her head and a new fringed and beaded belt around her waist. She smiles when she sees me, but immediately turns back to her work.

Hours later, everyone retires for the night. In my old corner, I lay out a new, larger mat that will accommodate me and Nikolai Isaakovich. The cedar mat walls are erected around the house, and the Kwih-dihch-chuh-ahts settle. The edges of the bedclothes of the people I can see are illuminated by light from the dying embers. Conversations are muted, children are hushed, and even though he's turned away from me, I wait for my husband to say something.

When I can wait no longer, I say in a low voice, "You've misunderstood. You don't know my side of it."

He burns with rage—I can feel it—but he says nothing.

"Makee is going to save us."

Tension presses against the edges of our contained space.

"Kolya, there are two ships on the coast. Two European ships. The koliuzhi have seen them. They could arrive any day now."

My husband rolls over and thrusts his face close to mine. His breath is sharp, like rusty metal. "Anna Petrovna, there are no ships. That's why the Tsar sent us. So we'd be first."

"But the koliuzhi saw them."

"And have you?"

Grey sea, grey sky, a grey horizon, all merged together, one single flat expanse that stretches as far as the eye is permitted to go—that's all I've seen offshore. The only two ships I have any certainty about are the *Sviatoi Nikolai* and the *Kad'iak*—they're ours—and one is wrecked.

"A ship will come. Makee promised we'll be rescued."

"Rescued? We're slaves. Thanks to you," he says in a voice too loud for this quiet house.

He doesn't realize what he's saying. What he knows of slavery and the serfs is what happens in Russia and in Russian America. He's not given the koliuzhi a chance. Besides, we're going home.

The fire pops.

"Kolya, please," I say softly. "You don't understand. Makee already arranged the rescue of an American. He told me all about it." I remember the metal cheetoolth, and his sister's silver comb. "He'll do the same for us."

"How dangerous of you to believe a toyon who calls himself Poppy Seed."

"Makee's virtuous—and kind—and there's plenty to eat. There are cabbages here, Kolya. Cabbages!"

"You would value our freedom less than a cabbage?"

"And you would value mine less than four muskets?" He seems to have forgotten the botched rescue on the riverbank, the intractability of the crew, and his own failure to take command.

"You don't know what you're talking about. You've betrayed not only me but the entire empire. We're doomed because of you."

But he's wrong. We were doomed from the moment the *Sviatoi Nikolai* ran aground. Good fortune has allowed us to make it this far, and now there's a way out. Why can't my husband see the truth?

"Kolya, please stop quarreling. It gets us nowhere. We have to be strong and stay together." I lift my hand and though he flinches, he lets me touch his face. With my thumb, I caress his cheek, what little of it shows through the even wilder tangle of his overgrown beard.

His eyes grow wide. I understand his apprehension. But when he gives Makee a chance, he'll see. Nikolai Isaakovich is an enlightened man, capable of acting practically and decisively. He will see the sense of our surrender.

Suddenly, he grabs my hand. He squeezes hard.

"Anya," he murmurs. The sharp odour of sweat wafts out from his armpit. He kisses the tips of my fingers. "I've missed you. You don't know."

"No, Kolya." Even though the mats are up and the fire burns low, there's enough light to put us on display. "We can't. Not here."

"If not here—then where? I can't live without you anymore." He slides closer and brings his lips to mine.

I turn my head. "But everyone will hear."

"We'll be quiet." He slides his lips down to my throat. The sound of the kiss he places there fills this quieted house.

I refused him that night in the tent in the forest, and I was successful only because he fell asleep. What's to be done this time?

"Kolya—I love you—but—"

He lays his fingers on my lips, then brings his mouth to my ear and moans softly. "I love you, too, Annichka, you can't imagine—"

He wraps his arm around my hips jerking me to his groin like I'm nothing more than a feather pillow.

"Please. I'm too tired," I whisper. "Tomorrow."

"No—today—right now—"

I could push him away now my hands are free. But I don't. Instead, I wrap my arms around him and hold on. I hold on not because my heart is in it. I hold on and pray that God may help him to lower his voice and that I'll have the strength to show my face in this house tomorrow morning. I hold on because if this passion is the form his forgiveness has taken, then it would be a mistake to push him away.

It hurts when he enters me. But not as much as it would hurt if I had to tolerate more of his punishing silence.

❧

In the morning, Inessa comes to the edge of our cedar mat and stands a respectable distance away. A basket dangles from her shoulder, but I don't want to go. I look away. Inessa hovers in silence.

"I'll come back soon," I finally say to Nikolai Isaakovich. He grunts. Last night has, I hope, brought us closer to a resolution of our differences.

Outside, Inessa gives me the basket. I follow her, and she stops at another house where she gets her own basket, and, for the first time, another girl joins us. She's no older than me or Inessa. Her cedar bark dress has long fringes that reach just below her knees. She tilts her head as she looks at me, then says something to Inessa, who responds briefly.

Then we head down the trail that leads to the sea.

All the way along the path, the girls talk and laugh. I don't know what they're saying but I think the new girl is teasing Inessa. She says something, Inessa cries out in horror, and the new girl shrieks with laughter and runs away. Inessa chases her, waving her basket high and wide as though she intends to hit her. I follow them but, since I soon lose sight of them, I don't know how their joking ends.

The path turns, and around the corner I see them again. They've stopped next to a tree trunk. They're picking off the gum, putting it in their mouths and chewing. When I draw close, Inessa says, "ku·, yałi?i·k łaƙitbis."[39]

She offers me a golden dollop. Gum is already smeared over her knuckles and the little scar on her hand.

I take it from her. It's very sticky and covered with bits of bark and a fly. She says something and gestures for me to put it in my

---

39 Here, have some gum.

mouth. I dig out the fly and flick it away, but I can't do anything about the bits of bark.

The gum tastes like the smell of the tree itself, like medicine, like a certain tea one of my mother's elderly friends used to drink in the winter. It's all crumbly but after only a moment, it turns soft and starts to stick to my teeth. I poke it with my tongue and suck using my cheeks. Inessa and the other woman laugh at the funny expressions I'm making.

But they're no different. They open their mouths to show each other, and then urge me to open mine. The gum is stuck to all our teeth. I laugh, too. With our mouths gaping open, we look like a nest of baby birds.

We take our baskets and continue down the trail, each of us sucking at our teeth.

We go much farther than I've ever been along this trail and finally take an abrupt turn and emerge from the trees onto a shoreline I've never seen before. It's rugged here, and much wilder than the coast near our houses. Tangled ropes of kelp are strewn about the slender beach that's covered with small stones the size of quail eggs. At one end, there's a reddish-brown headland with the sea churning at its base. At the other end, there's a smooth rock that bulges up out of the beach.

The girls throw their baskets down and run along the shore, kicking water at each other. Their shrieks rise over the sound of the sea. Seabirds float nervously offshore and watch them. Then, as abruptly as it began, their game ends. Panting and smiling, they lead me to the end of the beach where the bulging rock lies. A gull, startled by our approach, takes flight and disappears into the grey. The girls remove tools from the bottom of their baskets—some sharp, others blunt—and then they point. We're here for mussels.

"ƛuča·b!" cries the girl and waves her hand across the rocks. "ƛuča·b!"

"Kluchab," I repeat their word for mussels. They both laugh and Inessa nudges the girl with her shoulder. The girl beams. "Kluchab!" I cry and nod my head. They look pleased with me.

We clamber over and around the rock, collecting some large mussels, some small ones, but never stripping a patch bare. I watch them. They mostly don't use the tools. There's a way of twisting the shells that makes them snap right off, and I try it too.

After managing a few mussels, I cut myself. Despite all the work I've done with Inessa, my hands are still too soft.

What have I done with my hands all my life? There were the years of writing and reading at my father's side. The telescopes and the infinitesimally small moves needed to focus them. There was the needlework. Washing and beautifying myself. Eating. I'd held hands in a dance. Rubbed balm into them to keep them soft. I'd cut my fingers from time to time on sharp edges and thorns I didn't expect to encounter. My hands could tell a story of a life filled with pleasure and indulgence.

The white scar on Inessa's hand has stood out for me ever since the first time I met her. I'd felt sorry for her, as I knew how carefully all girls try to maintain a flawless appearance. But perhaps her scar, that perfectly shaped crescent moon, as pale against her skin as the real moon is in the night sky, might be an indication of her physical strength and evidence of all the things she's done with her hands during her lifetime. Perhaps her scar is precious to her. Perhaps she pities me my hands and the small, cramped life they reveal.

We leave many mussels behind, and yet we easily fill all three baskets. They help me once their own are filled. Then, it's time to head home. They slide the baskets onto their backs and slip the bands over their heads. I try to do the same, but because my basket is much heavier than I expect, it spills. The mussels clatter onto the stones, the entire morning's work lost among small rocks. Inessa and the other girl laugh, but they help pick up all the mussels, and then hold the basket on my back while I slip the band over my forehead.

When we reach the houses, I follow the girls down to the sea. We place our three baskets in sheltered waters near the shore, immersing the mussels. The baskets lean together. We bring some of what we collected to the women crouched over the cooking boxes. Perhaps for supper I'll get a taste. Perhaps by supper, the last of the tree gum will have dissolved from my teeth.

Nikolai Isaakovich returns to the house long after I've come back. His hair is straggly, his cheeks ruddy, and he smells of the ocean.

"They took us to hunt seals," he says. "You can't imagine how many were in the cove—floating, swimming, sleeping on the rocks—they were everywhere."

"Did you catch many?"

"My God, you could almost pluck them from the sea like they were pansies. They tied their canoes to the kelp, right in the middle of a herd. All we had to do was lean over the gunwales. They wouldn't let us use the harpoons, but they sure were happy we were there to help lift the carcasses into the canoes.

"Anya—a child—a little boy—he killed the fattest seal I've ever seen in my life. Just like that." He snaps his fingers and lowers his voice. "If the chief manager could see it. He'd have a schooner here in a fortnight and we'd fill its hold in even less time. The koliuzhi can only take a fraction of what's available. They don't realize what they've got."

Don't they? I think of Nikolai Isaakovich's seals—and of the number of mussels we left behind. What would happen if the schooners were to come? This is what the Imperial Decree tells us is our purpose. We'd become rich. We'd give the koliuzhi a fair trade—beads and cloth and iron tools and perhaps even a few muskets. What then?

Everyone thought sea otters were as countless as the stars. All along the coast that stretches from Russia to Novo-Arkhangelsk, they certainly seemed to be; then they disappeared from around Petropavlovsk. Next, they vanished from Kad'iak and all the other tiny islands. They're almost impossible to find along the shores around Novo-Arkhangelsk. Our own mission is to discover the next place where they're still to be found in abundance—and to take them before that place is as bereft of sea otters as the rest of the coast has become.

Would it be any different with the seals? The mussels? If the schooners were to come as my husband imagines, what would the koliuzhi do? Where would they get the shells and teeth and claws and whiskers and skins and stomachs and intestines—to make their knives and tools and bladders to store the oil and floats for whaling and blankets and clothing? What would they eat instead? And what would happen when the schooners come back for that, too?

When I make our bed at night and lie next to my husband, who falls asleep easily, my thoughts weave back and forth, constructing a useless garment that fits no one.

During the night, the rain starts and when we wake in the morning, it's thundering on the roof. Whoever ventures out, even for a moment, returns soaked, and when I go out to relieve myself, I also return cold and wet as a farmyard hen. I remove my cedar cape and lay it out to dry.

I join my husband, who sits near the fire and stares deeply into the small flames. Many of the Kwih-dihch-chuh-ahts also huddle around the fires, talking softly, sewing, making baskets, weaving, braiding cordage, waiting for the deluge to pass.

Timofei Osipovich, Kozma Ovchinnikov, my husband, and I sit together near the fire.

"It's terrible out there," I say. "I hope the others aren't wandering around in this."

"They should have listened to Timofei Osipovich and come with us," Ovchinnikov says.

Timofei Osipovich laughs, pleased with Ovchinnikov's continuing fidelity. "They'll surrender," he says, "soon enough." He looks smug and so certain that I almost expect him to crow. He doesn't add that he wouldn't be here, warm and sheltered from the rain, if it weren't for me.

"Maybe they found another cave," my husband says. "For their sakes, I hope so."

I imagine the crew, how wet and dejected they must be if all they've got to protect them are the tents made of sails. Even if they've found a cave, they must be miserable.

Ovchinnikov pushes a piece of wood deeper into the fire with his toe. He still has his boots. "What happened to old Yakov?" he says quietly, without meeting my eye.

I forgot—how could he know? He has no idea what's happened to us these past weeks. "I think he's all right. Maria told me he's back with the koliuzhi on the river—the Chalats—the ones who took us prisoner."

"Savages," my husband mutters.

"And Filip Kotelnikov?" Ovchinnikov asks.

"The apprentice is gone. But he's probably fine. Makee told me they sent him south to live with some other koliuzhi. They're Cathlamets, I think he said."

Timofei Osipovich nods. "Good people. He's lucky."

"He hates the koliuzhi," I say. The wind gusts and something outside bangs loudly on the roof. Two young men near the door slide beneath the mat that's covering the opening and go out to look.

I ask nervously, "What about everyone else? After that battle . . ."

Ovchinnikov folds his hands and drops his head so low, his hair casts thick shadows over the little of his face that's normally visible.

"We fared well," Timofei Osipovich says. "We lost only one."

I whisper, "One? Who?"

"Main Rigger Khariton Sobachnikov. God rest his soul." He blesses himself. "An arrow pierced his chest."

There are footsteps and banging overhead. They're fixing the roof in the storm.

I hold my silver cross. I think about all the evenings I spent together with Sobachnikov on the deck of the brig. Together and not together. How he always let me do my work in peace. How he brought my telescope to shore and didn't let a drop of water touch it. "How can that be true?" I say finally.

"We had to leave his body on the riverbank," Timofei Osipovich says. "It was too dangerous to go back for it."

The grey-brown mound. The hungry crows crawling over it, pecking at it, sailing overhead with strips of flesh swinging from their beaks. The stench, the repellent, pervasive stink of death left to the scavengers of the natural world to clean up. It was Sobachnikov. Ovchinnikov steals a glance at my husband, then Timofei Osipovich. My husband opens his mouth to speak, then thinks better of it.

"What? What is it?" I ask. "You must tell me!"

"Anya—" my husband says. "He was killed going back to get the bundle that had your telescope in it."

"What?"

"I told him to leave it. But he wouldn't listen. He didn't want to break his promise."

I crush my face in my hands and press until I think a bone will break, a bone must break. He should have broken that promise. He had nothing to fear. Everybody saw how vicious that battle was; every man did what he could. Who would find fault with him? There must be some restitution for Sobachnikov's senseless death. Where is justice? My telescope is gone and so is my star log. But they're not enough.

We must withstand this ordeal. We must endure in memory of Khariton Sobachnikov. We must not let his death be in vain. By the side of this fire, with the heavens opening overhead, I press my hand into my silver cross and vow to do whatever is necessary for us to survive and make it home.

"Anna? Please come," says Makee, in the afternoon, the rain still pounding on the roof. He's on the bench at his end of the house with the three men with whom he often confers. His metal chee-toolth is cradled in his hands. We've not spoken since his sister's been freed, and I dread this moment.

My husband glares at Makee and starts to rise. Timofei Osipovich looks at my face, then places a hand on my husband's arm and shakes his head in warning.

I cross the floor. It takes forever. When I arrive and stand before him, I feel like a child. He must think less of me. The only question is: How much less?

"Is your sister well?" I begin.

"Yes, she's at home. She seemed quite tired when I last saw her, but she was as well as could be expected."

"I'm sorry I broke my promise. I didn't mean to hurt anybody."

"She's not hurt. Thankfully. And neither are the others."

"I know I made a promise. But I realized as soon as I saw

everyone across the river that it was wrong. It was a terrible error for me to make that promise."

Makee and the men sitting with him look away toward the fire. I turn to see what's drawn their attention, but it's passed. There's only Ovchinnikov, staring at his hands, and Timofei Osipovich, his hand still resting on my husband's arm. The fire casts very little light, but it's enough to truly see how haggard they are, how everything between us is in disarray. It's a miracle that only one man is dead. "We need you, Makee. No one will get home without you." My voice cracks. "No one will survive."

He presses his lips together and frowns. "You thought only of your people. You broke your word and jeopardized my sister's life."

"She's free, isn't she?" I mumble. "Isn't that what you wanted?"

"Yes, that's what I wanted. But not like this," he cries. His hand sweeps toward the fire. "What am I to do with all of you until a ship takes you away?"

"We'll work. We'll try to live as you do. Just as you requested. Please—we won't be any trouble."

He turns the cheetoolth in his hands. A carved eye stares at me. "Your people have already caused a lot of trouble."

"It's only until the next ship. And you said there are already two ships nearby. Please—we need your help."

"Along the entire coastline, when there are too many babathid around, there is always trouble."

"I'll talk to my husband. He's in command. I'll tell him that everyone's got to listen to you."

He says something to the three men sitting beside him. One responds.

"And those who you left behind in the forest—who will tell them to leave us alone?" Makee says. "To stop shooting at us and stealing our food?"

"They're leaving. They're walking south. They think there's a Russian ship—far away. They're already gone."

He says something else to the three men. The same one responds, then another adds his thoughts. Makee listens while I try to understand what they're saying.

Makee speaks briefly then turns back to me. He sets his cheetoolth down on the bench.

"I forgive you, Anna. But you must speak to your husband. And from now on, I will hold you to your word."

CHAPTER FOURTEEN

———————————

"Why should I do anything for that Poppy Seed?" my husband says.

"Nikolai Isaakovich, there's no choice."

"Of course there's no choice. Anna Petrovna, we're slaves! Prisoners! And these koliuzhi are only waiting for a chance to murder us."

"They're waiting for a ship—just like us."

The sun is sinking into the ocean. The rain has ended and the heavy clouds have moved away, and now the sky is alive with pink and purple, the colour of boiled beetroot, the colour of the sea stars I saw in the pool beside the rock. There's a brush of gold hovering over the cobalt sea. It's a rare evening both for this sunset and for the fact that I'm watching it with my husband as though it's a display of Chinese fireworks and we're attending a gathering at a grand dacha outside Petersburg.

"Nikolai Isaakovich, if you don't order the crew to cooperate, we're never going to get out of here. Makee made me promise that we wouldn't make any further trouble for them."

"Make trouble—for them?" He laughs cruelly. "That Poppy Seed toyon is cunning. He has a scheme. You'll see."

I shake my head, no, but in the dying light—the sun is a

glowing dome about to disappear into the water—he's the one who doesn't see.

I'll have to find another way to fulfill my promise to Makee.

"Could I have a word with you—in private?"

Timofei Osipovich cackles. "With me? Are you sure? Whatever for?"

"We can discuss that when we're alone."

"Lead me where you will then," he says. "I put myself in your lovely hands."

I don't want to go anywhere with him, but since my husband refuses to agree and Makee's counting on me, I must find another way to convince the crew that cooperation with Makee is in everyone's best interests. My husband won't like it, but if I handle it skilfully, he need never know my part in it. I've seen it time after time on this trip. If I can persuade Timofei Osipovich, the others will follow, and it won't seem like I'm undermining my husband.

I lead him down to the stony beach where the canoes rest. There are some girls and boys playing at the water's edge not far from us. They toss fragments of dried seaweed into the wind. The seaweed floats for several seconds, then falls and scuttles along the beach until it comes to rest. The children run alongside the dark shards in a race against one another, against the seaweed. Other than a glance our way when we come to their attention, they pay us no heed.

"Timofei Ospiovich," I begin, "I must ask for assistance concerning a matter of great importance to our future."

"Our future? That's a weighty subject for a pretty girl. Or did you mean our future together—yours and mine?"

"Stop your ridicule or I'll leave."

"Leave? No, please, I can't live without you." He chokes on a sob and brushes fake tears from his eyes. How dare he mock my husband?

"Wait," he calls when I'm halfway up the beach. "Come back."

I stop and face him, trying to determine his sincerity. He's impossible to predict, and the fact remains that I need him. So, I plunge ahead. "Makee is concerned about having us here. He thinks we're going to cause trouble. I told him we wouldn't."

"Well, that goes without question," Timofei Osipovich says, as he strolls over to face me. "We've surrendered. The conquered are never in a position to declare war." The wind blows a strand of his long hair over his face, and he brushes it back and tucks it behind his ear.

"It's not just that. Makee expects us to live peacefully. And to work. To earn our keep until we're rescued."

"I'm happy to lend a hand here and there."

"No," I say, exasperated. "You don't understand. Makee's helping us and we have to help him. I've been collecting firewood and hauling baskets of water to the houses. This week, I'm gathering shellfish. We all have to work until we're rescued."

He laughs. "Tell your toyon he'll have my full cooperation. But between us—I won't be gathering, collecting, or hauling anything. I'm not his slave."

"You don't understand how it is here."

"And what exactly do you understand, Madame Bulygina?" He draws out the "madame" in a way that raises the hair on the back of my neck. "Tell me. What is your experience of slavery? Did your father keep slaves back in Petersburg?"

"They're not slaves," I cry. "They're house serfs." As the words leave my mouth, I think of the arguments of my father's friends. I think of Maria. I feel unsteady and wish I could stop myself, but Timofei Osipovich always knows how to provoke.

He laughs. At me. "And what about your dear husband? You don't actually believe the Aleuts are here with him of their own free will, do you?"

"That arrangement is between them and the company! My husband does not mistreat them!"

He hasn't stopped laughing. "And me? How long before your Tsar's reforms reach me? How much more time before he gives me an estate in the country where I can live like your father does?"

"You leave my father out of it! And tell the others what I said!" I speak so loudly the children on the beach stop racing the seaweed and look over. "Don't put our rescue in jeopardy." I stomp away like I'm no older than the children on the beach, and then chastise myself for failing, once again, to act like I'm eighteen years old. How does he manage to always make me feel so infantile?

"You're working far too hard," he calls.

Despite what he said, Timofei Osipovich must have spoken to the others. The next day, I see his loyal Ovchinnikov and the Aleuts helping the Kwih-dihch-chuh-aht men dig a hole near the houses. With long, pointed sticks, they hack into the soil, breaking it up, and using baskets they move the earth to nearby piles. Ovchinnikov's stick snaps, and he curses, but a man gives him another one. The hole grows deep and by the end of the day, it's a pit.

I see neither my husband nor Timofei Osipovich taking part in the digging and I wonder how they've been exempt from the task. I hope they're not idle, or, if they are, I hope Makee is not aware of their indolence.

In the evening, as we eat around the fire, I ask, "Where were you all day?"

My husband glances sideways at Timofei Osipovich and says, "We were on the other side of the headland."

"Working," says Timofei Osipovich. "I was told it would be advisable if we were to work." He looks at me, raises his eyebrows, and smiles.

He didn't say something to my husband. Did he? Nikolai Isaakovich keeps his eyes on his meal, and I know better than to ask anything further. They're working; that's all that matters.

The next day, I notice the Aleuts and Ovchinnikov helping make planks from a log that's washed up on the beach. With a heavy stone tool, a man pounds wedges into the wood. Each strike rings out across the bay. The Aleuts hold the plank and guide it away from the log, as it splits down its length. Its final release from the log is gentle; it comes apart with no effort. Then, Ovchinnikov and other men carry the planks from the beach up toward the houses. They must be heavy—it takes four men to carry each plank.

I watch them make the planks from down the beach, where I'm with Inessa and the other girl. We've pulled the baskets of mussels from the sea and we're removing their fibrous beards. They're coarse like dried straw, and sometimes so firmly fastened to the mussels that I can't detach them without a knife. I add each beard to a heap the girls started. Eventually, there's enough to stuff a mattress though it's not clear what use the Kwih-dihch-chuh-ahts have for the beards. I can see, now that I've done it myself, that they might be suitable for scaling fish or scrubbing the cooking ware.

After all the beards are removed, we put the mussels back into the baskets and carry them to the pit that the crew helped dig. Heat radiates from it—there's a fire buried deep below—and it's been lined with ferns. I prepare to tip my basket and pour the mussels in but Inessa stops me. She kneels at the lip of the pit and begins to place her mussels inside it. She leans in and positions each mussel beside the one she placed before it, leaving no room between. I lower myself nearby and begin to lay my mussels in the pit as well. We work slowly and deliberately, nudging the mussels up against one another. I bathe in the warmth that washes over my face and arms. When the baskets are empty, the dark ovals blanket the entire space and gleam like jewels. We lay more ferns over the mussels until they're completely covered, and, finally, on top, cedar mats that we tuck in at the corners.

Two women pour water from a large basket into the pit. There's a hiss, and a cloud of steam rises. They fetch a second basket, and then a third. Steam billows up as more water is added. After a few minutes, the steaming stops, and the smell of cooked mussels wafts up.

The mat is peeled back, and the ferns, now black, are removed. The acrid odour of wet charcoal is released. The shells gape, a frill of orange peeping out from each. We scrape out the flesh—still a bit gelatinous—and thread the mussels on sharpened sticks. Even the liquid in the shells is saved, poured into a cooking box.

The women who added the water to the pit look pleased when they see all the sticks of mussels lined up like orange soldiers at attention. One says something to Inessa and everyone laughs. Inessa blushes. Refusing to look up, she gathers the discarded shells, throwing them into the baskets, but she listens keenly to the women.

Eventually she calls, "Anna!" She motions me to come. We each carry a basket of empty shells to an area just beyond the edge of the village. There are thousands, maybe millions of shells already spread out here, bleached white by the sun. We each tip our baskets. When they spill, the river of shells rattles on and on, like it will never stop, just like the never-ending river that pours from the vase of Aquarius.

The world around us is starting to awaken. Thin, green shoots push through the surface of the damp earth. Buds swell at the ends of grey branches. Birds sing us awake, and flutter about with twigs and moss in their beaks as they fly away to build nests. Winter is coming to an end. The ships will be back soon.

On a rare afternoon when both Nikolai Isaakovich and I are idle, I say, "Let's go see how the garden is faring."

"Anya, gardens hold little charm for men of the sea," he complains.

"It's not far. Please?"

After a moment of hesitation, he nods and pushes himself to his feet.

I lead us along the winding path through the trees. The crows are cawing—we've startled them—and in the distance, the surf roars. New life is stretched out along the entire trail, in the buds and shoots and moss, vivid against winter's dull palette. The odour of growth is also sharp. It clamours for attention, and behind the hopeful pleasures it suggests, there's insistence, as the new season pushes against confinement. Spring wants to break free from the winter.

"How much farther is it?" my husband grumbles.

"We're almost there."

We pass the tree shaped like a chalice. The path veers closer to the sea. We bound across a rivulet channeling water toward the ocean. The water's etched a shape like the outline of an ancient oak tree in the sand.

When we reach the garden, I find it more overgrown, as indistinct from the plant life that surrounds it as it ever has been.

"This is it?" Nikolai Isaakovich says.

Upon closer examination, I find that the burst of spring growth has not forgotten the garden. A green shoot pushes through the grey winter debris like a knife blade. Beside it is another.

"Look!" I point. I pinch the tip off one of the shoots and let him smell it.

"Onions?" he says.

"Open up," I say, and I place the fragment in his mouth.

I pull the thatch back. It's too early but I can't resist. With a flat rock, I score a circle around the plant, trying not to get too close to the bulb. Then I dig away the earth. With my fingertips, I find the smooth skin of one small onion. There is another right beside it. I brush the earth from the first, and tug gently until it gives way and pops into my fingers.

It leaves behind a hollow space that's perfectly round as though it once held a giant pearl.

"Give it to me," Nikolai Isaakovich says and takes the root by its stubby stem.

He wipes it on his trouser leg. It's an impossibly white and glossy ball, with a hairy tangle of roots.

He sinks his teeth into it. It crunches. He chews. "God, it's delicious." He wipes his chin.

I laugh. "Give me a bite."

The juice rolls over my tongue. It's so sweet and tender. I take another bite before passing it back.

There are only three bites each. It's gone too soon.

"What else is here?" my husband asks.

I poke around, but it's too early, and I find nothing of interest. Not yet. There may be a few seeds that have yet to germinate, a few shoots that have yet to push to the surface and so, I pull the vines back into place for next time.

I sit back and my husband flops down beside me.

"The koliuzhi don't want anything from the garden," I say. "Except the potatoes. They like the potatoes."

My husband shakes his head in incredulity. "Why don't they

want it? They should take care of this garden. Make it bigger. They should make more gardens. They need farms. How can any civilization advance without producing its own food?"

"I thought the same thing when Makee showed me the garden. But now—Kolya—what if they don't need farms? They get everything from the forest and the sea."

"That's impossible."

"And anyway, they take care of the forest and the sea. They don't plant gardens, but they tend to things. It's not so different from the peasants tending to their land and livestock."

"It is completely different! Have you lost your mind?"

The afternoon presses in on us. The heat weighs us down. There's a bee humming and hovering woozily, and a buzzing in my ears, too, that might be the bees. Or it might just be me.

"Everything has gone wrong. Everything," my husband declares.

"Not everything," I reply softly. "We're alive—and together." I take his hand. It's cold and limp.

"We've lost the brig and everything on board. Khariton Sobachnikov is dead. Yakov and Filip Kotelnikov are gone. And who knows what's happening to the rest of the crew? If we ever get back home, what will the chief manager say?"

I tighten my grip. "What he'll say is: you've made the best of a disastrous situation. Under your command . . ."

"But we're slaves! I've failed!"

"Stop saying that," I cry. "You've done your best, and we've far more men alive than dead. We'll be rescued. You haven't failed at all." I draw him into my arms and kiss his cheek. I lean in and press my head against his. He softens and wraps his arms around me. I kiss his lips. Like me, he tastes of onion.

Perseus rescued Andromeda from the sea. He cut the chains at her wrists and ankles and set her free before the sea monster could take her. They married and had seven sons and two daughters. They whirl overhead and on any autumn night, if it's clear, I will see them together and be reminded of their message: that love's path has always been twisted and confusing, filled with hope—and fear. In the end, when we seek reassurance, we need only look overhead.

"Anya," my husband whispers. He lays me down at the edge of the garden. I close my eyes and the sun's so bright everything's deep pink. His hand runs down my side, and when it reaches my hip, it begins to tug at my clothing. He swings his leg over, and pushes it between mine.

His desire is quick and demanding. It beckons me to follow. If I do, I must skirt a ledge so narrow there's no space to turn around. I can't see the end of the ledge—I don't know how far it is and what lies beyond. There's nowhere to go except ahead. And that is the path I choose.

When he finally calls out, I'm glad there's nothing but a few birds and insects who've witnessed our coupling. I feel like one of the creatures here, wild and lacking the reason that would tell me how wantonly I'm behaving. We lie in each other's arms for a long time and a short time afterward, while in the air above us those creatures trace lazy paths.

❧

The next morning, the girls and I head into the forest. We carry smaller baskets with a tight weave, so I know we're gathering something new. We stay on the trail and pass alongside an area where many logs crisscross one another. One gigantic tree has put down its roots atop a fallen log. The roots wrap around the trunk and reach to the ground, forming the moss-covered bars of a cage. We eventually emerge into a level grove where the canopy has thinned. Spring is here, too, in the swollen buds and the pale shoots that push through the surface of the forest floor.

I've long lost track of the date, but we're close to the time of year when the peasants celebrate spring. My mother told me there's a ritual in which, on a certain day, they go into the forest to look for a fiery fern.

"It's not easy. It grows beyond the thrice ninth land, in the thrice ninth realm," she said. "And it shows itself only one day a year. But . . .whoever finds it will become steeped in wealth."

"Mother . . ." I said. "I'm not a child anymore." I was still a girl, yes, but already too smart to believe in such superstitions. "There is no thrice ninth land except in somebody's imagination. And people don't become wealthy from finding plants."

"Ah, you think so literally. I'm not talking about the kind of wealth they worship these days. The fiery fern promises prosperity in wisdom and an abundance of grace."

"People can grow wise and choose to behave with grace," I said primly. "They don't need a plant if that's what they desire."

She looked at me doubtfully. "Well, you'd best watch for it when you're in the forest. You're young still and the possibility of learning wisdom and grace certainly won't harm you."

My mother, if she were here today, wouldn't know where to look for all the ferns unfurling their fronds. As the days grow longer and hint of warmer days to come, they stretch out and open their pale arms.

The girls drop their baskets. Inessa gives me a shell knife.

I turn away from the ferns. The shoots we're cutting are faint green quills with only the hint of leaves. I guess the ones growing near spiny canes must be berry shoots. They have tiny white hairs that hint of the thorns to come, but, for now, the stems are so supple I could pinch them off without a knife.

"Anna," says Inessa. She holds a shoot and delicately peels back the skin in ringlets as pretty as freshly curled hair. Then she bites into the shoot and smiles as she chews.

She offers me a shoot. Nicking the end with my fingernail just as she did, I peel it. Then I bite into it.

"čabas," she says.

My mouth puckers—it's so sour—but as I chew, that taste diminishes and something as sweet and fresh as summer rain emerges. It's how I imagine waking up would taste if such a thing were possible.

She laughs at my surprise.

"Chabas," I repeat.

We work our way around the grove until we arrive at a damp hollow of shadows. Here, we shift our attention to a different kind of shoot. These look like tiny Chinese bamboo, their stems segmented into ever-decreasing lengths, dressed in frilly, brown skirts. The shoots are so slender, it will take many hours before we fill our baskets. Nevertheless, it happens and when the girls seem satisfied, we wind our way back along the trail.

Along a drier section of the path, I come across a big patch of chabas. The shoots, lush and pale, are everywhere. I can't believe we missed it on our way out.

"Chabas," I cry out and point. "Chabas."

The other girl smiles at me, then says something. Inessa agrees. I expect us to pick these shoots—surely we could squeeze a few more into the baskets—but the girls carry on.

In Russia, everyone believes the wilderness is free and open to all. The bounty of the land goes to the first man clever enough to find it and he'll take it all before anybody else can get it. The koliuzhi don't live the same way. Either we have enough already, or they want to save what's here for another time. In any case, they're not afraid somebody else will take it, which, in Russia, is how most people would feel before harvesting every shoot in sight before the sun had the chance to set.

We eat the shoots that night. The cooks steam them in shallow pits, similar to how we steamed the mussels. They're served with grease and a flaky white seafish that tastes of cedar and the smokehouse. They slide down my throat easily, but I think I preferred them peeled and raw on the side of the trail.

"My shirt was torn today," my husband says through a mouthful.

"Where?"

He twists away from me and with greasy fingers, points. There's a tear running along the shoulder seam, then down, forming a triangular flap of fabric. "It was caught on a branch."

"I can fix it," I say. I'll get Inessa to give me a needle and thread.

"Would you? While you're at it, some stitching is loose at the bottom."

I lean over and look more closely. "Tomorrow morning," I say. "There'll be more light, and I'll be able to see properly."

He runs his fingers around his bowl, scooping up a last shoot, and nods as he slips it into his mouth.

"Why does she come for you every day?" my husband grumbles.

Inessa's waiting with a basket, just as she does every morning. It's raining, but it's so light, barely a mist, it won't keep us from our work outdoors.

I start to rise. "I'll be back soon."

"No," my husband says. He grabs my arm and holds firmly. I can't stand. I'm hunched over, waiting. "You're supposed to fix my shirt this morning."

"I'll fix it when I come back." I struggle to keep my balance.

Inessa shifts uneasily and my husband glares. "There are other people here. Somebody else can go with her."

"I will make your shirt as good as new when I get back. I promise. I won't be long."

He pulls on me, but I resist. I refuse to sit. "Tell her you can't go."

I laugh. "How? I don't know her language."

"Stay here."

"You're making a scene. Let me go."

"If you won't tell her, I will." Nikolai Isaakovich thrusts me away. I stumble backward. He leaps up and grabs Inessa. "No. Go away," he shouts into her face. "She's my wife. She has work to do here. Leave us alone."

Inessa recoils. Despite telling her to go, he won't let her. She twists and tries to free herself, but he holds on. Her hair falls and covers her face. He screams. "She's not going. Do you hear me?" Inessa throws her head back, and her hair parts like a curtain. Her anguish drives me forward.

I thrust my body between them and try to force them apart. He smells of sweat and grease from his breakfast. She smells of smoke and cedar. "Stop, Kolya, leave her alone. It's not her fault." Inessa's head hits mine and she cries out. Everything goes white for an instant.

My husband tries to shove me aside, but I won't let go. "She's my wife. Don't you understand?"

Then the man with the scar on his chest is on us. His voice is like a blow. "hiyu·ʔaX̣!"[40] Strong arms do what I could not— he forces himself between Inessa and Nikolai Isaakovich and pulls them apart. The scarred man holds my husband's arms behind his back. Inessa pauses an instant, gasping, her face a mask of disbelief, and runs outside. Her basket, one side caved in, rocks back and forth on the floor where she dropped it.

"Don't come looking for her again," my husband shouts.

---

40   Stop!

"She's never going with you." He twists against the scarred man who finally lets him go and runs after Inessa.

"What do you think you're doing?" I snap. "You hurt her."

"I did not. Didn't you see the way she ran out of here? There's nothing wrong with her."

"You can't do that to people here," I say. "Nobody acts like that. They're not used to it. And now Makee's going to think we're causing trouble."

"All you care about is what that Poppy Seed thinks." His expression of disapproval makes him look like a toad.

"I'm going to work now. I'll fix your shirt later." I storm out of the house. There's no sign of Inessa, and without her, I have no idea what I'm supposed to be doing.

I walk away from the houses to the edge of the forest and stand beneath the shelter of the boughs. They're enough to keep me dry. The misty rain falls, but the sky is light, and I think it won't be long before it stops. Down on the beach, some men have gathered beside the canoes.

The scent of smoke in the air makes me want to go back to the house, where it's warm and dry. But I can't face the mess my husband's created. Let him deal with the Kwih-dihch-chuh-ahts. Let him explain to Makee. I should find Inessa, but I haven't any idea where to go look for her.

Somebody steps outside Makee's house. For an instant, I think it's my husband, but then I see it's Timofei Osipovich. He looks around and when he sees me in the shelter of the trees, he comes to me.

"You don't need to stand out here in the rain. Come inside."

"No," I say. "Please leave me be." I have no patience for him today.

He turns and watches the men on the beach, but he doesn't go. A gust of wind blows, and heavy drops of water fall from the boughs. One lands on my head and trickles down my face. It's cold.

The men on the beach have turned one of the canoes over. They're running their hands along the keel, deep in discussion.

"There's nothing you can do about it out here. Come back."

"Everything was fine," I blurt. "Things were finally working out for us." Tears press against my eyes, but I won't give in to them. "I thought he understood. He's been working hard, hasn't he? Just like Makee wanted?"

Timofei Osipovich peers at me, in disbelief, then laughs. "Yes, he's been working hard."

"Then why this outburst?"

He sighs. "Madame Bulygina, I must show you something. Come."

We go into the forest and follow the trail that leads toward the headland. We veer away from the sea and climb, then descend on the other side. It's the same trail I took with the girls to collect mussels.

When we've passed the headland, we turn off the trail and head toward the beach. Before we step out of the trees, he stops and points.

A huge patch of soil has been disturbed. All the shrubs have been torn out. Boughs have been collected and propped up against one another. We go closer. It's a hole in the ground that's covered with branches. There's a tiny opening with steps cut into the earth leading into the darkness. "What is this?"

"A house. A place to live."

"Who made it?"

"Your husband—and I."

"Makee asked you to build a house?"

"No, Madame Bulygina," he replies, enunciating each word.

"Makee did not ask us to build a house."

They have been working hard. It took a lot of work to build the hut. But this is not what I meant, not what Makee wants.

"It's almost finished. We'll move here in a few days."

"We can't!"

"We can."

"We'll never survive!"

"And why not? We'll eat fish. Snare a few rabbits. Get some mushrooms and roots. We'll make kvass!" He smacks his lips. "We'll trade with the koliuzhi for anything else we need. You may not realize it, but Kozma Ovchinnikov is more than a strong and loyal man. He's also a good carver."

"Does Makee know what you've done?"

He laughs. "Why? Are you going to tattle on us if he doesn't?"

"Does he?" I insist.

He shrugs carelessly. "Probably. There are no secrets here; he must have accepted it. He's done nothing to prevent our little project from proceeding."

"You shouldn't have done this."

He bursts into laughter. "Dear Madame Bulygina, your sanctimony is a never-ending source of entertainment. Even when circumstances are most dire, I can always depend on you to make me laugh."

A few hours later, Makee calls out from the bench. "Anna? Please come—and ask the commander to come as well." He's been in conference with the three older men all afternoon.

"Why should I go?" my husband mutters.

"Get up," I whisper. I nudge him with my knee, a little harder than I should.

Nikolai Isaakovich glares, and gets up as slowly as he can. Once up, he surveys the room as though it's something he must map but can't decide where to start. Lazily, he saunters over to Makee, every step defiant. When he reaches the bench, he says, "What is it—Poppy Seed?" He mispronounces Makee's name.

Makee's hands are folded over his cheetoolth. It rests lightly on his lap. The three men are stern. "Earlier," Makee begins, "there was a dispute in my home."

"We're sorry," I cry. "It was a misunderstanding, and it won't happen again."

My husband ignores my words. "Yes, there was a dispute—about how my wife is being overworked."

"I'm not overworked," I say. "Sorry, Makee. There's no problem."

"Yes, there is a problem," my husband says. "She's not your slave. She can't be performing menial tasks for you. She has other obligations."

To my surprise, Makee gives a short nod. "I understand. She's your wife. But you hurt that girl."

"She's fine. She walked out of the house. I saw her."

"She's hurt. I saw bruises on her arms." His spine stiffens. "She refuses to come back. Everyone is distressed. And for what? Why didn't you come to me first? We could have worked on a resolution."

"I told you both. There's no problem," I cry. "I can do whatever my husband wants—and whatever you need, Makee. There's plenty of time in the day."

Makee addresses me as though my husband is not here. "This is what I was trying to tell you. Whenever there are too many babathid around, the smallest feather transforms into the heaviest and most immoveable of rocks. Always."

"Makee—I'm sorry." I don't dare look at my husband.

"Did he tell you about the hut in the forest?"

Heat floods my face. "It's a mistake. Please—give us another chance."

"How many chances should I give? Tall mountains are built of many small rocks. The tragedy is already taking shape. I have a responsibility to my people."

"What are you saying?" my husband spits. "Speak clearly—all this talk of mountains and tragedy and responsibility—nonsense. What do you want?"

A gust of wind scatters drops of water on the roof that sound like soup on a slow boil.

"Tell me," says Makee coldly, "what is sacred to a Russian?"

I fear Nikolai Isaakovich's answer. I blurt, "God. God is sacred."

"The Tsar," says my husband as though I haven't spoken. "The Tsar and everything he stands for is sacred."

Makee presses his lips together and repositions the cheetoolth. When he raises his head again, he says quietly, "There is another village. They will take you."

"What do you mean?" I cry. "We want to stay here."

"You can stay here," Makee says, "but the commander must go."

"No!" I beg. "Makee, please!"

"I will slay the man who tries to separate me from my wife," my husband declares. He raises his elbows and clenches his fists. He takes a step toward Makee and holds his ridiculous stance.

I pull his arm down. "No, Kolya. Don't." He jerks his arm away.

Makee remains calm. He knows Nikolai Isaakovich's blustering will come to nothing. "There is no choice. We have decided."

The three old men watch. Their eyes dart from corner to corner of our little triangle. They can't know what's being said, but they certainly understand it.

"Then I want to go too," I say. I don't. But Makee's edict forces me to say I do.

"You can't."

"Why not?" my husband demands.

"They won't accept more than one babathid." He sighs. "Please go peacefully. I will try to bring you back together again—either there or here. But now it will take time. And it won't be possible if you keep fighting and causing trouble."

"In the name of the Tsar Alexander and the Russian Empire, I won't go!" my husband screams. "You hear me, Poppy Seed? You can't make me do anything! I'm in charge. Come on, Anya. We're finished here."

He tugs my arm so roughly that my teeth snap together. He drags me outside.

"What do you think you're doing? Have you gone mad?" I say. I reach for my silver cross, but it's gone. How long it's been gone, I can't say. Where I lost it, I don't know. I lay my hand against my heart, feeling the shape of absence. Where will it turn up? Who will find it? Whoever it is must not forget that the fate attached to lost necklaces found in the forest was determined long ago.

CHAPTER FIFTEEN

———————

"What are you crying about?" Timofei Osipovich scolds mildly. "He'll be back."

We're perched on the southernmost point within sight of Makee's village. The canoe carrying my husband—and fifteen other men and two women—disappeared in the mist a long time and a short time ago. I watched them transform from a rocking cradle of paddlers and singers to a silent, dark cylinder magically suspended against a grey background, to nothing when they slipped behind the dreary curtain.

My husband didn't look back but if he had, he would have seen me waving my arm until it ached like it was about to snap off. When I could no longer see them, I collapsed and landed on a sharp stone, but that wasn't what made me weep. I cried for my abandonment, for once again losing my husband. I imagined my tears channelled into a stream that ran to the sea. Salt to salt. If only I could have slid over the rocks and disappeared, too.

Timofei Osipovich found me curled up, with my head pillowed on a cold stone. The shroud of grey mist was the only thing that refused to leave me.

"Go away," I say.

"Go away? And leave a lady in distress? The damage would stain my reputation."

"Your reputation is well known, and there's nothing you can do about it."

He laughs. "Ah, you must be feeling better."

I watch the sea. The water moves gently like the ocean is breathing. Like it's an animal waiting patiently for something that no one could ever guess.

"He'll be back."

"Stop trying to cheer me up." I know I sound like a child, and I wish I didn't, but once he starts, I cannot suppress the words, cannot alter my tone.

"The sea will bring him back to you. One day soon, he'll float back here, and a strong wave will toss him into your waiting arms. It's inevitable—for it is impossible for a man to live without the sun, and equally impossible for him to live without his beloved!"

"Who sent you here?"

He grins again. "Your toyon is looking for you. And those slave girls you've befriended."

"Will you never stop?"

"Those girls have something to show you. A new trinket. Perhaps a jewelled locket. Maybe a scrap of white lace for your bonnet."

I lift my head, jump to my feet, and make for the path that leads to the village. His mockery follows me. "Or a bonbon from Paris. A satin ribbon for your neck? Maybe one of them has received an engagement ring. Maybe a golden—" until thankfully the wind carries away his voice and his silly sing-song chant fades to nothing.

Of course, no one is looking for me. Timofei Osipovich's tale was a fabrication, but if he meant it only to get me to return to the house and stop pitying myself, then perhaps, grudgingly, I must give him credit.

With the improvement in the weather, my thoughts go to the ship that will rescue us. Makee assures me one will come.

"They often stop at Mokwinna's village first. He has a reputation. Sometimes, if they find what they want, then they leave, and we never see them. They go straight to China to sell the furs."

"Can't we send a message to Mokwinna?"

Makee smiles. "We must never dream of it. Did you forget? He wouldn't let Too-te-yoo-hannis Yoo-ett go—remember the American I told you about? I had to get him released. It's better we say nothing to Mokwinna because once he's involved, your rescue will become more complicated."

"Is there no other way?"

"Be patient, Anna. You will get home."

One evening, as I'm eating with Timofei Osipovich and Ovchinnikov, I say, "I think a ship will come soon."

"Ha!" Timofei Osipovich cries. "Ships are out there every day."

"They are?"

"Indeed they are." A frown flits across the loyal Ovchinnikov's face and disappears so fast I almost wonder if it was ever there.

"Then why doesn't anybody see them? Why aren't they coming here?"

"Who knows? Perhaps there's no reason to stop here."

"What about trade?" I say. "Or maybe to look for us."

"Madame Bulygina," he says, his mouth half full of fish. "If you want a ship so badly, you better build one."

"Just like the hut you built?"

"No," he says dismissively, "I'm talking about a grand enterprise like in Petropavlovsk. Just think of the ships you could build!"

"I don't want to build a ship."

"You don't? Aren't you Russian? Have you no spirit?"

"Since you're so spirited, why don't you build it?"

"I just might."

"Have you ever built a ship before?"

"No! But neither have I been invited to the Tsarina's chambers for a private visit. Nor have I ever stumbled upon a cache of gold coins big enough to feed me on cream and jam until I die. But naturally I dream about such things."

Ovchinnikov laughs.

I say, "You're mad. You dream too much."

"And you, Madame Bulygina, don't dream enough. Imagine this," he says. "The koliuzhi cut down the trees. They make planks and beams and masts—whatever we need. Then I show them how to assemble it. And they build it. They can build one of their own while they're at it!" He grins.

"Why should they listen to you? They already have their own boats. They don't need Russian ships."

He looks at me like I'm the insane one. "They certainly do."

"Whatever for?"

"The toyons want everything we have to offer. They're smart. They're thinking about the future."

⁂

That evening, when I go out to relieve myself one last time, I walk down to the beach where the trees won't obstruct my view. It's the first time since finding out about Main Rigger Sobachnikov's passing that I've felt like looking at the stars.

The sky is clear, and the moon is waning. There's my Polaris, everlasting and strong. Who has depended on her since I last cast my gaze upon her? Countless men, I imagine. Traders, explorers, and wanderers of all sorts.

To her side lies Draco the dragon, dim as ever. With one finger, I trace his long back bent like the keel of a ship. My imagination must be spurred on by my longing. For next I see Polaris not as the tip of Ursa Minor's tail, but as the top of the mast to Draco's keel.

There was a ship constellation, the Argo Navis, but half a century ago, Monsieur Nicolas-Louis de Lacaille dismantled it because he thought it took up too much of the sky. He divided it into three constellations: the Keel, the Sails, and the Stern. And then he went on to name the Compass, the Clock, and even the Telescope. I've seen none of them—they're all in the southern hemisphere. Long ago, I pledged to see them myself and, one day, I will.

Without the Argo Navis, the night sky needs a ship. Has any astronomer thought to look for it in the northern hemisphere? How natural that Polaris, the Ship Star, would be part of it. How perfect that she would be the point around which the vessel's path would revolve. Such a ship would always come back to where it started. It would always get home.

How I wish my father were here. He appreciates thoughts like this, and the discussions they spur on. He might tell me that my imagination had run amok or point out the flaws in my discovery. I know they're there. He might say that even if the academy could ever be convinced to support my claim, the authorities at the French Royal Academy might not view it so favourably. I would know that what he really meant was that he was proud that here, in the land of the Kwih-dihch-chuh-ahts, a possible new constellation had just been named—by his daughter.

Dressed magnificently, the Kwih-dihch-chuh-ahts board the canoes. They wear clothing of fur and hide and cedar bark, much of it clattering with korolki and shells. Their dresses and robes ripple as they move, bringing to life the designs of animals and people that are woven into or painted onto their clothes. Their necks and arms are adorned with jewellery. Hats perch on men's heads, those men's faces, arms, and chests painted red and black. We're going to celebrate a marriage—so Makee informed me yesterday.

Makee has a freshly brushed sea otter cape draped over his shoulders. Timofei Osipovich sits just in front of him. He's tied back his hair with a sinew, and it hangs nearly to the middle of his back. He must have tried to trim his beard with a shell knife; it looks less disorderly than it did yesterday.

The Aleuts and Kozma Ovchinnikov are in the same canoe as me. Ovchinnikov's followed his master's lead and also done something with his hair and beard. I can almost see his eyes now. He and the Aleuts have paddles.

Inessa and the other girl wave from shore. They're staying home—as are some of the older people, three new mothers and their babies, and a cluster of young men who are already strutting about the beach like roosters. They'll watch over the village while we're gone. One of them is the man with the scar on his chest. He's watching Inessa wave at me.

A few days ago, when Makee told me about the wedding—and that I was to attend—he also told me I'd be given a new dress. When I later took the garment from his wife, it was much lighter than I expected. It draped over my arm like it was made of fine linen. It was much more delicate than the cedar robe I had to wear when I washed my clothing. Still, if anybody had told me in Petersburg that I'd one day own a dress made of bark, I would have thought her words in jest. I smiled. "Oo-shuk-yu—" I hesitated because I'd forgotten half the word. Enunciating each syllable, she said, "Oo-shoo-yuksh-uhlits." I thought that one day I'd get the entire word out without help.

Would my husband be irritated when he saw me in my dress?

Probably. But it made no sense to refuse. I'd been wearing the same clothing for several months now. The cuffs, collar, and hem were stained and shredded. The seams had all come apart and been stitched back together. There were tears where I'd caught my sleeve or hem on branches while I was working. I repaired my clothes as often as needed, but the fabric was so thin and had torn so often that, in places, my clothes were held together by mending and nothing more.

Besides, I now found the cedar dresses, with their fringes and the patterns woven into them, to be quite pretty.

Inessa and the other girl helped me dress. They showed me where the robe should sit on my shoulders and they tied a belt around my waist to hold the dress in place. Inessa patiently untangled my hair and fixed it in a single braid that trailed down my back just like hers. I felt nearly unclothed without my chemise, and with my limbs so exposed. My cedar cape would keep my shoulders covered and assure some modesty.

They circled me when they were finished, tucking in the dress where it protruded, and my own stray hairs. The only mirror I had was their faces. My doubt was alleviated for what I saw reflected back surprised and pleased me.

Once the canoes leave the shelter of our cove, the waves lift us like we're in a basket and set us down again on the other side. However, this canoe is so solid and heavy, it never feels like it will capsize. I sit still and low in the boat where the wind can't reach, and I listen to the songs that carry us with the current.

We pass the stacks and stumps with their fringe of trees, and the open arms of beaches. Gulls follow us then veer back toward the shore. A compact black bird shaped like a Chinese teapot floats in groups farther out to sea. On a pan of rocks, at the base of a stack, seals bask. They raise their heads and look, but as far away as we are, they deem us unworthy of their attention, much less important than the sun.

The ocean opens on our other side to a kind of eternity that's as timeless as the night sky, and, on a day like today, just as beautiful.

For a long time and a short time, we continue until finally, barely visible, a thread of smoke rises straight through the tops of the trees. The canoes turn toward it, toward the mouth of a river that will lead to it.

This is the Quileutes' village. Where I last saw Maria.

Beneath the cries of the seabirds, the faint sound of drumming rises, thin as that wisp of smoke. As we draw closer to shore and it grows louder, the paddles begin to dip and pull to match its rhythm. Finally, we're near enough to see the faces of the people waiting on the beach.

In a cluster off to one side, there's Maria. And Ivan Kurmachev, the carpenter. There's the American, John Williams, so pale and thin now that with his shock of red hair he looks like a candle. Do they see me? I wave. I didn't realize they'd all be here.

Maria comes to the edge of the water, her eyes all but invisible in their deep creases, her mouth stretched wide. "You said you'd be back, but I didn't expect it would be so soon." I take the hand she offers and sink into her arms once again, feeling the frail bones of her back.

Timofei Osipovich is pulled into the centre of the men. They wrap their arms around him and won't let go. Ovchinnikov and the two Aleuts are also dragged into the wild tangle. They look like a nest of octopuses. My heart swells.

And then I realize.

He's missing. My husband is not here.

I turn to Maria. I can't breathe.

"He's here," she says. "Don't worry."

"Where?"

"Fishing," she says. "Down the coast."

"When are they coming back?"

No one knows.

All the men are thinner and more worn down. They're dirtier and their clothes are even more ragged than the last time I saw them. Still, joy lights up their faces; it eases my worry. We're far from being the creatures we were when the brig ran aground, but the fondness they exhibit in their smiles and their embraces reminds me of their camaraderie on the ship. It renews my confidence. We will overcome this tragedy.

Maria's the least changed of all. The most conspicuous difference is a sinew with a beaded pendant she now wears around her neck. The pendant, made of those tubular, white beads and korolki, hangs between her saggy breasts like an artifact from happier times. It's hard not to look at that female part of her and wonder what kind of a young woman she was and what hopes she'd once nurtured.

When the men draw apart and there's space between their words, I ask, "Where have you been? What happened?"

They look at one another, and from the fear and pride and uncertainty and confusion in their gazes, I understand, without having heard a word, that much has happened—just as it has to me—and that it's hard to know where the story begins. The carpenter Kurmachev answers the challenge. "We were determined to stay free men," he says, "but as you can see, we failed. We planned an escape by sea. The moon was unfriendly that night, peeking through a rent in the clouds as though taunting us. There was so little light for a sea voyage."

They built a canoe. It capsized in the surf. They scrambled for their lives. They got back to shore. But they lost everything.

"From that moment, there was no choice," drawls the American. "We surrendered to these koliuzhi."

"If I'd heeded you, Madame Bulygina, that day on the river," says Kurmachev, "I'd still have my flask. But to each his lot is given!"

Every man speaks at once. Agreeing, disagreeing, explaining, qualifying, contradicting, exaggerating, and teasing. Multiple truths are set before me, and I'm invited to choose the ones I want. Some mesh with my story and some don't. Some are spoken quietly, others shouted with passion. I don't know which is most deserving, or what to believe. But I feel light as a feather, lifted up by the pleasure of hearing their voices once again.

The moustached toyon's house overflows with guests from the village as well as up and down the coast. Makee's sister with her silver comb sits with a group of women my mother's age on a bench near one of the posts. The Murzik has a long conversation with Timofei Osipovich. They've met before and I soon deduce that our prikashchik gave him the handkerchief that caused so much trouble with the Chalat Tsar. The injured eyebrow man is also here. Not only is he here but he's the bridegroom—marrying the moustached toyon's daughter.

He's wearing a breechclout, but covering it, and the top half of his legs, is a decorated apron. The queer koliuzhi creatures are woven into it—a big-snouted animal like a bear or a wolf stretched out along the top, and beneath it, a toothy creature with huge eyebrows that mirror his and a checkerboard neck. The apron is big enough to cover his scar. He also wears a new, red shirt that can only have come from us.

Nikolai Isaakovich returned from fishing just after we'd finished warming ourselves before the fire. The chill of the sea voyage had left my body. Timofei Osipovich called out to him as soon as he entered, and he stopped. He smiled, hearing the familiar voice, and when he found the prikashchik's face, he strode across the house and they embraced, pounding one another on their backs. When my husband pulled away, I had the chance to really see him. His face was ruddy, his hair wet and stringy, and he looked savage in a way that I know would have bothered his sensibilities only a few weeks ago. Timofei Osipovich said something else to him, and he looked up and found me.

I smiled. How did he see me? I'd taken great care with my appearance. Inessa and the other girl had let me know I was pretty in my new dress. But what did my husband think?

After a long, fearful moment, his lips pressed together in an uncertain smile. I rushed to his side and threw open my arms. He embraced me. He brushed his lips against my hair, and lowered his mouth to my ear. "My God, Anya, what happened to your dress?"

I hid my face against his chest.

The evening is filled with songs and stories and dancing. Though I'm tired from the journey, I can't look away. I press myself into the side of Nikolai Isaakovich and soak in the grand spectacle. The colourful masks. The regal clothes—sea otter capes over the shoulders of many men, and jewellery such as I've not yet seen anywhere. The drumming that shakes the walls. The smoke that, on a whim, conceals or reveals. The voices that soar into the rafters and plummet back down and squirm into our ears. I think our breathing has been harmonized, and our breaths together are part of the songs and stories. But not exactly a part—it's more like they're the canvas on which the songs and stories are embroidered. I try holding my breath to see what will happen, but as soon as I start breathing again, I follow the same rhythm as everyone else. To do otherwise would be like sailing against the wind and current.

At the end of one dance, two men begin to banter alongside a small fire. One of them is the groom—the eyebrow man. As they tease one another, women thrust kindling into that fire. It crackles and smokes for a bit, but then the wood catches and the fire flares, throwing light and shadows on everyone's faces.

Each man is given a dish—the dishes used to serve grease. The first man raises his dish to his lips and takes a sip. The groom does the same. Afterward, both have broad smiles and glossy lips and teeth—they *were* drinking grease. I look at my husband, but he's wide-eyed, watching the drama in disbelief.

The first man takes another drink—a longer, deeper mouthful. He swallows. And again, the groom does the same. The people in the house are calling out and laughing. In response, both men again drink—downing even bigger portions of grease.

"What on earth is this about?" my husband says.

They keep drinking from their dishes, back and forth, two gulps of grease, then three. Finally, the first man tilts his dish to the ceiling and drinks until the grease is drained. He tears the dish away and spits into the fire.

The fire unrolls toward the ceiling with a *whoomp*. Somebody screams. The faces of the nearest people are lit up like on a hot summer day. Many jump back. Everyone cheers. When the flame dies down, black smoke fills the house.

"That's madness," my husband says.

The groom tips his dish back and drains it, too. And then, with his head tilted right back, he gestures frantically until a woman gives him another grease dish. He drinks from it, too, the grease running down the sides of his mouth and neck, and all over his new red shirt.

He throws his head forward and spits into the fire.

The flames roar and touch the ceiling. I scream. And then it ends. The fire dies down, black smoke clouds the room—and the people cheer for the groom who has won the competition.

Glistening with grease, the groom calls out and circles the house. People laugh. Some brush him away. But one man raises his arm and steps forward. He's young—barely sprouting facial hair—but he's brimming with a combination of masculine confidence and bashfulness. The people cheer for him.

Two ropes that I hadn't noticed hanging from the rafters are released from hooks on the wall. They sway until they come to rest. They glisten. They're coated with grease.

A man starts to beat on a drum and when he stops, he calls out.

The young man and the groom run, jump, and throw themselves onto the ropes. The ropes swing. They start to climb.

Everyone shouts.

The ropes are impossible to climb. Neither man can get higher than one length of his arm before he comes sliding down to the bottom. But they keep trying. The groom wipes his hands on his shirt, but it's even greasier than the rope.

Their arms bulge as they squeeze and hold on. They twist the rope around their feet. Their toes grip like birds' talons. Still, they slide down more than they climb up.

Finally, when the groom's slid down once again, he lets go of the rope. He bends to the floor. He slaps his hands against the earth and something from there must stick. Because when he grabs the rope again, he climbs not one length of his arm, not two, not three. Something propels him right up to the rafters. He hooks one arm around the wood and hoists himself up. He waves in triumph.

The young man below just laughs and waves his hand dismissively. He knows, as does everyone in this room, that the winner of every contest tonight will be the groom, the eyebrow man.

I squeeze Kolya's hand. I hold on.

❧

When it's time to eat, serving dishes the size of the skiff are brought into the house. They're carved into koliuzhi creatures and painted: big heads with tongues that loll out at one end, and tails at the other. Feet and wings extend from the sides, and what would be their bodies has been hollowed out and filled with food.

Women ladle this food into trays until they're heaped with fish, clams, steamed roots, and grease, and distributed around the house. I sit between my husband, our arms and legs barely touching, and Maria. The others sprawl out around us, and dig into our food.

Nikolai Isaakovich tears off a fragment of fish and pushes it into his mouth. He chews. Swallows. He takes another piece. I feel these movements against my side.

"I will never understand why the koliuzhi gorge like this—and then have nothing for later. Don't they know anything about rationing?" Some of the others nod but their mouths are too full to reply. "Days of scarcity are always right around the corner. A wise man must plan—or suffer the consequences."

No one contradicts him, but he's wrong. The koliuzhi do prepare. When Makee caught the whale, we feasted, yes, but then we worked, preserving everything that wasn't eaten, dividing it up and storing it in boxes and bladders. Even after all these weeks, I wouldn't be surprised to know a few bladders of oil remain.

And it's not just the whale. Salmon, shellfish, roots, and berries, everything stored in boxes, baskets, and bladders, and buried in holes dug deep to where the air is as cold as an icehouse. They don't neglect to prepare for lean times. People work long hours at it. I do it, too. The planning Nikolai Isaakovich sees as absent must have been present for generations. Otherwise how would these people have survived?

When Nikolai Isaakovich is away from the houses, what does he think the women do? He's not here to witness it, but there's slicing and skinning and deboning and skewering, peeling, hanging, rendering, smoking, and though it's all fundamental to his survival, he's oblivious to it.

He's like the men of Petersburg. All the lotions and creams and washing and brushing and curling, the ironing and pleating and tying—all so we look presentable, and if we are lucky, pretty. No man could possibly realize how much effort is involved.

He says gruffly, "Eat, Anya. Eat all you can. You may as well. Are you not well?"

"I'm fine." I should eat, but words, stuck in my throat, won't allow me to swallow.

"I'm sick of these koliuzhi and their ways," my husband continues. "I'm hunting duck and geese in the rain and wind and cold—it's so unpleasant, you can't possibly imagine. And they become quite displeased if I can't kill the entire flock with a single shot. The toyon here is lazy and demanding and pompous—just like that Poppy Seed."

"Makee's friendly," I say. "And so is this toyon. When we first met, I sat across from him in the tent—"

"You don't see what's really going on here, do you?" He shifts his body away and is sullen the rest of the meal.

When the dancers and singers are exhausted and it's time to retire for the night, we Russians are divided among the houses in this village. My husband, Timofei Osipovich, and many of the rest of the crew are to stay in the toyon's house—along with Makee. I will go to another house to sleep alongside Maria once again.

While the arrangements are being discussed, I pull Nikolai Isaakovich to me and quickly kiss him. "Good night," I say.

He looks surprised and confused, but he kisses the back of my hand before I turn away, and before anybody notices.

Maria and I lie next to one another as the night noises of the house begin to unfurl—fires snapping and sighing as the embers die down in the darkness, children settling, hushed conversations, and tonight, the occasional smothered laugh.

I won't sleep until I know. "Why aren't Yakov and Kotelnikov here?" I whisper.

Maria says no one has heard from the apprentice since he was taken away—but Maria doesn't think he reached the *Kad'iak*. "It's been so long, he would have returned for us by now if he had," she adds. She's heard nothing about Yakov and thinks he's still with the Tsar's family.

"We'll find them," I say bravely. "They must come home with us."

She says nothing.

"Maria? They will. We wouldn't leave them here anymore than we'd leave you here."

Her head, outlined in the dim light, shakes slowly. "I think I'll live out my days here."

"No, Maria," I say. "You don't have to. You'll come home— with us. Don't you want to return?"

"To where?"

"Your home."

"I haven't been there in a long time. I don't even know who's there anymore. If I have anywhere to live." She sighs. "I don't expect you to understand. I know it's not like that for you." It's dark and she can't see my face flush. "Anyway, this is a good place for an old woman. They're very kind."

Long after Maria's deep and regular breathing indicates she's asleep, I'm awake mulling this over.

The Enlightenment has shown us the errors of our past when freedom was apportioned to men based on birth and status. The Tsar has set us on a path to eliminate hypocrisy at all levels of society, but my father's friends agree that we remain far from our destination.

What have the lofty ideas of the Enlightenment done for Maria? For Yakov, the Aleuts—for Timofei Osipovich? If I've learned anything from my time with the koliuzhi, it's that my father's friends are more right than they realize, as they perch in their comfortable chairs around a table full of food and drink brought to them by house serfs. We've fallen short of our ideals. We've not yet reached the place where our values and our actions are consistent and honourable.

I wish my father were here. He would understand my doubts. He would encourage me to keep struggling.

This much I do know. There is a truth that we are taught and another truth that we come to see. Though they should be, they are never exactly the same.

The following day, during a lull in the festivities, the old carpenter Kurmachev suggests we walk to a nearby beach. It's sunny and for the first time, the promise of summer hovers in the air. So Nikolai Isaakovich, Timofei Osipovich, and I accept. We head off following a trail that, contrary to expectations, leads into the forest.

We hike down and along a narrow, muddy path. The wet seeps through my boots reminding me it's time to apply another layer of grease. We then ascend the other side of this gully, past berry bushes starred with pink blossoms and two moss-covered trees that fell in the shape of an X. When the trail levels out again, it broadens, and I fall back to my husband's side.

"Do you know the beach we're heading to?" I ask.

"How could I? They drag me up the river or into the forest every single day. Visiting a beach is a luxury."

"I'm glad we'll get to see it for the first time together then." I shyly slip my arm around his waist and feel his scratchy greatcoat—now missing all its beautiful buttons—against my skin once again.

He leans over and kisses my cheek. His lips linger there, but not long enough.

"Be careful here," Kurmachev calls from far ahead.

"Where? We can't keep up—you're going too fast, old man," my husband calls back. He gazes at me but says to the carpenter, "Maybe you should go ahead without us. We'll catch up."

"No," calls old Kurmachev. "The trail's a bit confusing. I'll wait for you before we go down."

My husband pulls me close and kisses me on the lips, but I push him away and say, "No. Come on."

The descent to the beach looks steep. I start walking down on the heels of Kurmachev, who's surprisingly like a goat on the bumpy trail. My husband is right behind me, his breath in my ears. I cling to branches and place each foot carefully on the overgrown trail. Timofei Osipovich on the other hand releases himself, and with a holler, he hurtles down the hill, half sliding, half bouncing, ignoring the trail altogether. Brush crashes. He'll be scratched to bits if he doesn't break a leg first. He shouts when he reaches the bottom, "Hurry up, you feeble old men. You're taking the long way!"

"Nobody's feeble up here," calls Kurmachev, just ahead, and he winks up at me. "This way, Madame Bulygina, only a little farther now."

His friendly wink gives me confidence. I let the slope pull me down, two quick steps. One more. Then I slip and fall.

I slide through mud and over the rutted surface of a rock. My dress cinches up around my hips. I slip over a steep edge and keep tumbling. I reach for branches, but whatever I grab snaps off or comes out by the roots. The forest rushes by in a blur.

Then the ground levels and I come to a stop.

"Anya?" calls my husband.

"Are you all right, Madame Bulygina?" Kurmachev shouts.

"Yes—yes—I'm fine," I call back. I scramble to my feet and pull down my dress.

Just ahead, light extends through the underbrush. I part the branches like I'm opening curtains.

The sand shimmers in the sun. The sea's blue and green, as sparkly as a gemstone. Far to the right is the flat-topped island that dominates the view out to sea at the river's mouth. The arc of the beach is framed by rocky headlands around which the sea curls luxuriously as the waves are drawn to shore. There are fragments of shells bleached white by the sun, and driftwood bleached grey. Thick strands of bronze kelp lounge along the waterline. Birds drift lazily overhead or bob gently just a little way from shore.

The men emerge from the trail to join me at the lip of the forest.

"Kolya?" I turn to him, my hands clasped. "It's paradise. I fell down a hill and landed in paradise." I laugh. He smiles in return.

I run a little way toward the water then stop short. Should I take off my boots? I do. I throw them aside and dip my feet into the surf. It's freezing, and I run back up the beach, away from it.

I throw myself down on the sand and soak up the warmth through my palms. I squeeze the sand in my fist and let it run out like my hand's a sandglass. I fall back, stretch out, and close my eyes. I've been feeling tired the last few days, but it all slips away in the sunshine that laps against my skin and sinks into my cold bones.

My husband stands over me. "Come, Anya. Let's go for a walk."

I put my boots back on before I take his hand and we wander down the beach, leaving the others lying on the sand.

"I've missed you," he says when we're far enough away. His words are carried away in the wind.

"I've missed you, too." He drops my hand and slides his arm around me. He pulls me close, and I lean into his warmth. The surf breaks and sighs as the water runs back to the sea. Warmth from the sun cuts through the cool ocean breeze, and though it's much too early, it feels like summer has come to the wedding, too.

When we reach the end of the beach, there's a tall stump of a rock we can't see around. With a quick glance back at the others, he pulls me close and kisses me. His kiss grows deeper when the waves break on the shore, and tapers off as the water runs back out. "Let's go see what's on the other side," he says. I know what he's thinking.

The tide is out. If we pass the rock on the ocean side, and time our steps around the breaking waves, we'll get wet feet and nothing more. If we choose to pass on the side facing the shore, we'll need to climb some rock before we get to the other side. But our feet will stay dry. Nikolai Isaakovich releases me from his embrace, but holds tight to my hand. He turns and pulls me toward the water.

I shake loose his hand and laugh. "I'll race you," I say, and jump onto the rocks.

The rock is dry and there are many footholds. I scramble up as speedily as I can, knowing he's got to wait until the time is right. Every second is to my advantage. There's a pool of sea stars and other creatures, but I don't stop to look. I climb over this saddle of rock, picking my way across the protuberances and the hollows as quickly as I can, and start my descent to the sand on the other side. I'm going to get to the beach before him.

Then, ahead, movement catches my eye.

A wolf on the beach stares. Its ears lean forward, its neck extends, its head tilts. I hold my breath. I don't dare move. If I call for help, the wolf may attack. Would anyone even hear me? And what could they do anyway? The wolf is huge, its legs disproportionately long, and no one's armed.

The wolf also holds its position. Its manner is so reminiscent of Zhuchka's. Except for the eyes—two cold, polished opals set beneath a heavy brow. I never saw such a predatory expression on my sweet dog's face.

Old stories recount the risk of being the first to look away from a wild animal. It must not be me. Eventually my husband will come around the rock and see the wolf, too. Let him also have the wherewithal to stand tall before the wolf.

The wolf breaks eye contact. It turns its lanky body to the sea. It trots to the edge of the water, dips its head and laps, its pink tongue lolling out. Then it enters the sea, delicately lifting its heavy paws until it's slowed in the surf.

Where's Nikolai Isaakovich? Can't he see the wolf?

The wolf keeps going. It begins to swim. Its muzzle points into the waves like the prow of a ship, and its tail is a rudder trailing behind.

Where's it going? There's nothing but open ocean ahead.

It advances through the first line of surf. It swims and swims. Why isn't it turning back?

Where's my husband?

Then the wolf goes under. It bobs up for an instant, then submerges again. Only a ripple on the surface indicates it was ever there before it, too, disappears.

"Kolya?" I call. "Kolya!" Has he seen it? He must have.

Then the sea is slashed open. A dark, glistening object, hard and curved like a scythe, sails along the water's surface. It's the fin of a whale. It sails straight for a short time and a long time, before it's swallowed by the sea.

My heart pounds in my head. I can't move.

"Anya! Where are you?" My husband appears from around the stump. He looks up at me and beams. "I won!" he cries.

"Did you see that?"

"What?"

"That—wolf," I say. "There was a wolf here a minute ago."

He looks around. "Where?"

"It went into the ocean."

"Oh, Anya," he cries, "don't be such a poor loser. I beat you fairly. Now, come on down."

I climb down, keeping an eye on the sea. What just happened? Did the wolf drown? Did the whale eat the wolf? There was no struggle. As an enlightened woman, I know what's possible. There is no vodyanoy. No spirits exist in the sea or anywhere else. I also know what I saw. How could a wolf become a whale?

My husband helps me down the last two steps onto the sand. "Now that I've won, where's my reward?"

He pulls me close and kisses me, but I'm distracted. He slides his hands under the hem of my cedar dress and pulls it up around my waist. I watch the sea, I watch the forest. He bends and lowers me to the beach.

I'm afraid the wolf will reappear—and equally afraid it won't because it's no longer a wolf.

CHAPTER SIXTEEN

"What's wrong?" my husband asks.

I woke feeling ill and uncomfortable. My insides churned, my mouth was dry, and my tongue rose against the back of my throat. It was the second morning. Yesterday, nothing came up. This morning, I retched into the moss behind the bushes, hoping no one would see, knowing that many would hear.

After the nausea had almost passed, I went to the shore and breathed in the salty air. I rinsed my mouth with salt water and then returned to the house refreshed. But by the time I arrived at the edge of our mat, the salty taste had thickened and brought on a new wave of queasiness.

"I don't feel well again," I say.

"Are you feverish?" He sits up and pushes away our bedclothes.

"I don't think so. I don't know what it is."

"You should rest."

I shake my head. "I'll be fine. Look—everyone's getting up. Come on. It's a beautiful morning outside."

At the wedding feast, Makee brought my husband and me together again. He negotiated with the other toyons, and as soon as they finished distributing the baskets and boxes, the hats and shoes and dresses, the tools and utensils, the whale grease, the fish and food wrapped in fern fronds and cedar boughs, and as soon as the final dances were completed, he called over Nikolai Isaakovich and me to announce the good news. I'm disappointed we're not part of Makee's house—I already miss Inessa and the other girl—but at least I'm with my husband.

We're staying with the Quileutes, in the house of the moustached toyon. This is where I belong. How could it be otherwise? I love Nikolai Isaakovich.

Makee reassured me. "When the ship arrives, you'll all go. I promise no one will be left behind."

"Why is it taking so long?"

"Anna, this is not Boston. You must remain patient."

The negotiations were complicated and, up until the last minute, uncertain. The Tsar wanted nothing to do with us, Makee said, because we'd brought nothing but heartache to the Chalats—we'd stolen their fish, battled them and shot one of them, and then kidnapped three people. The only babathid he'd consider welcoming was Maria. At least she knew the medicine and could care for the sick.

She seemed unconcerned about going by herself.

"Wouldn't you rather have somebody else from the crew with you?" I asked. "Who are you going to talk to?"

She shrugged. "Perhaps Yakov is still there. Whatever happens, I accept God's will."

"We'll come back for you," I promised again. "That's God's will."

"I already told you—you needn't fret. They're good people," she said. "Good enough for me."

I held her hand in both mine. I smoothed the wrinkled skin with my thumbs. I thought of my mother and wondered whether

I'd ever hold her hand in mine again. Maria tried to pull away, but I wouldn't release her. Not until I said what I needed to say.

"Maria—I must ask you something."

"What is it?" she said suspiciously.

"A few weeks ago, I made a promise to Makee. I said we'd stop fighting, and that we'd try to respect the way the koliuzhi live and help out where we could." I lowered my voice. "But I don't feel confident. Sometimes, the promyshlenniki make trouble. Even my own husband."

"Don't expect me to do anything about that," she said. "No one's going to pay me any heed."

"Maria—please. You said the koliuzhi were good people. So, do it for their sake. Do it for mine. I'm indebted to Makee. If you have the opportunity, please make sure they don't hurt the koliuzhi anymore."

"I don't know how anybody could stop them."

"Try to find a way. If you can. Please."

She opened her mouth to say something, but changed her mind.

"Will you promise?"

She studied my face then gave a quick nod. When she did, I let go.

She left with the Tsar and the Chalats after the festival.

We're scattered now among different houses, in different communities. Timofei Osipovich, his devoted Kozma Ovchinnikov, and the Aleuts remained with Makee, and Timofei Osipovich gloated about it.

"I have your Makee right where I want him," he boasted. "We have a mutual understanding."

"What understanding? You mean that you take advantage of Makee's good nature."

"I'm moving into the hut your husband helped me build. I'm going to live there. Hunt my own game. I'm going to trade with the koliuzhi. Don't think I can't do it."

I thought of my promise to Makee. What could I do to stop this stubborn man? "That's not the way people do things here. Why should Makee do anything for us if you behave so selfishly?"

"When you want to know how it's done, let me know. I'd be happy to provide instruction."

"Please. Think about the rest of us. And what about Makee? Don't you care for Makee? If you don't like him, why are you always talking to him?"

He smirks. "I'm gathering information."

"For what? The chief manager is never going to listen to you after he hears how you've behaved."

"For the book I'm going to write."

They left the next day in the canoes. I watched them paddle into the fog. Except of course Timofei Osipovich wasn't paddling.

In the house of the moustached toyon, my husband and I were given a mat, a rare woolen blanket, musty smelling, but thick enough for the Tsarina, and we laid them in a place away from the draughty door. The carpenter Ivan Kurmachev and the American John Williams were to stay with us.

We started work the day after everyone left. The young man who'd lost the rope-climbing competition at the wedding came for us.

"Adidá! Hiʔolíɫka. Siyaḵalawoshísalas xʷóxʷaʔ. Áx̱as . . . wákiɫ k̓ʷisɫa ho! Ḵidíʔlo x̱áx̱i awí. Kitax̱ásdo xabáʔ,"[41] he cried, and gestured dramatically. It would be different living here with neither Makee nor Timofei Osipovich to translate. We'd be on our own to figure out what was being asked of us, and to ask for what it was we needed.

Eventually we understood that he wished us to go somewhere with him. He led us along a trail that wound through the trees, climbing, and then we followed a low ridge until we heard the

---

41 Wow! Come with me. Here's something to make hearts glad. We will be gut-full tonight. C'mon. Let's go, everybody.

surf and the gulls. We descended along a muddy path dotted with puddles. Then, light appeared through the trees and we emerged on a stony beach in a sheltered cove.

The sky was exploding with screeching gulls. They looped and dipped around one another, drawing circles and spirals overhead. One plummeted to the surface of the sea, and veered up again with a glittering fish jerking in its beak. The gull swung away, pursued by a dozen members of the flock eager to steal its catch.

Many people were already on the beach, while, out in the cove, canoes bobbed and clattered against one another.

The young man swept his arm across the scene and said, "Asáḵłi xʷóxʷaʔ. Wáli adá'dalásalas ti'l."[42]

Kurmachev offered me his hand and pulled me atop a rock from where I could look down on the scene. The cove was a strange shade of blue—cream and turquoise—and its surface quivered like aspic.

The cove was filled with fish. There were so many, I could have walked on their backs and not even wet my feet.

The canoes, I noticed then, were heavily laden. Their gunwales were barely above the water's surface. But they weren't loaded with fish. They were heaped high with white branches. The men in the canoes were pulling the branches out of the ocean.

The deep-sea forest of the vodyanoy is a myth—not even my mother would believe it—and I wasn't silly enough to think trees grew underwater. What were these branches? They weren't driftwood. Why were they white? Two loaded canoes separated from the group, and paddled away, back toward the houses. The youth who had led us called to us and waved. We followed him back along the trail through the forest.

---

42 How about this! I told you this was great.

Near the houses, we waited on the beach until the two laden canoes appeared from around the point. Before they reached shore, unloading began. Men, who'd walked into the ocean to meet them, filled their arms with branches. Water streamed down their limbs and chests as they waded in. One of them approached me. I opened my arms and he spilled the branches into them.

I staggered under the dropped weight. I licked the drops of seawater off my lips. As I tried to settle the pile comfortably, I looked down at the branches. They glistened with white, nearly translucent globules that were stuck everywhere on the needles of the branches.

Fish roe.

I recognized it. We ate it in Petersburg. It was herring roe.

The Quileutes must have put these branches in the water to give the herring a place to deposit their eggs. The Quileutes must have figured out where and when and how to submerge the branches so they could harvest all the roe without having to kill the fish.

I wondered what they'd say if they saw how we harvest caviar—the monstrous ancient sturgeon we hook or net, then kill for a few spoons of roe—female and male, we kill them both, for there's no way of knowing for certain until their bellies have been slit open. What would they say if they knew how sometimes the flesh is thrown to the dogs because it's too tough and it's only the caviar we want? For all our ingenuity and our enlightened thought, we still haven't found a way to harvest caviar that comes close to what the Quileutes have developed with the herring.

I turned and, lugging the wet, awkward load, followed the others toward the houses.

We suspended the white branches on the fish-drying racks attached by strong cords to the back walls of the houses. We passed the branches to children who carried them to the highest crossbars. When we'd emptied our arms, we went back to the canoes for another load, and another, until all the branches were hanging from the drying rack. It took most of that day.

After I urge my husband out of bed, he eats, but I don't. I don't feel like eating. The food, its aroma—just watching others chew—repulses me.

A woman brings me a huge ladle of liquid cloudy with particles of something. There look to be wood shavings floating on its surface. She says, "Ak\(^W\), tóliʔlol, hítk\(^W\)olt'sa t̓axíʔit. Yix t̓ók\(^W\)aʔ kiyatilwoxshíʔ x̣iʔ k̓axáʔa. Híx̣at áx̣ax\(^W\) łibíti choʔót̓sk̓."[43]

I accept the ladle and bring it to my lips. It's warm and reeks of a bedchamber badly in need of airing out, so I just hold it under my chin and let the steam warm my face.

After breakfast, Nikolai Isaakovich and the two promyshlenniki are led away from the house. I don't know where they're going, but neither do they. For a few minutes after they've left, men's voices rise, fall, and then fade away in the direction of the forest.

Before long, I, too, am led out of the house with a group of women and younger men, including the young man who took us to the cove for the herring roe harvest, the one who climbed the greasy rope at the wedding. We follow a trail upstream for a long time and a short time. It forks, and we leave the main trail and begin to climb. Our path rolls, up and down, but mostly up. My thighs ache and I regret that I didn't eat before we left. I fall behind, but the youth stays with me. He murmurs, "Hač̓hitsíliks. Pił̓ákłiliks."[44] Although I don't know what he's saying, I hear encouragement.

---

43 Here, poor little sick one. This will help you with the vomiting and make a strong baby.

44 You're doing fine. You can make this.

Though slow, I maintain a steady pace until we come to a rock fall. The shale that spills down the slope is not stable. I step on a flat, oval rock. It slips. I struggle to stay upright while it clatters down the slope. Once I regain my footing, I try again to focus. By the time we reach the opposite side of the fall, I must rest.

The young man says, "Was yapotala xáxi. Tsáʔdaslo xʷaʔwíkiɫ."[45] I smile and exaggerate panting. He stops and waits. I think he's understood.

Then he says something else. He repeats it. It sounds vaguely like cotton. He presses his hand on his chest as he says it again. It's his name.

"Holpokit," I repeat and nod.

He laughs—I must have mangled it—and he repeats his name. "Holpokit," I say again, but I can't say it the way he does.

Then I press my hand to my chest. "Anna," I say, trying hard to pronounce the "n."

He sounds just like the Murzik when he repeats, "Ahda."

"I'm pleased to make your acquaintance," I say.

We begin climbing again. We'll have to speed up if we don't want to lose the others.

My mother once told the story of a pretty girl she knew when she was young who had long, black hair. Galina was in the forest when she heard her grandfather call. "The problem was," my mother said, "that her grandfather had died the previous year." Galina knew it couldn't really be her grandfather, so she ran home as fast as she could. By the time she got there, her hair had turned to pure silver.

"How?" I cried. "Perhaps she only powdered it to fool everyone."

"Dear Anya," my mother said, "may you never come across the leshii yourself. But if you do, you may find out that Galina's story is true." She lifted a lock of my own dark hair and let it fall.

---

45 It's not hard from this point on. It's easy from here.

In this thick forest, it's easy to imagine Galina's story is true.
I follow close behind Holpokit, and wonder what it would be
like to hear my mother's voice calling from behind the fallen
logs. Would I, despite knowing she couldn't possibly be here, be
driven mad in my search for her? Or would I heed the story of
Galina and hurry away?

I wonder what my mother is doing right now. When we meet
again, the stories we share will be mine.

We catch up to the others on a slope from which many old trees
rise. Their trunks are impossibly straight, and far overhead, their
crowns spread like the arms of a chandelier. In Petersburg, a distant
cousin of the Tsarina had bolted to her dining hall ceiling an
elegant fixture that was the subject of much talk one winter. They
said it had a thousand Venetian crystals and two hundred candles
set in twelve tiers. It took two servants an hour to light it, and an
entire day to dust and polish it. These details spread and earned the
chandelier and the Tsarina's cousin much admiration. No one from
Petersburg society will ever see the crowns of these trees swaying
overhead, but they are magnificent and just as impressive.

The Quileutes have been waiting. Holpokit and I take places
alongside the others, closing up a circle. An old woman whose
hair really is all grey, whose voice is low and scratchy, sings. In
a moment, she finishes. Then she says, "O yix chikᵂ t́sik̓atít́ok̓ᵂ
kiyatilashít̓łich ishsik̓ᵂoyak̓ᵂá ʔal."[46]

The group scatters among the trees, laughing, looking overhead. There is a great deal of discussion among them.

The old woman who sang immediately goes to a tree right
beside her. Using a sharp stone, she cuts into it. She presses hard
and saws back and forth, revealing ropey muscles in her arms.
She cuts a straight line, perpendicular to the grain of the bark.
Though the incision is only the width of her palm, the bark is

---

46   Oh, the great Land, help me harvest some of your plentiful cedar bark.

thick, and it takes time. Then she pushes the blade underneath the cut until a corner lifts. She jams her fingers under the bark and begins to pull it off the trunk.

She leans back as she pulls, so far back I think her feet will leave the ground. The bark separates from the tree in a strip that ripples up the trunk. The tree releases it with a grudging squeak.

We're collecting bark—the bark that's woven into clothing, mats, baskets, hats, rope, and nets. It's rigid and I don't know yet how it will transform into the soft material of which dresses and bedclothes are made.

When the strip runs halfway up the trunk, the old woman calls Holpokit. He's taller. So, when he takes the strip from her and backs away from the tree, he gets extra leverage. He's also on the uphill side of the tree, so as he climbs the slope, the angle at which he pulls is wider, and therefore, more effective.

When I almost can't see the top of the strip, it falls, a flopping snake. Everyone jumps back. The newly exposed wood glows like a golden waterfall cascading down the height of the tree.

A woman lifts an end of the bark and, using another tool, begins to peel apart its layers. The outer bark comes off in large chunks and what remains is reddish-brown, like the colour Zhuchka was, and fibrous. It smells of potato. Now I feel hungry.

While the layers of bark are being separated, the old woman cuts the bark of a second tree. After she gets it started, Holpokit pulls it and she goes to a third tree. Around the entire slope, she moves from tree to tree, making only one cut on each tree. Holpokit follows her.

There are many trees here that have had bark harvested on previous visits. The exposed wood is smooth and nestles between outer bark walls that have swollen and closed tightly against the wood to protect it. Far above, the debarked trees look as healthy as any of the others. Are insects boring into the bare wood? I don't see any. It doesn't appear the trees are suffering.

The next strip of bark that Holpokit pulls down, he gives to me.

Separating the layers isn't easy. I chip off little bits looking for the right spot. The tool he gives me seems too blunt for the job, but it hurts the tips of my fingers if I try to do without it. When I finally find the right place, the pieces easily pull apart.

When all the cuts have been made and all the strips separated, the Quileutes fold the swathes over and over into small bundles. Each one is tied with a strand of the outer bark.

Though I carried nothing up to this grove, I have a full basket to carry down. Everyone does. Holpokit helps me position the loaded basket. When we get back, we put the bundles into vats of cold salt water, pressing them down to ensure they're immersed. By then, I'm starved and ready to eat just about anything.

My husband comes home when night falls. His return is just in time—the sky grew heavy in the late afternoon, and I expect it to rain throughout the night. By the door, he jokes with carpenter Kurmachev and the American, while Holpokit hovers shyly behind them, watching. He acts like he wants them to notice him, though they pay no attention to him whatsoever.

Kurmachev slips away from the group and slumps down by the fire.

"Where did you go?" I ask.

"We were hunting—for reindeer," says Kurmachev.

"Were you successful?"

"No," he says. "It was too hard."

"Hard? How so?"

"We only had bow and arrow—no muskets. And the arrowheads are wooden! They're sharp but there's nothing to them!

They're so light! We had to chase the reindeer first into a kind of channel the koliuzhi cut into the forest. When they were in the channel, then we could get a shot at them." He shakes his head. "That was clever—having the channel—but the bow and arrow are so impractical. That's the old way—and the old way is so backward."

"Perhaps hunters were more cunning back then," I say.

For old Kurmachev, the shift from carpenter to hunter has been awkward. He'd be much better at making bowls or boxes or handles for tools than he is at waiting in the cold and rain on the slim chance that his arrow reaches its target.

"Perhaps you should show the koliuzhi what you do. All this wood—" I say encouragingly.

"They have some good wood," he says. "I saw it in another house. It looks like they're drying it. I'm sure they intend to make something with it."

"You should try to get a piece."

His eyes slide sideways and back again. He fumbles in his pocket. "Look."

He shows me a lump of wood and, in the dim light, it takes a minute, but I soon realize what it is.

"It's a doll!" I laugh. "Did you make it?"

"A few days ago," he says. He's etched a little face on her, two dots for eyes and a crooked smile. Her belly is round and as big as her head. "I found the wood on the beach, and I used one of their tools. Just a piece of stone, but with a really sharp edge. I was slow." He turns the doll over, examining it. "But the wood is good. It's softer than birch, and I don't think it'll break easily."

He holds the doll to his nose. "It has a happy smell, this wood here. It's not like the smell of birch." He passes the doll to me.

Cold and wet, my husband and John Williams join us by the fire. I see dried blood from the hunt on the American's hands.

"What's that?" my husband says.

"Ivan Kurmachev made it," I say, as I show him. He takes it from me and rubs his thumb along its smooth back.

"Now you've got to make the others," I say.

"What others?"

"The rest of the family."

"Ah, I hope I'll get around to that. I'm slow without my own tools."

"You should make a bowl instead," says my husband. He hands the doll back to me. "The koliuzhi would be impressed if you made them a bowl. All they have are trays. Trays and these baskets."

He's talking about the woven bowls. We use them every day. I didn't think the Quileutes had any problems with them.

"If you make a really good one, then maybe you won't have to go hunting anymore," he continues.

"I need a much bigger piece of wood for a bowl," Kurmachev says sadly. Then, "You can keep it," to me.

"Keep it?"

"The doll."

"No." I try to pass it back.

"Then you don't want it?"

"No! It's not that! It's just—don't you want to finish it?"

He scrutinizes it. "It's finished. In any case, I'll make another."

I turn the little doll over in my hands. "I hope you do make another," I say. I tie it onto the end of my sash like I'm a peasant woman with a coin or a key.

As I had predicted, it rained throughout the night, pounding on the roof like the devil at the door. Morning brings no relief. The storm isn't finished with us yet. People fidget under their bedclothes, and talk in low voices, delaying the start of the day. Only a few push themselves out of bed to brave the cold air. They stir the fire and throw more wood onto it.

I close my eyes. Nausea washes over me. I pull the blanket up to my chin. My husband makes a weak effort to pull the cover back to his side, but when I won't relent, he rises and leaves the house. I seize the blanket and pull it up over my head wishing the day were over.

After a long time and a short time, I sense movement and when I peer out from under the blanket, a thick forest of legs encircles me.

"Ḳabaⱡiʔⱡóʔχaksh,"[47] says one woman.

"Tsixá ⱡa, dákiⱡ!"[48] replies another.

I wish they'd go away and leave me alone.

What could be making me so ill? I can barely rise again today. The smoke, the cold, the women—everything makes me nauseous. The tonics the women have given me are doing no good.

Maybe I'm dying. Maybe I'm—

I let the blanket fall back over my face. It can't be. Can it? How could it? And yet—why shouldn't I be pregnant? I'm already eighteen and a married woman—young married women have babies. It happens all the time.

I inch the blanket down my face and slowly look up. I scan the circle of faces, half of them upside down from my perspective on the floor, on my back. The women convey a strange mix of concern and delight, confirming my conclusion.

Nikolai Isaakovich and I had spoken often about starting a family. Back in Novo-Arkhangelsk, and in our cozy quarters on the brig, we'd have idle conversations about the son who'd distinguish himself in the Imperial Navy, about the daughter

---

47 Her face is so pale.

48 Well, of course!

who'd have a natural talent for mathematics. I'd only ever seen it as a possibility—distant and not pressing. The absence of my monthlies had been a blessing, and the way time had unevenly stretched and compressed meant I'd lost track of how many I'd missed. Beneath the blanket, my fingers lace together over my belly. Have I become more stout? Impossible to believe a child is only a layer of skin away from my touch.

"Hačháʔachid?"[49] a woman asks.

I smile, nod, and hope it's the correct response.

My husband returns from outdoors. The women scatter when he draws near. He shakes his wet head. Water dots the earthen floor.

"It's going to storm all day," he says. "The path's already deep with mud. Look at my feet." He stomps and more water sprays around. Then he looks at me bundled up on the mat. "Come on, Anya, get up."

I must tell him my news, but this isn't how I thought it would be. When we spoke about starting our family, I had imagined this moment. We'd be before a roaring fireplace or pressed against each other in our bed at home, or maybe even sharing our morning tea, the sun slanting in the window and cutting across the polished wood floor when I told him. I imagined the surprise, then delight flooding his face. How he'd scoop me into his arms, maybe even twirl me around in a little dance before he realized he'd need to be more careful with me.

I see myself right now—huddled beneath a stained and smoke-scented blanket, surrounded by the quiet morning chatter of the many people with whom we share a house, rain thundering overhead, a small smoky fire valiantly trying to catch in the chilly air.

"What's wrong?" He kneels at the mat's edge. "What is it?"

---

49 Are you okay?

I take his hand. He tries to pull it away, but I won't let go. "I know what's wrong with me. Why I feel so sick."

"Well—tell me. What is it?"

I should be planning a nursery. New furniture. I should be stitching blouses, knitting small mittens, slippers, and caps. Blankets as soft as fur. I should be calling the midwife. Preparing for my confinement. Looking for a nursemaid. And my mother should be at my side, her hand brushing back the hair on my forehead; she's the only one with the power to make this right.

"Anya?" He pales. "What?"

"Remember how you said you wanted a family?"

His hand tightens. He's not breathing. "It's impossible," he says. "It can't be."

I nod and shrug.

"Oh my God," he says. He tears his hand from mine. "Oh God."

I think Nikolai Isaakovich has never really considered a family beyond it being something he would like to have one day. He never expected to receive this news in a place like this. He never expected he'd have to consider the future of a child when his own future is so beyond his control. Now everything has changed. His abstract idea has transformed into a reality. I put my hand back under the blanket.

"Anya—are you sure?"

"Yes," I whisper. "You're happy—aren't you?"

"Yes! Very happy! Of course," he cries. "I just—"

I close my eyes and feel the swell of tears.

"No," he cries. "No, Anya, don't. That's wrong." He grabs the blanket and finds the shape of my hand. He squeezes hard. "Don't worry," he says. "Anya, I'll take care of you. I'll take care of everything."

The place inside that desperately needs reassurance accepts his words. Though I still long for my mother, he's here now and whatever needs to be done, we'll do it together.

That afternoon, I finally learn how bark is transformed into the soft fibres the koliuzhi weave into clothing and blankets. The folded slabs that have been soaking in salt water have been laid out on flat stones. The cord that held them in place has been discarded and each one is partially unfolded.

I work with a group of women from my house. Each of us has a little hammer that's made from the porous inner bones of the whale—just as Makee had told me several weeks ago. My hammer is very light, but when I run my thumb along the ridges carved into its head, I feel how sturdy it is. With the hammers, we pound the bark against the flat rock. It grows flatter and flatter, and the ridges cut and separate it into strands. I don't look up for fear I'll strike my own fingers.

The pounding warms the bark, releasing the scent of potatoes and salt water. The strands become as supple as silk. I watch how the women position their bark, and I do the same. The strands fall away from my hammer onto my lap. I work my way up the strip of bark, and create threads as long as my hair, and then much longer. When I reach the top of my slab, and all the strands are detached, I follow the other women and twist the threads into skeins by winding them around my outstretched fingers until they are transformed into fibrous loops.

More than any other job the koliuzhi have given me, I'm able to perform this one well. The threads I've created feel just like silk embroidery threads, and the way they respond to the winding and tying is no different.

The women converse, voices raised so they may be heard above the sound of the pounding. I grow alert when from the corner of my eye I notice one woman glance in my direction as she's speaking. Is she talking about me? Many of the women look, then go back to pounding the bark.

After a short time and a long time, my head aches with the constant thud of the hammers and the nearly shouted conversation. The nausea grows intense. I have to go. I drop my hammer and run.

Afterward, I stay on my knees behind the bushes, not sure if I'm finished. I lick some drops of water off a broad leaf and savour the sensation of the cool liquid in my sour mouth. What were the women saying about me? Did they understand why I ran away?

Then I hear shouting. One of the voices is my husband's. I run back along the trail.

Outside the houses, my husband is in the centre of a circle of men, screaming at all of them. His arms are wrapped around a woolen blanket. It drags in the dirt. Nearby, the new bride—the moustached toyon's daughter—is weeping while the women with whom I was shredding bark are trying to console her.

"Kolya," I call, "what's going on?"

"These savages," he cries. "They're trying to take my blanket."

I look at the blanket. It's white and has lines of blue and black trim running through it. There's a pretty fringe along the edges. I've never seen it before. The eyebrow man tries to snatch it, but my husband turns his shoulder to the man and pulls it away.

"Where did you get it?"

"She gave it to me," he cries, and points at the crying bride.

"What happened to our old blanket?"

"Nothing happened to our old blanket. But it's old. It's worn out. We need a new one."

I look at the bride, leaning into the women, and sobbing. "But I think it's her blanket."

"Whose side are you on?" he spits. "I asked her. I told her I needed the blanket. For you. In your condition. She has lots of blankets."

"Kolya—no," I cry.

There's been a terrible misunderstanding. Obviously, she has lots of blankets. She just married. The blanket's a wedding present. Maybe it's part of her dowry.

"She said yes," he insists.

"She didn't understand."

"We need a new blanket. They have to give us a new blanket."

He's got to give it back. "Kolya—I don't need a new blanket. I'm fine."

He looks as if I've slapped him. "Well, what about the baby then? Are you thinking about the baby?"

I haven't stopped thinking about the baby. Not for one second.

"Kolya, please. Give her back the blanket."

The men have backed off, but they're watching every move. The eyebrow man is breathing heavily. He's coiled and could spring with the least provocation.

"Kolya!" I cry harshly.

He drops the blanket, and it flops into the dirt. "I did it for you, Anya," he cries. "For you and the baby." He pushes his way out of the circle and disappears down the trail into the forest.

It's dark now. I haven't seen my husband or the promyshlenniki since this afternoon's disaster. The bride took her blanket from the dirt and disappeared into the house, with the other women trailing behind her. I ran back into the forest, swept up in another wave of nausea. I vomited again and sat on an old log for a long time.

When I finally dared to venture back to the houses, I looked for my husband. I could find no sign of him, but also no sign of old Kurmachev or John Williams. I thought this was hopeful. Perhaps everything had blown over. Perhaps they'd gone to work.

As the hours passed, my theory made less sense. And now it's far too dark for anybody to be working. Where could they have gone? The house is subdued. As I sit in my usual place, people glance over at me, then look away.

The evening meal is served. There are two chunks of fish and some tiny roasted roots. I feel hungry for the first time today. The roots are fibrous, and their edges are charred. They're bitter, but I find that taste appealing.

I eat all I can and still my husband and the promyshlenniki haven't returned. When everyone settles for the night, Nikolai Isaakovich is still not back. If only I knew a few words in the Quileute's language. If I knew how to say, "where," and "husband," that would be enough. What words might appear in their answers? I'd need to know those as well. *Fine*—maybe. *Coming back*—likely. *Home soon*—that's what I'd like to hear.

I go to our mat and curl into a ball trying to warm up before I fall asleep. I clutch the old blanket, the good-enough old blanket around my throat and close my eyes. The fire whines, then pops and exhales.

A crowd has gathered on the beach. Three canoes with long silver trails are heading for shore. Is it Nikolai Isaakovich and the others returning? I throw aside the firewood I'm carrying and run to the beach.

The first canoe pulls up to shore. He's not in it. But it's loaded. There are baskets, boxes, bladders, and packages wrapped in leaves and branches. The Quileutes begin unloading the cargo. My husband is not in the second canoe either. But the American is. His red hair always makes it easy to identify him, even from a distance. As the canoe lands, he wraps his arms around a box that, from the way he lifts it, must be full. He wades through the water bringing the box to shore.

I look to the third canoe. He's not there either. But one of the koliuzhi men is wearing a black-green greatcoat with no buttons. It droops off his shoulders.

"Where's my husband?" I cry to John Williams.

He squirms and shifts the heavy box. "Alas—"

"He's dead?"

"No, no, no," drawls the American. "He's alive—God willing."

The carpenter Kurmachev has climbed out of the third canoe. He pushes through the surf toward us. "Madame Bulygina—the koliuzhi took him away." He pants like he's been climbing mountains.

"Where?"

"We went north."

"Why?"

The American's box is carved and painted. The shells set into the wood glitter like chips of ice. The face on my side has sharp teeth and a heavy brow. "We don't know," he says in his flat voice. "It was many versts from here—on a huge sandy beach. Some other koliuzhi were waiting for us."

"Is he hurt?"

Kurmachev says, "No one's hurt. The koliuzhi gave us these things." He nods to indicate the box and all the other goods being ferried up the beach. "And they took away the commander."

"It was a trade," the American says.

I look from the face of one to the face of another. I hope to see something I've missed—an explanation, some qualification—he's coming back, isn't he? I find only what their words stated. My husband is gone—again.

"They kept his coat," John Williams adds.

"Madame Bulygina?" Kurmachev says, and he reaches his tired old hand toward me.

"Leave me alone," I say, and I brush him aside, knowing, even as I say the word, that alone is exactly what I am, and I certainly don't need to ask for it.

CHAPTER SEVENTEEN

As the night noises of the house diminish, I try to understand my husband. I can't discount his intentions, his concern for me and our child. But has he learned nothing in the months since we've been living with the koliuzhi? Sometimes he exhausts me. He's enlightened, yes, but when it comes to the koliuzhi, he's senseless. Some block stands in the way of his understanding of our situation and the people who've taken us in. Would he, in Petersburg, open the cupboard doors in a home to which he'd been invited, help himself to the contents—and be angry when the hostess objected? Does he think so little of the koliuzhi that he believes such outrageous behaviour would be acceptable here?

Now what will I do? I need him. Without Makee, without Timofei Osipovich, there is no one I can ask to bring him back. To take me to him.

The months ahead stretch out like a serpent in the grass. I pray that a ship will arrive soon. And if it doesn't? I'll be the mother of a new baby here. Who will be the nurse? The women here nurse their own children. Can I? What do babies do all day? What if mine cries all the time? The koliuzhi will help me—won't they?

What if they hate my baby? And what if it gets sick? What if the baby is born sick?

How will I ever work? Without a mother, a sister, who will take care of my baby while I'm away? Will I be one of those women forced to juggle my child and basket over the fallen logs and buckled tree roots as I follow trails that lead to where I must collect shellfish or cut shoots or separate bark? Those women move like ancient tortoises, slow, deliberate, indifferent to their burdens. Will the moustached toyon lower his expectations of me?

I fold my hands across my belly. The fire whistles and pops. Smoke hovers over the mat.

Maybe the baby won't be born here. Surely a ship will arrive first. The season is right. We could be home in Novo-Arkhangelsk long before the birth.

That fills me with an equal measure of dread. For who will help me there? The promyshlenniki? And what if the baby is born on the ship? At least the koliuzhi houses are filled with women like me, women older than me, and girls younger than me, all eager to wrap their arms around the new babies, to shower kisses and caresses on the children.

Without my husband, my nausea grows worse and when it does, I go to the sea. Cold ocean air makes me forget my queasiness. It has a quality that contradicts its physical form. It feels dense and pliant, as though you could cup your hands around it and shape it into something you could keep in your pocket. It feels strong, and yet I know its physical properties. It's nothing.

I'm on the beach, near the place where the river and sea meet, seeking respite in that air when I hear my name.

"Ahda!" A man's voice surfaces through the air and finds me.

It's Holpokit. He's walking from the houses toward me, waving his arm to catch my attention. A woman is with him.

The stones that lie high up the beach crunch as they cross over. Their faint voices grow stronger as they come closer. Holpokit beams.

But I'm hardly conscious of him. It's the woman who's attracted all my attention.

Koliuzhi Klara.

She wears a cedar dress so new that it blouses around the belt. Her hair's been cut. It now falls to her shoulders, barely long enough to tie back. One stubborn strand whips across her face. She's wearing soft brown shoes made of animal hide. When they arrive, she smirks and says, "Wacush."

I attempt my own smirk. "Wacush," I answer back. She laughs.

"What are you doing here?" I say. She should be with the Tsar and the Chalats. And Maria.

"Ahda," she says, and then begins to speak. When she's finished, I smile, but she's knows I haven't understood anything.

Holpokit says, "Kitaxásdo, wiwisaťsópat. Tix\u02b7alísdoḵ\u02b7álo lobá?a."[50] Then, he turns and heads back toward the houses. After he takes a few steps, Koliuzhi Klara grabs my arm and pulls. "Where are we going?"

She says something, and it's not "wacush." I go with her.

Digging roots is as repetitive as hauling water and collecting firewood. Squatting on the damp earth with a slender tool, I work my way across meadows in the pale sunshine of early summer, overturning lumps of soil. Despite having the digging tool, I follow the ways of Koliuzhi Klara and the other women and finish extracting each root with my fingers. Dirt lodges beneath my fingernails and when they split, I return to the digging tool.

---

50   Come on, ladies. We have to get home.

By midday, it's already hot. The grass sways and the insects buzz and the air doesn't move. The glare off the bright green meadow makes me long for the sombre shade of the forest. The baskets fill slowly.

The roots we dig are from the same brown lilies that grew all around my house in Novo-Arkhangelsk last summer. Their heads nodded so beguilingly in the breeze that blew onshore, and I tried to encourage their growth, pulling back the weeds that grew over them, adding a cup of water when the earth seemed dry—though that wasn't often, thanks to the rain. Their season seemed so short.

I hadn't known the roots were edible. If I had, we'd have been eating them. I could have put them in my piroshki. They're white clusters smaller than the Spanish potatoes I ate at Makee's and they break apart into little fragments like the dough of pastry.

While we're in the meadow, we dig another root as well. Koliuzhi Klara shows me a plant with long roots that are thin and straight, like nails that have been hammered into the earth. They take much longer to dig out.

As she's showing me, a little girl jumps all over her, playing with her hair, tickling her, stealing her tools, until Koliuzhi Klara leaps at her with a roar, trying to grab her. The girl dashes away with a squeal. But she returns a few moments later and helps dig up the long roots. She flicks the freshly dug earth at Koliuzhi Klara, making sure each handful stops just short of hitting her. Koliuzhi Klara ignores her.

Back at the houses, we wash the roots and lay them in firepits for a long time and a short time. As they roast, they give off a nutty aroma that renews my nausea. I go away from the firepit to where some children are playing.

They sit in a circle around a heap of fern fronds. A boy inhales deeply then picks up one of the ferns. He says, "Pila," and pulls one leaf from the frond. "Pila," he says again, and plucks another leaf. "Pila. Pila. Pila," he repeats, pulling off one leaf each time he says the word. The children lean in and count as he plucks. When he finishes one frond, he picks up another. When he's running out of breath, his plucking grows furious. "Pila. Pila. Pila!" he gasps. He throws what's left of the frond down and falls backward, gulping in mouthfuls of air. The children cheer and laugh, then recount the leaves he's torn off. I try to keep up. I think they reach forty-seven.

Next, a little girl gets a turn. It's the same girl who was digging roots with me—the one who jumped all over Koliuzhi Klara. "Pila. Pila. Pila. Pila," she cries, wisely keeping her voice soft and her head down. Her fingers fly, and the leaves collect in front of her. "Pila. Pila. Pila," she continues. The pile grows. The boy whose turn is finished leads the count. Finally, she gasps her last "pila," and with a flourish, throws down the nearly bare stem.

Fifty-two.

The children cheer. The boy leaps up.

"Wacush!" I blurt. The children turn, some surprised to see me. They laugh and tease the girl. The boy holds out a frond to me.

They make room for me in the circle. I sit and look over the heap of fronds. I smile. Perhaps one is my mother's fiery fern. She'd be disappointed, I think, to discover that her rare and divine fern did not require a journey across the thrice ninth land, but was so easy to find and pick, it was part of a children's game, and that they treated it no differently than any other fern frond.

I choose one and slide it from the pile. I twirl it in my fingers. It will do.

Finally, I inhale, and I pluck a leaf. "Pila," I say. And I pluck and pluck, quietly repeating, "Pila. Pila. Pila." When I think I won't be able to go another second without breathing, I cry my last "pila" and throw down all that's left of my frond.

Twenty-nine.

"Wacush," says the girl and everyone laughs.

When evening comes, and the meal is ready, I'm still repelled by the smell of the roasted roots, so I offer my share to the carpenter Kurmachev.

He divides it in two, and tosses some to the American.

"You've taken the biggest serving for yourself," cries John Williams.

"What are you talking about? I have not."

"Yes you did—you swine!"

"I did not! Madame Bulygina—you saw, didn't you?"

"Hush," I say, before their voices grow any louder. "There's enough for both of you. Stop behaving like children."

Before there can be any further debate, Kurmachev pops all his roots into his mouth and chews. The nutty aroma wafts over, and I turn away.

When I do, I find Koliuzhi Klara watching us. She's kneeled before the tray she shares with the others. Her eyes flit from me to Kurmachev to John Williams. They stay there. Focused on the American. She stares for so long that, if he was aware of it, he'd be uncomfortable. She's not yet become accustomed to his red hair, or his pale eyes and skin. No one has.

John Williams runs his fingers around the section of the tray in front of him, picking up whatever fragments of fish are left. He chews while he goes back again in case he missed something. He's blind to Koliuzhi Klara's intense scrutiny.

Then the little girl pops up out of nowhere, and with a shriek, leaps on Koliuzhi Klara. Koliuzhi Klara cries out and reaches for the tray to steady it and prevent it from spilling. The girl rolls to the ground, then curls into and presses her body tight against Koliuzhi Klara, who looks bemused. She finally nudges the girl away—but not far away—and only then she begins eating.

Jumpy and doe-eyed, the little girl is just like a rabbit. I name her Zaika.

Koliuzhi Klara comes for me after the morning meal. She has no baskets or tools. We head toward the sea, accompanied by five young women, all carrying paddles. The women chatter as we head toward the canoes.

Two young men are already there. They give paddles to Koliuzhi Klara and me.

We push our canoe out to sea. The bow points down the coast. We are heading south.

In Petersburg, I once rowed a little boat across a pond in the park. I pestered my father until he relented and allowed me. My parents sat at the stern, my father instructing me to keep us on course. "Pull on the right. More. Now straight ahead. Hard." I didn't dip one oar deep enough and it skimmed the surface. Water sprayed my parents. "Anya!" they shrieked, and we all laughed.

But I've never paddled anything before. I dip the blade into the water and pull. We push against the waves that break on the beach and try to force us back. I try to time my stroke to match that of Koliuzhi Klara, but she's fast. We pass the headland and on the other side lies a long sandy beach and more rocks. It takes a long time and a short time before we arrive at an island I've never seen before.

It's much bigger than it looked when we were approaching. The helmsman steers toward a shelf on the inland side where the water is calmer, the waves are not breaking, and we can pull up the canoe. We all climb out.

The gulls shriek. Their yellow beaks are fiery slashes against the grey sky. They dive at us. Some women bend their arms to protect their heads. The gulls are so close, I hear the *huff-huff-huff* of their beating wings and feel the air they stir against my cheek.

I follow Koliuzhi Klara over the rocks. They're slippery near the water and I'm slower than usual; my new small belly has already unbalanced me in a way that's disproportionate to its size. The old peasant women would watch me and say I'm going to have a boy.

We arrive before a steep face of rock. The women grab onto it and begin to climb.

The first woman disappears over the top. She comes back an instant later and pokes her head over the edge. "Ishaḵʷá kʷalíl-čhoʔ. Kʷŏł axʷół!"[51] she says, barely raising her voice, as though she's conveying a secret.

The small plateau up here is scattered with nests of twisted grass and grey feathers. Each one contains two or three green-brown speckled eggs. No doubt they belong to the gulls whose cries have become even angrier, whose diving is so close now, I could touch them if I dared.

The woman who arrived first on the plateau steps on a nest. There's a pitiful crunch. Then everyone joins in. The gulls scream and dive as the women move across the plateau, breaking the eggs and flattening the nests. The women say not a single word.

I'm baffled. This is not the way the koliuzhi do anything.

Koliuzhi Klara stops her stomping and peers at me. At my feet is a nest with only a single egg. She stomps her foot to show me what I must do.

I shake my head no. She frowns, then steps over to the nest and crushes the egg herself.

When all the eggs have been broken, we climb back down the rock and go home. Every stroke of the paddle, I hear the thud of Koliuzhi Klara's foot and the crunch of the one egg that lay before me. I can't reconcile what she did, what they all did, with what I know of the koliuzhi.

---

51   There are so many gull eggs! Hurry!

Two days later, Koliuzhi Klara hands me a paddle and leads me to the beach again. This time, there are two canoes waiting for us—one quite deep but much shorter. The young men tie the small canoe to our large canoe. Only two women climb into the smaller vessel. They are towed behind us, but paddle to lessen our load. The bow is pointed, once again, out to sea, and once we pass the headland, I'm certain we're returning to the gull island.

We destroyed everything there. There are no eggs left. I don't know why we're going back. When the canoe bumps up against the rock, the gulls are once again furious.

I follow Koliuzhi Klara and the others. I pull myself up the steep part of our path. I'm the last to reach the top. When I do, I look around. Every nest is once again fluffed up, lined with feathers, and filled with eggs. It's as though we were never here.

Koliuzhi Klara bends over and picks up an egg. Then she turns to another nest and takes a second egg. The other girls join in. Quietly, they move from nest to nest, ignoring the gulls, and removing only a single egg from each nest. The eggs are placed in small baskets they've brought. They stuff dried lichen around the eggs to cushion them.

Every egg is fresh. We know that because we destroyed all the eggs three days ago. The gulls had no problem laying more eggs—they're no different from hens in Russia—and when we leave they'll lay again to replace the ones we're taking. When we eat the ones we've taken, we'll know with certainty that they're not spoiled.

The gulls will hatch their young in a few weeks and after they get their feathers, they'll fly away, and then they'll come back here next year and do it all over again. The survival of this bird is tied to the survival of the koliuzhi. Just as it was with the mussels and the herring roe and just about everything the koliuzhi gather from the land and sea, a cycle of give and take governs their actions. What I'd judged to be wanton destruction is part of a system that stretches out like a spider web, and just like a spider web, unless seen from the right angle, it's invisible.

I bend before a nest. The egg is as smooth as porcelain and warm. I gently place it in my basket before moving on to the next nest.

When we return to the canoes, our baskets full, there's a fire blazing on the rock shelf near where we disembarked. The men are tending it. The women show off the eggs, then gather around the fire. The wind gusts and pushes smoke into my face. I cough and rub my eyes. I wonder why we're not yet going home.

Then the women rise and retrieve their cooking tongs from the bottom of the big canoe. They dig stones from the orange coals and carry them to the small canoe. Plumes of steam rise when the rocks tumble into the boats. I hadn't realized there was water in the small canoe.

Koliuzhi Klara takes her basket of eggs and gestures to show me that I should take mine as well and follow her to the canoe. We place the eggs alongside the rocks in the hot water. Once all the eggs have been placed in the small canoe, we all climb into the large canoe and turn our bow to shore.

When we land, we remove the eggs from the water and put them back into the baskets. Then, we go house to house, giving the eggs to the oldest people. They receive them with open hands, and broad smiles that crinkle the skin around their eyes. When we get to the moustached toyon's house, the women gesture to show me that I should give an egg to old Ivan Kurmachev.

He takes it so gingerly the women laugh. "What is it?"

"It's a gull egg. It's cooked."

"What about me?" says the American.

"They're only for the old people. You're too young." Then I say to Kurmachev, "Go ahead. Try it."

He cracks the egg against his leg and peels the shell. Everyone's watching. With his thumb, he digs into the white and slides a bit into his mouth. After a moment, he grins. "It's good," he says.

"What does it taste like?"

"Here." He offers me a morsel.

"That's not fair," the American says. "You're not old enough either." I hesitate. What I said was true.

Koliuzhi Klara catches my eye and gestures, putting her fingers to her mouth. So, I take the piece of egg and put it in my mouth.

It's fishy and greasy and a bit chewy, but warm as it is, it's also pleasingly rich. It reminds me of turkey eggs, but only if they were eaten with dollops of caviar and sour cream.

The women watch me expectantly. When I smile and nod, still chewing, they laugh. I swallow and say, "Oo-shoo-yuksh-uhlits." I know it's Makee's language, not theirs, but it's the only word I know for "thank you." The women shriek with laughter, but from their expressions I believe I've done something that has pleased them.

As our group moves to the next old man in the house, I see Koliuzhi Klara slip a gull egg to the American when no one's looking. His face is surely as shocked as mine. He rolls the egg into his sleeve before anybody notices.

One afternoon, as I head to shore to wash my hands, I find the beach crowded with children, Holpokit is in the centre of their high-spirited play.

"Ahda!" he calls when he sees me. He says something to the children and they laugh. Zaika, the little girl who clings to Koliuzhi Klara, runs over and grabs my hand.

"Wait," I cry. "Where are you taking me?"

Holpokit laughs at me. She's just a child—why should I resist? I let her pull me to the others. Holpokit leads them in a kind of a chant or rhyme that they all know. When he finishes, everyone except him—and me and Zaika—runs away.

Zaika pulls on my hand and shouts desperately.

I look to Holpokit for guidance. "What's going on here?"

Holpokit says, "Hiʔiláʔalo kaʔkadiyáskٖal. Aʔlitítaʔχas chaʔ lítiksh híχat kaʔdiyáskٖaliksh. Dákił hi'adasákalawóli."[52] He points to the forest.

I look at Zaika. We run.

Zaika and I slip into the forest. We follow a narrow vale until she pulls me up its other side. We head deeper into the forest. I hope she knows where she's going—we're no longer on the path. We dart among the tallest trees, avoiding the fallen logs and the thickets of berry bushes. Wet foliage sparkles like jewels. The shrubs must have dressed for an evening out.

I hear rustling near my feet. The boy who won the fern game squats beneath a moss-covered log. When our eyes meet, he puts his hands on the back of his head and pulls his face down until his hair falls like a curtain and he's nearly invisible in the shadows.

Zaika says something in a low voice.

We arrive at what looks to be a sheer drop. The underbrush is thick, and it's impossible to judge how deep this chasm is. There may be a path down. I see a narrow ledge that disappears into the foliage. I shake my head. It's too dangerous.

Still, Zaika urges me forward.

"I don't think this is a good idea," I say, attempting to extract my hand from hers. But she squeezes my fingers until they hurt. Then she jumps. "No!" I cry. She lands on that narrow ledge. Only by bending awkwardly am I able to stay on the edge and hold onto her.

"You're going to pull me over." I slide down until I'm beside her. We share a tiny space that has barely enough room for our

---

52 We are playing hide and seek. It means that you run and hide, and I look for you.

feet. Then she leans over and parts a wall of ferns. There's a cave.

She pulls me inside. The ferns bend back into place.

"What is this?" I say, incredulous, and my voice echoes. The cave is cool and dark—but not entirely black. It must be deep. She tugs my hand, hard, and I think she wants me to be quiet.

This is a serious game of Cache-Cache, and Zaika has a perfect hiding spot. How she ever found it is a mystery. Whoever is looking for us—it must be Holpokit—will never find us.

She squats against a wall and pulls me down next to her. The wall is cool. She shivers.

We wait. After a few minutes, my eyes adjust. The floor of the cave is earth and toothy rocks that force their way up through the ground. It's very wet and there's a slow *plop-plop-plop* of dripping water. The little light that filters through the ferns at the cave's mouth is not enough to enable me to see much more.

Is the girl scared? She turns her head, and I see her eyes and her smile flash white in the sparse light. She's been here so many times she's not afraid.

We wait. I try to imagine what's happening outside. Has Holpokit found the boy hiding under the log? Who else has he found? Do the children set boundaries on how far away they can hide? Unless Holpokit knows all the secret places, we might be waiting a long time.

I shift to get more comfortable for the tedious wait ahead and I feel a jab in my hip. It's the small wooden doll that the carpenter Ivan Kurmachev made and gave me. It's still tied to the end of my sash because I have nowhere else to keep it. I reel in the belt.

Zaika watches me unknot it. When I show her what's there, she's surprised. I offer her the doll. At first, I only mean for her to hold the doll, but when I see her expression, I want her to keep it forever.

She turns the doll over and over in her hands. She whispers,

"Waʔaxʷ xʷóxʷa aʔachidáʔal. Kʷotałasichíd. K̓ʷópatk̩ʷali."[53]

She gazes into the doll's plain face then touches it to her forehead, her eyes closed. Then she pulls the doll away and tries to give it back. I shake my head, no. "I want to give this to you," I whisper. "I hope you like it."

She cups both her hands around the little doll. Again, her teeth are a flash of white.

Suddenly, from the back of the cave, there's rustling—and then it stops. Zaika is rigid. Is it an animal? It could be a mouse. But it could be a wolf. Or a bear.

Should we run? Would we have time to get through the narrow opening and climb up the ledge? Perhaps we're better off staying very still. The creature may go away.

I carefully put my arm around Zaika. Her fear seeps into me like I'm a sponge.

What if it's not an animal? What else could it be? In all my mother's stories, did she say anything about a cave?

Something bangs. I jump and yank Zaika by the arm so hard she cries out. I drag her to the mouth of the cave. I duck between the ferns. I barely look at the narrow ledge as I fling myself up to the earth above. I swing Zaika by the arm in a way that makes no sense. Where we're safely on top, I scoop her up and run.

I dodge between two tall trees. I slip on moss but use the motion to push myself in a new direction. I can't look back. My head is filled with noise: my breathing, Zaika's breath, the pounding of my feet, and the rustle of whatever is after us. I force myself to go faster. I scrape my leg against something. It hurts.

I come up against a wide tree trunk. I dart around it.

I slam into Holpokit. He grabs me by the shoulders. Zaika's wedged between us.

---

53   That's not a rock dolly. Where did you get it? I like it! NOTE: Traditional Quileute dolls are made of thin, round, flat beach rocks. Eyes, a nose, and a mouth are scratched on that face. The dolls wear dresses of woven cedar bark.

"Let go! We have to get out of here," I cry. Pain shoots through my leg.

I twist. But Holpokit won't let go.

"No! Stop it!" I push against him, squeezing Zaika. She cries out.

"The game's over!" What's wrong with him? He still won't release me.

Zaika pushes herself out of my arms and slides to the ground. She wraps her arms around my legs and won't let go. And then there's rustling all around. I scream. A child appears. Then another. Then a third. They pop out from behind the trees and bushes. They smile. Some laugh.

"No," I cry, "there's a bear—or a wolf—I don't know—" I'm crying. No one knows what I'm saying.

Holpokit peers into my face and when he has my attention, he points.

The smiling face of a boy is poking up out of the ground. His arms appear. He boosts himself up and squirms out of a deep hole concealed by foliage. Another boy pops out of the same hole. They stand side by side before the hole, waiting. Then the second boy slowly extends his arm and opens his hand. In his palm rests the little wooden doll.

And I understand. The cave has two entrances.

"What's going on?" I ask Zaika.

She laughs but she's nervous. Holpokit says, "Kidatlíswali dixá tich baya?á. Hitkʷotaítilili."[54] In his face there's the same combination of humour and contrition.

He probably initiated the prank. All the children were in on it.

When they see that I've finally understood, everyone laughs and shrieks. They jump into the knot that's me, Holpokit, and Zaika. There's no bear, no wolf. No creature from my mother's stories. Of course not. It was only ever us.

---

54 I misled you to make you laugh. My heart is sick.

That night, I go to the beach to look for my Polaris. The ocean sighs softly; I think the last of the winter storms has blown itself to exhaustion. The sky is clearer than it's been in a long time, and I easily find her, perched in the arms of Draco. My ship constellation. Surely, it's a portent. When we're back in Novo-Arkhangelsk, I'll write to my father and tell him about the constellation, but when I write to my mother, I'll tell her about how it foretold our rescue.

Corona Borealis, the northern crown, is a little to the south. Many think it's the crown that Theseus used to light his way through the labyrinth, and that he wouldn't have found his way home without it. I have often wondered about its shape, which I see not as a crown, but as an unfinished circle.

How perfect its arc, how tempting to try to identify stars that could complete the circle. But they are not there. They are not where one would hope to find them.

If I were on the brig right now, I would hear my husband's footfall. From behind, he would call out, "Anya!" And before I could lower my telescope, I'd feel his arm slip around my waist and pull me toward him. I'd lean back into his solid form. Right away, I'd be warmer. His beard would scratch against the side of my face as he nuzzled into my neck. Those short moments when we stood like that, quiet, together, our faces pointed to the sky, those were the bright moments that held the possibility of making that circle complete.

I will find a way to bring us together again.

The berries are at their prime. Because of last night's rain, they're plump and with the slightest touch, they tumble into my fingers. The berries are as orange as salmon, each one a tiny cluster of jewels worthy of the Tsarina's collection of jewels. The ripest dangle from high above, forcing me to stretch if I can or, if I can't, to bend the thorny branches toward me. The canes arc, making incomplete circles that mirror Corona Borealis.

Koliuzhi Klara is here, Zaika, too, and many other women. This is the largest group with whom I've ever gone into the forest. Three men have come: two Quileutes, our guards, and John Williams. He tells me he's only here to carry back one of the large baskets—there are three—all of which we aim to fill today.

The Quileute men have their bows in hand, and talk softly to one another as we weave through the bushes picking berries. John Williams, on the other hand, seems at a loss for what to do. He wanders around, stopping every once in a while to eat a berry. His hair is a brighter colour than the berries.

The dappled sun reaches through the forest canopy and warms both us and the berries. The insects hover and buzz around my ears looking for opportunities to land and bite. I swat them away, but they're back in an instant. I pop a berry into my mouth. It bursts with a sharp sourness that slides over my tongue and turns sweet before I swallow.

Tonight, we'll eat berries—of this I'm certain—but most of what we'll pick today will be preserved. All winter long, we ate last summer's berries. I'll see how they press the berries into loaves, and how they keep birds, rodents, and insects from eating them while they dry. The children will be involved. I can imagine their delight, flinging sticks and stones and shouting at the birds who, being very clever, will dodge whatever they throw and still manage to steal a few berries.

Some of the fruit are very hard to reach without getting scratched. But the reward of a particularly plump berry or a branch that droops with the weight of many berries makes us all endure a few prickles. It seems we must risk the thorns if we want the sweetness.

Koliuzhi Klara and I move to opposite sides of a bush, picking, picking, picking as we go. We drift farther and farther away from the group. The rustling, the conversation, and the low laughter tell me we're not alone. Eventually we lose sight of Zaika. Then we can't see the watchmen.

I spot a heavily laden branch, and I pull it toward me. I hear a soft laugh nearby. The branch I've pulled aside reveals Koliuzhi Klara and John Williams. They're not speaking but the way they're looking at each another makes me blush. They're so attentive to one another they don't even notice me. I let the branch spring back up again.

I turn away from them and pick from another bush. I keep my head down and tread softly. I don't want them to know anybody's spotted them. I pick and pick without looking behind. The signs have been there all along. I've been slow to see the truth. I'd told myself that his red hair and pale skin were the only reasons anybody here would stare at him, and I thought giving him the gull egg was simple kindness. But I knew in my heart that there was nothing simple about it.

She's so preoccupied with him, and he with her. I have no time to think about that. Putting aside their feelings, the possibilities and impossibilities, I see they've presented me with a chance. I take two steps back. Three more. They're not coming. They're not calling. No one is. I edge farther away until all the berry bushes are behind me. I pause at the lip of a slight depression, set down my basket, and slip over the edge.

I'm going to find my husband.

I try to keep my step light as I run through this vale. I climb the other side of the depression and head straight. I aim to find a path. And if I'm lucky, it'll be a path that leads to the sea. From there, I need only turn right to go north.

I can't think beyond that.

I stumble upon an old, rutted trail. Judging by the overgrown branches, it's rarely used. I hope I'm not misreading the thick brush. If the trail's been abandoned for long, it may lead nowhere, and I may get lost. Ahead, the thick undergrowth ripples in a slight breeze. I choose to take my chances with the trail.

The minutes slip away. Have they noticed I'm missing? Are the watchmen looking for me? Has anybody run back to the village to alert the others? I force myself to go faster. I must get as far away as I can before they notice.

Finally, my overgrown path meets another. This new path is wide and clear. I run. I step on a branch and it cracks. The sound echoes off the trees. I stop—but there's nothing more.

Off to the side, the forest thins a little. I see sunlight. I head toward it.

I find a clearing, scented with an indescribable perfume, blanketed with wildflowers. There are the purple ones whose roots we eat. There are the tiny pale clusters of blossoms at the top of fragile stems, looking like candlesticks. There are the starry white ones with butter and sunshine in their centres. They lead my eye around as I find shapes and see the constellations they form.

But I've no time. I plunge back into the forest.

Using the light and shadows to guide me, I try to head in the same direction. At times, I'm blocked by the land or a fallen tree or one of countless streams. The little creeks are as tangled up as yarn, and I wish I could give one end a good, strong tug and turn them into a single long, powerful river. The kind of river that leads to the ocean.

As dusk approaches, I hear running water. I head toward it and find a fast-flowing creek. The water is glossy where it curls around the logs and rocks. It flows to my right. This is it—my path to the coast.

A shadow falls across the little stream.

One of the guards? A bear? My mother's leshii?

No.

Koliuzhi Klara on the opposite bank. Alone.

It's over. I'm going back. "Please," I say. "I just want to be with my husband."

She smiles. Her eyes glitter. "Wacush," she says. She raises her head and swivels away. She merges into the shadows of the forest.

In a moment, I don't hear her at all.

CHAPTER EIGHTEEN

———————————

I shelter under a low overhang at the foot of a cliff. I pull my knees up to my chin and wait for sleep to come. Mosquitoes pester me and some bite before I'm able to swat them away. I try not to think too much about what I'm doing. What matters is that I'll soon be back with Nikolai Isaakovich.

The night air sags with moisture, but the ledge above prevents it from settling on me. In a few hours, before the sun rises and erases the stars, I'll leave. Polaris will point me in the right direction. When she fades away, I'll find a stream, and eventually, following Polaris by night and water by day, I will reach the ocean. From there, I'll go north until I find him.

Is my child cold? I hum one of my mother's lullabies, one about a crying duck, careful to keep my voice low in case the Quileutes are looking for me. I don't know why Koliuzhi Klara let me go—whether it was pity or kindness or whether her own new feelings guided her decision—but I will remain indebted to her for all my life. I drift in and out of sleep, and then, when I think enough hours have passed, but the sky is still dark, I go back to the creek where I might get a better look at the sky.

The trickling water seems louder in the dark. I take a drink, then look up. Mercifully there are no clouds.

In a break in the treetops, through a hole that's as round as the opening of a telescope, I spot Polaris. I stretch out my arm and I measure fist by fist as my father showed me, arriving at a number somewhere between forty-five and fifty. That's my latitude. Then I line up Alpha Cassiopeia—the brightest star in the Queen of Ethiopia—with two branches sticking out high overhead, and I wait. When the star sinks out of alignment, I know I'm facing west.

It's difficult enough to walk in the dark, and even harder to walk along the riverbank. Shrubs with sharp branches compete with grasses and reeds for water and light. This is why so few koliuzhi trails follow the waterways. I walk a few sazhens into the trees where there's less undergrowth. I can't see the water any longer, but its sound is not far. It's a friend who's agreed to accompany me on my voyage. There's no path, but there's more space. Eventually, I'll find a trail.

Are the Quileutes looking for me? I wonder what Koliuzhi Klara told them. That she couldn't find me? Would she be audacious enough to tell them that she saw me running away—in a southerly direction? If she gets caught in a lie, they'll punish her. Should I go back to prevent that? What if she told them that I'd gone back to my people on a ship? Or that she'd seen a wolf or a bear dragging my corpse away to its den? My sudden return could make things worse for her.

I must get much farther away, for her sake, too.

When the sun starts to rise, I'm hungry. I snap off spruce buds as I go and eat them. I stop to pick some tiny scarlet berries that I recognize. They grow in a spray and pop like fish roe when I bite them. Only half are ripe, and I don't have time to pick very many anyway. I must carry on. I scratch gum off a tree and chew as I walk, remembering the day I did the same thing with Inessa and the other girl.

When the brig ran aground, and we first stepped into the forest, I had no notion there was anything here to eat. It was empty wilderness—nothing more. But the koliuzhi live in a kind of Eden with an abundance of berries, roots, mushrooms, and shoots. It has ponds and rivers stocked with fish, and an ocean full of seals, whales, halibut, clams, mussels—and more. Thanks to the koliuzhi—and the night sky, and the good sense my father nurtured in me—I know I can survive until I find my husband.

When the mud is deep, and when I have to walk a long way to circumvent a heap of fallen trees, and when I come up against a stream too wide and deep to cross, I wonder if I've made a mistake. Sometimes, I think I should turn back. Then the landscape changes, and my path grows easier, and every time, I decide I must not give up.

Late this afternoon, a gorge that's gradually grown deeper forces me farther into the forest, distant from any stream. I miss the company of the flowing water, but I must go where the land permits. When the light starts to fade, and I know evening is not far, I look up. The clouds are moving in.

By the time night falls, there's no sense continuing. There's no stream to follow. I can't see the stars. I might be walking back to the Quileutes.

I pray it doesn't rain.

I look for shelter. The land is flat, and there's no overhang that I can hide under until the sky clears. I remember the boy in the game of Cache-Cache—the one who hid beneath a fallen log—and I try to locate a log of my own, one that's big enough and dry underneath. When I see one that's suitable, I crawl under and prepare for another night in the forest.

I'm so exhausted I fall asleep right away. But mosquitoes wake me—and I decide to check the sky, but it's even worse—so I crawl back under the log. I bend a bough toward me and wedge it into place, thinking it might deter some mosquitoes and maybe even keep my burrow warm. I don't fall asleep again.

In the early morning, I decide there's no sense staying. Even if I don't know exactly where I'm heading, at least walking will keep me warm, and eventually I will find another stream. If I'm lucky, the sky will clear and tonight I will have the stars to guide me once again.

I stop to eat a few berries, but otherwise, I walk and walk, for a long time and a short time. Then I hear water. I follow the sound until I come across a slow-moving, murky creek. I walk downstream, along its mucky banks, until it widens, and the water is clear enough to drink. I gulp handfuls of it and head back into the forest.

On a hump of land in a clearing, I find some leaves that I recognize. They're pale green pliant bowls that grow low to the ground, each no bigger than a fingertip, and each one with a speck of a white flower in its centre. I pick the leaves as the koliuzhi taught me, pinching them from their stems so the roots remain intact, and when I have a handful, I eat them.

I walk on. For a while I think the clouds are lifting. A few minutes later, I look again and find the grey as thick as yesterday.

I'm far from water. Hours have passed since the murky stream and while it's been muddy in places along my route, I've seen no other flowing water. The land starts to flatten; ahead, the forest canopy is a little lighter. I walk in that direction, pushing branches aside. And then I find the devastating sight of the log under which I spent last night and the bough I bent to close off my burrow. "What have I done now?" I whisper and hold my head in my hands. I've been walking all day, and here I am, back where I started.

What is the sense of this? What foolishness made me think I could find my husband in this wilderness? I'm so lost, I couldn't even go back.

Then I hear the crunch of a rotten branch that's been stepped on.

They can't have seen me—otherwise they'd be calling out. I lean into the fallen tree beside me. I put my hands on its moss-covered bark and creep down until I'm on my knees. Slowly, I lie down.

When I'm as low as I can go, I try to look around. I keep my movements slow and slight. I listen so hard my head roars.

Then a dry branch cracks right behind me. I leap up and turn around.

It's a wolf.

Its eyes lock onto mine. Its nostrils flare, and its sides quiver. Its sharp ears point forward.

Should I run? If I do, it will chase. Its legs are long, its paws huge saucers. It knows this place and I don't. I wait for it to move. If it attacks, I'll stand no chance. *Go away*, I urge the beast. *There's nothing here for you. I'm a girl looking for a trail to the sea. I mean you no harm.*

Its eyes are impossible to read.

Let me go, I urge. *Please. I just want to find my husband.*

It breaks off its stare. It turns its head and trots away.

I exhale. I don't move. I'll wait until there's enough distance between us. And then I must move far, far away from here. Any direction will do.

When the wolf is only nine or ten paces away, it stops. It looks back.

Keep going, I again urge. *You have to keep going. Somewhere far from here you have unfinished wolf duties.*

It turns around and faces me again. It tilts its head and watches. Like it's listening.

Like Zhuchka.

I nearly laugh. She held her head at exactly that angle when she wanted something. When she wanted me to follow.

But that's lunacy. This is not Zhuchka—it's a wolf. I can't follow a wolf into a forest. The old stories tell me everything I need to know about allowing a wolf to lead me into the forest. Those who have been foolish enough to follow wolves were eaten or doomed to another painful fate. *Go away. I have no business with you.*

But it doesn't go anywhere.

So, I take a hesitant step forward. And when I do, the beast turns, and steps ahead. Should I run now? The wolf turns back and, again, watches me.

What do you want? What do you want, my Madame Zhuchka?
The wolf tilts its head.

Warily, I step toward it. The wolf turns and also advances one step.

I can hardly stop myself from fleeing but I'm equally scared to not follow. So, I decide to go against the old stories, to do what this Zhuchka seems to want, praying this creature is more Zhuchka and less wolf. Leaving a safe distance between us, I follow.

The beast leads me through the imposing trees. It finds ways that are clear of the thorniest brush and the spongiest bog. It leads me along ridges, circumventing rocky, uneven ground. When we must cross a stream, the wolf finds a place where it's shallow and calm. This is its land, and the creature knows it well. It never gets so far ahead that we become separated. When I fall behind, it waits patiently.

As night reveals its face again, I'm exhausted and terrified. We've made unbelievable progress—much more than I ever could have made on my own. I've put so much trust in this wolf, but I still don't really know what it wants. As the shadows grew, I began to wonder if I was making the biggest mistake of my life. Was this wolf leading me to its den? What other motive could it have?

My mother's friend Yelizaveta recounted a story told by a strange man at a party. A few years before, he'd attended a wedding and even though the host had properly assembled the requisite twelve-member wedding party, still some ritual had not been carried out properly, and the entire party was transformed into wolves. "The sources of human vice are idleness and superstition!" my father had cried. "You're excelling at both." He left the room. My mother quietly asked Yelizaveta to continue. The transformed wolves ran with the real wolves for seven years and over that time, one by one, they were killed and eaten because the real wolves could tell by their scent that they were really human. One man survived—the man Yelizaveta met. He'd always lie downwind from the pack so they could never smell his humanness. And after the seventh year, he returned to his village. The villagers were terrified and threw rocks and sticks to drive him away. But he persisted. Finally, somebody in his family thought it could be him and that he might have been enchanted. So, they left a heel of bread out for him. He ate it. And every night afterward, they left more bread, and every night he ate it all, until he'd eaten so much bread, his pelt opened like a cloak and fell from his shoulders and he transformed back into a person. All that remained of his years as a wolf was a long tuft of grey hair that grew on his chest and never went away.

Yelizaveta swore the tale was true. At a dinner party, he'd told his story, then boldly unfastened his jacket and his shirt. He showed everyone in the room the tuft of grey hair. Until that moment, Yelizaveta herself had doubted.

I was ten years old, and I didn't believe her. My mother's friend tended to embellish, and, besides, I agreed with my father. Her story was impossible. It was exactly the type of superstitious nattering that spread among the peasants, which the Tsar was so anxious to purge from our society. It had only been a couple of years since my illness and that strange blindess that had afflicted me. The visions of that night were still fresh. And my mother listened so earnestly I could tell that in her heart, she believed Yelizaveta.

In this forest, where everything seems possible, I wonder if my mother heard something in Yelizaveta's story that she'd caught and I'd missed.

When it's so dark that we can no longer see very well, the wolf stops. It's dry, and the mosquitoes seem less numerous here. I sit with my back against a tree while the wolf curls next to a nearby log. We stay within sight and watch each other. When sleep overcomes the creature and it settles its head on its paws, I allow my own eyes to close. Just for a minute I tell myself. One minute is all.

When the birds wake me in the morning I'm astonished to find myself alive. The wolf sits by its log and watches me. It's been waiting for me to wake up.

Good morning. Where are you taking me today?

The wolf's ears are cocked. Very carefully I walk away and relieve myself without taking my eyes off it. Its ears twitch at the sound of my water hitting the earth.

When I've risen, it trots ahead, and, having little choice, I follow.

We stop to drink from streams but otherwise continue for a long time and a short time. Then, just ahead, I see expansive light and wonder if we're near the sea. I don't smell salt water, but this amount of bright light is unusual.

When we emerge through the trees, we come upon a huge lake. It's the biggest lake I've seen in the koliuzhi territory. The wolf trots to its edge and wades in. It laps at the water. I walk across the spongy ground until I'm a short distance down the shore. I hear the plop of a frog, but it's gone before I see it. Water ripples out in rings marking the place where it vanished. I splash cool water on my face and neck and arms. I drizzle some on my head. I hear the *krya-krya* of a duck; a flock bobs near shore. I'm surprised the wolf pays it no attention—Zhuchka would have been off on a chase—but this creature's only waiting for me.

You've missed your chance for a big breakfast. I wouldn't have stopped you.

The shore of the lake is too boggy and overgrown to follow, so the wolf leads me back into the trees. Still, I'm sure, from the marshy smell, that the lake's not far. The path the wolf chooses is flat and only slightly moist, so we cover much distance. The sky remains grey throughout though I sense that it's lightening and perhaps by tonight, I'll be able to find Polaris again.

Where is the seashore? Show me the seashore so I can head north. But the wolf only continues through the forest.

Dusk eventually arrives, and the birds frolic, then settle. I'm very tired, and the more tired I feel, the more I can't cast away my doubt. I've been foolish to come this far with a creature all because the tilt of its head reminded me of a dog I once loved. I've trusted this beast for two days, but I still I don't know where the ocean is.

I stop walking.

The wolf pauses and looks over its shoulder.

Why can't we stop?

It trots ahead a few paces, then turns and tilts its head.

All right.

I follow. It makes no sense to give up now. I've trusted this wolf. Maybe it's trying to take me to shelter for the night.

The mosquitoes come out. Dusk crosses the threshold and becomes night. The sky is not clear. The way ahead is obscured.

Let's stop. Please. That's enough.

What I'd give now for a warm fire. I'd dry my feet. Put some boughs next to it and sleep. I'd wake up periodically to stoke it. I'd keep it going all night for the warmth and for the comfort. I can almost smell the smoke.

No.

I can smell the smoke.

"Zhuchka?" I cry. "Where are we?"

Ahead there's a flicker. Light. A fire.

I go forward cautiously. Whose fire is this?

When I finally come to the edge of the trees and peer into the clearing, I see a row of about a dozen houses, whale bones gleaming around their perimeter, a wall of tall drying racks, stacks of firewood, canoes pulled up on the shore, and four totem poles facing the ocean, one, with wings stretched out, that resembles the Holy Cross. I understand. I understand, but I don't believe it.

It's Tsoo-yess. I'm back at Makee's.

And the wolf is gone.

⚜

I stumble toward Makee's house. When I almost reach the threshold, a figure is silhouetted against the door. It's a woman. She screams.

It's Inessa. She screams again.

"It's me," I cry. "It's only me."

She runs back inside, still screaming. I hear shouts—from both her and the other Kwih-dihch-chuh-ahts.

I enter the house. I'm nearly blinded by the light from the fires. Everyone's moving. Some are clustering around Inessa, others around their children, and still others have turned to the doorway or climbed the benches, so they can see. My vision returns to normal. In people's faces, I see shock and fear.

And there he is. Nikolai Isaakovich.

Disbelief fills my heart and his eyes. I run, my arms stretched out, and throw myself against him. He enfolds me in an embrace, and only then do I believe it's him. I let my body sink into his.

"Anya?" he says. "Where—how did you—?"

To respond is impossible. I don't know the words to explain what happened these past four days.

I cling to him and remember all the times I've pressed up against him. None has been before so many people. There's the brooding Kozma Ovchinnikov who's almost smiling. There's Makee's wife. There's the old woman who saw me unclothed and washed me in the pond. I feel far more exposed to her now. There's the man with the scar on his chest; he has his arm around Inessa. On her left, the other girl is stroking Inessa's hair and the instant she removes her hand and lays it against Inessa's belly, I realize Inessa is pregnant, too.

"Where are the others?" I ask.

"Gone to the mountains to hunt," Nikolai Isaakovich says.

"And Makee?"

"He took them. He's with them." He shifts and peers into my face. "Anya—I don't understand. How did you get here?"

"Kolya—I'm exhausted." I bury my face in his shoulder and try to shut out everyone who's watching us. I let him lead me to our sleeping mat. He lies down with me, tucks the cedar blanket around us, curls into my back, and holds me. Mercifully, he stops talking and leaves me alone.

The next morning, I'm left alone to wander the beach. Everyone—including Nikolai Isaakovich—has eaten and gone to work. How will I explain my sudden appearance? I know what happened, but, even to me, it sounds like a fiction as dubious as any of Timofei Osipovich's stories. Have I gone mad? Maybe. But even with Polaris, even with all the enlightened good sense in the world, I never could have found my way here on my own. That wolf was real.

The hunting party returns near midday with a commotion. The Kwih-dihch-chuh-ahts rush to meet them and cry out in excitement and real pleasure. The hunters have brought back two reindeer that have been butchered into haunches and shoulders, barrels of ribs still attached to the backbone, legs with black stony hooves that look like elegant boot heels, and two heads with their antlers splayed like the crown of an oak tree.

Timofei Osipovich gapes when he sees me. But his shock flits away in an instant. He smiles and calls out, "Madame Bulygina! What a delightful surprise! It's a good thing I brought dinner." He raises his hands, which are caked with dried blood. "I hope you're hungry."

Makee doesn't see me right away. He's dealing with the meat. He points and gives instructions. One set of ribs is carried into his house. A man kneels beside one set of antlers and begins to saw it apart.

Finished, Makee turns toward his house. Before he reaches the door, I run up to face him.

"Anna? What are you doing here?"

"I came back last night." I've said nothing false, but I already feel as guilty as if I had.

"Who brought you?"

"No one." I redden. "Makee—I want to stay. Please let me."

Until now, I've never seen him lost for words. "Give me a few minutes," he says finally. "We shall talk."

I pace along the length of the village while I wait, back and forth, the totem poles on one side, and the line of houses on the other. Timofei Osipovich slides into step beside me. "Congratulations!" he cries heartily.

"For what?"

"You've succeeded in surprising everyone."

"That was not my intent." I start to walk faster, but he matches my pace.

"They say it's only seven versts to heaven, but the path is all forest. Have you arrived in your heaven?"

"They also say that a fool's tongue runs before his feet," I reply, and he laughs. "You haven't moved into your hut, I see."

"We're waiting for our furniture to arrive from Petersburg. You must know what that's like. It could take a while."

A boy comes from the doorway of Makee's house. His feet slap the earth. He stops before me and says, "šuʔuk. da·sa·ƛ̓idic łax̌."[55]

"What misfortune," says Timofei Osipovich, "Your toyon is calling."

"He's not *my* toyon." His laugh follows me and the boy inside.

Makee's on the bench, holding his metal cheetoolth on his lap. He's washed and put on fresh clothing. I approach, slowed by the weight of a hundred thoughts of what's going to happen to me now.

"I am surprised to see you," he says. "What are you doing here?"

"I came to find my husband."

"You knew he was here?"

"Not exactly. I only knew he was somewhere to the north."

I tell him most of the truth. What the promyshlenniki told me about the trade. How I ran away, hid in the forest, found Polaris, pointed myself in the right direction, followed streams—and how I stumbled upon Tsoo-yess by chance.

---

55 Come. He wants to see you now.

I say nothing about the wolf.

A silence stretches out between us. He shifts his hands on the cheetoolth, and it glints in the firelight.

"Makee—please—we're expecting a child." I redden.

His eyes flicker for an instant. Then, he purses his lips thoughtfully, and gives a short nod. "A child! I wish you and the commander great happiness."

"Could I stay?" My voice comes out small and helpless, like I'm a little girl again.

"The Quileutes will be looking for you. They must be worried."

"I'm sorry. I have to think about the baby now," I say softly. "Try to understand."

"A child is such happy news," he says. "And happy news is hard to reconcile with what the toyons are saying." He sighs deeply and says, "I will talk with them. But they won't be pleased with me. I keep telling them the situation will improve. They don't believe me anymore."

"I'm very sorry, Makee. I promised you, and now all I've done is make more trouble."

He sighs and sets aside the cheetoolth. "For the child's sake, I'll try. But the disruption your people are causing is nearly insupportable now. Order must be restored."

❧

After everyone's back from work—my husband was near the rocks all day with some men harpooning octopus that they'll use for bait tomorrow—we share the evening meal: there's reindeer, naturally, that was roasted in a pit near the beach. I saw the smoke spiralling gently upward and bending over the forest, and smelled the cooking meat. The bones are splintered and I suck out the marrow. We eat berries with it—the same orange berries I was picking when I escaped.

Timofei Osipovich blusters through the whole meal. He tells stories about the hunt that make it sound as though he tracked, cornered, killed, and slaughtered both animals by himself. The Aleuts don't contradict him, and, as usual, Ovchinnikov only laughs. My husband sits so close to me I can feel him chewing. He says little.

Then Timofei Osipovich says, "Well, speedily a tale is spun but with much less speed a deed is done! Congratulations are in order. I ought to have said something earlier, but I wanted to wait until we were all together. To the glory of offspring!" He raises an imaginary goblet.

Ovchinnikov nods and cries, "To your health and happiness."

I look across the house. Inessa and the other girl are watching. Inessa's belly is big enough that it must be uncomfortable for her to get down and up from the floor. I smile at her, and she gives me a little smile before turning and saying something to the other girl. After that, they both focus on their meals. There's no sign of the man with the scar on his chest, but I'm certain now he's become Inessa's husband.

Well before the sun rises, my husband is stirred from sleep to go fishing. The octopus bait awaits.

"Why so early?" I whisper sleepily.

"We have to get out to the halibut banks before dawn," he says.

"Who's we?"

"The koliuzhi. Ovchinnikov is coming, too, but not Timofei Osipovich."

"They'll be heartbroken without one another," I murmur and stretch, and he laughs. "I wish you were staying instead of him."

"I can tell them I won't go."

"No!" I cry, fully awake, thinking of Makee.

He laughs softly. "I'll be back early. Don't worry."

"Kolya—before you leave—would you find Polaris and wish her good morning from me?"

"I will." He kisses me.

Two men start digging up the earth. We're a long way from the houses, in a huge meadow. The grass is as dry as tinder, and it ripples when a breeze catches it. But the breezes are slight today. It's the hottest it's been since we arrived on this coast. I'm sweating after our long walk, most of which was uphill. Women, children, and men all carried something: long-handled tools, large baskets for carrying water, and a meal. And it's because of that meal I know we'll be here awhile.

Timofei Osipovich and the Aleuts are here, too.

The meadow is warm and smells of the dried grass and the freshly turned earth. Copper-coloured butterflies with gold flecks on their wings flit about. Small black flies cluster around us. I brush them away as best as I can, but each one is replaced by another three.

Many of the people hover and talk while the two men dig. They overturn the dark earth in clumps, and in one, there's a startlingly pink earthworm that squirms until it finds its way back to the cool underground.

"What are they doing?" I ask Timofei Osipovich.

"They're going to burn the field."

"Why?"

"You don't know? Even old serfs like me know," he scoffs. "It's ancient practice."

"So, what's it supposed to do?"

"It makes the soil richer. The ash goes into the dirt. Whatever is growing here will grow stronger next year because of it."

"Won't they burn down the forest?"

"I doubt it."

"It doesn't make sense."

"It doesn't matter whether you think it makes sense. It works. People figured it out a long time ago. Long before your Tsar started preaching about the Enlightenment, and stopped listening to the people."

He sounds like my mother when my parents would disagree.

The men who are digging create a narrow ditch as long as a koliuzhi house. Then they start to curve the ends of the trench inward. Two men join them, starting a parallel ditch some distance away. They eventually curve the ends of their trench inward as well, until the two meet and form a large circle.

The Aleuts and a couple of Kwih-dihch-chuh-aht men are sent away for water. The baskets bounce on their backs until they disappear into the woods.

The women clear away dead grass. We comb with our fingers like we're brushing hair and make a pile. When our heap grows tall, the youngest children stomp it down. They throw themselves into their task, rolling, laughing, and pushing one another. A girl shrieks when she uncovers a snake. It slithers away, children chasing it until they lose sight of it.

While they're picking dry grass from their hair and clothing, and throwing it at one another, the water bearers return.

Then I smell smoke. An older man with a hide breechclout rises from a crouch. He's just lit the heap of dry grass. The children cluster around the tiny flames and tease one another. How did the old man manage to light a fire? Did he bring an ember?

Does he have a tinderbox?

Smoke billows toward my face. I back away, and circle around until I come to the other side. The flames are spreading rapidly toward me, but the smoke flies in the opposite direction. People poke the fire with sticks, not stirring it up, but containing it. They stay one step ahead of the fire's leading edge. Whenever a wayward flame extends like a tongue beyond the outside of the trench, it's doused with water. The burning edges sizzle and black smoke rises.

The flames are cleverly shepherded into a circle that burns in on itself.

Everyone's drawn to the fire. It's easy to come close because it's so contained. Right at my feet, a fern catches and flares, as copper as the butterflies' wings, and it remains copper-coloured while everything around it turns black and grey. What strange alchemy. It should have fallen as ash. But it continues to hold its feathery shape, glowing like it's being forged at the blacksmith's.

I haven't seen a calendar in many months. It's not spring. But I know.

"Timofei Osipovich!" I call.

It's my mother's fiery fern. I'm certain of it.

"It shows itself only one day a year," she'd told me. "The one who finds it will become rich."

I hadn't believed her. There were many ways to become rich and none of them involved finding a fern in a forest. But she'd told me to stop thinking of wealth so narrowly. "These days, that's what they'll tell you, but the old, old peasants, they know better. And they all say the fiery fern promises prosperity in wisdom and grace."

Everything about the koliuzhi's place has surprised and confounded me. I was told this land was barren and desolate and sometimes it is, but mostly it's not. I was also told the people are brutal and unforgiving—perhaps some are but I've seen generosity that I'll never be able to repay. Our Enlightenment has given us knowledge and harmony, but perhaps it's just a raindrop falling into an ocean. Why shouldn't the fiery fern show itself here?

"Timofei Osipovich!" I cry again. I look around, trying to locate him.

Smoke envelopes me. Ash fills my throat. I cough and choke. The smoke billows up again, a grey wall, and all I can see through it is the glow of the fiery fern. I must not lose sight of it. This thought sticks with me as I tumble through the smoke and into the fire.

Light. Smoke. Crackling. A jerk on my arm so strong it could tear me apart. I'm thrown like an old sack. I roll and roll and roll and roll. Then I stop.

"Madame Bulygina!" Timofei Osipovich bends over me. He leans so close his hair brushes my face and each strand feels like he's plunged a knife into my cheek. "Are you all right?"

Pain radiates everywhere in my body. My knee. My elbow. My belly is being torn out. Shadows surround me.

Timofei Osipovich grits his teeth and shouts, "Say something!"

Then he disappears. Everything goes black.

CHAPTER NINETEEN

———————

An old woman with a face like wrinkled velvet gently pulls my
lower lip open. She hums a song I've never heard. With a
mussel shell ladle, she dribbles liquid into my mouth. I'm dying
of thirst, but what she feeds me burns my throat. I cry out, and
make no sound. Only a hiss of air escapes.

It's silent here, wherever I am. It smells of smoke and cedar. I
can't recall coming here. The old woman's face swims into focus.
It's so large it fills my field of vision. Her eyes are like bright stars
that pierce the velvet.

"Help me," I try to say, but nothing comes out. The old
woman watches me. I try to sit up, but the mere thought exhausts
me. I reach for her, but my arm won't move.

"What happened?" I want to say but my throat is as dry as
sand and my words are nothing more than puffs of air.

Despite this, the old woman answers. "You fell into the fire—
or perhaps the children pushed you. Do you remember? They
were playing and they may have knocked you down by accident.
Now rest. Everything will be just fine."

Pain undulates through my body, a cat's paw scuttling across
the surface of the ocean, a serpent with two heads pulling in
opposite directions.

The old woman with the ladle disappears.

The path is so wide and clear that I begin to doubt the certainty with which I set off on this journey. It's unnatural. The trees, the undergrowth, the moss, the mud—they're here—but they're far off the path, a distant shadow that means nothing. But then all trails change with the seasons, don't they? Perhaps I just can't recognize this path yet.

The trail begins to climb. It's easy at first, just a slight incline, but then it becomes steeper. Rocks have forced themselves through the earth. They're teeth that chew up the path. Still I follow, setting one foot in front of the other, trusting that this is the way to go. Then the path turns sharply and climbs in the opposite direction, and I doubt myself once more.

For a long time and a short time, I keep walking. My feet are cut and bruised. They're on fire. What happened to my boots? My bones ache and press against my skin as though trying to break free just like the rocks on the trail.

I turn with the footpath again. Something ahead glitters.

It's my silver cross. I should be surprised, but I'm not.

I must recite the incantation first. I picture my mother's face, her rosy lips. I don't really need them. Ever since I promised, I've never forgotten.

"Earth, earth, close the door
One necklace, nothing more.
Earth, earth, I command
One necklace in my hand."

I open the clasp and once more fasten the chain around my neck.

The pain comes in waves like the surf, roaring up my body, then falling back down again in a rush of sand and stone. The old woman's hand is like my mother's—cool against my forehead and light as a feather. I don't need the medicine in the ladle. Her hand will cure everything, and as long as she leaves it there, I can bear this pain.

"Where's Kolya?" I ask. Or, I want to ask.

"It's too soon," she says. "Relax. Don't be afraid. You're doing very well." She resumes humming.

She drips more medicine into my mouth. There's always more, and each time, it sets my mouth on fire. Sometimes, she gives me water so cold I think my teeth will crack. She rubs a salve into my hands. She's trying to be careful, but my skin will peel like I'm an overripe peach if she doesn't stop.

The pain in my abdomen is like lightning. It cuts from side to side, top to bottom. My spine is going to break. My head, too heavy for me to move, is filled with thunder.

The old woman faces the thunder with me. "No, no, no," she says gently. "No. You're too early."

Who is she talking to? There's no one here but me.

The old woman's face disappears. I can't see her anymore but her hands flutter over my body, the wings of butterflies in a sunny meadow. Another hand—it's made of iron and it belongs to no one—is squeezing me out of my own body. The old woman pushes apart my knees. The pain explodes.

She touches my woman parts. I should be ashamed, but I feel only desperately afraid that she'll leave me. "No, my child," she coaxes, "there's lots of time."

"Kolya!" I scream. Or, I want to scream.

Her hands clamp around my legs. She's stopped humming.

"Are you so determined, then?" she says softly. "Is there no talking sense to you, little one?"

How is it that I can understand what she's saying?

The old woman pulls. It's me and it's not me.

The western horizon grows dusky. The path enters a dried-up meadow. As darkness creeps in, the stars leap out one by one. Sirius. Arcturus. They're the brightest stars this evening. Pretty blue Venus sparkles near the horizon and the faint light of Jupiter flickers on and off. Eventually, it will be dark enough that Jupiter will remain alight for the rest of the night. If I had my telescope, I could count his moons. My Polaris isn't visible yet, but she will be soon.

I see Vega, Altair, and Deneb. These stars form a perfect triangle. When we were married only a few days, Nikolai Isaakovich pointed it out to me. "All the navigators know it. Don't you?" I knew the names of the stars, but I'd never seen the triangle they formed, never heard a name for it. There are so many possible combinations of stars in the night sky, they could never all be seen, never all be named.

"Then I shall name it," he declared, "and I shall name it after you, Anna Petrovna." He wrapped an arm around my waist and pulled me close. All summer long, the starry triangle revolved overhead and with each degree of rotation, I fell more deeply in love with my husband.

It takes only a few more minutes in the meadow before my Polaris reveals her beautiful face. She's clear and especially strong tonight, as if she knows I need her. As soon as I see her, I feel the tiredness slip off my shoulders like a too-old mantle.

I stretch out my arms and make fists, and then count. I line up Deneb with two distant trees, and as soon as it falls out of alignment, I turn north and walk.

It takes a long time and a short time to cross the meadow. The grass is stubbly, but my feet feel nothing. When I reach the edge of the meadow, there's no choice but to enter the forest again. I look through the bushes for a path, but I can't find one. Eventually, I give up and just push my way through, and then I'm among the trees.

High overhead, the wind plays music in the canopy. There are the usual heaps of mossy, fallen logs, grey shadows whose outlines I can still see. Some of the ground is boggy, and my feet sink into the muck. But the way forward feels easier now that I know my direction.

I stop and look up every once in a while. If there's enough of a gap in the trees, I see dear Polaris shining down. She gives me courage.

"Anya!"

Nikolai Isaakovich bends over me. His face, like the old woman's, fills my field of vision. I can't see anything else. His eyes fill. "Anya, what happened?"

"I don't know," I try to say, but the words are nothing but a hiss. "Where were you?"

"I can't hear you." He seizes my arms.

I cry out. His hands burn.

"Oh God!" He lets go and turns away. "Do something!"

The old woman is back with the ladle. She offers me medicine, but I won't open my mouth. I can't take any more pain.

"Anya—we have a son! Did they tell you?"

Then I notice, for the first time, that my body is different. The lightning pain inside has gone, and my stomach has collapsed. The thunder has left my head, and now it's so light it could float away.

"The baby is fine, Anya." I hear tears in his voice. "The baby is fine."

The baby. I start to shiver.

My husband pulls the cedar blanket up to my chin. "Timofei Osipovich is worried." He gently tucks it around my neck. "He carried you back here. Did you know that?"

Timofei Osipovich carried me across a beach. I bounced along, his shoulder cutting into my belly, until we saw the koliuzhi. And then he fired a musket to scare them.

"You must not worry anymore." He lifts my hand but gently this time. He holds it to his chest. "I'll take care of you."

"The baby?" I cry. Or try to.

"Just rest, Anya," he says. "I'm here. I told you I'd come back and I did, and I'm here now."

I climb for so long I must be on a mountainside. The trees are more spread out. The canopy is thinner. Night is here, but with the forest becoming less dense, the light from the night sky makes my path slightly more visible. What lies ahead, I don't know yet. A meadow? A lake? A beach?

I quicken my pace. Then, the underbrush thickens. The trees are shorter and even more dispersed. I'm close to the edge of the forest. I can't see beyond the shrubs. I push aside the branches and step out of the blackness.

A wave rolls from my toes all the way up my body and ends in my head, where it washes back until it reaches my toes again. It's not water. It's fear.

"Kolya!"

I'm on a cliff so high above the sea that if the masts of six schooners were stacked one atop the other, they still wouldn't reach my feet. I grab onto the brittle branches behind me. The wind whips my face.

Moonlight reflects off the surface of the ocean, which builds, then falls in lines of foam that crash against the foot of the cliff I'm balancing on. Far below where I stand, boulders as big as carriages face the waves, but they're submerged with each upsurge. The sea roars like a monster. Something—a log?—smashes against the base of the cliff with a hollow thud that reaches the soles of my feet. The land shudders.

I desperately want to step back. But the bushes have knit their brittle fingers together and they won't allow me.

"Kolya!" His name flies into the wind and is lost.

***

The old woman has changed my medicine. Now it's warm and sweet like honey. I crave more, but when the ladle is finished, she turns away. She does not offer me another drop.

There are men's voices at the door. They're talking. I close my eyes. Trying to understand their words empties me.

Makee. In his beaver hat.

"Anna," he says, "how are you feeling?"

I meet his eyes for a moment. They're wide with worry. I quickly close mine. It takes too much effort to be in his gaze. He calls out in his language. I hear the rattling of shells or bones. There's somebody singing.

"You must rest," he says. "These are terrible days. You must get better. Your son is counting on you."

I remember the day I was swept under the wave when the brig

ran aground and we were all running to shore. What everything sounded like from beneath the water—the roar of the surf and the people's voices calling out. Makee's voice sounds like that—though I know he's here, he could be in another world.

"I have good news. The ships are coming. There's an American ship at Mokwinna's."

There's drumming, loud as thunder. My bed shakes, my bones rattle.

"You can go home, babathid. Floating woman, you have a destination."

"Makee—I'm sorry," I say. Or at least, I want to say.

"Get better, Anna. The ship is on its way."

I lean back, pressing into the bushes, and when I do, a curtain is drawn, and the night sky opens. Where is my beloved Polaris?

There. She glimmers. Draco the Keel is sailing a never-ending circle around her. The sea tosses him, but he can depend on her. She is the tip of the mast on the ship that will traverse the northern hemisphere forever.

Of the countless possible combinations of stars, I found this one. My ship.

It's arrived.

It rocks gently. The sail billows.

"We're here!" I cry. I wave. I stand on my toes and my arm sweeps the sky. "Can you see me?"

The ship is lifted on a wave and plummets down the other side. A rooster tail of spray splashes its deck. Its sail swells, then flops, once, twice, before filling again. The ship is tacking. They've seen me.

The boat swoops down. "Here!" I cry. But it sails past. It missed. A wave of grief washes over me. "Come back!"

The wind drives it away. Then the sail flops once more. It's tacking again. The ship swoops back down and blackens the sky.

It's close. Closer. The bulwark is almost out of reach but—I jump. It takes a long time and it takes a short time. Then my hands close around the bulwark. A wave throws itself against the hull and water sprays and soaks me. I throw my leg over. I pull myself onto the deck. I look up.

Polaris glitters.

AFTERWORD

Aﬅer Anna died in August 1809, the surviving Russians continued to live among the coastal First Nations. The record
tells us that her husband, Nikolai Isaakovich, died in February
1810 from a combination of consumption and a broken heart.
Kozma Ovchinnikov and two Aleuts also died of unknown causes
at unknown dates.

On May 6, 1810, the US vessel *Lydia*, captained by Thomas
Brown, approached the shore near Tsoo-yess. The man known
in the novel as Makee immediately took Timofei Osipovich
out to the ship where they were surprised to find another of
the Russian crew, Afanasii Valgusov. He had been traded to an
unidentified First Nation community on the Columbia River
and subsequently traded to Captain Brown. Makee then brought
to the vessel as many of the Russians as he could and traded for
them. The negotiations were not easy. Makee asked a higher price
for two men, one of whom was Ivan Kurmachev, fictionalized
in this novel as a carpenter to explain the higher asking price.
In the end, in return for each person, Makee's people received
five blankets, five sazhens (about 35 feet) of woolen cloth, a
locksmith's file, two steel knives, a mirror, five packets of gun
powder, and the same quantity of small shot. In his account,

Timofei Osipovich Tarakanov calls this an outrageous sum, but when measured against what would have normally passed hands when trading a slave at that time and the trouble to which the Makahs, Quileutes, and Hoh went to feed, clothe, and house the Russians, it is not so outrageous. Though it took a year and a half, Makee kept his promise. The *Lydia* took the surviving Russians back to Novo-Arkhangelsk.

Makee is identified in the Russian account as Yutramaki, a name whose pronunciation somehow eludes Anna and the Russians. Furthermore, this intriguing man appears in *The Adventures of John Jewitt, Only Survivor of the Crew of the Ship Boston, During a Captivity of Nearly Three Years Among the Indians of Nootka Sound in Vancouver Island,* where he is named Machee Ulatilla. In the Jewitt account, Makee plays a key role in Jewitt's rescue, just as he explains to Anna when he shows her the metal cheetoolth.

Yakov and the apprentice Filip Kotelnikov were not among those rescued by the *Lydia*. The people with whom Yakov was living after Anna's death traded him to Captain George Washington Eayres, commander of the American vessel *Mercury*. It is not known what happened to him after that time, but it is likely that he did not return to the Russian-American Company but instead worked for the Americans. Filip Kotelnikov was sold to "a distant people." Despite his revulsion for the Hoh people when he was first captured, there is evidence to suggest he married an Indigenous woman and had children and may have lived at the Russian Fort Ross in California for many years. There are Kotelnikovs living still in California; the surname can also be found in the Seattle area.

Maria, to whom I assigned the fictional job of cook, was among those rescued. She also has an extraordinary postscript to the story. The oral tradition of this incident, recounted by Ben Hobucket of the Quileutes in the early 1900s and finally published in 1934, states that Maria lived with the Hobucket family until the rescue Makee arranged. But several years later, a Russian ship returned to the mouth of the river looking to capture Quileutes as slaves. The curious Quileutes who paddled out to the ship without this knowledge were startled to see Maria on deck. She shouted in the Quileute language to the people in the canoes, telling them of the ship's intent. "Go away from this place!" she called. "If you come aboard, you will be carried away as slaves. You will never see your people again." According to the Hobucket account, the people heeded her advice and returned to shore.

NOTE FROM THE AUTHOR

———————

I came across this story more than ten years ago at the Fisgard Lighthouse National Historic Site in Victoria, BC. There was a display about Pacific west coast shipwrecks, and in that display, a single line about the *Sviatoi Nikolai*. That single line said that a Russian woman had been onboard, and that as a result of the wreck, she was probably, in 1808, the first European woman to set foot on the Olympic Peninsula.

Because of where I live, because of my Russian ancestry (my mother is Russian), I was instantly curious.

The story is not well known. It took me a couple of years just to find Anna's name. When I discovered that she hadn't wanted to be rescued, I became hooked.

But, very quickly, I realized that telling Anna's story would mean writing characters who were Indigenous and representing them in my narrative. As a non-Indigenous writer, this felt especially daunting given the history of non-Indigenous writers misrepresenting Indigenous people and the terrible legacy that has left behind.

So, I first stepped back from the story and tried to inform myself about this legacy. In studying cultural appropriation, I thankfully ran into the work of Dr. Jeannette Armstrong

(Syilx-Okanagan). Her 1990 essay, "The Disempowerment of First North American Native Peoples and Empowerment Through Their Writing"[3] became a foundational document for me. In it, Dr. Armstrong asks non-Indigenous writers to imagine creating new works that are courageous and honest about colonialism and imperialism. This, she writes, would require tackling and explaining the roots of the racism that's inherent in many of the structures and practices that still exist today. She challenges non-Indigenous writers to interpret the prevailing thinking that sustains domination—instead of trying to interpret Indigenous stories. She likens this to a process of turning over and examining the rocks in one's own garden while leaving your neighbour's garden alone.

As I worked, I imagined Anna and those rocks. I gave names to her rocks. Colonialism. Imperialism. Individualism. Unfettered pursuit of wealth. Spiritual void. Disconnection from the land. The Enlightenment. Serfdom. The Napoleonic Wars. Globalization. I let Anna kick at the rocks and, when she was ready, turn them over—or at least peek underneath.

Anna's rocks had an immediate effect on the Makahs, Quileutes, and Hoh River people who took her and the other Russians into their homes for a year and a half. That effect ripples out and reaches across the decades, touching us even today. History still characterizes the Russians' experience using the terms "captivity" and "enslavement." However, even a cursory glance suggests this choice of words is flawed, and that using them only serves to keep the rocks firmly in place.

In seeking a respectful way of writing Indigenous characters, I approached the Makahs, Quileutes, and Hoh River people first through their tribal councils. Through various means, and not always through the councils, I received help that allowed me to glimpse history, language, and culture through an Indigenous lens. I hope this view is reflected in the narrative. But I know this information does not qualify me to speak on behalf of any Indigenous people. This is a work of fiction, and I have endeavoured to represent the Indigenous characters with as much integrity as I am able, and always from Anna's point of view with all of her assumptions and cultural baggage.

The path I took was far from straightforward, and my experience is not a road map. I certainly learned more about the *Sviatoi Nikolai* incident. But I also learned:

- Indigenous people are constantly asked for review, input, and opinion on agendas that are set by outsiders (like me).

- No one person should be put in a position in which she has to speak for an entire community.

- Asking for permission in a colonial context puts a burden on the Indigenous person you're asking.

- I had to consider that the people I was asking might have more pressing things to do with their limited time.

- Some questions might be painful to answer.

- Some questions where the answers are not known might be equally painful.

I let these lessons inform my approach and tried to remember to go gently. White settlers must no longer allow Indigenous peoples and communities to carry the burden of fighting against harmful colonial practices alone. The path we must share is necessary, urgent, and inevitable, but how we're going to walk it has yet to be determined. Writing this book has helped me on my own path to decolonization, and for that I am grateful.

ACKNOWLEDGEMENTS

I'm deeply indebted to Kenneth N. Owens and Alton S. Donnelly for their book, *The Wreck of the Sv. Nikolai*, which contains the original accounts of Russian fur trader Timofei Osipovich Tarakanov and Quileute elder Ben Hobucket.

I'm also indebted to the Olympic Peninsula Intertribal Cultural Advisory Committee and Jacilee Wray, editor of *Native Peoples of the Olympic Peninsula*; Charlotte Cote, author of *Spirits of Our Whaling Ancestors*; Joshua Reid, author of *The Sea is My Country: The Maritime World of the Makahs*; Hilary Stewart, who annotated and illustrated an edition of *The Adventures and Sufferings of John R. Jewitt: Captive of Maquinna*; Erna Gunther, author of *Ethnobotany of Western Washington: The Knowledge and Use of Indigenous Plants by Native Americans*; Ruth Kirk, author of *Ozette: Excavating a Makah Whaling Village*; and Linda Ivanits, author of *Russian Folk Belief.*

The Makah Cultural and Research Center in Neah Bay, otherwise known as the Makah Museum, contains many valuable treasures that show some of what life was like for the Makahs before contact with the Europeans. I enjoyed every minute I spent there and encourage others to visit this gorgeous and eye-opening facility. Thanks to Janine Ledford, the centre's executive director, and to the Makah Language Program team for patiently and thoroughly assisting with both language and culture. ƛeko· ! ƛeko· !

Gracious thanks to the Quileute Tribal Council who responded positively to my project. Through tribal publicist Jackie Jacobs, I was blessed to spend many hours with Jay Powell and Vickie Jensen with whom the Quileute elders have entrusted much of their language and cultural teachings. I'm grateful for the extensive reference materials they provided, the translations, advice, and their willingness to discuss their work and their lives.

Warm thanks to Hoh elder Viola Riebe for sharing her memories of growing up in the Hoh River area and offering sage advice that informed the passages in this book that are set among the Chalats, now known as the Hoh or the Hoh River people.

I'm grateful for all the time I spent in La Push and Neah Bay. These were quiet visits, sometimes with my son, sometimes alone, when I experienced the warm hospitality of the community during Makah Days and Quileute Days and was invited to share salmon, watch games, listen to music, see the dancers, and thrill to some of the best fireworks displays I've seen in my life. In winter, I trekked the trails to Cape Flattery, to Tsoo-Yess Beach, to Rialto, First and Second Beach, and to the site of the *Sviatoi Nikolai* Memorial, completed during the writing of this book, to get a sense of what Anna might have seen and felt in the days after the shipwreck.

In Sitka, Alaska, I would like to thank Hayley Chambers, then-curator of the Sitka Historical Society and Museum, and Jackie Hamburg of the Sheldon Jackson Museum.

I'd like to thank the Maritime Museum of British Columbia for giving me my first hands-on experience of a sea otter pelt. I'd searched high and low only to unexpectedly discover several hanging on the wall in the old museum in Bastion Square in Victoria, BC.

My team of early readers graciously ploughed through my first draft, and their suggestions improved the text in many ways.

Thank you, Susan Gee, Rita Parikh, and Meg Walker, for your courage and wisdom.

Taryn Boyd, publisher at Brindle & Glass, has been behind this project for much longer than anyone could imagine. She also critiqued an early draft and over coffee we spent many hours discussing not only the novel and my struggles, but also cultural appropriation, truth and reconciliation, the too-often overlooked work of Indigenous novelists in Canada (two thumbs up for Ruby Slipperjack), and our own family histories. Our discussions gave extra dimensions to the text, and I thank her for encouraging me to go deeper.

Thanks to Claire Mulligan, my extraordinary editor, who helped steer this novel in a direction that's true—in so many senses of the word.

It's been a joy to work with Tori Elliott, Colin Parks, Renée Layberry, and the rest of the team at Brindle & Glass. Warm thanks to Tree Abraham for the creative genius that generated the book's cover and Kate Kennedy for her sharp eyes.

The Canada Council for the Arts and the BC Arts Council both generously provided funding during the writing of this project. This funding allowed me to travel to Neah Bay, La Push, and Seattle, Washington, Sitka, Alaska, and Vancouver, BC. Moreover, it gave me the time and space to be able to research and write.

Thank you to D. M. Thomas for his kind permission to quote the lines from "You Will Hear Thunder" that appear in the epigraph. That poem is published in his collected translations of the poetry of Anna Akhmatova, titled *You Will Hear Thunder*.

Thank you also to Kerry Tymchuk of the Oregon Historical Society for kind permission to quote or paraphrase certain passages from *The Wreck of the Sv. Nikolai*, edited and with an introduction by Kenneth N. Owens, translated by Alton S. Donnelly. These brief passages appear on pages vii, 32, 49, 58-60, 154-155, and 219-221 in the text. Deep thanks to Sally Owens who, under particularly difficult circumstances, facilitated this permission.

There are many others who offered encouragement, meals, drinks, rides, roofs, books and articles, advice and sympathy, and put up with my obsession. Know that you are in my heart, and I thank you for your contribution. Any errors in the book are my responsibility and not those of the people who've touched this project over the years.

ENDNOTES

1. Vasilii Mikhailovich Golovnin (English translation by Alton S. Donnelly), *The Wreck of the Sv. Nikolai*, "The Narrative of Timofei Tarakanov" (Lincoln, Nebraska, University of Nebraska Press, 2001), 59.

2. Anna Akhmatova (English translation by D.M. Thomas), *You Will Hear Thunder: Poems by Anna Akhmatova*, "You Will Hear Thunder" (Athens, Ohio, Ohio University Press, 1985), 86.

3. Armstrong, J., *Gatherings of the En'Owkin Journal of First North American Peoples, 1*(1) "The Disempowerment of First North American Native Peoples and Empowerment through Their Writing" (Penticton, BC, Theytus Books, 1990) 141.

NOTES ON LANGUAGE
AND GLOSSARY

Long before Europeans came to the shores of the Olympic Peninsula, there was active trade up and down the coast. There was also a lot of movement of people through, for example, frequent and widespread socializing, marriage, sharing of songs, and the movement of prisoners and slaves.

There were (and are) also dozens of languages. These are not simply dialects of one common language. The Makah language is very distinct from what is spoken by the Quileutes and Hoh. Thus, it is widely accepted that many coastal Indigenous people were (and are) bilingual, if not multilingual. Children of exogamous marriages were raised speaking both their mother's and father's languages.

Fur traders such as Timofei Tarakanov often used this multilingualism to their advantage. By learning a few words of one coastal language, they were able to make themselves understood. There were reportedly various lists of "Nootkan" words published in Europe and shared among the European traders starting from the visit of Captain James Cook to the Pacific coast in 1778.

This is different from what we know today as Chinook Jargon. Chinook Jargon originated as a trade language that, according to anthropologist Dr. Jay Powell, did not develop until after the arrival of J.J. Astor's traders in the lower Columbia River in 1812—a few years after Anna's time. Chinook Jargon has deep roots in the coastal Indigenous trade language, but includes contributions from French and English.

During her time on the coast, Anna dealt with language in this multifaceted context.

A couple of notes on the Russian language: adding 'i' to the end of a Russian noun makes it plural; and, Russian naming conventions are used throughout the novel. Anna is known as Madame Bulygina, Anna Petrovna, Anya, and Annichka, in decreasing formality. Her husband is known as Nikolai Issakovich and Kolya, a diminutive for Nikolai.

Babathid: (Makah babaɬid) white people living in houses on the water

Bast: (Russian) reeds or grass

Beze: (Russian) meringue cookie

Blin: (Russian) pancake

Cache-Cache: (French) hide and seek

Chabas: (Makah čabas) sweet, tasty

Cheetoolth: (Makah čiɬu·ɬ) war club

Cingatudax: (Unangam Tunuu or Aleut) yarrow. Maria would know *Achillea millefolium* var. *borealis,* but this is more likely the similar *Achillea millefolium* var. *californica.*

Dikari: (Russian) savages

Domovoi: (Russian) spirit of the house

Hamidux: (Unangam Tunuu or Aleut) yellow avens. Maria would know *Geum calthifolium,* but this is more likely the similar *Geum macrophyllum.*

Khorovod: (Russian) folk dance, a combination of circle dance and chorus

Kizhuch: (Russian, origins Inuktitut) Coho salmon

Kluchab: (Makah ƛuča·b) large mussel

Klush: (Nuu-chah-nulth) good, pretty

Koliuzhi: (Russian) Indigenous people. This word originates from the Sugpiaq-Alutiiq word "kulut'ruaq," which means wooden dish. The Russians derogatorily used it because of the practice of some Indigenous Alutiiq women of putting a wooden labret in their pierced lower lip.

Korolki: (Russian) blue glass trading beads

Kotel: (Russian) kettle

Kvass: (Russian) a fermented beverage, usually made from bread. The Russians used other ingredients while in Russian America, such as wild celery or various berries.

Lamestin: (Chinook Jargon) medicine

Leshii: (Russian) spirit of the forest

Makee: (Russian) poppy seeds

Makuk: (Nuu-chah-nulth) buy, trade

Pahchitl: (Nuu-chah-nulth, Jewitt's list of Nootkan words) to give. The word "potlatch" originates from this word.

Prikashchik: (Russian) supercargo

Promyshlennik: (Russian) fur trader

Putchki: (Russian origins, but widely used in English) cow parsnip. *Heracleum lanatum.*

Quartlack: (Jewitt's list of Nootkan words) sea otter

Reindeer: (English) Russians use the word "elk" to describe what Canadians know as moose. Anna would never have seen a Roosevelt elk, and would most likely have confused it with a reindeer.

Rusalka: (Russian) spirit of the ponds

Ryba: (Russian) fish

Sazhen: (Russian) 1.76 metres, using makhovaya sazhen or swung sazhen

Shchi: (Russian) cabbage soup

Sviatoi: (Russian, abbreviation *Sv.*) saint

Too-te-yoo-hannis Yoo-ett: (Makah) John Jewitt

Toyon: (Yakut) chief. This word was brought from northeastern Siberia by the Russians and used when referring to leaders of the Unangan, Alutiiq, Tlingit, and subsequently, other Indigenous groups.

Ukha: (Russian) fish soup or stew

ʔušu·yakšʔalic: (Makah) thank you. A personal thank you for something someone has done for you. There is a slightly different word for thanking a group, and an entirely different word for a public thank you.

Verst: (Russian) around 1 kilometre (sing. versta)

Vodyanoy: (Russian) old spirit man of the sea

Wacush: (Nuu-chah-nulth, Makah (wayke·š [also wake·š]) bravo. Applied to a task well done. Used by European anthropologists to name the language group to which the Makah belong: Wakashan.

Zaika: (Russian) bunny. Used affectionately.

Born in Toronto and raised on a farm near Tottenham, Ontario, Peggy Herring felt the first taps of love for the written word as a young girl when her grandfather gifted her with her first typewriter. This love led her to study journalism at Carleton University in Ottawa, and after graduation she embarked on a career with the CBC, which took her from the east coast of Canada to the west. With her similarly nomadic husband she traveled to Bangladesh, where she volunteered with the United Nations, and travelled throughout India. After working in Nepal, London, Dhaka, and New Delhi, Peggy and her family returned to Canada, and currently reside in Victoria, British Columbia. She is the author of *This Innocent Corner* (Oolichan Books, 2010), and her short fiction has been featured in a variety of publications, including *Antigonish Review*, *New Quarterly*, and *Prism International*. Visit her at peggyherring.ca.